PRAISE FOR ABBY JIMENEZ

PART OF YOUR WORLD

"[A] layered, soul-stirring romance... Jimenez dexterously tackles class difference and shades her endearing side characters with as much care as her lovable leads. The result is an emotional roller coaster centered on love as a source of empowerment."

—*Publishers Weekly*, starred review

LIFE'S TOO SHORT

"A hilarious, tender, and altogether life-affirming gem of a book. This is the kind of novel that leaves you a little better than when it found you. Jimenez is a true talent."

—Emily Henry, *New York Times* bestselling author

"Jimenez masterfully blends heavy issues and humor, lacing the tear-jerking heartache with sass and sarcasm."

—*Publishers Weekly*, starred review

"Abby Jimenez's knack for tackling heavy subjects with humor and care shines through in this exquisitely written story about love, difficult family relationships, and living life to its fullest."

—Farrah Rochon, *USA Today* bestselling author

"Jimenez continues to burnish her well-deserved reputation for delivering truly unforgettable love stories."

—*Booklist*, starred review

"This story was nearly flawless!"   —*The Nerd Daily*

THE HAPPY EVER AFTER PLAYLIST

"*The Happy Ever After Playlist* tackles love after loss with fierce humor and fiercer heart."

—Casey McQuiston, *New York Times* bestselling author of *Red, White & Royal Blue*

"A perfect blend of smart, heart-wrenching, and fun."

—*Kirkus*

"A powerfully life-affirming love story...and a dangerously addictive sense of humor."   —*Booklist*, starred review

"Sparkling wit and vulnerable characters bring this story to life. Jimenez tackles deep emotions without ever losing sight of fun."

—*Publishers Weekly*, starred review

"Delightfully adorable."   —*Library Journal*

THE FRIEND ZONE

"Your next favorite romantic comedy.... *The Friend Zone* is that rare beach read with tons of heart that will make you laugh and cry in equal parts."   —PopSugar

*Part of
Your World*

ALSO BY ABBY JIMENEZ

Life's Too Short
The Happy Ever After Playlist
The Friend Zone

Part of Your World

ABBY JIMENEZ

FOREVER

New York Boston

Copyright © 2022 by Abby Jimenez
Reading group guide copyright © 2022 by Abby Jimenez and Hachette Book Group, Inc.

Cover design and illustration by Sarah Congdon. Cover copyright © 2022 by Hachette Book Group, Inc.

Forever
Hachette Book Group
1290 Avenue of the Americas, New York, NY 10104
read-forever.com
twitter.com/readforeverpub

First Edition: April 2022

Forever is an imprint of Grand Central Publishing. The Forever name and logo are trademarks of Hachette Book Group, Inc.

The publisher is not responsible for websites (or their content) that are not owned by the publisher.

The Hachette Speakers Bureau provides a wide range of authors for speaking events. To find out more, go to www.hachettespeakersbureau.com or call (866) 376-6591.

Print book interior design by Jeff Stiefel.

Library of Congress Cataloging-in-Publication Data
Names: Jimenez, Abby, author.
Title: Part of your world / Abby Jimenez.
Description: First Edition. | New York : Forever, 2022. | Summary: "People expect big things from Alexis Montgomery. She's a thirty-seven-year-old doctor from a wealthy and prestigious family full of world-renowned surgeons. Only, Alexis is tired of living up to her family's dreams for her. Now she's about to take her bravest step yet: start living her life for herself. Daniel Grant is a twenty-eight-year-old small-town carpenter with a heart of gold and a legacy of his own. He may not have gone to college, but he's always known just what he wants for his future. What he never counted on was meeting the woman who would make him question all he'd ever believed he needed. One fateful night their worlds collide, and soon the two are spending all the time they can together. Their families, their friends, and their lifestyles are worlds apart...yet something about being together just clicks. But when word of their new relationship gets out, they are not at all prepared for what happens next"— Provided by publisher.
Identifiers: LCCN 2021041710 | ISBN 9781538704370 (trade paperback) | ISBN 9781538704363 (ebook)
Classification: LCC PS3610.I47 P37 2022 | DDC 813/.6—dc23
LC record available at https://lccn.loc.gov/2021041710

ISBNs: 978-1-5387-0437-0 (trade paperback), 978-1-5387-0436-3 (ebook)

Printed in the United States of America

LSC-C

Printing 1, 2022

To Jeanette, Terri, Dawn, and Lindsay.
I can't imagine being able to do half of what
I do without your tireless support.
This one's for you.

CHAPTER 1

ALEXIS

Moths fluttered in my headlights over the long grass of the ditch. I was still clutching the wheel, my heart pounding.

I'd swerved to miss a raccoon in the fog and careened into a shallow embankment on the side of the road. I was okay. Shaken, but okay.

I tried putting the car in reverse, and my tires spun uselessly. Probably mud. *Ugh*. I should have bought the SUV instead of the sedan.

I turned off the engine, put on the hazards, and called roadside assistance. They told me it'd be an hour wait.

Perfect. Just *perfect*.

I was still a two-hour drive from home, stuck on some lonely stretch between the funeral home I'd just left in Cedar Rapids, Iowa, and my house in Minneapolis. I was starving, I had to use the bathroom, and I was in shapewear. Basically the grand finale to the worst week ever.

I called my best friend, Bri. She answered on the first ring. "So? How was hell week?"

"Well, I can tell you how it ended," I said, reclining my seat. "I just drove my car into a ditch."

"Ouch. Are you okay?"

"I am."

"Did you call a tow truck?"

"I did. An hour wait. And I'm in Spanx."

She sucked air through her teeth. "Satan's underwear? You didn't change before you left? You must have run out of there like you were being chased. Where are you?" she asked.

I peered out the windshield. "I have no idea. Literally the middle of nowhere. I don't even see streetlamps."

"Did you mess up your car?"

"I don't know," I said. "I haven't had a chance to get out to check. I don't think so." I shifted uncomfortably in my seat. "You know what? Hold on. I'm taking these off."

I got unbuckled and reclined the seat as far as it would go. I took off my heels and tossed them on the passenger side, then reached around to unzip myself. I wiggled out of the attached bra straps and leaned all the way back and pulled my black cocktail dress up around my hips, hooking my thumbs into the top of my Spanx.

There was nobody out here. I hadn't seen another car on this road in a half hour. But just as I started to wrestle the nylons down, headlights poured through my back windshield—because of course they did.

"Shoot," I breathed, moving faster.

It was like trying to get out of a full-body compression sock while being timed for speed. I heard a car door slam and I got frantic, fighting my Spandex restraints down to my knees under the steering wheel and then kicking out of them just as someone came up to the window.

A large shaggy dog popped out of nowhere and jumped up on my door to look in at me. Then a bearded white guy in a denim jacket with a wool collar came up behind him. "Hunter, down." He pulled the dog off my car and tapped on the glass with a knuckle. "Hey, you okay in there?"

My zipper was still half undone, and my dress was hiked almost to my underwear. "I'm fine," I said, tugging my dress over my thighs, pivoting to put my bare back to the passenger side. "Raccoon."

He put a hand to his ear. "I'm sorry, I can't really hear you."

I cracked the window an inch. "I swerved for a raccoon. I'm fine," I said again, louder.

He looked amused. "Yeah, we've got a lot of those around here. Want me to tow you out?"

"I called a tow truck. Thank you though."

"If you called a tow truck, you're waiting on Carl," he said. "You might be waiting awhile." He nodded down the road. "He's six beers deep at the VFW."

I closed my eyes and let out a tired breath. When I opened them, the man was smiling. "Give me a sec, I'll tow you out."

He didn't wait for me to reply, just walked back behind my car.

I hurriedly zipped myself up. Then I picked up my phone again. "Some guy is towing me out," I whispered to Bri.

I angled my rearview to try to see his plates, but his headlights were in my eyes. I heard metallic clanking from outside. The dog jumped back up to look at me through the window. His nubby tail began wagging, and he barked.

"Is that a dog?" Bri asked.

"Yeah. He belongs to the guy," I said, shaking my head at the dog. He was licking the glass.

"Why are you so out of breath?"

"I was in the middle of trying to get my Spanx off when he showed up," I said, grabbing them from the floor and balling them into my purse. "I was half naked when he walked up to the window."

She laughed so hard I had to pull the phone away from my ear.

"It's not funny," I whispered.

"Maybe not to *you*," she said, still laughing. "So what's that guy look like? Some creepy old dude?"

"No. He's kind of cute, actually," I said, trying to see the activity behind me in the side mirror.

"Ahhhhh. And what do *you* look like?"

I glanced down at myself. "Hair and makeup done, black funeral dress—"

"The Dolce one?"

"Yeah."

"So lookin' hot. I'm gonna stay on the phone with you in case you get murdered."

"Ha. Thanks." I leaned back in my seat.

"So did the funeral suck?" Bri asked.

I let out a long breath. "It sucked so bad. Everyone kept asking where Neil was."

"What'd you tell them?"

"Nothing. That we broke up and I didn't want to talk about it. I wasn't getting into it. And of course Derek was a no-show."

"What a time to be in Cambodia. He's missing *alllll* the fun," Bri said.

My twin brother had a penchant for avoiding the family drama. I couldn't say he knew Great-Aunt Lil was going to die suddenly in her nursing home, and that I was going to be thrust alone into the lion's den at the three-day family reunion/funeral that followed—but it was very on brand for him nonetheless.

I rolled the window down another few inches so I could pet the dog. He had bushy old-man eyebrows and wide golden eyes that made him look startled to see me.

"Mom did a really nice job with the eulogy," I said, giving the dog's ear a scratch.

"Doesn't surprise me."

"And Neil texted me the whole time."

"*Also* doesn't surprise me. That man has nothing but the audacity. Did you reply?"

"Uh, *no*," I said.

"Good."

More clanking from outside.

"All right, so listen," Bri said. "I was thinking we could do a double date thing when you get back."

I groaned.

"Hear me out. It's not at all convoluted."

This was going to be convoluted.

"Both of us pick the hottest guys we can find on Tinder. Probably someone posing with a fish, but that's not important. We take them to the café outside of Nick's office, the one where he gets his lunch every day at eleven-thirty? And then when Nick shows up, we act totally surprised to see him there. You pretend to trip and spill some red wine down his shirt by accident while I make out with my date."

I choked on my laugh.

"As much as I'd like to help you destroy your soon-to-be ex-husband's clothes," I said, still tittering, "I'm not dating for the foreseeable future. I don't need any men in my life right now. Or ever."

She scoffed. "Yeah, well, we're all strong-ass women until a smoke alarm starts chirping at three a.m. on a high ceiling and there's no one to hit it with a broom but you."

I snorted.

"Seriously though," she said, "we've never been single together before. We should embrace this. Hot girl summer. It could be so fun."

"I think I'm more in the mood for *Golden Girls* summer..."

She seemed to mull this over. "This could work too."

I heard more clanking from outside and felt the car move, like something was being attached to the bumper.

"Wanna get drinks tomorrow?" Bri asked.

"What time? I have Pilates."

"After."

"Okay, sure."

I noticed movement in the side mirror. The man had started to walk back over. I stopped petting the dog and rolled my window back up to almost closed.

"Hey," I whispered to Bri. "The guy's coming. Hold on."

The man pulled his dog off my car again and leaned down to talk to me through the glass. "Can you put the car in neutral?" he asked through the one-inch crack.

I nodded.

"When I pull you out, put it in park and turn off the engine until I get the chains off."

I nodded again and watched him walk to his truck. A door slammed, and his engine started. Then my car lurched, and I slowly rolled out of the embankment and back to the road. He came around the car with a flashlight and looked at the fender.

A dragonfly landed on my hood. It sat there completely motionless while the man crouched to examine my tires. Then he clicked off the light and went back behind the car. More clanking chain noises and a minute later he returned to the window. "I looked the car over. I don't see any damage. You should be fine to drive."

"Thank you," I said, sliding two twenty-dollar bills through the crack.

He smiled. "This is a freebie. Drive safe."

He went back to his truck and honked, putting up a friendly hand as he drove past me into the fog.

CHAPTER 2

DANIEL

A hundred bucks if you get her to leave with you," Doug said, nodding at the redhead sitting at the bar.

It was the woman I'd pulled from the ditch half an hour ago. Fifteen minutes later, she'd walked into the VFW.

It was nine o'clock on a Tuesday night in April, which meant the whole town was crammed into the bar. The snow had melted, and it was officially the off-season. Everything except for Jane's Diner and this place was shut down until the river heated up, and Jane's had closed at eight o'clock. The tourists were gone, so this poor unsuspecting woman was not only sticking out like a sore thumb, but she was also one of the only women in this tiny town who wasn't either related to us or had grown up with us. She was going to be relentlessly pursued.

I scoffed at my best friend, chalking the end of my cue stick. "Since when do *you* have a hundred bucks?"

Brian laughed from his barstool. "Since when do you have five bucks? And if you do, you better give it to me. You still owe me from drinks the other night."

"Good luck with *that*," I muttered.

Doug flipped us off. "I have it. And I have your five bucks too, dick," he said to Brian. "Besides, I'm not paying the whole bet. Losers each put in fifty, and whoever gets her to go home with you takes all."

"Leave her alone," I said, taking my shot. The balls bounced around the table, and the six ball went into the corner pocket. "That woman is not going home with anyone in this bar. Trust me."

Women like her wanted nothing to do with guys like us.

The car I'd pulled from the ditch was a Mercedes. It was worth more than all three of us probably made in a year. Not to mention she was dressed like she was headed to a cocktail party on a yacht. Fancy dress, huge diamond studs in her ears, diamond tennis bracelet—she was clearly on her way through town and had no intention of stopping for a layover. In fact, I was surprised she'd stopped here at all instead of driving the forty-five more minutes to Rochester to eat. The VFW wasn't exactly fine dining.

Doug was already fishing money out of his wallet.

"I'm not interested," I said, putting the eight ball cleanly into the side pocket. "I don't like betting on other human beings. She's not an object."

Doug shook his head at me. "At least *try* to have fun."

"I'm having fun."

"Oh yeah? When's the last time you hooked up with someone?" Doug asked. "It's been what? Four months since Megan?"

"I'm not looking to hook up. Thanks though."

Seeing he wasn't getting anywhere with me, Doug turned his attention to Brian. "What about you? Hundred bucks."

Brian almost immediately glanced to Liz, working behind the bar.

Doug rolled his eyes. "She's married. *Married*. You need to get over it. It's getting depressing. Get on a dating app or something." Doug tipped his glass of Sprite at Brian. "I met twins on Tinder last week. *Twins*." He bounced his eyebrows.

I took my shot. "Oh yeah? You got to disappoint two women at once?"

Brian laughed.

Doug ignored me. "I'm serious, man. She's not gonna leave her husband. Do your thing."

Brian peered back at Liz. Then, almost on cue, the door to the VFW opened, and Jake sauntered in wearing his police uniform.

We all stopped to watch him walk to the bar. He made his way through, slapping backs and saying hello louder than necessary, just to make sure we all knew he'd graced us with his presence.

He went around the counter like he owned the place, strode over to Liz, and pulled her into a dramatic kiss. Hooting erupted in the bar, and Doug and I shared a glance. What an asshole.

I looked back at Brian, just in time to see the hurt move across his face.

Hell, maybe Doug was right. I wasn't saying that betting on women was the answer, but Brian did need to get over this shit. Liz wasn't leaving Jake—even though she should.

Mike walked by on his way to the bathroom, and Doug nodded at him. "Hey, Mike! Hundred bucks if you get her to leave with you." He pointed to the woman at the bar.

Mike stopped and peered over at her in his glasses. He must have liked what he saw because he fished out his wallet.

"Almost doesn't seem fair. I get a hundred bucks *and* a beautiful woman."

I laughed and checked my watch. "I have to go. I need to feed the kid," I said, putting my stick away.

Doug groaned. "Every damn time." He waved me off. "Fine. Get the hell outta here then." Then he looked over my shoulder at the bar and nodded at the woman. "Hey, put in a good word for me on the way out, yeah?"

"So you want me to lie to her?" I asked, shrugging on my jacket.

Brian and Mike laughed.

Doug ignored me and put his pool stick on the table. "'Bout to get my secret weapon."

I chuckled and headed to the bar, shaking my head.

CHAPTER 3

ALEXIS

Whatcha thinking?" asked the bartender, wiping down the counter.

She had blond hair, a tattoo of a rose on her wrist, and hot-pink lipstick. Pretty. Her name was Liz.

I looked over the menu she'd handed me. "What's good?" I asked, not loving the options. Almost everything was fried.

"The chili's homemade," she offered.

I twisted my lips. "I don't really love chili."

The fog outside had gotten so bad, I knew I wouldn't be able to make it home before the need to eat and use a restroom got desperate. The only gas station in town had been closed, so I couldn't use the bathroom or grab a snack. Google kindly directed me to the one open place within fifty miles—the VFW that Truck Guy had mentioned.

The place was—*worn*. The tables were mismatched with cheap chairs. There were broken vintage-looking beer signs on the walls, along with framed medals and black-and-white pictures of veterans. "Bennie and the Jets" blared from an old jukebox against the wall. A huge deer head was mounted over the bar with rainbow Christmas lights strung through its antlers. It was all very tired and junky. I couldn't imagine being in here under any other circumstances, not in a million years.

A very pregnant young woman came up next to Liz and swiped a key card into the register with a hand on her lower back.

"Heading out, Hannah?" Liz asked, pouring an IPA from the tap.

"Yeah." She grimaced. "The baby's got a foot right on my bladder."

"I'll put your tips in the office," Liz said. Then she looked back at me. "It's too bad you didn't drive through before the diner closed up for the night. Pickings are kinda slim until it's summer and the tourists come back."

"Tourists?" I asked.

"Yeah. We're on the Root River. Plus, we're only a two-hour drive from the Twin Cities, so we get a lot of weekend warriors. Right now, though, it's just the townies. And they're all here. *Alllll* three hundred and fifty of us." She laughed, nodding at the packed bar.

I pivoted on my stool. It was true. There wasn't an empty seat in the whole place.

As I scanned the crowd, I spotted the guy who'd towed me out, over by the pool table.

He really *was* cute.

Now that his jacket was off, I could see he had a nice body too. He had that rugged lumberjack thing going on. Beard, dark brown hair, hazel eyes, dimples. Tall. He wore a flannel and jeans. His sleeves were rolled up and he had colorful tattoos on both forearms.

I turned away before he noticed me looking.

A bell chimed, and Liz looked up over my head. Something nervous flickered across her face, but she smiled. I turned to follow her gaze. A police officer was coming in—a handsome one. He was tall, well over six feet. Brown eyes, thick brown hair. A fit body pressed against his tan sheriff's uniform. A gun sat holstered on his hip, and a gold badge was pinned to his chest. He wore a wedding band.

"Hey, baby." Liz smiled at him as he came around the counter.

He leaned in and planted a kiss on her. A few people whistled.

He tipped up her chin. "I brought your sweater," he said, speaking to her eyes. He put a bundle of white fabric into her hands. "You left it in the cruiser."

"That's so sweet." Liz looked down at it. "Oh, Jake, this is..." She stopped, realizing I'd never told her my name. Jake turned to me and seemed to notice me for the first time.

"Alexis," I said. "Nice to meet you."

"Welcome to Wakan." He pronounced it wah-kahn. "I gotta get going," he said to his wife. "I'll be here to get you at midnight." He kissed her and tipped his head at me before leaving.

I puffed air from my cheeks and looked back at the menu. I was considering leaving without ordering. Nothing looked good. "So besides the chili, what else should I try?" I asked.

"Hey," a male voice said, coming up behind me, talking to Liz. "I need to close out my tab."

I glanced up. It was Truck Guy.

Liz smiled at him. "Turning in early, huh?"

"I have to feed the kid," he said. Then he turned to me and smiled. "Hi."

"Hello," I said, moving to face him. "We meet again."

"And under much better circumstances," he said.

I smiled. "Thank you for earlier. You didn't have to do that."

"I think I did." He nodded at a man at the end of the bar, looking red-eyed and disheveled with seven empty beer glasses in front of him. "That was your knight in shining tow truck."

I sucked air through my teeth. "I would have been there all night."

"Nah, one of us would have stopped. Five or six hours, tops."

I laughed, and he smiled at me. "I'm Daniel." He offered me a hand.

"Alexis," I said, taking it. His palm was rough and warm.

"I think I should give you a heads-up," he said, giving me back my hand and leaning on the bar. "You see those guys over there?" He nodded to three men huddled around the pool table. "They have a bet going that they can get you to leave with one of them."

Liz made a groaning noise from behind the register. "They're such assholes," she muttered, swiping his card. "Brian too?" she asked.

"Nah, just Mike and Doug." He pointed. "You see the guy with the glasses?" he said to me.

I twisted in my stool to look over at the men. "Yeah..."

"Questionable rash."

I snorted and Liz let out a laugh.

"The tall white guy in the Carhartt jacket lives in his mom's basement," he said, going on. The sandy blond man was grinning in our direction and waving. "In about five minutes he's going to procure a guitar from somewhere." He looked at me. "He's going to play 'More Than Words' by Extreme and he's going to do it very, *very* badly."

Liz was laughing as she slid his charge draft in front of him. "It's true. God, why is it true."

While he signed his receipt, I glanced at it. It was only ten dollars, but he left a ten-dollar tip. He flipped it upside down and pushed away from the bar. "Anyway, good luck." He started for the exit.

"Wait," I said after him.

He stopped and looked back at me.

"How much are they betting?"

He shrugged, pulling out his keys. "A hundred bucks."

"And what about you? You're not in on this bet?"

He shook his head. "That's not my thing."

"No? Well, what if I left with you? Would you win the money?"

He wrinkled his forehead at me. "I don't follow."

"I think I'm going to leave anyway. You could walk out with me. Win the bet."

He smiled. "You'd do that?"

I shrugged. "Sure."

He glanced over at the men across the room.

Carhartt Jacket was holding a guitar.

Daniel's eyes came back to mine, and a smile played at the corners of his lips. "If we do it, we split the money."

I turned to Liz. "Liz, on a scale from one to serial killer, how dangerous is this man? Am I safe to walk out into a dark parking lot with him?"

She smiled. "Daniel is the *only* guy I'd leave this bar with."

"I don't know how I feel about that," he said. "You're my cousin."

She laughed. "He's harmless."

"And he'll keep up his end of the bargain and pay me?" I asked.

She dried a tumbler with a rag. "Even if those idiots don't keep up their end of the bargain and pay *him*, he'll pay you. It's the kind of person he is."

I looked back at Daniel, and he shrugged. "I'm not an asshole. It's my favorite thing about myself."

I felt my smile reach my eyes. He was funny.

"Okay," I said. "We have a deal." I nodded at the barstool next to me. "But sit and talk to me for a bit. Otherwise they won't believe you wooed me."

He looked at his watch. Then he seemed to decide he had time and took a seat.

"So, tell me about yourself," I said. "What do you do?"

"I'm a property manager," he said.

Liz laughed from behind the counter where she was pouring beer from the tap. "He's the mayor."

I arched an eyebrow. "Wow, the *mayor*?"

He gave her a look. "It's more of an honorary title. This is a small town. My duties are very minimal."

Liz shook her head. "He's being humble. He's sort of everything around here. Calls bingo on Saturday nights, volunteer firefighter. He's even Santa." She nodded to one of the framed articles above the cash register.

Santa Comes to Wakan.

The article was accompanied by a color photo of a fat Santa Claus with a little boy on his knee.

I looked back at him with a smile, and he changed the subject. "And what do you do?"

I shrugged. "Nothing worth mentioning."

I didn't like giving out my personal information to a stranger. He didn't push it.

"Okay," he said. "And what brings you to Wakan?"

"I'm coming from a funeral."

His face went serious. "Oh. I'm sorry to hear that."

"Aunt Lil was ninety-eight, and she had a very good life. Many lovers, as she liked to say."

He smiled.

"I live in Minneapolis. I'm just driving through. Hey, is it always this foggy out here?"

"There's fog outside?" Liz asked, looking surprised.

Daniel shook his head. "Never. It's weird, actually."

"Huh. So you have a kid?" I asked.

He looked at his watch again. "I do. Chloe."

"How old?"

"One week."

"Oh," I said, pulling my face back in surprise. "She's little."

He wasn't wearing a wedding ring—not that that meant anything. He could have a kid without being married.

"So you have a girlfriend?" I asked.

He shook his head. "I wouldn't have taken this wager if I did."

"Well, you're not *actually* taking me home," I pointed out.

"But I'm pretending to. I wouldn't disrespect my theoretical girlfriend." He grinned.

I had to stifle a smile. "So you're not with your baby's mother?"

He looked amused. "Definitely not. I'm fostering."

Liz smiled. "Chloe is *soooo* cute. He's such a good daddy to her." She nodded at him. "Show her a picture."

He pulled out his phone and swiped. Then he held it out to me.

A laugh burst from my lips. "Your kid is a baby *goat*? In *pajamas*?"

"She is. She goes home in a few weeks. She belongs to Doug.

The guitar guy. Mom has mastitis and Doug couldn't do middle-of-the-night feedings, so I volunteered to help."

"So let me get this straight," I said, crossing my legs. "Doug is trying to seduce me with a poorly sung version of 'More Than Words' when he has an entire baby *goat*? If you have a baby goat, you *always* lead with 'I have a baby goat.'"

He chuckled. "Technically *I* have the baby goat."

Liz put ice into a tumbler. "I keep telling him his Tinder profile could be nothing but a picture of Chloe and an address."

I laughed.

Daniel smiled and nodded over his shoulder. "Are they watching us?" he asked.

My eyes flickered over to the pool table. "Oh, yes." I looked back at him. "Carhartt Jacket Doug is tuning his guitar. So how much time do you think we have until I'm serenaded?"

"I'd say another minute or two."

"Okay." I leaned forward. "I'm going to pretend that you just said something *really* funny and I'm going to laugh. Then we can wrap this up."

He put a hand to his chin. "What kind of laugh?"

"What *kind*?"

"Yeah. In theory whatever I'm saying to you has to be good enough to make you leave with me after only knowing me for five minutes. It's going to have to look pretty convincing. I'm thinking Julia Roberts?"

This actually *did* make me laugh, which made *him* laugh—and it was adorable. His warm golden-green eyes creased at the corners and it lit his whole face.

God, he had a nice smile. *Really* nice. Something about it darted me right in the heart, took a little of my breath away.

We sat there, still cracking up, and I found myself biting my lip and leaning into him a little, and I realized with shock that I was *flirting*. Like, actually flirting, not pretending.

I'd been with Neil seven years. I thought Neil would be the last man I'd ever be with. Then I'd broken up with him and I told myself that I was done. No more men. I didn't need one. I didn't need the hassle. I completely rejected the idea of dating ever again. I'd bought a very nice vibrator and I'd retired myself from the pool at thirty-seven. Zero interest.

And now I was *flirting*.

It was like finding out a plant you killed was alive after all and just needed water.

"Uh-oh, Doug's coming," Liz whispered.

I tore my gaze away from Daniel. Doug had begun weaving his way through high-top tables toward the bar, guitar in hand.

"Time to go," Daniel said.

Then he took my hand, helped me down from the barstool, and walked me out.

CHAPTER 4

DANIEL

I grabbed her hand. We were trying to look comfortable with each other. I figured it was in character. Brazen, but in character.

She didn't pull away.

The guys watched me with slack jaws as we made our way out of the bar. I put my other hand low and flipped them off.

When we got out into the parking lot, I let go of her. I pulled the bills out of my wallet and handed them to her.

She took the cash, counted it, and then tucked it into my shirt pocket.

"Uh, the deal was fifty-fifty," I said, digging for the money to give it back.

"I'm paying you for the tow service."

"Nope. I don't accept," I said, handing her the wad of bills.

She crossed her arms.

"You did the lion's share," I said, holding it out. "You earned it."

"I wouldn't even be here if you hadn't hauled me out of the ditch. I would have paid Drunk Carl a lot more than fifty bucks.

And I get to decide what to do with my ill-gotten gains. That's how ill-gotten gains work." She gave me a wry grin.

I shook my head with a smile. I could see she wasn't going to fold, and I didn't fight her too hard because if I wasn't going to be out fifty bucks, I wouldn't hit the guys up for the money tomorrow. Finances were tight for everyone in the off-season. And anyway, this had been well worth the entertainment value alone.

"So do you do this often?" I asked, putting the bills back in my wallet. "I have to say, this was the highlight of my week."

She smiled. "Must be a slow week."

I laughed a little.

A soft breeze blew a strand of hair across her face and she dragged it away with a finger. God, she was gorgeous. Red hair, fair skin, freckles peppering her nose. Deep brown eyes. Athletic. I'd seen more than she probably intended when she was getting changed in her car. I could smell her perfume. I didn't know what it was, but my guess was it was something expensive.

This was a woman so far out of my league it wasn't even funny. It was hard to believe that she was even here, standing in this parking lot full of cracked asphalt in the middle of nowhere, wearing that dress and those heels. Like a model had wandered away from a photo shoot for a fashion magazine and gotten lost.

And she was right about the fog. It hugged the edges of the parking lot like there was an invisible force field around the VFW. It was weird. And not great to drive in, that's for sure.

We stood there for a moment. Then she nodded to her car. "Well, I better get going. You have to feed your kid—hey, is there anywhere to get food close by?"

I shook my head. "No. Rochester's the closest city to Wakan, and that's forty-five minutes north."

She pursed her lips. "That's what I thought. Okay, well. It was nice hustling your friends with you."

"Yeah, you too."

She smiled at me for another moment. Then she turned and headed for her car, and I stood there, watching her.

"Hey," I called.

She turned. "Yeah?"

"I could make you something to eat. At my place."

"What are you going to make me? Because I'm a *very* picky eater," she said without skipping a beat.

I smiled. "Well, I don't have any dinosaur chicken nuggets if that's what you're hoping for."

This drew a laugh, and I grinned.

I mentally scoured the contents of my fridge. "Probably a grilled cheese? With fresh tomato and basil in it?"

She arched an eyebrow. "Fresh tomato and basil?"

"I have a garden."

"I don't do one-night stands."

I laughed. "Well, *that* escalated quickly."

"I'm serious. I've never had one and I never will. If your goal is that, you're going to be severely disappointed."

"My goal is not that," I said honestly, smiling at her.

She nodded, taking a few steps until she stood looking up at me. "Okay. But I have to inform you that I'm bringing my Taser."

"Fair enough."

"And I will definitely use it if I have to." She gave me a stern look.

I made a matching serious face. "You won't have to. But I believe you. You look violent."

She fought a laugh, trying to keep her serious expression. "And I'm taking my own car. You're not driving me."

"Of course."

"One last thing." She cocked her head. "Is there anyone out there under the impression that they are in a relationship with you?"

I laughed. "It's just a grilled cheese, you know. It's not that serious."

"Oh, I know. But if I was under the impression that I was in a relationship with someone and I came home to find them making a grilled cheese for another woman, I would not be happy."

"I said I didn't have a girlfriend."

"Completely different question."

"No," I said, smiling. "Nobody is under the impression that they're in a relationship with me. Is there anyone out there who is under the impression that they're in a relationship with *you*?"

She laughed. "No."

"Okay."

She smiled. "Okay."

I woke up the next morning at six a.m., naked and happy after having the best date of my entire life.

And then I realized she was gone.

CHAPTER 5

ALEXIS

I tiptoed into my own house without turning on the lights like a teenager sneaking in after curfew.

It was six-thirty in the morning, I had one shoe on, my hair was a tangled mess, I was caked in mud and farm animal fur, and I was wearing a hoodie I'd stolen on the way out.

I'd panicked.

I'd panicked, and I ran while he was asleep.

I woke up in a strange man's bed in a dusty garage in a town in the middle of nowhere after having what was admittedly the best sex of my entire life—with a twenty-eight-year-old.

He was twenty-*eight*.

I'd gotten up to use the bathroom and put on his hoodie. When I was washing my hands, his wallet fell out of the pocket, open to his driver's license.

I knew he was younger than me. I just didn't realize he was almost a decade younger than me.

I'd had a one-night stand with a total stranger, who was a *decade* younger than me.

What was I *doing*? I didn't do things like this. I didn't have casual sex. I didn't *do* risky behavior. I'd made Neil wait two months before I'd slept with him, and when I finally did it was during a very well-planned romantic trip to Mexico. I'd spent a week picking out the lingerie I was going to wear, and I got waxed and exfoliated, and there were petals on the bed. I'd never had sex with anyone who wasn't my boyfriend in my entire life. And now I'd just made an exception with a guy I'd just met who was almost as young as Neil's son.

I completely freaked out.

I'd gotten dressed and fled in the night, stepping in dog poop on the way out. Or maybe it was pig poop? Or goat poop? Whatever it was, there was so much of it that it sucked my shoe right off my foot and I left it like a lizard shedding its tail to make its escape.

I hobbled into my dark living room, tossing my keys on the credenza.

"Where were you?"

I gasped at the phantom male voice coming from the direction of Neil's favorite armchair. And then a light flicked on and my heart started beating again.

"Derek! Oh my God, you scared me half to death."

My twin brother beamed at me from the recliner. "Hey, sis." Then he looked me over and sat up, worried. "Are you okay?"

I scoffed and looked down at my destroyed dress and bare foot. "Yeah." I blew out a breath. "I'm fine. How'd you get in here?"

"Your alarm code is the same one you use for your phone."

"You know the code to my phone?" I reached back and took off my lone heel.

"I know all your codes. Even when you change them."

I laughed dryly. My brother and I had a touch of twin telepathy going on. Always had.

"What are you doing back?" I asked, padding across the room in my bare feet and flopping on the sofa. "I thought you were in Cambodia for another six weeks."

"Came back early."

"But not early enough to save me from half a week in Cedar Rapids alone with our parents," I deadpanned.

"Wild horses couldn't have dragged me there."

I laughed again, leaning my head back on the sofa and closing my eyes.

"Is that a *hickey*?"

My head shot up. "WHAT!?" I bolted off the couch and ran to the mirror over the credenza, looking at my neck.

"Damn," I breathed, seeing the quarter-size purple blotch by my ear.

"That's a little tenth-grade retro, don't you think, sis? And I'm slightly pissed at you for not telling me you got back with Neil."

I groaned, touching the splotch with my finger. "I didn't."

Derek eyed me. "Then who gave you that…" He seemed to notice my hoodie at the same time. "And since when do you wear camo?"

"I don't," I said, groaning at the mark. I was going to have to put a Band-Aid over it, it was so big. I pulled the hoodie open and rolled my eyes. There was a hickey on my breast too. I looked again. Both of them.

Derek waited in silence for me to elaborate.

"I met someone. It's over," I said, abandoning my examination, dropping back down on the sofa, and scrubbing my hands over my face.

"You met someone? When?"

I lolled my head to look at him. "About ten hours ago?"

He blinked at me. "Okay. You're having a midlife crisis. I've seen this before. We can get you help."

I laughed. God, I probably *was* having a midlife crisis. How else could I explain this?

"My car got stuck on the way home from the funeral and this guy towed me out. He was nice and very cute, and I went home with him to eat a grilled cheese—which was really good, actually. He made it from stuff in his greenhouse. Then there was this loose pig running around and it got mud all over me—"

"A *pig*?" He looked amused.

"Yeah. It came running out of the woods. Scared the crap out of me. It was like three hundred pounds. I guess it got loose from a nearby farm or something? It was friendly. I petted it. Then a dog jumped on me too. The guy had a baby goat in pajamas and—"

He put up a hand. "Say no more, that explains everything."

I laughed tiredly.

"Anyway, it's not going to be a thing," I mumbled. "I didn't even get his last name."

"Did you use protection?"

"Yes. Of course. I still have my IUD and he used a condom."

A few of them, actually... I blushed thinking about it.

"Good. Well, I'm glad you're having fun—and that it wasn't Neil."

I scoffed. "Yeah, same."

"I see his stuff is still here." He nodded to the garage.

I rubbed my forehead. "I packed it all up, but he refuses to come get it."

Derek leaned forward with his elbows on his knees. "I'm sorry I wasn't here when it happened," he said seriously.

"It's fine. You were saving the world," I said wearily.

Derek had been gone for six months doing volunteer work with Doctors Without Borders. He was a plastic surgeon. A good one. He was out there treating burn victims and children with cleft lips. I could hardly be upset that he wasn't here to tell Neil to go to hell in person—though as I understand it, he definitely did via satellite phone.

I looked over at him. "Why are you back? They let you out early?"

A slow smile crept across his face. "I can tell you, but you have to sign an NDA."

I laughed, thinking it was a joke, but he reached into a messenger bag resting on the side of the chair and pulled out a piece of paper and a pen.

I blinked at him. "You're kidding me."

"Look, I wouldn't ask if it wasn't to keep a promise." He slid it across my coffee table at me.

I eyed him. "You want me to sign an NDA before you, my brother and closest confidant, can tell me why you're in my living room."

He pushed the paper toward me another inch and tapped an index finger on the signature line.

I shook my head and picked it up, scanning it. "What is this?"

He put up a hand to quiet me. "Just sign, and then I can tell you everything."

I sighed. "Okay," I mumbled, scrawling my name on the dotted line. I set it back on the table and tossed the pen on top. "You have your paperwork. Tell me."

"I got married."

I bolted straight up. "WHAT?!"

He was beaming. "Last weekend. I've been seeing her for six months."

I gawked at him. "And you didn't *tell* me?"

"I couldn't. I promised. It was important to her."

"But...but you tell me *everything*," I said, incredulous.

He nodded. "I know. Which should tell you how important her trust is to me."

I sat deeper into the sofa, my eyes moving back and forth across my lap. "Married..." I breathed. I looked up at him. "To *who*?"

"Her name is Nikki. She's a recording artist. A famous one. She was in Cambodia setting up a women's home for survivors of sex trafficking."

I scanned my limited knowledge of current recording artists. "Nikki...Nikki who?"

"Her stage name is Lola Simone."

"*No*," I said.

He was grinning.

"You are not married to Lola Simone."

"I am." He pulled out his phone and handed it to me.

I stared at the picture of the two of them together in what appeared to be a wedding photo.

Lola Simone was a huge, Lady Gaga–level rock star. Only she didn't look the way she did in the tabloids in these pictures. She looked normal. Shoulder-length brown hair, a modest white dress with a flower lei. Derek was in white linen, beaming.

"She's incredible, Ali. The most remarkable woman I've ever met."

I raised my eyes to him. "And you married her. Without me there?"

His smile fell the slightest bit. "No one was there but her agent, Ernie. We had to keep it small," he said, taking his phone back. "Her privacy is super important to her. She gets recognized everywhere she goes. She has no anonymity. The paparazzi hound her constantly. It was just easier to do it there and do it quietly."

"Well, when am I going to meet her? You didn't bring her?"

"She's too busy with her project to leave. And she doesn't like coming back here."

"Well, she's going to have to come back eventually. You live here, and your volunteer work ends in a few weeks."

His smile fell again. "Ali, I'm not coming back."

I blinked at him. "*What?* What do you mean you're not coming back?"

"I'm moving to Cambodia to be with my wife."

The news punched me right in the gut. "Moving to Cambodia..." I said, disbelief in my voice.

"To get her women's home up and running. To do more volunteer work. They need surgeons and there's a lot of good we can do there."

I sat back into the sofa. Then the true impact of what he'd said hit me. I raised my eyes to him. "No. You can't leave me here with him."

He managed to look even sorrier than he already did. "You'll be okay."

I shook my head. "No. No, I most definitely will *not* be okay. You can't do this to me, Derek. I can't keep working with Neil. I can't. I tried it. I'm already applying to other hospitals. I can't see him every day."

He dragged a hand down his mouth. He didn't answer me. He studied someplace behind me. He couldn't look me in the eye.

I was a Montgomery.

A Montgomery had worked at Royaume Northwestern Hospital since the day it was built in 1897. I came from a family of legendary doctors who made huge strides in medical advancements over the decades. They were powerful philanthropists who made possible the bulk of the programs and clinical trials that Royaume was famous for. It was my family's legacy. We were the Vanderbilts and the Carnegies of the medical world. Last year the History Channel made a documentary about it as part of their Titans of Industry series. Half the hospital was named after us. There was a Montgomery Memorial Garden. A Montgomery Pediatric *Wing*. There had never been a single day in almost a hundred and twenty-five years that Royaume *didn't* have a Montgomery on staff. It was more than a tradition, it was an institution.

Mom and Dad had been there, but they retired in March. Derek was there and so was I. But with Derek leaving...

It was going to have to be me. I was going to have to stay.

I couldn't be the Montgomery who undid it. I couldn't dismantle the franchise. It would literally go down in the history books.

It was like I'd just been handed a life sentence. And he *knew* it.

"Look," he said. "Maybe it's time to break the chain. The hospital isn't going burn down if a Montgomery isn't on staff—"

"Great. Good idea. How about *I* leave first and *then* you quit." I cocked my head, and he pressed his lips into a line. "That's what I thought."

He averted his eyes. "Any chance Neil will move?"

"He's the chief of surgery. He's been at Royaume for twenty years. I think we have a better chance of him getting struck by lightning than him going anywhere else."

He looked back at me and sat quiet for a moment. "I'm sorry. I know the position this puts you in."

I looked at him, hopelessness washing over me.

"You don't know what it's like, Derek—the way Neil chips away at me. He'll start to gaslight me, make me feel like I deserved what he did, and I'll get so confused and broken down and tired that I'll let him back in out of sheer exhaustion. I *have* to leave, Derek. I don't have any other way to protect myself."

He paused for a long moment. "I have to live my life, Ali. And that's with Nikki, doing what I know I'm meant to do."

I put my face in my hands.

We went quiet for a long time.

"How did I not feel it?" I whispered. "How did I not know that you were falling in love and deciding something so big? I should have sensed it. It should have felt like a glitch in the matrix."

"How did I not know Neil was hurting you until you told me?"

I sniffed and took my face from my hands, but I couldn't look at him.

"He spent so many years taking pieces of me," I said quietly. "I'm trying to put myself back together, and now I have to do it without you? And with him always there?"

He inched closer to the edge of the sofa. "You are strong enough for this. And all your friends are at Royaume. Don't let him run you off. You deserve to be there if that's where you want to be."

Yes, my friends were there. Jessica, and Bri, and Gabby. But that didn't outweigh having to work with Neil for the rest of my life—and it *would* be the rest of my life. There was no one else.

Right now Neil was playing the remorseful ex. But it wouldn't last. Once he saw he wasn't going to get me back, he'd switch strategies, and it would get mean.

He *always* got mean.

I put my face back in my hands. "Why am *I* the last in the dwindling Montgomery breeding program? It's like some cruel joke."

Mom and Dad had me and Derek for the sole purpose of continuing the family line. Bred, molded, groomed, and told from my earliest age that I was destined to work at Royaume Northwestern and I was not to take my husband's name if I ever got married. But it wasn't supposed to be me in the limelight. It was supposed to be *Derek*.

I felt a hand on my arm. "Don't let them decide the life you're going to live. You only get one."

The words hung there between us. But I was too weak to pick them up.

Derek knew the truth. I had no choice in the matter now.

I'd never, ever get away.

CHAPTER 6

ALEXIS

Six days later I sat with Bri at the nurses' station in the emergency department at Royaume Northwestern. I hadn't seen her over the last week—mostly because we didn't have any shared shifts, and I was too busy with my brother to talk on the phone or do the drinks we'd planned. Derek left on Saturday, back to his new wife, after telling our parents that he was leaving for good.

Dad, as expected, completely lost it.

He didn't say it, mostly because I don't think he had time to gather his thoughts in the chaos of Derek's NDA and marriage announcement, but I could sense the disappointment descending on me, like he was realizing that I was all that was left of the great Montgomery/Royaume legacy, and all was to be lost.

Derek had always been the golden child, so it hadn't mattered that I was always mildly disappointing in terms of my accomplishments. I didn't want to publish papers in medical journals or do speaking engagements, like he did. I hated the spotlight. I just wanted to help people.

But now as the only Montgomery on staff, anything other than complete and total professional domination would be considered an embarrassment to my prestigious lineage—and I was already off to a bad start. I wasn't a surgeon, I wasn't pioneering any medical advancements, my face would not appear on magazine covers. It was like Dad just found out the most useless princess had ascended the throne.

Bri clicked away at her computer next to me. She was charting her patients. Her brown hair was tied up into a loose bun, and she had her stethoscope draped around her neck. She looked like the results of a Pinterest search for "beautiful physician."

Briana Ortiz was an ER doctor like me. We'd met in med school. She was thirty-four, Salvadorean, and *very* good at her job.

"So," Bri said, "are you going to tell me what happened? The rumor mill's chugging out a story that Derek quit?" She did a final tap and turned to me.

I looked at her over my reading glasses. "It's not a rumor."

"They're also saying he was wearing a wedding ring." She gave me a raised eyebrow.

"*That* I cannot discuss," I said, doing my own final tap on my keyboard. "I signed an NDA."

"Your own brother made you sign an NDA," she deadpanned.

"He did. It's been a whole week of firsts."

A nurse came out of room four. "Nunchuck Guy's here. Again."

I groaned.

"Send him to CT," we called in unison. Bri looked back at me. "So what'd you do all week?"

I sighed. "Hung out with Derek and my parents. We went to that new restaurant in Wayzata on Friday, and Mom decided it was the time and place to give me her Team Neil speech about going with him to couple's counseling. Said he deserves a second chance. I feel like he's asking people to talk to me. This is the second attempted intervention this week."

"The man boned an anesthesiologist. Who you have to *work* with. What doesn't your family get?"

I rubbed my temple tiredly. It wasn't just Neil's cheating. Bri and Derek were the only ones who knew the real reason why I wasn't giving him another chance. Bri wouldn't pee on Neil if he was on fire after what he'd put me through the last couple of years.

But everyone else? Everyone *loved* Neil. My parents, our friends. He was the life of the party, everyone's buddy.

"I mean, they all started off sympathetic enough," I mumbled. "*How could he? I hope you threw him out on his ass.* Blah blah blah. But then Jessica's birthday came up and everyone went to the lake house, and Neil and I weren't there, and I think it finally started to hit everyone that life as we all knew it for the last seven years is over. Then it suddenly flipped to, *Well, have you considered counseling? It was just that one woman, he made a mistake and he knows it.* I think he's sleeping on a futon at Cam's," I added wearily.

Bri made a disgusted noise. "The man's a surgeon. He's gotta sleep on his twenty-two-year-old's sofa? He can't get a damn apartment?"

"I think the second he does, this whole thing suddenly becomes real."

"Good. I hope his dick shrivels up and falls off. For real." She picked up her iced coffee. "What did your dad say about it?" she asked, talking around the straw.

"It's going to piss you off," I warned.

"Tell me."

"He said that Neil is brilliant and that sometimes brilliant people make mundane mistakes."

She scoffed. "Yeah, well, you're brilliant too, and I don't see you humping anesthesiologists."

"He also said he hopes I come to my senses soon because the summer holidays are coming up."

"He *didn't*." She gasped.

"Oh, yeah. He did. And Derek left me alone, trapped for three days in Cedar Rapids with *this*."

"I want to cage fight your whole family."

I snorted. "Yeah, me too."

"Why didn't you just tell your dad to go to hell?"

My laugh was for a joke much funnier than this one.

"You do *not* tell Dr. Cecil Montgomery to go to hell."

No one did.

I was raised to have an almost godlike deference to my legendary father—I didn't know anyone who didn't. You did not argue with him, you did not disagree with him, and you certainly did not tell him to go to hell.

I went to the university my father told me to go to. I pursued the career he demanded. In fact, the only time, and I do mean the *only* time, that I ever dared disregard my dad's wishes was when I went into emergency medicine instead of surgery. He only let it go because Derek was the family front-runner anyway, so I didn't really matter.

That backfired.

Bri poked at her ice with her straw. "Your dad terrifies me. When he used to come to the ER, everyone would scatter like cockroaches. And then your mom would come in after him to do a spinal consult, all sweetness and light, mopping up the tears of the nurses. Why's there always a nice one and a mean one?"

"Because there are two types of people in the world, difficult ones and easy ones, and they marry each other."

"Ha."

She paused for a moment and eyed me. "Okay. So tell me about the hickey. Telling everyone you burned yourself with a curling iron—are we in tenth grade?"

I laughed.

"Did you have hate sex with Neil?"

I recoiled in horror. "No! Why would you ask me that?"

"Because you've been avoiding talking to me, so I can only assume that's because you don't want to tell me the hickey origin story. And the only kind of sex I'm gonna begrudge you is sex with Neil."

I let out a deep breath. "I did not hook up with Neil."

She waited. "Well?"

I made eye contact with her for a long moment, and she made a give-it-to-me gesture with her hand.

"I met someone last week."

She pulled her face back. "You did? When? Where? What app are you using?"

"No app. Remember the guy who towed me from the ditch?"

"The middle-of-nowhere guy?"

"That's the one. I went home with him."

She blinked at me. "You *didn't*..." she breathed.

"I did. And then I ran out at four-thirty in the morning without waking him up." I cocked my head at her.

"Why the hell did you do that? Something wrong with him?"

I shook my head. "No. There was absolutely *nothing* wrong with him. He was nice, and sweet..." I looked over at her. "And twenty-*eight*."

She grinned. "Daaaaamn! You get it, girl."

"Shhhhh," I said, hushing her, looking around. "I can't date a twenty-eight-year-old, Bri," I whispered. "He's a baby."

"He's not *your* baby."

"Cam is twenty-two," I said.

"Yeah, well, Cam is not your kid, and the only reason your ex had a twenty-two-year-old son was because you were dating a man ten years older than you."

I shook my head. "I didn't even date twenty-eight-year-olds when *I* was twenty-eight."

"Well, you missed out. They're just old enough to not be annoying and they have all that sexual energy. And you can train them. They're so eager to learn at that age, like puppies." She dipped her head to look me in the eye. "Does he have any friends?"

I laughed.

He did have energy…My cheeks went hot thinking about it.

"I'm going to be thirty-eight this year," I said. "I can't date a guy that young."

"Who says? If you were twenty-eight and he was thirty-seven, nobody would bat an eye. Nobody batted an eye when you dated Neil—and they should have, that guy was an asshole."

I pressed my lips into a line.

"Look," she said, going on. "You're new to this whole single-in-your-thirties thing so you don't know what it looks like out there, and I'm here to tell you, it doesn't look good. It's like picking through a garbage heap looking for the least disgusting thing. Last week I had a guy bring me funeral flowers. Like, they were a cross and they had a picture of the dead guy in the middle."

I barked out a laugh.

"I don't think he noticed until I pointed it out," she said. "Oh, remember the Hawaiian-shirt guy with the porn 'stache and all the cats who kept saying I looked like his next ex-wife? Like, seriously? These are the men we're supposed to get a UTI for? If you found someone you like, date him. Trust me."

I was still laughing about the funeral flowers. "I didn't even get his number," I said.

"You get his name?"

"Yeah. His first one."

She shrugged. "So go find him. You said the town is small. How hard can it be?"

I didn't answer her.

"Was the sex good?" she asked.

I scoffed. "The sex was incredible. In-*credible*. He did this thing where he lifted me against a wall," I whispered. "We went three times. He was back up in under two minutes flat. *I* got tired before he did, and he was doing all the work."

"See, that's some twenty-eight-year-old shit right there. You think your cognac-drinking, receding-hairline, pushing-fifty-year-old Our Time date is gonna give you that acrobatic sex? He's not. He threw his back out playing golf."

I laughed so hard a nurse wheeling someone into a room turned to look at me.

I was still snickering. "Okay, but really though. I can't. I mean, what the hell am I even doing? What does he have in common with my friends? My family?"

She looked me dead in the eye. "You know you can just fuck him, right?"

I gasped.

"I'm serious. You do not need to marry this man. You can just use him for sex. You are aware of this option?"

"Of course I'm aware of the option," I whispered. "But it wasn't like that though. I kind of liked him. He was charming."

"You had a one-night stand with a man you knew for how long?"

She waited.

"Well?"

I glanced at her. "Three hours."

She nodded. "Three hours. And it wasn't like that?" Her face called bullshit. "You are very capable of casual sex, I promise you."

I blew a breath through my lips.

"So what's this guy look like?" she asked.

I scoffed. "Scott Eastwood in *The Longest Ride*, only with a beard. Oh, and he had a baby goat in pajamas."

"He *didn't*."

"He did."

Her eyes were wide. "I'd follow a clown into a storm drain if he had a baby goat in pajamas."

"His hands were rough," I said, somewhat distantly. "I know it's weird to say, but I *really* liked it. He smelled good too. I stole his hoodie."

She arched an eyebrow. "You stole the man's hoodie? That's a serious crime."

"I'm going to hell, I know."

I couldn't stop wearing it. It smelled like him and it smelled *good*.

My friend Gabby told me once that she sent a blanket over to the breeder where she got her Lab, so the puppy could get used to her smell before he came home. I felt like it was like that. Like I was getting used to Daniel via his sweatshirt pheromones, and he wasn't even here.

I'd be lying if I said the fading scent wasn't making me want to go back and smell the real thing...

I seriously couldn't stop thinking about the sex. I was thinking about it more now, almost a week later, than I had the day after it happened, like I'd developed a taste for it and now I was craving it.

"How old do you have to be to be a cougar?" I asked.

She laughed. "Older than you."

"I can't believe I had a one-night stand," I whispered. "Who *am* I?"

"You know, it's only a one-night stand if you don't go back and do him again."

I had to cover a snort, and she laughed.

"What? It's true," she said.

I shook my head. "There has to be science behind that kind of attraction," I said quietly. "Something with the genes."

"That good, huh?"

"That good," I said, turning to look at her. "And it felt *extremely* mutual."

It had been so long since I'd been made to feel like I was irresistible. Come to think of it, I wasn't sure I ever had.

I was never this horny with Neil. Well, not unprovoked anyway. Our sexual relationship had always required lots of lead-up. Foreplay and wining and dining. But with Daniel...

It didn't escape me that I'd wanted to see him naked an hour after meeting him.

I'd pulled out my vibrator last night. The one that a week ago I was perfectly satisfied using as a full replacement for an actual sex life. I stared at that little pink contraption and realized that the one reason why I'd been ready to hang up my dating belt was because I'd never had sex good enough for me to go in pursuit of it. Now I *had*, and a vibrator wasn't going to cut it anymore.

It sort of made me wish I'd stayed blissfully ignorant.

"You should have seen how I came home," I whispered. "I got accosted by a loose pig while I was there—don't ask. My dress was caked in mud. I had a snout print directly on my ass, goat fur all over me. Then I stepped in a pile of dog poop in my black Manolos. The motion sensor lights went on and I panicked, so I ran and left it there."

"You left your shoe," she deadpanned. "Like Cinderella."

"Yeah. I did. And the hoodie I was wearing was camouflage."

"So you came home in a muddy two-thousand-dollar dress wearing one shoe and your fuck buddy's camo hoodie."

I nodded. "That is correct."

"Like an Old MacDonald walk of shame. Did you have hay in your hair?"

I started laughing. "Shut up."

It was sawdust, actually, but I wasn't telling her that.

"I would pay to replace that dress for one screenshot of you coming home in the Ring camera."

"Well, your birthday *is* coming up..."

We were still giggling when a small huddle of brand-new first-year residents touring the hospital came down the hallway and froze to stare at me, wide-eyed.

"Oh, God," Bri groaned. "Yes, it's a Montgomery," she called. "You will be seeing them on occasion, this one is your attending, be happy she's not her dad. Please move it along." She made a shooing motion with her hand and they scurried off. She rolled her eyes.

"Do you ever get sick of that?" she asked, turning to me.

"I don't even notice it anymore."

She leaned back in her seat. "God, you guys are like the royal family. So what are you gonna do about all that? Derek's gone, so you're sort of 'The One' now, right? You have to, like, kiss babies and christen pediatric wings?"

I squeezed my eyes shut. "I hate this so much." I looked over at her. "You know the *Star Tribune* called me yesterday? They wanted to know what my plans were for the hundred-and-twenty-five-year anniversary now that the 'torch has been passed on to the new generation.'" I put my fingers into quotes. "Apparently I am now delivering the keynote speech at the quasquicentennial gala in September."

She made a face. "Damn. Can you just not do it? Say no?"

I shrugged. "Sure. And then the hospital will lose a million dollars for cancer research, the Montgomery scholarship program will cease to exist, half the initiatives for low-income families will be defunded, construction on the new transplant center will grind to a halt, and I'll become the shame of the Montgomery legacy."

"Wow. No pressure."

"Seriously. Mom made sure to remind me that the international donors won't fly in for the galas unless a Montgomery is in attendance. So I will be expected to be at every fund-raiser to schmooze the elite from this day forward."

"Derek *loves* to schmooze the elite."

"Well, right now Derek is loving something else far more important." I sighed. "I love what we do, I just hate the pageantry of it. It's like this unrivaled, bottomless tool for good and I'm the last one that can wield it, and I just wish it wasn't me."

"With great power comes great responsibility."

I smirked, but she wasn't wrong.

"That's kind of cool though. You can save lives just by showing up in a cocktail dress. Hey, remember when *Forbes* called you guys the last great American dynasty and then Taylor Swift used that as the title of a song?"

"STOP."

"What?! It was hilarious. You're fancy. I'm proud of you. Also, can you autograph a few Post-its for me? I sell them to the first-year residents. I have student loans."

I flicked a pen at her, and we cracked up.

Then Neil rounded the corner.

The second we saw him, our humor ground to an abrupt halt.

He made his way to the nurses' station in his sky-blue scrubs.

At forty-seven, Neil had a full head of silver hair, a strong square jaw, and a chin dimple. He was annoyingly good-looking, and what was more annoying was that he knew it.

I saw him almost every day that I worked. He was the chief of surgery so I was constantly handing patients off to him. But we didn't have any today, so this was probably a personal call. Yay.

Bri crossed her arms as he approached. "Dr. Rasmussen. What can we do for you?" she asked dryly.

He ignored her and looked at me. "Alexis, I'd like to speak to you."

"You can say anything you need to say to her in front of me, Wreck-It Ralph," Bri said. "She's gonna tell me everything anyway. Saves her from having to do the sleazebag accent."

I saw the flicker of annoyance on his face, but he pushed it down.

I crossed my arms too. "What do you want, Neil?"

He glanced at Bri and then back at me. "It would be better if we talked in private."

"Better for who?" Bri said. "You?"

His jaw ticked. "We need to discuss the house."

The house. Actually, we did need to discuss it.

We hadn't been married, but we had bought the house together five years ago. We were both on the title. He'd paid his portion of the mortgage the last two months, but it wasn't fair to expect him to keep doing it given that he wasn't living there—even though in my opinion it was the least he could do.

"I'd like to buy out your stake in it," he said.

My arms dropped. "*What?*"

"I'd like to buy you out. I want the house."

I stared at him, incredulous. "I'm not selling you my house."

"It's not your house. It's *our* house. My friends are there, it's close to work when I'm on call, it has the running trails I like—"

Bri pressed her lips into a line. "Uh-huh. Well, guess you should have thought of that before you boned what's-her-face over there." She gestured vaguely to the exit.

"You're not getting the house," I said again. "I'll buy *your* share, and you can buy something else."

His eyes narrowed. "You don't need it. It's too big for you."

"But not too big for you?" My voice was a touch too high. "Fuck you, Neil."

I felt Bri jerk in her chair and stare at the side of my face.

Nobody was around but the three of us. Nobody heard it. But I hardly ever stood up to Neil. I didn't know what was fueling this momentary surge of bravery.

No—I knew *exactly* what was fueling it. It was the clarity from months of therapy. The realization that he was a manipulative, emotionally abusive asshole.

And something else.

For some reason knowing that Neil wasn't the last man who'd given me an orgasm fortified my courage. I think it did more for this situation than any of the rest of it. The other night was proof that I was attractive and desirable, despite everything Neil had tried so hard to make me believe.

Bri smirked, and we tag teamed glaring at him.

His jaw set. "You don't know how to deal with the house. The pool needs to be opened for the summer, the sprinklers are shut off and blown out, there's a dead tree that needs to be removed before it falls on the roof, you need to put salt in the water softener—"

"You don't do any of that," I snapped. "You hire someone to do it."

"Hiring someone to do it is part of what it takes to run it. There's a hundred and one things I manage there that you have no idea about. You're not capable of running a property of that size."

"My answer is no," I said. "I will not have you uproot my life." I leaned forward. "And anyway, if you got the house, how would you ever get the smell out?" I cocked my head and watched him take the hit. It was an inside jab that only he and I understood, and one that made its mark.

He pressed his lips into a line. Then he turned and stalked off.

"Oh, my God!" Bri whispered when he was far enough away that he couldn't hear her. "Holy shit, I've *never* seen you tell him to fuck off like that."

"What happened?" I muttered. "I blacked out."

We watched Neil push through the double doors and disappear.

Bri shook her head with a grin. "Look at that man-trum. Eight thousand nerves in the clitoris and still not as sensitive as a white man not getting his way." She beamed at me. "I *like* this new you."

"My therapist says being consistent is the only way to deal with someone like him. That what you allow is what you teach. I have to set clear boundaries and enforce them."

"I'd say that was pretty damn clear. God, he's annoying. He's like that hair stuck to your shirt and you know it's there 'cause you can feel it on the back of your arm but you can't get rid of it?"

I laughed. "I'm *never* giving him that house."

"You shouldn't."

"I'm not. I spent an entire year furnishing it. I use those trails more than he does, and my friends live there too. That is *my* damn house."

Then we sat there for a minute.

I faced her. "I think I need to call that guy."

"I think so too."

"I mean, I should return his hoodie, right? That's the right thing to do. What if it has sentimental value?"

She looked amused.

"What?"

"Let's call this what it is. It's a booty call. You need this rebound. Someone to make you feel safe and beautiful and give you all the good sex you didn't have for the last seven years. And he sounds perfect for the job. Too far away to be up in your shit. Too young to want a commitment."

"And we have nothing in common, so no way I'll get attached," I added.

She nodded. "Not even a possibility."

CHAPTER 7

DANIEL

I sat at a high-top table in the VFW, nursing a warm beer. Doug was being annoying. This meant his anxiety was high. I was used to it, but my patience had been shorter than usual this week.

April was one of my favorite months. No tourists, so I got to shut down the rental property and focus on my carpentry full-time. The weather was starting to get good and the leaves were budding, which I liked. But I was in a bad mood anyway.

I couldn't stop thinking about her. About why she'd left. I felt like I'd frightened away some beautiful creature I'd never lay my eyes on again.

I ran the night through in my mind over and over, and so many stupid fucked-up things had happened, I couldn't put my finger on the one that had done it. Was it the pig? My loft? *Me?*

I knew what it *hadn't* been. It hadn't been the sex. *That* had been amazing. For both of us. At least that was obvious.

Her hands had been so soft. I'd threaded my fingers through

hers when I was on top of her—but then I wondered if my hands were too rough for her. If she noticed the calluses and if it turned her off. Or maybe it was the massive pile of dog shit that Hunter had left like a present directly outside my front door—that she'd stepped in. I knew this because she'd abandoned her shoe in it.

I'd cleaned it. Not like I had any expectation that she'd come back for it. It had been a week.

I never minded living in Wakan. It never bothered me that we only had a pizza place open during the summer, or that I had to drive forty-five minutes to get to a Walmart or a Home Depot. But dating here was difficult. The small town didn't exactly have a singles scene, and sleeping with tourists was never a means to an end. I didn't do Tinder or whatever the hell Doug was doing these days. I dated a girl named Megan from Rochester for a while, but there had never been that spark between us. Eventually she told me she was seeing someone else and broke things off with me. I hadn't even cared enough to be disappointed.

But Alexis...I was disappointed about her.

I don't know what else I expected. Chances were she would have left the next morning never to be seen again, even if she *had* stayed the whole night. But I hated it anyway.

Everything about her had drawn me in. Her personality, her sense of humor. The curve of her body, the smell of her hair...

I had to stop thinking about it. Especially because there was nothing I could do.

"Hey," Doug said. "Let's do pull tabs."

"I think I'm going home," I muttered, setting my beer on the table.

He scowled at me. "Man, what's your deal? You still crying over that girl?"

"You know what? Fuck you. Maybe if your pig hadn't been out running all over the yard—"

"Hey, don't blame your lack of game on me." He laughed into his glass of Coke. "Not my fault you couldn't close the deal."

I didn't tell anyone we'd slept together. I told them she'd come home with me, I'd made her something to eat, and she left. I didn't want to cheapen our time together by making it fodder for Doug's jabs. And the truth was, even though it *had* only been sex, it didn't really feel that way. We'd had a connection.

At least I'd *thought* we did.

I'd probably imagined it. I had to have, right? Otherwise she wouldn't have left without giving me her number.

I got up and started to pull on my jacket.

Doug cleared his throat. "You can't just stay another twenty minutes?"

He glanced at me for a quick second, then looked away.

Doug struggled with some mental health issues—depression and PTSD. It's why I was taking care of Chloe for him, because he needed his sleep. When he didn't get it, it made his symptoms worse.

The off-season was hard on him. He needed interaction and projects, and when the tourists left he had neither. It had gotten so bad last year Brian and I had to take turns staying at Doug's house because we were worried he was going to hurt himself.

This was another thing that sucked about Wakan. We had nothing. No dentist's office, no urgent care. The closest mental health professional was almost an hour away, which meant we usually just dealt with our shit instead of getting help for it. He'd taken the drive down to the veterans' hospital a few times. They gave him some meds and offered counseling. But they wouldn't refill his prescription unless he kept seeing a doctor, and it wasn't really practical to keep schlepping out there to keep it up, so he didn't.

I was glad he was asking for help. Even if it was just asking me not to leave him alone.

I sat back down. "Yeah, sure. I can stay a bit."

He took a swallow of his soda and nodded. "Thanks." He paused a moment. "So what happened with her?" he asked, softer now. "The girl."

I blew out a breath. What *didn't* happen?

"Well, let's see. We got to my place, and I had to explain that I lived in the loft above the garage and not the beautiful historic mansion that we parked in front of. So that was fun. Then your potbellied pig came crashing out of the woods and got mud all over her dress. Like, *all* over it. I had to throw tomatoes down to get him off her."

"I'm sorry, man. I fixed the fence," he said, looking genuinely apologetic.

"It's fine," I mumbled. "She was pretty cool about it, actually. She petted him, once she realized he wasn't dangerous. Then when we got inside, Hunter jumped on her too. I think the whole thing was just too much."

But *had* it been? Because even after all that, she'd stayed. I made her dinner, and she played with Chloe. We talked.

We did other things...

It was weird because I felt like we'd spent the whole time getting to know each other, and at the end I still knew nothing about her. I didn't know her last name, where she worked, what she did. She was sort of cagey about it, so I didn't press it. Not that knowing would have helped. She obviously didn't want to be contacted or she would have given me a way to do it. I'd just look like a creeper tracking her down.

Liz came by with a tray. "Anything else, guys?"

"No thanks," I said as she picked up an empty peanut basket from between us.

"So what happened with Alexis the other night?" she asked.

She hovered, giving me a twisted-lipped smile that I didn't have to look up to know was there. I knew my cousin. She was trying to poke me.

I grunted into my beer glass. "Didn't work out."

"Really? I thought she liked you. She was giving off some *very* interested vibes."

I scoffed quietly.

The phone started ringing, and Liz gave up her interrogation and went back to the bar to get it.

"Pull tabs?" Doug asked again.

"Ten bucks," I said, fishing my wallet out of my jeans. "That's it. And then I go home."

Liz shouted at me from across the room. "Daniel! You've got a phone call!"

I looked over at her in confusion. "A phone call?"

She was grinning, holding her hand over the mouthpiece. "Alexis!"

I stared at her for a few disbelieving seconds. Then I ran to the phone so fast I tripped over a barstool and almost went flying. I limped the last few feet and took the cordless from Liz. "Hello?"

A tentative voice came over the line. "Hi... Hello. I don't know if you remember me. We met last week? Alexis?"

A huge grin ripped across my face. "Of course I remember you. Hi."

"Hi."

"I didn't think I was ever going to hear from you again," I said, walking the phone over to the hallway by the bathrooms where it was a little quieter. "I thought maybe I did something wrong."

She laughed. "No. You didn't do anything wrong. At *all*."

I smiled.

"I, um...I'm calling because I have a little confession to make," she said, sucking air through her teeth.

"Yeah?"

"I stole your hoodie. I've been feeling really bad about it."

"So let me get this straight," I said, my smile so big there was no way she didn't hear it in my voice. "You feel bad about stealing my hoodie, but not for running off on me in the middle of the night?" I teased.

"Yeah...about that. I'm sorry. I'm a hoodie thief *and* a runaway."

"Well, you should know that one of those things ruined my whole week. The other thing was just a hoodie."

She laughed. "Can I mail it to you?"

I shook my head. "Nope. Not fast enough. I'm gonna need that back immediately. Tonight preferably. I can come get it, just give me your address."

"Tonight, huh?"

"Definitely. Poor hoodie, confused and lost. You're probably keeping it in a dark closet."

"Oh, no, your hoodie has been *very* well cared for, I promise you."

I smiled. "Are you wearing it?"

"Well, you don't steal a hoodie and *not* wear it. Otherwise it's just another senseless crime."

The idea of her wearing my hoodie made my heart pound.

"You know, I have a theory," I said, switching the phone to my other ear.

"Oh, yeah, what's that?"

"I think you took that hoodie because you wanted a reason to come back here."

"*Reeeeally.*"

"Yeah. And I think I know why. The baby goat. Are you using me to spend time with my kid? Because if you are, I have to be honest, I get it."

She laughed, *hard*.

"Well, if I do come back there, am I going to be accosted by the pig again? Because that was a lot of excitement for one night."

"Okay, first of all, that pig has a name. It's Kevin Bacon. It's rude not to use it."

She was laughing again. "Kevin Bacon?"

"Yup. Doug has a petting zoo, and he names them stuff like that."

"Like what?" she asked. "What else?"

"Well, there's Scape Goat—that's Chloe's mom. Chloe's full name is Chloe Nose Bleat." I ticked off on my fingers. "The chickens are Mother Clucker and Chick-a-Las Cage, there's Barack O-Llama, the miniature horse is Al Capony—"

She howled.

I grinned. "The rabbits are Rabbit Downey Jr. and Obi Bun Kenobi—"

"STOP," she begged. "You're kidding me."

"That's Doug for you," I said, grinning. "So what's your address? I can leave in thirty minutes."

I heard her let out a breath. She paused for a long moment. "I'm sure you realized this, but I'm a lot older than you."

I shrugged. "So?"

"Don't you want to know how old I am?"

"Not really. It doesn't change anything for me."

"I'm going to be thirty-eight in December."

"Okay," I said. "I don't care."

I didn't.

She paused. "Daniel, this isn't really a good time for me to get involved with someone. I'm not really emotionally available right now."

"No problem. We can just hang out."

"And you should know that I don't do what we did the other night. *Ever.*"

Yeah, she'd said that the other night. A few times, actually. "Well, you should know I don't do it either. Ever."

And I meant that too. I didn't.

She went quiet again.

There was something fragile in the silence. I got the feeling that if I hung up without getting her to agree to meet, I was never going to see her again. Like she would just disappear back into the universe. And something told me she could go either way.

I cleared my throat. "You are not going to believe this," I said. "Doug just bet me a hundred bucks that I couldn't get you to see me tonight. Wild, right?"

She laughed, and I felt her decision tip.

"Okay," she said finally. "But I'll come to you. I won't be able to get there for another three hours though. I don't live close."

I looked at my watch. It was four o'clock. "So what I'm hearing is you're staying the night."

"Uh..."

"I'll tell you what. I'll put you up in the B & B," I said quickly. "Your own room. It's closed for the season, so you'll have the whole house to yourself."

"Are you sure?"

I felt myself deflate a notch hearing she didn't want to sleep next to me. But beggars can't be choosers, and this was obviously something that had freaked her out the last time. "I'm sure. And come hungry. I'll make us dinner. I got dinosaur nuggets."

She laughed again. "Okay."

We exchanged cell phone numbers and I gave her the address to the house. Then I hung up and turned around to Liz and Doug standing directly behind me. They were both beaming.

"She's coming?" Liz asked, looking excited.

I dragged a hand down my mouth. "Yeah." And then the anxiety hit me. "What the hell am I gonna do with her?"

Doug scoffed. "I think you know what to do with her, buddy."

I gave him a look. "You know what I'm talking about."

It was the off-season. Nothing was open. We didn't even have a movie theater. I couldn't even take her for ice cream, nothing.

What the hell did people in big cities do? What did *we* do? Bonfires? The VFW? Drive around?

"Take her for a drive," Doug said, like he was reading my mind.

Panic ripped through me.

"She likes you," Liz said. "She's coming here because she wants to see you. That's good enough."

Was it? I mean, what the hell did *I* have to offer a woman like her?

Well…there was one thing. And I must have done a pretty good job of it if she was driving two hours to have it again. At least there was that.

"Just keep her laughing," Doug said. "When a woman laughs, her eyes are closed more. She won't notice how ugly you are."

I snorted, despite myself.

"Call Brian," Liz suggested. "See if he can help."

I nodded. That was a good idea. "Okay. Okay, what else?"

Doug threw back the rest of the Coke he was holding. "I'll make the food. I can drop off a basket in a couple of hours."

"Really?"

He grabbed his jacket off the back of a barstool. "Yeah, really. I'll even throw in the good cheese."

I nodded, feeling slightly better. Doug did wine tastings at his farm in the summer. He was a beekeeper and made his own goat cheese and honey. He actually knew how to put together a nice spread.

"Pick her flowers," Liz said. "Women like effort."

I nodded. Effort. Got it.

With that figured out, I ran home.

Three hours felt like a lot, but it wasn't. I had to open the house up and get the best bedroom ready. I cleaned out my truck, which sounded like less work than it ended up being. I don't think I'd ever washed it—it was a work truck almost as old as I was. I cleaned my loft, my bathroom. I had to feed Chloe and change her pajamas. By the time I got in the shower, I had thirty minutes left.

I was so damn nervous. I felt like I was getting a second shot at—I didn't even know what.

She sent me a "be there in five" text, and I came outside with Hunter and grabbed Chloe from her pen. I crouched in the driveway and looked my dog in the eye. "Okay, buddy. No more messing around, got it? No jumping—hey! Look at me.

NO JUMPING. You see how good Chloe is? This is the kind of energy I need you to bring to this situation."

Hunter leaned over and licked Chloe on the nose, and she made a cute little bleat noise.

"And do your business in the woods. We've got a whole forest. You don't need to do that in front of the garage. *Best* behavior."

Hunter didn't look like he had any idea what I was talking about and started scratching his neck. His collar made a jingling full rotation, and then he stopped and blinked at me. His ear was inside out.

Hunter was a six-year-old retired hunting dog I'd gotten from a rescue. I'd only had him three months. He was a Wirehaired Pointing Griffon. He looked perpetually confused and was the worst listener I'd ever met—which was weird, because the previous owner told the rescue he was fully trained. Hunting dogs were strong-willed by design, but this one...

I eyed him. "Some help you're gonna be," I mumbled.

I heard the sound of wheels on gravel and stood. My heart started to pound.

I had a quick second of what-if. What if the chemistry was gone or the attraction didn't feel the same, or I'd built her up in my head and she wasn't like I remembered?

And the second I saw her, I knew I hadn't imagined a thing.

CHAPTER 8

ALEXIS

I'd called him. I'd called him, and I was going back down there. *What in the world* was I doing?

It was such a spontaneous thing, I didn't even really think it through. One minute I was standing in my living room, debating what to order from Grubhub for dinner, and the next I was Googling the VFW in Wakan and calling the number.

I had no idea if he'd actually be there. He was. And the second I heard his voice, I knew I was spending the night in a bed that wasn't my own.

I'd scoured my closet for the right thing to wear. I checked the weather in Wakan. It was sixty today, so I picked jeans, some plaid rain boots that could be hosed off if I stepped in poop again, and a flannel with a white tank top underneath it. I looked exactly like someone *trying* to look woodsy.

I debated calling Gabby to ask her for help with what to wear, but then I'd have to explain why, and I wasn't ready for that talk at *all*.

Daniel was not someone I could introduce to my friends. Ever. They would never get it. Frankly *I* barely got it.

My set of friends didn't know people with tattoos. Or beards. Or goats. Gabby's husband, Philip, was some big money manager guy, and Jessica's husband, Marcus, was a hotshot lawyer. Daniel was too young and too different from the men they were used to. He was too different from the men *I* was used to.

Maybe that was the allure...

There was definitely something very non-demanding about him. I didn't feel like I had to summon stimulating conversation or dazzle him. And he was so fun. Neil would have never hustled his friends in a bar.

Neil would have been horrified to *be* in that bar.

I packed some silky sleeping shorts and a matching black tank top. Not too sexy, but definitely not frumpy. I didn't want to look like I was coming there solely to seduce him—which I totally was—but I also didn't want to look like I wasn't making an effort.

I showered, shaved my legs, did my hair and makeup, packed a quick overnight bag, and headed south before I had time to talk myself out of it.

I listened to Lola Simone the whole way down.

I decided, since I couldn't get to know my new sister-in-law in person, I'd do it through her songs. She had eleven albums, and I started with the first one. It wasn't really my kind of music. Sort of pop rock. Very early Britney Spears, which I guess made sense, since according to her Wikipedia, Lola was sixteen when she made this. But her lyrics were pretty good.

This time when I drove through the tiny town of Wakan, I looked around. Half the businesses were closed on the sleepy main street. An ice-cream and fudge place, an old-timey photo shop, two boutiques, and half a dozen restaurants had unlit neon open signs and "gone for the season" posters in their windows. The motel I'd seen the other night on the drive in had a "closed for the season" message on the marquee, and the RV park next to it looked abandoned too. But even in the off-season, Wakan was charming.

The town was nestled between a river and bluffs. All the buildings were redbrick with old-fashioned lampposts lining the sidewalks. Almost every shop had a black metal historical land-mark plaque, though I was too far away to read the inscriptions. I crept past an antique shop, a bakery, and a pharmacy that looked like it'd been there since the 1800s, with a faded mural of Paul Bunyan and Babe the Blue Ox painted on the brick side.

There was a tiny bookstore, a barbershop, and a single café called Jane's Diner with an OPEN sign hanging from a chain on the inside of the door.

I drove half a mile more and finally turned down the gravel drive of Daniel's rental property. A sign I hadn't seen the last time was illuminated on the corner. The Grant House, 1897. The same year Royaume Northwestern was built, I noted.

Daniel was waiting outside—holding the baby goat.

My heart leaped the second I saw him.

I didn't know how I was going to feel seeing him again—if it would be awkward or whatever had attracted me to him might be gone. But the moment I laid eyes on him standing there, my pulse zinged.

He was even handsomer than the last time—maybe because he had warning? He was wearing jeans and a black Jaxon Waters T-shirt with a loon on the front, a thick brown leather bracelet on his wrist. His hair seemed more styled. Sort of coifed up. He looked like he'd gotten ready.

It was funny that Daniel's version of getting ready was a level of dressed down that I'd never seen on Neil. But it fit him. And God, was it attractive.

Daniel had that lithe, toned body type. Not a bit of fat on him, but he was muscular enough for it to not look lanky on his tall frame. I remembered he had broad shoulders sprinkled with freckles. Every time he'd lifted me, his abs had crunched like an accordion...

My face flushed thinking about it.

I parked. As I got out, Daniel came up to the car door to meet me.

The dog bounded between us, tail wiggling back and forth. He stopped in the middle of his excited greeting and let out a long *rooooooooooo!*

Then he jumped on me.

I caught him with an *oomph*, staggering back.

"Hunter, down!" Daniel pulled him off me with his free hand, still cradling Chloe. "Sorry," he said.

"It's okay. I came dressed for it this time." I smiled at the kid. "You're really milking this, aren't you?"

"I know what I have." Then he leaned in and kissed me.

It was sort of surprising. I mean, I was here for this, so I expected kissing at some point. But the sensual kiss as a greeting made this feel oddly familiar. Like I'd been here a dozen times and was just coming back again.

Chloe was pressed between us, and she began nibbling on my shirt button. I started laughing, and Daniel smiled against my lips. "Are you hungry?"

"Starving."

He leaned away from me. "Let me put her away. Hunter." He eyed his dog, who was sitting obediently at my feet. "No jumping. We talked about this." He made the fingers to the eyes motion like he was watching him and then headed to the back of the garage.

I smiled after him and grabbed my overnight bag from the passenger seat.

When he came back, I was peering up at the house.

It had been dark the last time I'd been here, so I hadn't gotten a good look at the place. It was getting dark now too, but the up-lighting on the house was on this time and I could see it was a gorgeous Victorian, green with white trim. It had a wraparound porch, a swing, rocking chairs, and red geraniums hanging from flower boxes over the banisters. There was a historic landmark plaque by the front door with the same year as the sign in the driveway.

"This is beautiful," I breathed.

"It's been in my family for six generations," he said, taking my bag for me.

"You didn't want to live in it?" I asked, walking with him to the steps.

"I can't afford to live in it," he said.

He didn't seem embarrassed by the question, but I kicked myself for asking it anyway.

It was like I'd forgotten that not everyone can just casually live in mansions. It was a disconnected Let Them Eat Cake moment, and it was the first time since I called him that I thought maybe I'd made a mistake coming here. I was so different from him that I didn't even know how to not carelessly insult him. I was afraid I was going to accidentally do it again.

I still was internally beating myself up for this when he let us into the house.

"This is it," he said, closing the door behind us.

I peered around the entry. It was beautiful. I sort of knew it would be, just based on the outside.

There was a small check-in counter just inside the foyer and an impressive dark walnut staircase behind it with a switchback leading to the second floor. The banister was like a functional piece of art. Hand-carved floral appliqués twisted along the railing. A beautiful period piece, probably original to the historic house. Stunning.

The formal dining room on the left featured a long wooden table that would seat twelve. A living room was on the right with a fireplace framed by green mosaic tile. Colorful glass Tiffany lamps, rich red curtains, antique Victorian furniture. The house was exquisite.

I beamed down at my feet. "Original hardwood floors?"

"In a maple wood herringbone mosaic," he said, proudly. "My great-great-great-grandfather did these. See how he inlaid oak for contrast in the switchbacks? Finished it with a colorless filler, white shellac, and a light-colored wax to preserve the natural color of the wood grain." He smiled. "He knew what he was doing."

And Daniel knew what he was talking about...

"Did he build this place?" I asked.

"He did." He nodded. "Come on, I'll show you the rest."

He went into what sounded like a well-rehearsed tour as he walked me through the rooms. He pointed out Baroque antique monumental Italian wood tole wall sconces, a German wall clock, a nineteenth-century Victorian hair wreath.

It was like the place was frozen in time, trapped in the 1800s. I was totally in love with it. I *adored* antiques. I always wanted to buy some, but Neil complained they didn't match the style of the house.

The Grant House had four bedrooms and bathrooms, and a view of the river out back, though it was almost too dark to see it. There was a four-season porch with wicker chairs and another hearth. The landing on the switchback to the second floor had a huge stained-glass window of a blue underwater river scene with swimming fish and diving loons. We viewed the bedrooms upstairs. Each one had a beautiful fireplace. In the fourth bedroom, he set my bag down. "This is your room for the night. It's the best one in the house."

I looked around, smiling. It had damask wallpaper, a four-poster bed, and a crackling fire. This was a *huge* upgrade from Daniel's loft.

I remembered when I walked into his garage that first night. It had smelled like cedar. Like the lumber section of a hardware store. The jagged teeth of a power saw had glinted on a table in the middle of the room and various furniture projects had been cluttered around the concrete floor and walls. There was a weight bench that he obviously used and a row of muddy men's work boots carefully lined up by the side door. To the right was a small kitchenette where he'd made me that grilled cheese.

To the left a metal spiral staircase had led up to an enclosed loft with a tiny bathroom, a queen-size bed, and a large window that overlooked the garage. It had probably been an office once, but Daniel had converted it into a small bedroom.

To his credit, the room had been spotless. The bed was made, and there weren't clothes thrown around. He hadn't known he was bringing a woman home, so it spoke to his cleanliness. And so did this... The room he'd put me up in was immaculate—and there were fresh flowers on the nightstand.

I'd Googled reviews of the property on TripAdvisor before I headed down.

Five stars. A *solid* five stars.

Every single review gushed about Daniel and how he'd gone out of his way to make them feel at home. Tales of practical heroism abounded. He'd gotten the pharmacist to open the store at two in the morning to buy Tylenol for a sick kid, and he'd changed a tire when a guest had a flat. He did things like leave a box of graham crackers with chocolate and marshmallows by the fireplace.

He had guests on their fifth year of vacations on the property because they were so loyal to him. It went on and on and on.

He was thoughtful. And generous. I knew this already, having experienced his selflessness in our very first meeting, but it was nice to be able to attach a star rating to the man as well.

"It has so much character," I said on the way back down, almost more to myself than to him.

He waited for me at the bottom of the stairs, then he opened the front door for me.

"So what are we eating?" I asked.

"We're eating out, actually."

I paused on the porch. I wasn't sure I liked this. The town was small. I didn't want to advertise this liaison to everyone he knew. Did he?

"Where?" I asked.

He looked up at me from the bottom of the steps, amused. "Are you afraid to leave with me?"

I crossed my arms. "No."

"You *do* have the Taser."

"I don't think you're going to murder me. Though statistically speaking you're much more likely to be murdered by someone you know, so my chances are actually higher this time."

He laughed. "You think I saved you from the raccoon ditch

the other night just to murder you now? And technically aren't *my* chances of getting murdered higher now too? Should *I* be concerned?"

I fought a smile.

"I planned a picnic. Just us. But my friend Brian will be around to call an ambulance for me if you assault me."

I laughed, relaxing. "Okay. Also, while we're on the subject of bodily injury, no hickeys this time."

He pulled his face back. "I gave you hickeys? You gave *me* hickeys."

"What? No, I didn't."

He pulled his shirt down and showed me a fading purple blotch on his collarbone.

My jaw fell open. "I did *not* give you that."

"What? Who else would give me this?" He held his arms out and peered around with a grin. "How much action do you think I get around here? I'm not making out with anyone but you."

I crossed my arms. "Okay, but seriously, I didn't do that."

"Yeah, you did. I have scratches down my back too."

I gasped, and his eyes twinkled.

I *did* remember clawing at him a bit...

He climbed the steps between us and slipped his hands around my waist. "It's okay, I liked it," he said, his mouth a fraction of an inch from my lips.

I would have laughed if my entire body hadn't turned to jelly in his arms.

God, he was *so* sexy. I think he knew it. He grinned at my breathlessness and whirled me off the porch to the ground. "Your chariot awaits."

CHAPTER 9

DANIEL

I went around and opened the door of the truck for her, and immediately started second-guessing my plan. I also regretted calling it a chariot.

The bench seat she got in on had duct tape over the cracks in the leather. Damn. I should have put a blanket down on it. Even clean, the inside of my truck smelled like gasoline and oil. I never really noticed it before, but I was noticing it now.

I pulled out of the driveway, overthinking everything.

I couldn't give two shits what any of my last girlfriends thought about my truck, but Alexis was too fancy for this. Even out of the cocktail dress and heels, she was too fancy.

It was in everything about her. She was so polished. The clothes she wore for Hunter to jump on looked like they'd never been worn before. The denim was too dark to have been washed even once. Diamond earrings, perfectly painted fingernails. Even the duffel bag she brought was a brand name so far out of my reach, I couldn't even afford it at a yard sale.

Once, a cardinal flew down into the chimney in the living room, and I remembered how startling it had been to see this beautiful, bright red bird perched in the ashes. It was just like this. The ruin of my shitty Ford just highlighted the contrast, how out of place she was.

Women like Alexis didn't live in ashes. They didn't live in small towns in the middle of nowhere where you couldn't get a damn steak in the off-season. They didn't ride around in tired work trucks and hold hands with men who had calluses. They lived in big cities with accomplished men who had important jobs.

I stared at the road, feeling for the first time in my life like I wished I was the kind of man who owned a tie—or a nicer car.

She must have been thinking the same thing, because she put a finger to the hole where the radio dial used to be. "I've never been in a truck before."

I glanced at her. "You've never been in a truck? Ever?"

She shook her head.

"Well, you're gonna love the tractor ride later."

She laughed, and I felt a little better. At least she thought I was funny.

"So where are we going?" she asked.

"It's a surprise."

I slowed down and turned onto the dark, unpaved, wooded road to our destination, and she sat up a little straighter. Then she saw the sign illuminated at the entry of the lot, and she broke out into a dazzling smile. "A drive-in?"

I grinned. "I got Brian to open it just for us."

"I've never been to one," she said, almost in awe. She beamed at me, and all my reservations about the night slipped away.

"You've never been to a drive-in?"

"No. We never really did this kind of stuff growing up."

I pulled into the lot and parked us with the bed of the truck facing the screen.

"What kind of stuff did you do?" I asked, putting us in park.

"Not stuff like this," she said.

I guess that tracked. She didn't really strike me as a swimming-hole, pinball-machine-in-the-pharmacy-during-the-summer kind of woman. But I liked that I was giving her an experience she'd never had. It somehow seemed impossible that I *could*.

"Stay here for a second while I set us up," I said.

I jumped out of the truck and went to the bed. I blew up a twin-size air mattress and covered it with a thick, red, patterned Aztec blanket. I'd brought some heavy blankets and pillows and propped them against the back window so we had something to lean on. I lit a citronella candle for the one or two mosquitoes that might be out this time of year and put it on the roof. Then I plugged in some white Christmas lights to a portable power inverter and ran those along the sides to give us some light to eat by. When I was done, I went to get her.

I opened her door for her. "All ready."

She hopped out and came around the back. "Oh wow," she said when she saw it, smiling.

I helped her up and climbed in after her. Then I grabbed the picnic basket Doug dropped off and started pulling things out.

Doug had outdone himself. There was homemade goat cheese with sliced pears drizzled in honey, dried fruits, bruschetta sandwiches on his fresh baked crusty bread that he made himself with his own sourdough starter, two thermoses with hot chocolate in them—Doug was a lot of things. But when it came down to it, he was a very, *very* good friend.

Annnd I think he was trying to make up for the pig.

She watched me set it all up. But when I handed her her thermos, I noticed she looked a little serious.

"What's wrong?"

She shook her head. "This is all so nice."

I sensed a "but" coming.

"But I feel like I do have to remind you that I'm really not looking to date right now. You didn't have to make such a big deal about me coming," she said.

I stopped what I was doing. "Okay. We need to clear something up," I said, looking her in the eye. "When you come down—no matter what you come down *for*—I'm going to make a big deal over it. Because it *is* a big deal. You're driving four hours, round-trip, to be here. That's not nothing. And if you're staying the night, this isn't going to be a quickie situation. While I'd like to say that I could spend all twelve hours of your stay pleasuring you, I can't."

She laughed.

"We're going to do other things," I said, going on. "We're going to eat, and we're going to hang out. And I'm going to put effort into that because you're putting in effort to be here. And it's going to be like that every time. Okay?"

The corner of her lip twitched. "Okay."

I smiled.

Part of this was my hospitality background and my upbringing. It was in my blood. I was raised to cater to the needs of tourists. My life and the lives of everyone in this town were dependent upon people enjoying themselves while in Wakan. But the other part was something else.

I liked her.

I wanted her to like coming here, because I wanted her to come back. I knew the second I saw her pull into my driveway that this couldn't be the last time.

If all she wanted was sex for now, it could be just sex. I preferred sex with someone I liked and looked forward to seeing. This worked for me.

But there was a connection. I'd sensed it before, and it was the same now. I couldn't explain it. I didn't know if it meant anything or if it would lead to something else. Probably not, all things considered. All I knew for sure was that she needed to come back.

"What are we watching?" she asked, sitting with her legs crossed under her.

"We can pick. Here are the options," I said, swiping open my phone to read the text Brian sent. "Okay, we've got *Gremlins, Pretty Woman, Breakfast Club, Princess Bride*—"

"*Princess Bride*," she said quickly.

"As you wish."

She smiled, and I shot a text to Brian, who was waiting in the projection room above the closed snack bar. A moment later the movie flickered to life.

A message came up on the massive screen:

HE MUST REALLY LIKE YOU. HE BEGGED ME TO DO THIS. ENJOY THE SHOW.

Alexis laughed.

Fucking Brian. I felt my cheeks heat. I was grateful for the dim lighting.

"You begged him, huh?" She smiled.

"He didn't fold until I cried."

She shook her head, still laughing.

The screen went into a pre–movie reel. Silent ads for places in town that were closed until June.

Black bugs zipped around in front of the screen.

"What are those?" she asked, nodding at them.

"Dragonflies," I said, wiping my hands on a napkin. "Though it's a little early for them. It's been kind of warm this spring."

She squinted at them. "There's so many."

I leaned back on my hands. "My grandma used to say that dragonflies mean change is coming."

She went quiet for a moment. "Must be a lot of change."

"It must."

I kept glancing at her while we ate in the white glow.

She was so beautiful. I couldn't believe I'd gotten her to come back here. Made me a little proud of my sex skills.

"Does Brian own the drive-in?" she asked, eating a dried apricot.

I nodded. "That and the grocery store."

"And you're the mayor, and you run a bed-and-breakfast?"

"We all wear multiple hats around here. Liz works at the VFW and waits on tables at Jane's three days a week. Doug does odd jobs. And the mayor thing really isn't a big deal. It's mostly town hall meetings."

"For what?"

I snorted, picking up a cracker. "For me to resolve petty squabbles."

"Like?"

I chewed and swallowed. "Well, like telling the Lutsens they can't have chickens on the roof of the barbershop because the feathers are blowing into the candy store across the street. Barking dog complaints, judging the butter carving contest in Doug's barn on Halloween. You know, important stuff like that."

She laughed.

I took a sip of hot chocolate. "So are you going to tell me what *you* do for a living?"

She gave me hooded eyes. "I mean, isn't it more fun if I'm mysterious?"

"I think it's more fun if I get to know you."

She twisted her lips.

She didn't want to tell me.

"Is there something nefarious you think I'm going to do with this information?" I teased.

She tucked her hair behind her ear. "I'm in the family business."

"Which is..."

"How about I give you three guesses."

I smiled. "Okay. And what do I get if I guess right?"

She arched a playful eyebrow. "What do you want?"

"I want you to come back next weekend."

She gave me an amused smile. "Okay," she said. "You have a deal."

I rubbed my hands together. "Do I get any questions before I guess?"

She shook her head. "Nope. You have to go in cold."

Crap. This was going to be hard. I tried to think of the little I knew about her. She was polished and elegant. Smart. My guess was a white-collar job. She obviously came from money, so she probably made a lot, whatever she did.

"A lawyer," I said.

She tilted her head. "Do I seem like someone who negotiates for a living?"

"You hustled Doug," I pointed out.

She laughed. "No. Not a lawyer."

"CEO."

"Nope."

"Damn," I whispered.

"That's two," she said, smiling. "One more."

I pursed my lips.

"Banking?"

She shook her head. "No."

I puffed air into my cheeks. "So what are my chances of getting you to come down next weekend anyway?" I gave her a raised eyebrow.

"Not good."

"So you're saying there's a chance…"

She laughed at the movie screen. "Let's just see how tonight goes."

We finished the food right as the movie started, and I put everything in the picnic basket and pulled out a blanket so we could lie down. I was glad it was a little cold, because she needed me for warmth. She scooted over and let me put an arm around her. She snuggled into the crook of my elbow, and it was so familiar and comfortable I had to remind myself this was only the second time we'd been together.

And damn, she smelled good. It was intoxicating. I didn't even want to watch the movie, I just wanted to put my nose to her neck, and I knew if I did, both of us would end up with hickeys again before we drove out of here.

I tried to behave myself and watch the show, but I got the sense her attention wasn't faring much better. I made a mental note to take her upstairs before taking her out next time. Neither of us could focus.

Westley was sword fighting Inigo Montoya when I glanced down at Alexis again. But she wasn't looking at the screen. She was looking at the sky.

She noticed me and turned so her lips were an inch from mine. "I don't remember the last time I looked at stars," she said quietly. "Maybe never. It's so peaceful here."

"We don't have the light pollution," I said. "The stars are always really nice in Wakan."

I dropped my eyes to her mouth.

She cleared her throat and looked down at the arm I had lying across my stomach. "Tell me about your tattoos."

I held up my arm to show her. "It's roses on both sides."

"Why?"

"These are the flowers from the banister on the stairs. They were one of the first things I remember as a kid. One of my favorite things in the house. And Grandpa always brought Grandma roses."

She traced a finger over a petal, and I watched her. I felt my heart picking up just from this tiny contact, like even this minor attention from her was enough to put my body on alert. When she got to my wrist, I threaded my fingers in hers. She closed her hand around mine and I smiled.

Maybe women like this *did* hold hands with men with calluses…

She tipped her head up again to look at me. "Why don't you have a girlfriend?" she asked.

"What?"

"You're sweet. You're thoughtful. You're not hard to look at, and the sex is… why don't you have one?"

"The sex is what?" I beamed.

She propped herself on her elbow, our hands still clasped between us. "Well?"

I propped myself too. "I was seeing someone up until a few months ago. It wasn't serious."

"Why wasn't it serious?" she asked.

I shrugged. "I don't know. I just couldn't ever see her past a day I guess."

"What does *that* mean?"

"I never envisioned her in the future. I only ever wanted to see her the day I wanted to see her. You know how when you like someone, you want to make plans with them? I never wanted to make plans with her."

"But you want to make plans with me next weekend, huh?"

I grinned. "Busted."

She laughed. "I get that whole day thing," she said. "At the end I couldn't even see my ex past a minute."

"Oh yeah? What was he like?"

She gave me a one-shoulder shrug. "Arrogant. A surgeon."

I felt myself deflate. So I'd been right about the kind of men she liked. Educated. Accomplished.

The opposite of me.

Surgeon. Maybe that's what she did for a living?

"Are you a surgeon?" I asked.

Her smile fell a little. "That's four guesses. But no."

There was something a little tight about the way she said no. I didn't know how to respond, so I did the only thing I could think of to fill the silence. I leaned forward and kissed her.

Turns out, it was the right move.

I'd had chemistry with other women, but I'd never experienced animal magnetism before. It's the kind of thing that's unmistakable when it's happening—and it happened with her. The same as last time, only stronger. The sexual tension between the two of us was like a sunflower turned to the sky. I'd felt it even when she was gone, I realized. Like my body was looking for her even though I didn't know where she was. It was a shift in gravity. Two bodies in a hammock, or an old mattress that dips in the middle. I could feel us rolling toward each other.

It's the kind of pull that's easier to give in to than it is to get out of.

CHAPTER 10

ALEXIS

We'd just gotten home from the drive-in. He'd chased me giggling up the steps, and I had my back pressed against the door of my room.

"That was fun," I said, biting my lip. "I love *The Princess Bride*. I think we could have paid better attention though..."

Daniel closed the space between us, and his body heat bore down on me. "Inconceivable," he said, crushing his lips to mine. His kiss was warm and wet and perfect, and a rock-hard boner pressed into my stomach.

I broke away, breathless. "You keep using that word. I don't think it means what you think it means."

He laughed, and firm hands slid around my waist and down my back.

Oh, my God...

I'd made out with a boy in the bed of a truck.

We probably would have done a lot more than that if Brian hadn't been in the projection room and we'd had a condom.

I'd reverted back to sixteen years old—only I'd *never* done this stuff at sixteen. At sixteen I was taking AP chem courses and volunteering at the hospital. I was not making out with good-looking small-town boys in the beds of trucks.

Daniel pulled away an inch from my mouth. His hot breath rolled over my lips. My underwear was drenched.

"Good night," he whispered.

Then he pushed off me and started down the hall.

I stared after him in shock. "Wha—you're not...?"

He turned to look at me. "Not what?" He blinked at me innocently.

"I thought...I mean...you're not going to stay?"

"Oh, for that? I want to. Obviously." He gestured to the front of his pants and made a face like any other idea was ridiculous. "But I can't. That was my grandparents' bedroom. I wouldn't be able to do the things I want to do to you in there. Wouldn't feel right."

"Well, there's three other rooms..."

He shrugged. "They're not made up." He put a thumb over his shoulder. "Of course, we could always go back to my loft." He smiled. "I can't really think of a single thing I wouldn't do to you in my own bed. All night. As many times as you want."

So that's what this was about.

I crossed my arms. "You really want me to spend the night with you, don't you?"

"I want you to do whatever you're comfortable with. And you could always come back here to sleep later." He put a hand up. "Unless I make you too tired to walk the short distance from the garage to the house. Which you should know is my goal." His dimples popped. "Also, this place is haunted. I wouldn't sleep here alone." He made a fake scared face.

I laughed, and his eyes sparkled, and he knew he had me. Not because I believed in ghosts, but because he was too adorable to refuse.

Daniel somehow managed to be charming and completely down-to-earth while also exuding pure sex. It was the most baffling combination.

And one I wasn't capable of refusing.

CHAPTER 11

DANIEL

The phone woke me up at seven-thirty.

Alexis was still here, naked and curled up next to me in my bed. I filed this away as a victory.

I didn't want her to get used to staying in the big house. It wouldn't always be available, and it wasn't where I lived. Where I *did* live wasn't great, but it *was* where I lived. And the sooner she got comfortable staying at my place, the better, because she had to keep coming back. She *had* to.

The sex was un*real*. It was like finding the perfect dance partner and then only getting better because now you were practicing together.

I couldn't keep my hands off her. Hell, she couldn't keep her hands off *me*. I was going to have to start keeping Gatorade on the nightstand.

I leaned over and picked up my ringing cell with a smile. "Hello?"

"Hey, hon, it's Doreen. Hope I didn't wake you."

"It's fine," I said, rubbing my eyes. "What's up?"

"Popeye didn't come in this morning. Now, I know sometimes he runs a little late, especially if Jean's dog's been doing her business on his lawn and he's gettin' into it with her, but it's almost twenty past and he's not here. I didn't want to call for the sheriff, 'cause you know how Pops feels about Jake."

Shit.

"All right, thanks for letting me know. I'll head over there now." I hung up.

Alexis sat up on her elbows. "Everything okay?"

I threw off the covers and started jumping into pants. "I have to run out," I said. "I don't know what time I'll be back. I need to check in on someone."

"Is it medical?"

"I think so."

She got up too. "I'll go with you."

I didn't argue. One, because I didn't like losing time with her, and two, because if Popeye was still alive, I could probably use the help. He was a handful. He always took to women, so he'd probably put up less of a fight if she was there.

She got dressed quickly, and Hunter followed on her heels right up until she jumped in the truck. "What happened?" she asked, slamming the door.

I fired up the engine. "Popeye didn't come into the diner this morning," I said as I backed down the drive.

Pops was like clockwork. He was at the diner by seven o'clock every single day, rain, sun, or snow. If he didn't come in, something was seriously wrong.

"Popeye?" she asked.

"He squints with one eye. Kinda looks like him," I said as I turned onto the road. It was only a two-minute drive.

"How old is he?" she asked.

"Ninety at least."

"Any preexisting conditions?"

I shook my head. "I don't think so."

"Dementia, high blood pressure, diabetes?"

I glanced at her. "I don't know. Nothing he's ever mentioned. He's pretty sharp."

"Any idea what medications he's on? Has he ever been hospitalized?"

I blinked at her. "No . . ."

I wanted to ask her about the questions, but I didn't have a chance because I was pulling up to his tiny one-story house. I put the truck in park. "Stay here."

She got unbuckled. "I'm not staying in the car."

"What if he's dead?"

"I think I can handle it."

I arched an eyebrow. "What if he's naked?"

"Nothing I haven't seen," she sang and got out.

I smiled after her, then jogged up the walkway and knocked. "Pops? You there?" I gave him a minute. When he didn't answer, I fished the spare key to his house off my key chain. Popeye was armed and not afraid to shoot, so I knocked and called out as loudly as possible as I opened the door. I pushed it in slowly and peered inside. "Pops?"

A moan came from the bedroom. I ran through the dark, musty house and burst through the door. Popeye was on the floor next to the bed. He was awake and sitting up, still in his pajamas, his back propped against the front of his nightstand.

"Hey, you okay?" I crouched next to him.

"I fell gettin' outta this damn bed. Couldn't get my feet under me to get back up. Well, help me for God's sake!"

I put an arm behind him and helped him to the edge of the mattress. He smelled horrible. Acrid sweat and ammonia. My eyes started to water. "Jesus, Pops, you're ripe. When's the last time you had a shower?"

He yanked his arm away. "Who the hell are you, my wife?" he snapped.

Well, at least he wasn't injured enough to stop barking at me. "Do you think you broke anything?"

He glared at me under his thick white eyebrows, stark against his black skin. "No, I didn't break anything. Gotta piss like a racehorse though. Took you long enough to get here."

Alexis knocked on the doorframe and came up next to me. "Hi, Popeye. I'm Dr. Alexis. Is it okay if I have a quick look at you?"

I stopped and stared at her. "You're a doctor?"

"I am." She smiled at Pops. "Does anything hurt?"

He eyed her like he was trying to decide if he should trust her. "No."

She pulled out her cell phone and turned on the flashlight. "Just a quick light here." She flashed it in his left eye, then his right. "Good. What's your full name, Popeye?"

He looked at me and then back at her. "Thomas Avery," he grumbled.

"Can you tell me what day it is?"

"It's Wednesday," he said grumpily. "Tuna melt day at Jane's."

She looked at me for confirmation on the tuna melt, and I nodded. Then she took his wrist and put two fingers on his pulse, looking at her watch.

It was like she'd transformed before my eyes. Everything about her shifted. She was a professional all of a sudden, going through a routine I could tell she'd done a million times. I just stared at her.

"What were you doing when you fell?" she asked Pops.

"Just gettin' out of bed."

"Do you have any conditions you can tell me about? High blood pressure? A history of strokes? Heart attacks?"

He shook his head. "Fit as a fiddle."

She smiled and peered over at his nightstand. "Are these the only medications you're on?"

"Far as I know."

She picked up the two bottles and studied them. She shook one. "Did you take this with food?"

"I take it like I always take it. With water before I get up."

She smiled. "If you don't take this one with food, it can make you dizzy. Do you have some crackers you can keep by the bed? Something to put in your stomach next time?"

He shook his head.

"Okay. Well, we'll get you some. I think you're in good shape. But you need to follow up with your primary care physician, okay? A fall at your age can be a big deal."

"Fine. Mind if I take a piss now?"

She grinned at me.

I helped him stand so he could use the toilet. He shuffled into the hallway bathroom, mumbling to himself. As soon as the door clicked behind him, I looked at her.

"I'm going to check around for other medications," she said, walking out of the bedroom.

I stared after her.

A *doctor*?

I felt like the chasm between us had just deepened. It was like every time I thought I was leveling up, I realized I wasn't even close. A damn *doctor*.

I blew a breath out and looked around. The place was a mess. "Pops, is Jean still cleaning for you?" I asked through the door. "When's the last time she was here?"

The long sound of Popeye relieving himself tinkled from the bathroom.

"I told her to piss off weeks ago."

I dragged a hand down my face. "This place looks like shit." I started gathering all the clothes on the floor and tossing them into a pile. "Who's doing your laundry?"

The bathroom door opened, and he came out, grumbling. "I'm doing it. She did a crap job. Made my T-shirts smell like petunias."

"We need to get you in the shower," I said. "Do you need help?"

He nodded in the direction of the kitchen, a white caterpillar eyebrow raised. "*She* could help me."

I saw Alexis stifle a smile through the doorway.

I slapped a hand on his shoulder. "Okay, old man, let's go."

He had a hard time stepping over the rim of the tub. I had to brace him, and he almost had another fall. "I'll come get you when I hear the water turn off. Don't try getting out without me," I said.

"Yeah, yeah. Get the hell out."

I went over to talk to Alexis while the shower was running, leaning on the counter by the sink.

"Does he have any bruising?" she asked.

"Not that I saw."

"Does he have any family? Who takes care of him?"

I rubbed the back of my neck, looking around the dim house. "Nobody? All of us? It's sort of a group effort."

"Daniel," she said, her voice low. "He's going to need more help than he's getting. He needs food in the house and someone to make sure he's showering."

I dragged a hand down my beard. "He told me he fell getting in the tub last week. I think it scared him."

"You can put a call in to Adult Protection Services. Try to get him a personal care assistant, Meals on Wheels."

I shook my head. "It's hard to get help out here. I'll work out a schedule. I'll get someone in here once a day to clean, check on him. And I'll install a railing in the bathtub. Maybe some treads on the floor of the shower."

She nodded. "And he needs to take those pills with food. He probably fell because he got dizzy."

"Okay. I'll give them to Doreen. She'll give them to him with his breakfast when he comes into the diner."

She smiled.

"What?"

She shook her head. "It's just...I don't know. I like that you guys take care of each other."

"That's how it is here. It's what we do." I tilted my head, noticing something. "Did you put makeup on?"

We'd ended up in the shower last night. She didn't have any on when she went to bed, and she got up when I did. At least I *thought* she did.

"Yeah," she said, tucking her hair behind her ear. "Why?"

I looked at her, confused. "When?"

She paused. "Before you woke up."

I blinked at her. "You got up just to put makeup on? Weren't you tired? You didn't want to sleep?"

She didn't answer me.

"I hope you didn't do that for me," I said. "I don't care what you wake up looking like."

I meant it. I didn't.

Her face called bullshit.

"I don't care about that stuff," I said. "I'd rather you sleep. If we're gonna be pulling all-nighters, I need you to keep your strength up."

She laughed. Then she bit her lip. "Okay."

I nodded at the house. "I'm gonna clean up a little. When he's ready we can take him to go eat at Jane's."

But she shook her head. "I think I'm going to head out."

My lips fell. "You're not going to stay for breakfast?"

She slipped her hands into her back pockets. "No, I have stuff to do at home. You don't have to drive me back to the house, I remember the way, I can walk. It's not far, and you didn't lock the garage. You take him to eat."

She didn't want to be seen with me.

Not out in public anyway. She'd been perfectly willing to stay for breakfast when we were back at the house . . .

I didn't know what I expected. I guess it *was* a tall order, asking her to go around town with me. Things were new and we didn't really know what this was yet. But it still bothered me.

"Okay," I said. "When can I see you again?"

She gave me a noncommittal one-shoulder shrug. "I don't know. I'll text you." She stood on her tiptoes and gave me a quick peck. "I had a really good time." She smiled. "Thanks for having me."

"Yeah. Thanks for coming."

I watched her let herself out, disappointed that the visit was over.

While I waited for Pops, I went around combing for dishes. Then I grabbed a trash bag and started chucking old newspapers and take-out containers. The place was wrecked. Dusty and cluttered.

A long double-barrel shotgun lay across the coffee table. It was bigger than Popeye was. He'd been cleaning it, and a metal rod and oil-soaked rags lay tossed around next to a box of shells.

I hoped he wasn't planning on shooting Jean's dog.

Or *Jean*.

I came back into the kitchen and pulled out the kitchen trash. When I heard the shower shut off, I went to get him, and a few minutes later he came out dressed and clean.

Popeye wouldn't let me help him into the truck. The diner was only a block away, but I could tell by how slow he was moving that he was a little sore from his fall. The second giveaway was that he didn't fight me to let him walk there. I pulled up as close to the door as possible without it looking like I was trying to baby him, which he'd hate.

Doreen was relieved to see him, and we sat at the counter.

Doreen poured coffee in our cups, and when she was gone, Popeye mumbled at me. "She'll come calling."

I poured half and half into my mug. "Who?"

He pivoted to look at me. "The doctor! Acting like you don't know who I'm talkin' about..." he muttered. "The town'll get 'er back."

I wrinkled my brows at him. "I don't follow."

"The town! It'll get 'er back! It picks who it wants. I've known every lifer going back ninety-six years. I know one when I see one. Your grandparents, you, Doug, Doreen. Not your mama. I knew it the moment she came into the world, she weren't for here. The town knew it too, let her leave."

I blinked at him. "Let her *leave*?"

He looked at me for a moment, squinting with his good eye. "It's alive, you know."

"What's alive?"

"This place. It breathes like you and me. It's got magic in it."

I grabbed the sugar jar, amused. "Magic, huh."

He glared at me. "Go ahead, poke fun at me. But when things start happenin' you can't explain, snow in July, lucky coincidences, you'll change your tune. There ain't no coincidences here, boy. It's the town, protecting itself. And I'm tellin' ya, it likes that girlfriend of yours and it'll get 'er back."

I sighed. Maybe he *was* getting a little confused in his old age after all.

Not that I couldn't use some mystic intervention . . .

She was a *doctor*.

We didn't have people like that here. Hell, I think there were less than a dozen college-educated people in the whole town. We were all in the service industry—we didn't have white-collar jobs in Wakan. We didn't have a clinic where she could work, let alone a hospital. We didn't even have a blood pressure machine in the pharmacy.

I finished breakfast and took Popeye home. When I got back to my place, Alexis was gone. I sat on the bottom of the spiral steps, looking out into the garage. Hunter trotted over and sat next to me.

I looked at my dog and scoffed. "Please tell me you're kidding. Is this how you looked when she came back? We're trying to make a good impression and both your ears are inside out."

He blinked at me, and I had to laugh. He had a pink lipstick kiss on his forehead.

I smiled and flipped his ears back and let out a long breath. "How you think we did, buddy? Think she'll call us?"

He looked over at me, his tongue lolling out of his mouth.

Then I noticed my black hoodie was missing from the hook by the front door.

CHAPTER 12

ALEXIS

I was on a run with my next-door neighbor, Jessica, on the trails by our house. I'd gotten home from Daniel's a few hours earlier. My friend Jessica was forty-five and statuesque. She was an OB-GYN at Royaume Northwestern and married to a lawyer named Marcus.

She hated him.

"How can you tell when it's time to put salt in the water softener?" I asked.

"My hair tells me," she said flatly. Jessica was always a little crabby.

"What?"

"When my hair stops feeling soft, I know the thing's out of salt. Why?"

"I have to do it now that Neil's gone."

"I'll come over and show you. I'm the one who does it at my house. Heaven forbid Marcus lift a finger." She checked her watch. "So where were you?" she asked. "You missed bunco at Gabby's last night."

"I know," I said. "I was out of town."

She looked straight ahead. "If you're getting work done, I want to know where."

"What?"

"New York? L.A.? You're glowing. Was it that new light therapy? A peel? Don't be selfish, we share this information."

"I didn't get work done."

She looked over at me and studied the side of my face. "Okay. Then where were you?"

I went quiet for a second. Mostly because her legs were longer than mine, and I had to run harder to keep up and I couldn't talk through it like she could. But also because I needed to gather my thoughts.

I'd called Jessica because between her and Gabby, she was the one who'd be the most receptive to what I was doing with Daniel. And I was going to have to tell them eventually.

My neighbors saw everything.

Everything.

They watched their security cameras from their phones at work like it was their favorite channel.

If I came home late—or not at all—it was only a matter of time until they noticed. And I'd rather get ahead of it. Especially because I was pretty sure this Daniel thing was going to keep being a thing. Not a serious thing. Not a forever thing. But definitely a frequent thing, at least for now.

I liked him. He was fun. And the sex had been even better this time, if that was possible.

I didn't stay for breakfast.

There was only one diner in town, and I didn't want to advertise the whole "Hey! I woke up here! With him! We had sex!"

thing that would be very obvious if we'd shown up together. We weren't dating—this was a fling. We didn't need to let everyone know about it.

"I was at a guy's house last night," I said finally.

Jessica stopped running. "Well?" she said, not looking in the least bit surprised. "Who is he?"

I put my hands on my hips, catching my breath. "I met him a week ago. I've seen him twice. I'm going to keep seeing him, I think."

"Okay." She looked at her heart rate on her Fitbit. "And where'd you meet?"

I pulled out my water bottle and took a drink. "I met him after the funeral last week, driving through his town."

"Have you told Gabby?"

I shook my head. "No. Not yet. You can tell her if you want. It's not really a big deal. I just figured I should tell you guys before you start to notice me not coming home at night."

"Does Neil know?"

"Nope," I said, making a popping noise on the P.

"Good," she said dryly. "Get all your rage sex out of your system and then you two can get back together with an even score."

My smile fell. "Jessica, I'm not getting back with him. Ever."

"Uh-huh," she said dismissively, stretching her hamstring.

"Jessica…"

I gave myself a long moment.

"Do you know what he used to do?" I asked, looking over at her. "He used to tell me I smelled bad."

She wrinkled her forehead at me. "What?"

"Right before we'd walk into a party or a restaurant or something he'd lean in and go, 'Did you take a shower today?' And you know me. I'm compulsively clean. I'd be half an hour out of a bubble bath, and he'd wrinkle his nose and tell me my deodorant wasn't working. I'd go to kiss him, and he'd turn his face and ask me if I'd had onions for dessert."

"You don't smell," she said. "I would tell you."

"Yeah, well, I was so freaked about it, I had Bri give me a full physical to see if something was wrong. Came back with nothing. I went to the dentist to see if I had an issue with my mouth, same thing, nothing.

"He wouldn't touch me or kiss me. I was taking three, four showers a day at the end, brushing my teeth constantly. I was on the verge of a nervous breakdown. And you know what my therapist said? She said it's a form of abuse. That he was purposely lowering my self-esteem."

Someone on a bike chimed their bell, and we stepped onto the grass shoulder. We waited for them to whiz past us before I continued.

I rubbed my forehead. "It's so much to unpack, Jessica. I feel like I've toppled down a therapy rabbit hole over the last six months.

"It was good in the beginning. He was nice. We got serious, bought the house. He was kind of cranky sometimes, but it wasn't bad. Then he started making these little comments about how I looked. Didn't that used to fit better? Why do you look so tired? Joking that if he'd known how much I was going to let myself go once we were living together, he would have never moved in with me—"

"Let yourself *go*?" She sounded annoyed. "I don't think I've ever seen you without lipstick."

"Yeah, well, it just kept getting worse. After a while he wouldn't even talk to me in the morning until I had my face on. I'd wake up and he'd lean in and sniff and shake his head and then he'd be irritated all day like I'd picked a fight with him. I started getting up before he did to get ready. Six a.m. and I'm showered and in full makeup. And if I didn't do it and he made some comment I'd find myself apologizing, like his reaction was completely reasonable. He was always in these bad moods. I never knew which Neil I was going to get. One day he's cooking me a nice dinner, my favorite bottle of wine, and the next he's mad at me for God knows what because he won't even speak to me. It was like he *liked* me on eggshells. Like as long as I was running after him, begging him to tell me what was wrong, what I could do better, he was happy.

"I could never relax, I started getting depressed, I had anxiety all the time. I was miserable and I felt totally trapped while at the same time feeling *grateful* that he was with me, because who else would want me?"

She shook her head. "Ali, I had no idea."

I scoffed. "*I* had no idea either. It started so gradually, I didn't even notice it was happening until it was so bad it was my whole life. It wasn't until I had a therapist breaking it down for me that I even realized what he was doing. It was like I'd been brainwashed into thinking this was normal."

Two joggers passed us, and we went quiet until they were out of earshot.

I let out a long breath. "I almost died of relief when he had that affair, because now I didn't need an excuse to leave him. 'Neil cheated, so I left. He's the bad guy, I'm out.' Cut-and-dry. Only it's not, because now he's playing the whole remorseful ex thing and everyone feels sorry for him. And I don't think he even expected me to break up with him. I think he actually thought I was going to stick around and keep what he did quiet like I always did because I'd be so embarrassed that I was disgusting enough to drive him into the arms of another woman."

Her face was hard. "Who else knows?" she asked. "Bri?"

I shrugged. "I told her after, when I was starting to understand it myself. I mean, she never liked him. But he never did it in front of anyone, and it's sort of hard to explain. Can you imagine me trying to tell you guys this? Convince you that Neil was mean to me? Everyone's favorite guy, *Neil*? Complain about him being a good boyfriend and letting me know that my breath smells bad? You'd probably be more inclined to think that he was trying to help me out than to believe that he was being purposely cruel. It wouldn't even surprise me if you didn't believe me now—"

"I believe you," she said flatly.

I blinked at her.

"Ali, men are two things. Disappointing and consistent. I believe you."

I don't know what it was. Saying it out loud to someone I'd hidden it from for so long. The tiny victory of claiming one of our mutual friends to my side, or just having someone else know it and believe it—but my chin started to quiver.

"I should have known, right?" I whispered. "I know what abuse looks like. But I just thought it was different, you know? Someone hitting you, calling you names, yelling. I didn't know it was like *this*." I wiped under my eyes with the side of my hand. "Honestly, he did me a favor with that woman. I should send her an Edible Arrangement."

"You should. Use his credit card."

I laughed weakly.

She gave me a moment to compose myself. Then we turned and kept walking along the tree-lined trail.

"So you're seeing someone," she said, circling back to the beginning.

"Yeah." I sniffed. "It's not serious."

"Just do me a favor with your new boy toy. Be safe. Bring your own condoms, watch him put it on, and make sure it's still on when you're done."

I glanced at her. "Why would it not be on?"

"Because they take it off."

I pulled my face back. "Like, on purpose?"

She scoffed. "Ali, never underestimate what a man will do for five percent better sensation. My days are filled with unplanned pregnancies and STDs—from husbands. Men are shit. It's why I stay with Marcus. He's too busy to screw anyone else, let alone me," she mumbled.

I wrinkled my forehead at the trail. "That's...*sad*."

"The devil you know," she said dryly. "Oh, which reminds me. You're not going to like this."

I glanced over at her. "What?"

"Marcus's birthday next weekend?"

"Yeah?"

"He invited Neil."

I stopped walking. *"Why?"*

"He said it's *his* birthday and Neil is *his* friend, and he wants him there. Believe me, I tried to talk him out of it."

I scoffed. "Well, guess *I'm* not going."

"No, you shouldn't. I don't wanna go either. Screw 'em, they can make it a boys' trip."

I looked at her gratefully.

"We should just find a day spa or something and go do that. A bed-and-breakfast. Gabby will go where we do. She always does."

I smiled. "Thank you," I whispered.

"Don't thank me. God, what a dick."

She squinted at the houses ahead of her and stopped walking. "Why are the police in your driveway?"

I froze. We were a few houses down from mine. She was right, there was a cop car in front of my garage.

They were there with *Neil*.

"What's going on?" Jessica asked as we approached the two men.

Neil turned and gave me the practiced look of contrition he gave the families of his patients when they didn't make it out of his operating room. "Ali, let's go have a private conversation."

"What are you doing here?" I asked, crossing my arms. "If you wanted your stuff, you should have just texted me."

"I'm moving back in."

The words hit me like a freight train.

"What?"

"I have a legal right to be here. I'm on the deed, and I'm a resident of the property."

"You moved out!"

"We had a disagreement," he said to the officer, not to me. "I stayed with my son for a few weeks. I continue to get my mail here, and the utilities are under my name. She doesn't have a restraining order." He was handing him documents. "We co-own the property. I live here."

I stared slack-jawed between them. The officer thumbed through the paperwork. Then he looked up at me. "If he's a legal resident of the property, I can't ask him to leave."

"You're kidding me…" I breathed.

Jessica crossed her arms. "Neil, you can't be serious."

"Jessica, this is my house, and Alexis is the woman I love. I'm not walking away from either of them."

"Don't you *dare* pretend this is about me," I spat, feeling my face grow hot. "You're *not* living here."

He looked back at the officer. "I'm going inside now. Is there anything else you need from me?"

He shook his head. "No. Have a good night."

Neil turned and walked into the garage. I'd changed the locks, but I'd left the garage code the same so he could get his stuff. I didn't lock the inside door, since I was just on a short jog, so Neil walked right into the living room.

Jessica looked at me in shock.

"Ask Marcus if this is legal," I said, my voice shaking.

I turned and ran inside after Neil. He was carrying one of the clear plastic containers that I'd packed his stuff in, heading down to the basement where we have our biggest guest room.

"Neil!"

He ignored me.

A mild wave of hysteria bubbled inside me. This wasn't happening.

I paced in the living room, frantically texting the group thread with Gabby and Jessica. Gabby had just got home and saw the cop car pull away from the house. I told her what happened as Neil came back up for another container.

"Neil! Why are you doing this?"

His face had dropped the friendly, placating look he'd reserved for his audience outside. "This is *my* house. I told you, I want it. I have a better chance at getting it if I reside here. I have every right to do so. If you don't like it, *move*."

He grabbed another bin and went back down.

I watched him go in shock. My chin quivered, and I ran up the steps to my bedroom and slammed the door.

My phone was pinging in quick succession in our group chat. Gabby, Jessica, Gabby, Jessica. And then almost comically, right in the middle of it, Daniel texted.

Daniel: I just wanted to say that I really enjoyed seeing you again.

Jessica texted. According to Marcus it was all legal. There was nothing I could do.

I dropped my phone on the bed and put my face into a pillow and screamed.

CHAPTER 13

DANIEL

She never texted me back.

It had been eight days since the last time I saw her, that morning of Popeye's fall. I'd sent her another text two days ago. She didn't reply to that either. I figured two unanswered messages was the max before I started to look desperate, so I left it at that.

I'd taken Popeye to Rochester to see his doctor after his accident. He was fine. I'd gone down to the hardware store while I was there and bought him the railing and tread for his tub. Installed that yesterday. Helped Doug dig a trench. Made a coffee table.

I would have rather seen Alexis.

To say this was a disappointment was an understatement. I thought things between us had gone well.

I guess they hadn't.

It was seven a.m. and gloomy outside. I was sitting in the four-season porch of the house having a coffee when Amber—*Mom*—called.

Mom wasn't really my mom. Not for any practical purposes.

She'd had me when she was fifteen. My dad had been a sixteen-year-old tourist whose family had no interest in me. Grandma and Grandpa raised me.

I had only fleeting memories of ever seeing Amber as a kid. She took off as soon as she could drive. We didn't really have a relationship until after my grandparents died.

They'd left the house to *her*.

My aunt Andrea, Liz's mom, and Aunt Justine, my cousin Josh's mom, didn't want it. They both lived in South Dakota and had no intention of coming back to Wakan. So my grandparents had left the house to Amber, probably thinking they'd change their will to me when I was old enough, but they'd never gotten around to it. So Amber took all.

I begged her not to sell it. At twenty-three, I hadn't had the means to buy it. I convinced her to let me run it as a rental, that she'd get a deposit every week, and she could always sell it if it didn't work out. She'd agreed, and we'd entered into the arrangement that I'd been living under for the last five years.

When she called, she called about money.

"Amber," I said, answering on the third ring, trying not to sound as moody as I felt.

"Hi, Daniel, it's Amber."

I rubbed my forehead tiredly. Sometimes I thought she wasn't all there.

"What's up?" I asked.

"So, are you gardening right now?"

"What?"

"What are you doing?"

She was making small talk. That was weird. "I'm just sitting here, in the four-season porch. Why?"

She paused.

"So, I don't know how to say this without just coming right out and saying it? I'm selling the house."

I froze. "What? What are you talking about?"

"I'm listing it. Like, today."

I stood. "Wha—*why*?"

She was making shuffling noises. She seemed distracted.

"Amber, you can't."

"I already have an agent. That Barbara lady? The one from Root River Real Estate or whatever? She says it's worth five hundred thousand dollars!"

I shook my head. "But…it's going well as a rental, it's making money."

"I'm tired of owning it. It's too stressful. I have to deal with the taxes—"

"*I'll* do it. Let *me* do the taxes—"

"Nah. It's just too much work. I don't have time."

Bullshit. She didn't lift a finger, I did *everything*. She wanted the money.

I went outside and started to pace.

"Why don't *you* just buy it?" she asked.

"Amber, I don't have the money for a down payment on a house like this. It's going to be tens of thousands of dollars." My mind was racing. "The house has been in this family a hundred and twenty-five years," I said. "You can't do this. Grandpa would—"

"Grandpa would what, Daniel? Roll over in his grave?" I could tell she was rolling her eyes. "It's being used by strangers. Don't be so dramatic. It's not like you live there or something."

"I *do* live there!"

"You live in the *garage*. Why don't you ask whoever buys it if you can just stay there? Like, rent it or something. And anyway, Barbara says it'll probably just get bought by an investment company who wants to keep it as a B & B. So maybe they'll keep you. You could have the same job and everything."

"And if they don't? If a family buys it to live in? You'd let that happen to the house? I'll lose my job, apartment, my workshop—"

I stopped at the side of the house and peered up at it. The twisting vines and oak trees on the stained-glass window shone emerald under the hand-wrought eaves that my great-great-great-grandpa carved with his bare hands. My great-great-grandpa had been born in the bedroom with the four-poster bed. My grandpa proposed to my grandma in the living room in front of the fireplace with the green tile mosaic.

I knew every nook and cranny of this house. She couldn't sell it. I couldn't let her. This was my home. My entire childhood. Generations of Grants had been born here, raised here, *died* here.

"Look," I said. "Give me a few months to get a down payment together. Please. So I have a fighting chance at a loan."

I had no idea where I'd get the money. I got a percentage of every rental in exchange for managing the property, and I sold my furniture when I completed a piece. But it was a hobby, not a stable source of income, and the house wouldn't rent again until at least May. I lived modestly. I had a couple thousand saved up, but not nearly enough to put down what I was sure the bank would ask for.

She sighed. "I don't know—"

"I'll open it up for the off-season," I said before even thinking about it. "You'll get all that added income. Plus, there's work it needs," I added quickly. "There's water damage in the Jack and Jill room, the roof needs to be replaced. If that stuff doesn't get repaired, it'll just lower the value, and it's going to take me a few months to fix anyway."

She was quiet for a moment.

"Amber. I have never asked you for anything. *Please*. Give me this."

There was a long pause. "All right. Fine. Six months. But that's it. I need the cash. I'm opening up a bike shop with Enrique."

And there it was.

I squeezed my eyes shut. I had no idea who that was. Probably some guy she just started hooking up with who was going to take her money and run. I couldn't even care at this point. Nothing I could do about it either way. She always did what she wanted, and this would be no different.

I nodded, even though she couldn't see me. "Okay. Thank you."

I hung up with her, only half believing she'd even keep the promise.

Six months. I had six months to raise fifty thousand dollars.

After the phone call with Amber this morning, I'd been to the bank. The good news was the B & B had five years of stable earnings that would more than cover the amount of the mortgage if I were to take it on, and my five years as a property manager and my good credit could definitely secure me a loan. The bad news was I had to have fifty thousand dollars as a down payment.

It might as well have been a million. It didn't seem possible.

I stood in my workshop, inventorying. Projects were stacked up floor-to-ceiling along the walls. Grandpa's work from before he died. He was notorious for starting something and losing interest. Sanded rocking chairs that needed to be stained, dining room tables with missing legs, dressers without knobs, bed frames that just needed to be assembled.

If I could power through the backlog, finish what was already started, maybe add a few of my own artistic touches to the pieces to raise value, I could take it all down to the indoor swap meet in Rochester and sell it. There might be enough here to raise the money.

Maybe.

This, coupled with the seven thousand I already had set aside, might do it. It would be an exhaustive amount of work. I'd still need to run the damn B & B on top of it. But I could do it. I could do all of it.

I *had* to.

I'd never hated someone in my entire life, but right now I *hated* Amber. It was hard to believe we'd been raised by the same people, given the same values, and grown up in the same place. How could she not love that house? Feel protective over it? It had a soul, it *breathed*. It was our responsibility.

I guess I couldn't really be surprised. I'd known Amber and I were going to end up here eventually.

Amber needing money was the hallmark of my childhood. Amber calling Grandma and Grandpa and them bailing her out, no matter what she did. I remember the calls every couple of months, begging for wire transfers. Grandma sitting in the pantry on the phone with her daughter, the curly phone cord pulled taut and shut into the door, the conversation muffled and whispered. Grandpa was more tough love with her, but she could always get Grandma to fold.

I used to wonder exactly what my mother would have to do to

fall from my grandmother's good graces. It was like the standard was so fucking low, even the most heinous of her crimes were just followed by a sigh and a head shake.

When she visited, she stole things. She'd go down to the VFW and get shit-faced and end up in a bar fight with someone, and Grandpa would have to go get her out of the drunk tank at the post office. When she wasn't in Wakan, she jumped from one deadbeat guy to the next. She almost never had an address.

I think the only reason this arrangement lasted as long as it had was because a reliable source of income got deposited directly into her account during the busy season. She never had a steady job. She waitressed and was a flight attendant once, but she could never hold down a position for more than a few months. Then I'd get a phone call asking me to advance her money.

Sometimes she'd claim she had some health issue that she needed cash for. A thousand dollars for a root canal, or money for a down payment on a new car because she'd crashed the last one without insurance. It was always something. Only now the something was so big, she had to sell the house to cover it.

I updated the website to show the B & B had availability starting on Friday and gritted my teeth as I hit Enter.

Being open in the off-season was almost pointless. At best, we'd be at half capacity, and the amount of work this meant for me with only half the payout wasn't worth it. I was tied to the property when I had guests. I couldn't even make a trip to the hardware store in Rochester when I had people in the house unless I was able to get Liz or Doug to fill in for me. I had to have coffee out by six a.m. for the early risers and a gourmet breakfast ready by nine o'clock. Checkout at eleven, then cleaning the rooms, stripping beds, checking the next guests in at three o'clock. It was a never-ending hamster wheel. And I had to do all those things whether I had one room booked or all four. But I had to make it work. Because if Amber didn't see the money, she'd probably list the house now instead of in October.

I sent out an email blast to our guest list. I mentioned some fun new spring breakfasts I'd make, the leaves budding, a complimentary wine-and-cheese hour in the foyer that I'd be adding to the stay. Then I started in on the pieces in the garage. I was about an hour into it when my cell phone pinged. I was in a shit mood, but the second I saw who it was, that changed.

Alexis: Sorry, just realized I never replied.

I grinned. Then I called her.

She answered on the second ring. "Uh, hello?"

"Hi."

"Did you just call me? On purpose? Without texting to tell me first like a normal person?"

"Yeeessss." I smiled. "Isn't that what you do with phones?"

"That's not what I do with mine."

"You make it sound like I sent you an unsolicited dick pic."

"The dick pic would have been less shocking."

I laughed.

"What if I'd been in the middle of something?" she asked.

"Then you wouldn't have answered. Wild, I know."

I could tell she was smiling.

"I'm working on something," I said. "I can't text right now."

"Oh, yeah? What are you working on?"

"A chair."

"You're fixing it?"

"I'm making it."

"*Wooow*," she said. "You know how to do that?"

"I'm a carpenter," I said. "The whole family is. All my cousins. Liz too. My grandpa taught us."

"Cool. Do you have an Instagram for your woodworking? I'd love to follow it."

I shook my head. "No. I don't do social media."

She paused. "Like, at all? *Ever?*"

"Nope. It's a waste of time. I spend two hours on TikTok, and I lose two hours. I spend two hours in my workshop, and I have a chair. I prefer the chair."

"But...how do you keep up with people if you don't do social media?"

"I call them."

She laughed.

That chemistry...it was like the second we reconnected, there we were.

I heard the sound of a door opening and closing.

"Where are you?" I asked, grabbing my measuring tape and getting back to my project.

"I'm sitting by the pool on a recliner."

I arched an eyebrow. "You have a pool?" The only pool we had around here was the river.

"Yup. I just came home from a friend's house."

I liked this. If she was at a friend's house and she remembered she never replied to my text, it was probably because they were talking about me.

"Which friend?" I asked.

"Eh, just one from across the street."

She always answered my questions like this, I realized. She gave me the same vague response whenever I asked her anything. I didn't know her last name, what hospital she worked in. Hell,

I hadn't even known she was a doctor until the Popeye thing. But I figured she'd open up to me when she was ready, so I didn't push it.

"So," I said, "what have you been up to?"

"Not much. Working mostly." I heard the *pith* of a can opening.

I put in my earbuds so I could have both my hands. "So what kind of doctor are you?" I asked. I hadn't had a chance to ask her before she took off on me the other day.

"I'm an ER physician."

"Ah," I said, measuring the chair leg and marking it with a pencil. "Why'd you pick that?"

She sounded like she was stretching. "I didn't plan on it. I was going to go into neurosurgery, but I met my best friend and she was pursuing emergency medicine and she got me into it. It's fun. And I like being there on someone's worst day. I like saving people."

I smiled. "Any interesting cases?"

"Oh, *lots*."

"Like what?"

She made a humming noise. "I pulled a Barbie shoe out of a kid's nose yesterday. And some guy used a nail gun to shoot a three-inch nail into his foot this morning. He was stuck to the floor. The paramedics had to use a hammer to pry him off."

I sucked air through my teeth. "Ouch."

"Once this guy swallowed a Fitbit. He was cheating and he got a text from another woman on it. His girlfriend demanded he show it to her, so he ate it. It was still tracking his steps from his stomach. We have Nunchuck Guy. He comes in once a month with a concussion. There was the guy with a flashlight stuck in his rectum—"

"Why is it always guys?"

"I don't know, Daniel. Why is it always guys?" I pictured her grin.

"Hey, *I* have never been to the ER. Doug does my stitches."

"*Doug* does your stitches?"

I nodded. "Yup. He was a medic in the army. Saves me a two-hour round-trip to Rochester every time. Uses a barbless fishhook and a ten-pound test line."

"Please tell me you're kidding…"

"Nope. He does a good job too. Straight."

"Oh, my God," she breathed. "What do you use for the pain?"

"Gin?"

She laughed.

I needed to use the saw, but I couldn't do it with her on the phone, so I decided to stain some headboards instead. I got up and grabbed some brushes. "So, back to the flashlight thing. Does this happen often?"

"You have no idea. People *love* putting stuff up their butts. And they always want you to think they fell on it in the shower. About fifty percent of my job is keeping a straight face."

I chuckled. "Same. Someone spray-painted dicks on the bike trail yesterday. Mrs. Jenson came to tell me, and she kept mouthing the word 'penis' because she couldn't bring herself to actually say it out loud and I had to look very concerned and nod a lot."

"Any leads on who did it?" she asked, a smile in her voice.

"Eh, it's teenagers. It's always teenagers. Firecrackers in mailboxes, stealing wine coolers from the grocery store, nature peeing—"

"Nature peeing…" she deadpanned.

"Yup." I pried open a paint can. "It is exactly what it sounds like. The businesses are either closed for the season or they don't want kids in their stores using their bathrooms, so they just go where they can. The alley outside of the pharmacy was starting to smell like a urinal."

"And you have to deal with this? This isn't a police issue?"

"I suppose it is if Jake can catch them," I said. "Which he can't. Evading the police is a time-honored Wakan tradition," I said, stirring the stain. "That's half the fun."

"Ah. So what are you going to do about this crime spree, Mayor?"

"I'm working on a volunteer program for the off-season, actually. Stuff to keep them busy. Doug's going to teach them bee-keeping, I'll do a woodworking workshop. If they do community service, they get credits to use at the rental place for bikes or kayaks. We're having a fund-raiser for it in a few weeks."

"Nice. I thought you said the mayor thing was honorary."

I shrugged. "It is. I mean, I was elected. But the town's too small for it to be a paying gig, so I always feel like it doesn't really count. It's just sort of something the Grants have always done."

"Well, you sound like a very good mayor," she said. "Even if you don't feel like it's a real thing—which it sounds like it is. You could have punished the kids instead."

I shook my head. "Nah. Grace costs you nothing," I said, brushing stain on a headboard.

"Huh?"

"Grace costs you nothing. My grandma used to say it. She especially liked to say it to herself when I was being a little shit."

"I somehow doubt *you* were ever a little shit."

"It's hard being a teenager here," I said. "It can be very

boring. Actually, it's hard being an adult here too. You know, if the population is less than a thousand, it isn't even a town. It's a village."

"So you're a villager," she said, sounding amused.

"Yup. Any chance I can get you to raid my village tonight? Because I'd like to see you."

"I can't." I pictured her putting out a bottom lip. "I have a girls' weekend thing. I'm leaving tomorrow morning."

My smile fell a fraction of an inch. It had already been over a week. I wanted to see her.

"You'll just have to settle for talking to me instead," she said, a smile in her voice.

I grinned "Okay. What do you want to talk about?"

"I don't know."

"How about we play a game?" I asked.

"A game? What *kind* of game?"

"A get-to-know-you game."

I pictured a shrug. "Okay. Sure."

If history was any indication, she'd deflect the questions I really wanted to know the answers to. So I decided to keep it light.

"If you could go back in time, when would you visit?"

"Hmmmmm," she said. "That's a good question. Am I a ghost? Or do I actually have to live back then?"

I shook my head. "Why would you want to be a ghost?"

"Too many diseases. Diphtheria, smallpox, bubonic plague. People back then lived to the ripe old age of childbirth."

"You could be anyone," I said. "Any gender. You could be a king."

"You think kings had it any better? What about Charles II of Spain? He was so inbred he could barely eat. His jaw was horribly disfigured, he had rickets, hallucinations, an oversized head, he was impotent and infertile. Henry VIII had an ulcerated leg from a jousting match that was so putrid you could smell him coming from three rooms over. And some think he went mad from syphilis."

I smiled. "So a little syph and you're out, huh?"

"Are we still talking about the king thing, or is this a dating question? Syphilis is highly treatable and nothing to be ashamed of. A single intramuscular injection of long-acting benzathine penicillin will take care of it."

"Okay, we get it, you know how to cure syphilis."

She laughed again.

"Yeah, you're right," I said, dipping my brush in the can and tapping it. "I read a lot of historic nonfiction. I guess it *was* pretty brutal back then."

"Historic nonfiction?" she said, sounding a little surprised.

"My favorite kind of read."

"Me too. I like the medical aspects. I always think about how I'd do it differently if I lived back then, knowing what I know."

"I like it because it happened," I said. "Can't get frustrated with the plot if it's a true story. And you learn something."

"Yeah. You know, reading makes your penis look bigger—don't quote me on it, the science is really new."

"Is that what's going on down there? I was wondering. Just finished *War and Peace*, by the way."

She laughed so hard I think she spit out her drink.

"I like to read," I said, grinning. "It's the only way I get to live somewhere that isn't Wakan. I read three, four books a week. A lot of audiobooks. That way I can work and read at the same time."

"I've never done an audiobook," she admitted.

"Oh, you should. It's like a movie for your ears. You could listen on your drive down to see me. Which is when again?"

"Daniel, you know how much I love watching you work. But I've got my country's five hundredth anniversary to plan, my wedding to arrange, my wife to murder, and Guilder to frame for it. I'm swamped."

A line straight out of *The Princess Bride*. I was cracking up.

God, I liked talking to her. I couldn't remember the last time I'd liked talking to someone this much. I liked seeing her more, but this was a close second for sure.

I checked my watch. "I gotta feed Chloe."

"Oh," she said, sounding a little disappointed. "I guess I should hang up with you then."

I set my brush on the lid of the can. "Nope, I'm taking you with me. Took me a week to get you on the phone, I'm not hanging up with you now."

I didn't hang up with her later either.

We talked for five hours straight.

CHAPTER 14

ALEXIS

We were on our way to our girls' weekend.

The men had gone north to Grand Marais, so we went south. Some bed-and-breakfast Gabby had booked.

Gabby was driving, and Jessica was in the passenger seat. I was sitting in the back of the black Escalade like the kid. Jessica was the grumpy dad and Gabby was the perky mom.

Gabby had a cheerleader thing about her. She was thirty-four, blond, and stood only five feet tall. She was a pediatrician. Of the three of us she was the only one who was in a happy relationship. Philip was totally devoted to her.

Gabby turned to Jessica from behind the wheel. "You're sure Marcus didn't care that you didn't go? It's his birthday."

"The man hasn't touched me in six years," Jessica said, her tone bored. "He barely remembers I exist. I don't think he cares where I do it."

Gabby looked in the rearview mirror at me. "So Jessica told me what happened. Neil is *such* a jerk. I had no idea. Seriously, why didn't you tell us sooner?"

I blew a breath through my nose.

These were my friends. I spent more time with them than I spent with Bri, mostly because of the couples thing. We vacationed together and worked together and lived on the same street. But I couldn't talk to them about everything, like I did with Bri.

Gabby was a little gossipy and could be a tiny bit shallow. Jessica was moody and tended to be negative.

I loved them, but I saw them for what they were.

"It was hard to explain," I said, shutting down the discussion. Gabby already knew everything I'd told Jessica.

Gabby gave me a mischievous smile. "So this guy you're seeing…"

This was another thing I couldn't discuss with them.

I'd kept my relationship with Daniel as close to my chest as humanly possible. I gave them no details other than he lived far away. But I knew their interrogation was coming. We had a whole weekend.

"I've only seen him twice," I said dismissively.

"Yeah, but what's he like?"

I shrugged, looking out the window. "I don't know. He's nice."

"What does he do?"

"Uh, he's in property management," I said vaguely.

"Is the sex good?" She glanced at me in the rearview, and her eyes sparkled.

Good didn't brush the surface of how amazing the sex was. But if I told her the truth, she'd want more details.

I shrugged again. "It's okay, I guess."

"There's an antibiotic-resistant strain of chlamydia going around," Jessica said flatly.

Gabby made an *ewwwww* noise.

"I'm using protection," I said.

"When do we get to meet him?" Gabby asked.

"It's seriously just a hookup thing."

It wasn't.

Well, not entirely. I guess technically if it was just a hookup thing, we wouldn't talk like we had last night. The time had gone by so fast, I didn't even notice how late it had gotten, and I'd only hung up with him because Neil came home, and I saw the light flick on in the office.

I *really* liked talking to Daniel. It was easy, and he made me laugh. Surprisingly enough, we had more in common than I thought.

Gabby made a left into a gas station. "I need to use the restroom. Anyone want coffee?"

Jessica got unbuckled. "I'll go."

My phone started to vibrate. Bri was calling.

"I'll wait in the car," I said, answering it. "Hey."

"I just got stood up. Again," she said. "Do you think they're showing up, seeing me, and then bailing? Or are they not coming at all? I can't decide if I'd rather be so hideous I'm causing them to flee, or so boring they literally forgot we had a date."

"You're not boring or hideous," I said, watching Gabby and Jessica go into the gas station. "It's their loss."

"Is it? Because I feel like contouring my cheekbones on my day off is sort of my loss. Do you want to meet for dinner? So my outfit isn't a total waste?"

"I can't," I said. "I'm doing that weekend thing with Gabby and Jessica."

She groaned. "Crap. I forgot about that."

"Why don't you come down? If the place is booked, we can share my bed."

She scoffed. "Uh, pass. There's only so much of Gabby's complaining and Jessica's eye rolling I can take. It's fine. I'll just go see Benny or something."

"How is he?" I asked. Her little brother was having some pretty serious health issues.

"It's starting to affect his kidney function."

My lips curved down. Benny was only twenty-six—younger than Daniel, and Daniel was a baby. Too young to be this sick.

Benny's deteriorating health was hitting Bri pretty hard. It was like she felt she needed to fix it because she was the doctor in the family, which was totally unfair.

"This isn't your fault, Bri."

Benny had excellent care, and his condition was progressing anyway. Sometimes medicine was like that. There was only so much you could do.

"So what's up with the guy?" she asked, changing the subject.

I shrugged. "Not much. I talked to him last night."

"Oh yeah? Phone sex stuff?"

"No. Just talked. Nothing serious. I left him on read for like a week. I was so overwhelmed with the whole Neil squatting in my basement thing I kept forgetting to call him back."

"Are you going down there again?"

"Eventually. Maybe next weekend?"

"Okay. Well, just remember not to name his penis. Once you name it, you get attached."

I laughed. Gabby and Jessica were coming out of the gas station. "I gotta go," I said, still cracking up.

"All right, call me later."

The girls got in the SUV, and Gabby turned back onto the road. We drove for thirty minutes, Gabby and Jessica talking about the new hot pool guy everyone was hiring and some Butter Braid fund-raiser Gabby's kids were in. I wasn't really paying attention. I had one earphone in listening to audiobook samples Daniel had recommended.

"Ugh, gas station coffee is so gross," Gabby said, dropping her cup into the drink holder. "I don't even know why I bother."

Jessica sighed loudly. "Maybe you can get something better when we get there. So where exactly are we going again?"

"Oh, my God, you guys are gonna *love* this place I found," Gabby said, making a right near a cornfield. "It's on the Root River. They have this epic bike trail. It used to be a railroad track and they paved it. We can rent bikes in town. Kayaks too."

I pulled out my earbud and leaned over to look out the windshield. "The Root River? I thought we were going to Red Wing."

"We were. I'd already booked a different place, but I canceled it for this one when it popped up. It's this small town, it's super cute. Grant County. It's this bed-and-breakfast I've had my eye on. I got an email saying it was opening for the spring."

"What town?" Jessica asked.

"Wakan."

Wait. *WHAT?*

My heart started to pound.

"Wakan?" I asked, trying to keep my voice steady. "Are you sure?"

"Uh, yeah." Gabby laughed.

"Not Wabasha? Or Winona?"

"Is something wrong with Wakan?" Jessica asked, bored.

"No. I don't know, never been there," I said, my voice a touch too high.

Daniel's bed-and-breakfast wasn't open. He closed it in the

off-season, so I didn't have to worry about ending up there. But if I was in Wakan, chances were good I'd run into at least one person who recognized me from that first night, and I wasn't ready to tell Gabby and Jessica about Daniel. I wasn't ready for these worlds to collide. Not yet. Maybe never.

I knew unequivocally that if Gabby and Jessica met Daniel, it would get back to Neil. Jessica could keep it from Marcus. They didn't talk. But Gabby would tell Philip, and Philip would absolutely tell Neil—especially if the story was the dramatic one I was sure Gabby would give him about my "boyfriend" being a tattooed twenty-eight-year-old who lived above a garage in a town with more corn than people.

Neil would make it a joke. They all would. And I didn't want Daniel to be a joke. I didn't want it to be anything. I just wanted to have fun and enjoy him and not think about my friends' opinions on it or have Neil laugh and make it an example of how far I'd fallen since him. He couldn't have this. None of them could. Daniel was mine and I wanted him to stay only mine, because what we had was good and it was making me happy and it wouldn't survive the scrutiny.

And that was really it—it wouldn't survive the scrutiny.

It wouldn't hold up under their inspection. My friends wouldn't approve. And this hadn't really mattered too much to me, since I'd never imagined that they'd ever be in a position to.

We drove down a winding road that I now recognized as the final leg into downtown. "Where in Wakan?" I asked, trying to sound casual.

"It's called the Grant House," Gabby said.

Panic ripped through me. I felt like I was going to hyperventilate. No. No no no no. This couldn't be happening.

I looked at Gabby's navigation. We were less than three minutes away. I started frantically texting him.

Me: I'll be there in two minutes. Please act like you don't know me. I'm sorry.

When the car crunched down the gravel drive, I strained my neck peering out the window to see if Daniel was outside. I didn't see him. My text said Delivered but not Read.

My mouth was dry.

"We're here!" Gabby sang, putting the car in park.

Jessica looked up at the house through the windshield. "Cute."

"Right?" Gabby turned off the engine and got out.

They went around to the trunk to get their bags, but I didn't get out. I was pretending to look for something in my purse, stalling for as long as possible, praying for a text from Daniel letting me know he'd gotten my message.

"Umm . . . are you coming?" Gabby called a moment later. They were both standing with their luggage in front of the steps.

I poked my head out the window. "I dropped my earbud. Just go ahead. I'll be there in a second."

Daniel still hadn't texted.

CHAPTER 15

DANIEL

I heard my weekend guests pull up to the house. I took my spot inside next to the small check-in counter by the stairs and looked down at Hunter. "All right, listen up. I'm letting you meet guests so you can get practice being a gentleman. But there's rules." I gave him a stern look. "You have to sit." I gave him a raised index finger for the sit command.

He sat and I smiled.

"Good boy. No jumping. And no sniffing anything either—you know what I'm talking about. Understand?"

He gave me one of his goofy looks, his tongue lolled out.

I'd leashed him to the check-in counter, just in case, but with the exception of Alexis, he really didn't jump on people.

He needed this socialization. With me running the B & B full-time, he was going to end up locked in the garage for most of the day if he couldn't get his act together. The more interaction I could give him, the better.

The door to the house opened, and I put on a smile as I

came around the counter to grab luggage handles. It was two women.

"We've got one more outside," the brunette said, her tone bored. "She'll be in, in a minute."

They let in a dragonfly that zipped around the foyer. Hunter watched it, but he stayed put, and I gave him an approving pat on the head.

I fired up my laptop and started to check them in. I'd lucked out. I'd booked three of the four rooms with this reservation—and they'd booked the Jack and Jill room, which was a bonus. Those two rooms had an adjoining bathroom between them, so I could only book them with the same party. This meant I still had an extra open room that could get picked up last minute. I needed it. If I was able to send Amber fat checks every week, she might actually keep her promise not to list the house until fall. Not to mention, I'd be able to save faster for the down payment.

"Is there a good place to have dinner?" the blonde asked, texting into her phone.

"There's a complimentary wine and appetizer hour starting at five," I said. "As for dining, I recommend—"

The door to the house opened with a slow creak, and the third woman came in. I looked up to smile at her—and it was *Alexis*.

I blinked at her in surprise, and she pressed a quick finger to her lips. She looked almost panicked. I didn't really have time to process this, because Hunter saw her and lost his ever-loving shit. He *dove* at her.

The counter jerked sideways with the sudden yank of his leash, and my laptop fell to the floor with a clatter. Then he dragged the hundred-pound counter across the wooden floor of the foyer like some deranged sled dog and pummeled her.

He was going so wild in the confined space, the other two women retreated shrieking into the dining room to escape.

"Hi...*dog*," Alexis said, petting him, clearly trying to hold him so the check-in counter massacre of the parquet floor would stop.

Hunter was crying like a puppy at the sight of her. Then he let out a long, excited *ROOOOOOOOOOOOOO!*

"Wow...that dog really likes you," the brunette said from the dining room.

Alexis laughed nervously. "Yeah, I must have one of those faces."

What the *hell*? What was she doing here? And why was she acting like she didn't know us?

Red-faced, I grabbed Hunter by the collar, unclipped his leash, and put him quickly outside. He immediately circled around to the window next to the door and jumped up, whining and crying to be let back in.

I looked at Alexis. She was disheveled after Hunter's lovefest. She wore a spaghetti-strap yellow dress and sandals. Her cheeks were pink and one of her straps had fallen down her arm. I registered even in my confusion that she looked beautiful.

She held my eyes for a split second. Then she glanced away.

I turned back to the other guests. "I'm, uh...sorry about that. He has a thing for redheads."

The other two women laughed, and Alexis smiled uncomfortably at the floor.

Not knowing what else to do or what the hell was going on, I picked up my laptop. The screen was cracked.

Dammit, Hunter.

I felt like the house had just been hit by a meteor. An unexpected cyclone of chaos.

The counter was sitting sideways in the middle of the foyer. It had gouged a large scratch into the wood floors that would need to be sanded and refinished.

Hunter made a pitiful *rooo*oing noise from outside like being banished was some sort of torture I'd just inflicted upon him for no reason.

I cleared my throat. "Uh, let me show you to your rooms," I said, giving up on checking them in. I grabbed the keys from the drawer in the counter, my face hot.

I carried their luggage up the stairs, giving them a disjointed version of the tour. My brain was misfiring. I couldn't focus.

Ali Montgomery.

That's the name the blonde had made the reservation under for Alexis's room.

I'd talked to her for five hours last night. I'd been on two dates with her. I'd had my hands on every inch of her body, and I didn't even know enough about her to circumvent this messed-up situation by knowing her full *name*.

The absurdity of it bounced around my brain with everything else that just happened. She trailed at the back, quiet, and I could feel her there like a drop in the air pressure. I wanted to pull her into a closet and ask her what the hell was going on, what was she doing here?

After pointing out each of their rooms, I smiled, hoping I looked collected. "My cell phone number is in the guestbook on your nightstands if you need anything."

The other two women went into their rooms. Alexis made eye contact with me, and then closed her door. I blinked at it for a second. Then I pulled out my phone. I had a series of rapid-fire texts from her.

The last one said: I'm sorry.

CHAPTER 16

ALEXIS

The explanation was too much to text. I just apologized and told him I'd come talk to him as soon as I could.

What a *mess*. And the ironic thing was, all I could think when I walked in was how much, despite my panic, I actually liked the surprise of being here and how cute Daniel looked. GOD.

The girls wanted to relax in their rooms until the appetizer hour, so I took the opportunity to sneak out.

When I let myself into the garage, Daniel was sitting at his workbench. He glanced up and then went back to his project, jaw tight. I made my way over to him and nudged his thigh with my knee. "I'm sorry."

He looked up at me. "What *was* that?"

"I didn't know they were bringing me here. It's a girls' weekend, and they booked the room. Besides, I thought this place wasn't open in the off-season."

"I opened it," he said shortly.

"Are you mad at me?"

He peered up at me. "Imagine if I showed up with my friends at your hospital. You're the doctor treating them. And I act like I don't know you. Does that sound okay to you?"

I let out a breath. "Daniel, I'm not ready to tell people about us yet."

"I'm not asking you to tell people. But to pretend you don't even *know* me?"

"You don't..." I blew out a breath. "If I say I know you, they'll want to know *how* I know you, where I met you and when. Jessica, the brown-haired one? She knows I've been coming to see someone who lives south. They're like gossip detectives. They'll figure it out."

He pressed his lips together, and I knew he was wondering why it mattered if they did.

I knew *his* friends. He was willing to take me to breakfast in front of everyone. He wasn't hiding *me*.

I'd hurt his feelings.

I licked my lips. "Daniel, I know we haven't talked about this yet, but I'm coming out of a really bad breakup. Really, *really* bad. Their husbands are having a boys' weekend with my ex. And without getting into details, my ex is not someone I want knowing about my life right now. My best friend Bri knows all about you. But these friends just... *can't*."

He studied me like he was searching for the truth. So I gave it to him. "I was so happy when I realized I was getting to see you today."

His face went soft for the first time since I'd come into the garage.

He looked away from me, but he put the tip of his finger to my bare knee like a tiny little olive branch.

"Please don't be mad at me," I whispered.

His eyes came back to mine, and he blew out a long breath. Then he pulled me onto his lap. He put his arms around me in a hug that was so sweet, it made my heart skip.

Daniel was really affectionate. He liked to cuddle, like a big teddy bear. I bet he was good with children. He was definitely good with baby goats.

I nuzzled his nose with mine. "You looked really handsome when I walked in," I said quietly.

The corners of his lips quirked up. His eyes were on my mouth. "Do you have my hoodie?" he asked, his voice low.

I nodded.

He smiled. "You brought it, even though you didn't know you were coming to see me?"

"You have to wear a stolen hoodie," I said.

"Otherwise it's just another senseless crime?"

"I like the way it smells," I whispered.

He grinned and kissed me, and I was immediately forgiven.

God, I missed him. I realized it almost retroactively, but I had.

It was weird to miss someone you'd just met. But I think it was because I hadn't gotten enough of him, either time I came. My mood improved, realizing that I had an entire weekend here—because I needed it.

This whole week had been horrible. I had to get a lawyer and a real estate agent. I was dodging Neil in my own freaking house. But I'd *missed* Daniel. Being on his lap, letting him hold me, smelling his warm, piney scent—it was a *finally* moment. Like arriving at a finish line or letting go of a breath you've been holding—or coming home.

It's the release that happens when you don't have to think about anything at all.

❧

Thirty minutes later, Daniel had to go set up the appetizers. I snuck back into the house through the four-season porch. Hunter followed me all the way through the yard pushing his head under my hand, and when I let myself in, he tried to come in after me. I had to wrestle him back out and close the door in his face.

I was starting to develop a theory about this dog, but further observation was needed.

Jessica and Gabby were there sitting on the wicker chairs.

"Oh, hey. I went for a walk around the house. I didn't know you guys were out," I said, sitting in the open lounger, trying to look casual, like I hadn't just been making out with our host in the garage.

"We knocked on your door, but you didn't answer," Gabby said. "Figured you were taking a nap or something. God, that dog is obsessed with you."

I looked and laughed. Hunter had his nose pressed right on the window, breathing heavily. There were two foggy breath trails under his nostrils on the glass and his ear was inside out. He had a dragonfly on his head.

"Was the guy out there?" Gabby peered around me to the yard. "Chopping wood or...?"

"What guy?" I asked, playing dumb.

"Uh, the hot check-in guy? With the tattoos?"

I shrugged. "Didn't see him."

Jessica flipped through a magazine. "Maybe you should go look. Put another toy into the rotation."

"I bet he's outdoorsy," Gabby said. "He looks outdoorsy. He probably smells like campfire smoke."

"Motor oil," Jessica said dryly. "He screams 'I can change spark plugs.'"

Gabby laughed, and I pressed my lips into a line.

"My boyfriend before Philip was like that," Gabby said. "He was a contractor. Handy. Did all the woodsy stuff, hunting, fishing. They bring ticks into the bed. Actual wood ticks. It's like letting a dirty dog sleep next to you."

Jessica chuckled.

"I'm serious," Gabby said. "And they're always bleeding." She made a face.

I gave her a look. "Bleeding?"

"Yeah. They have cuts on their hands and bug bites. Perpetually. They just bleed, all over your thousand-thread-count Egyptian sheets." She shivered.

Jessica talked to her magazine. "Don't discourage her. Those guys are fun to play with."

Gabby gave a one-shoulder shrug. "Yeah. They're in shape, they're low maintenance. They'll churn you like butter. Just take them to a hotel, don't bring them home."

"Why the hell would she bring him home?" Jessica winced.

"What's wrong with bringing him home?" I asked, looking back and forth between them.

They both stared at me like I'd just told a joke.

"Your dad would *love* that," Jessica mumbled, going back to her magazine.

Gabby guffawed. "Can you imagine? 'Dad, I know my last boyfriend was chief of surgery, but here's this guy who can build me a deer stand.'"

They both laughed.

"He could be really nice," I said, a little too defensively.

Jessica lowered the corner of her issue of *Vogue*. "You think your dad cares one ounce if he's *nice*?" She scoffed. "Remember that lawyer I set you up with at Marcus's firm? Adrian? Right before Neil? *He* was nice. Your dad acted like you brought a registered sex offender to brunch. He gave you so much crap, you never saw him again. And Adrian was a lawyer, not a guy with a GED, tattoos, and wood ticks."

Gabby looked at her nails. "Your family's like royalty. They'll only marry you off to someone who will strengthen a medical alliance."

I snorted, even though it wasn't funny.

"I hate to say it, but your next guy is going to have *very* big shoes to fill," Jessica said, looking back at her page. "If he doesn't have the words 'world renowned' on his résumé, don't bother."

Gabby nodded to the house. "Forget your parents. Could you imagine bringing a guy like that home to Philip and Marcus?" She sucked air through her teeth. "They'd eat him *alive*."

Jessica shook her head at her article. "Philip would probably talk to him about stock portfolios just to be a dick."

Gabby laughed. "Marcus probably wouldn't talk to him at all."

My face fell, and I sat back in my chair and twisted my bracelet around my wrist. I felt like someone had pushed all the wind out of me.

They weren't saying anything I didn't already know. But to hear it in no uncertain terms was sobering.

"He *is* cute though," Gabby said. "Kinda looks like Scott Eastwood. If he's single, you should play with him." She bounced her eyebrows.

I rubbed my forehead. "Yeah, I don't know if I'm gonna be up for it. Actually, I think I'm getting a migraine." At this point it technically wasn't even a lie. This discussion was making my head hurt. "I might let you guys go to dinner without me tonight."

Gabby frowned. "Seriously?"

"Yeah, I—"

Daniel poked his head into the patio. "Sorry to interrupt. The appetizers are out in the foyer." He smiled handsomely, then disappeared.

Jessica dropped her magazine on the coffee table with a slap. "Good. I could use a glass of wine." She got up.

I followed them, feeling tired in a way that I hadn't in a very long time.

CHAPTER 17

DANIEL

I t was hard not to look at her.

I didn't like faking this, pretending I didn't know her. But more than that, it was hard not to look at her because she was beautiful and I liked doing it.

While the women got wine and plates of the caprese bites and goat cheese I'd put out, I highlighted a map for them for the walk to Jane's for dinner. I circled the bike rental place for tomorrow, since they said they wanted to do the trail. Not much else was open.

If Alexis had let us be introduced—the way we *should* have been introduced—I would have shown them around town, made sure they had a good time. Taken them wine tasting at Doug's farm, even though he was closed for the season, maybe get Brian to open the drive-in again. But Alexis didn't want that. So I stayed quiet.

After I handed over the map, I retreated to the kitchen to give them some privacy, but I could still hear them talking in the foyer.

It was a little too early to judge, but I wasn't sure I liked Alexis's friends. The younger blond one, Gabby, seemed kind of shallow. I'd come into the dining room to bring more crackers, and she was bragging about firing a nanny and how the woman had cried. She rolled her eyes when she said it.

Jessica looked like she hated even being here. She kept scowling around the house.

I mean, I guess Doug wouldn't really pass the first blush test either. You had to get to know him to like him, that's for damn sure. But these women didn't really fit what I knew of Alexis. They did, but they didn't. They looked like her. Like they came from the same place. But they didn't *act* like her.

I came back into the foyer when I heard them start talking about walking into town for dinner, just to get one more second with Alexis before they left. I pretended like I needed to get something from behind the check-in counter.

The two friends had purses under their arms, but Alexis was sitting in a chair rubbing her temple.

Jessica checked her phone. "Want us to bring you something?" she asked Alexis, her tone bored.

I poked my head out from behind the counter.

Alexis shook her head. "No, I'm good. I'm just going to go to bed early."

She was staying with me. I did my best to hide my smile.

"I'm sorry," Alexis said. "I don't know what's wrong with me."

Jessica pressed her lips into a line. "Probably hormonal. Women are three times more likely to have headaches than men." Then she turned to me. "Must be nice to be a man. *Our* reproductive organs are like painful rusty gears that eventually stop working—if they even work at all. Enjoy your penis."

She walked out with Gabby right behind her.

When the door clicked closed, Alexis looked at me and shrugged. "She's really fun at parties?"

I started to laugh. Then I grabbed her wrist and pulled her out of the chair and into my chest. "The question is, do *you* enjoy my penis?"

She bit her lip. "Oh, yes."

She smiled and leaned to kiss me, but I pulled my face back. "You don't really have a headache, do you? Do you need something?"

She laughed. "No, I made it up so I could stay with you."

My grin was enormous. "How much time do you think we have?"

She wrinkled her nose. "An hour?"

I slid my hands down her back and cradled her ass. "Well, we'd better get started..."

CHAPTER 18

ALEXIS

We were all over each other before we even got the door closed to his room.

The second he touched me, the chemistry between us burst out like a rip cord being pulled. It was zero to ten, instantly.

I *loved* his body. His wide, muscular shoulders, his defined stomach, the curve of his collarbone when I tucked my nose into his neck while he was on top of me. His scent was like an aphrodisiac.

I kicked out of my sandals as he peeled his shirt off.

It was incredible how he transitioned from the polite young man of a few minutes ago to the virile, hungry male in front of me now.

This was no boy. This was a *man*. And he was pure sex, six feet tall and an erection pressing against his zipper. His eyes hooded and looking at me like he wanted to eat me. A thick trail of hair descending into his pants...

I loved the way his hands felt on my skin. I didn't care if they had cuts or bug bites on them, they made me feel feral. It was the same way he made me feel every single time he got me alone, like I couldn't scale him fast enough.

I wondered offhandedly if this is how most people felt during sex. This must be the reason why it's such a big deal.

It wasn't like I didn't enjoy sex. I did. Neil could give me an orgasm most of the time—I'd never had a problem getting there. But it wasn't this all-consuming, driving need that it seemed to be for everyone else.

I could never understand why people would fight about it or cheat looking for it or end things because there wasn't enough of it. It was always dead last on my list of important things in a relationship.

But *now* I got it.

If this was the kind of sex everyone else was having, it all made sense, because this? This was *incredible*. It was like Daniel had flipped some broken switch inside me, and now all the parts were running like they should and I hummed like a well-oiled machine.

I was becoming addicted to him. I wondered how much sex I'd need to have with him for him to actually satiate this need he seemed to bring out of me. I kinda wanted to figure it out. Seemed like a fun experiment...

I was slipping an arm out of my spaghetti strap, and he came up behind me. "Don't," he said in a husky voice. He started kissing the side of my neck. His beard and his tongue raked across my bare skin. "I like it."

I leaned back into him. "You like it, huh?" I ground into him, and I felt his breath shudder.

Then a hand was pushing my dress over my hips, tugging my underwear down my thighs. The clink of a belt buckle, pants dropping to the floor, and a hot erection pressing against my ass...

Need ripped through me.

He whirled me onto the bed and reached into the nightstand. He tore the corner of a condom with his teeth and I watched him roll it on. Then he was climbing over me.

And then he slowed down...

He hovered, hands on either side of me, nothing touching me but his lips, his breath on my skin.

"You smell so good," he whispered into my collarbone.

I hooked an elbow around his neck to pull him toward me, but he held his body off me, and like he saw the complaint coming he crushed his mouth to mine to keep me quiet.

The kiss was everything, and it was torture because I wanted more than this. I wanted his weight on top of me. He was all over me and all around me, but still too far away. The heat from his body pressed into mine, I could feel it through my dress.

I'd never in my life wanted someone to rip my clothes off until this moment. I wanted nothing between us. I hated the very existence of the fabric, I wanted to feel his skin on my skin. I wanted his sweat and the pounding of his heart and his fast breath. It was some sexual claustrophobia. I was starting to feel frantic.

I ran a palm down his chest following the trail of hair under my fingertips and took him into my hand, and he sucked in a breath against my mouth. He squeezed his eyes shut and let out a shuddering noise as I moved back and forth. He lost his resolve and lowered himself onto me.

When he eased inside of me, it was *fireworks*.

I gasped at the deepness of it, the internal thump. I felt desperate for it, like I wanted to claw at him, get him closer.

He rode me with his rough hands on my thighs, his tongue plunging in and out of my mouth, my dress bunched around my hips. I slipped an arm out of my dress strap and uncovered a breast and it made his motions more frantic.

I turned him on. He was ravenous for me.

Every time I was with him, he built me up. He gave me back something that Neil stole.

I rolled my hips just the right way and threw back my head and in one fluid movement he made his final thrusts between my legs. I could feel him pulsing inside of me, and I wished in my delirium that there was no condom.

With Neil, I hated the cleanup. But with Daniel the thought of him filling me up, him dripping down my thighs—I wanted it. I couldn't *have* it. I'd never have unprotected sex with someone who wasn't my boyfriend. It was amazing I was even having sex with someone who wasn't my boyfriend at all. But, God, the thought of it made me quiver.

I realized that I would try things with him that I hadn't tried with anyone. He made me feel uninhibited like that—and safe.

I think the safe thing was the biggest part of it, actually.

He hovered, still inside of me, catching his breath. His heart was thudding against my bare breast like a jackhammer.

"Fuck..." he breathed. "You're gonna give me a heart attack."

"Well, you seem like a decent fellow. I hate to kill you."

He laughed so hard into my neck, I broke into giggles.

He started kissing me softly, still chuckling, and I tipped my head back.

I hated that we only had time for this quickie. The second time would last longer. We'd take everything off. We'd play a little. Draw it out.

This was the night I wanted. It was the *weekend* I wanted. I wished I could just stay here, stay with him. I didn't want to spend two days with Gabby and Jessica when this was the alternative. I didn't want to ride the bike trail or sit in a chair on the four-season porch reading a book or get my nails done at the lone salon in town. I just wanted to do this. And it was weird because until I got here, I'd been looking forward to spending time with my friends. But Daniel had just risen to the top of a quickly shifting priority list.

Huh.

He kissed his way up under my chin. "I didn't know your last name," he said.

"What?" I said absently.

He came up to look at me, his earnest hazel eyes peering into mine. "It was on the reservation, but I didn't know it was you." He paused. "I've never done this with someone I didn't know," he said quietly.

The way he said it made me instantly feel bad. Like I'd defiled him. Made him lower his standards for intimacy. I mean, he hadn't asked me my last name. But then he probably thought I wouldn't have told him. And honestly? I probably wouldn't have. I'd sort of had one foot out the door since the start of all this.

But I didn't really have one foot out the door now...

I was going to keep seeing him. At least for the time being. He didn't need to know my whole life story, but I could give him a little more than I had been.

I gave him a gentle kiss. "Alexis Elizabeth Montgomery."

He smiled so that his eyes twinkled. Then he leaned in. "Alexis." Kiss. "Elizabeth." Kiss. "Montgomery."

I never knew hearing my name could make me smile so much. I arched an eyebrow. "Are you going to Google me now?"

"Not if you don't want me to," he said. "Did you Google me?"

"Well, yeah. What if you were a registered sex offender?"

He looked amused. "And? What did you find?"

"Five-star reviews."

He laughed.

My cell phone pinged from wherever I'd dropped it on the floor. Daniel nodded over his shoulder. "Are you gonna check it?"

"I probably should," I said, running my hands through his hair. "What if they're coming back."

He gave me a final peck and got up and handed me my phone from the floor. Then he went to the bathroom to clean up.

I checked the text and grinned. "They're going to the VFW," I called out. "Something about trivia night?"

Daniel smiled coming out of the bathroom, zipping up his pants. "It goes until ten."

"So we have three more hours?"

He climbed onto the bed. "We have three more hours."

He wrapped around me in the biggest, sweetest teddy bear hug, and again I marveled that he was both this cuddly boy and the guy who'd screwed me senseless a few minutes ago.

He planted a kiss on my neck, then propped himself up on an elbow and looked down at me. "Why is it a bad breakup?" he asked.

I wrinkled my forehead. "What?"

"Your last boyfriend. You said you're going through a bad breakup. Why is it bad?"

I hadn't planned on talking to Daniel about Neil. It wasn't really information he needed. But now that it was the reason I was pretending I didn't know him in front of my friends, it seemed like a fair question.

I drew in a long breath and let it out slowly. "The relationship was...abusive."

His brows drew down. "He hit you?"

I shook my head. "No. He was mean."

Daniel studied me. I couldn't interpret the look on his face.

"What?" I asked.

He shook his head. "I would never be mean to you."

The comment hit me right in the heart, it was so earnest.

No. I didn't think he would ever be mean to me. Daniel couldn't be mean to anyone, I suspected.

Whoever got him one day was going to be a very lucky girl.

When I didn't answer, he looked at his watch. "I wasn't expecting company, so I'm going to have to get creative with dinner," he said. "I should probably feed you."

He got up.

"Need any help?"

"Nope. But you can come hang out with me while I cook."

He put on a shirt, and I followed him downstairs.

He had a pot of coffee on the kitchenette. "Mind if I have some of this?" I asked, already grabbing a mug.

"I can make you a fresh one."

"No, this is fine," I said, pouring it. "I got used to old coffee during my residency. Now I kind of like it. Reminds me of the little bit of downtime I used to get."

He watched me take a sip. "No cream? No sugar?"

"No."

He shook his head. "How can you drink that?"

"It's coffee. You're supposed to taste it. You can't taste it with cream and sugar in it."

He looked at me dubiously. "That's like saying you can't taste your eggs because you add salt and pepper." He took my mug from my hand and put it to his mouth. He winced, handing it back to me. "This tastes like a burned tire."

I laughed.

He looked amused. "I guess this proves strong coffee doesn't put hair on your chest. Actually, maybe I should get a closer look." He pulled the front of my dress open with a finger and I laughed, swatting him away.

It was amazing how good I felt. Like I'd had a full body and mind reset. And I didn't think it was only because of the sex either. I was happy to be here.

Come to think of it, I'd felt like this last night after we'd hung up too. I'd slept better than I had in months.

Daniel was a vacation for me, I realized—like a break from my own brain or the reality of my current crappy situation. And we had that easy flowing conversation that you so rarely find with someone. I had it with Derek and Bri, but I'd never had it with Neil. With Neil, I always felt like I needed to say something important or smart for it to be worth bringing up. We spent a lot of quiet meals together.

At the time, I thought this meant we were good with comfortable silence. But now I realized it meant something else. Some strange, stiff, unnatural dynamic that I'd dealt with for so long, I didn't know it wasn't normal. It wasn't a comfortable silence, it was just...silence.

I started wandering the garage looking around while Daniel rummaged in a fridge. Hunter walked with me, pushing his head under my hand until I resorted to walking with a palm between his ears.

I saw the headboard Daniel had been working on last night. It was propped to dry. He had chairs hanging from the walls in various stages of completion. A dresser set and a pair of nightstands sat by the garage door.

He had a stack of books on a stool by his workbench. I picked up the top one. *The Circus Fire.*

Daniel looked over at me. "That's a good one. Have you read it?"

I shook my head at the cover. "No."

"It's about the deadly Ringling Bros. and Barnum & Bailey Circus fire of 1944. You'd probably really like it—severe burns, emergency situation, mass casualties. Your kind of thing."

I laughed.

"You can borrow it if you want."

"Thanks. We like the same books," I said, looking at the rest of the stack.

I knew he liked history, but most of these weren't big titles. Self-published books about Alaskan homesteaders and stories of Native Americans. A memoir about a man who ran a dogsled team in the 1940s.

I liked lesser-known books too. I'd even read a few of these. It was a little surprising. I didn't really know anyone who read the exact same kind of books I liked.

"What's the last book you read?" he asked, pulling out a frying pan.

"Well, I actually just finished this one," I said, showing him one from his stack. "But right now I'm reading *The Great Influenza* by John M. Barry."

"Oh yeah, I read that," he said, setting some carrots, garlic, and an onion on the counter. "About the Spanish flu of 1918. You know my great-great-grandfather Wilbur Grant saved the whole town from that."

"Really?" I said. "How?"

"Cut down trees to block the roads into Wakan. Kept everyone in, everyone out. Didn't lose one person. They were pretty pissed at him though at the time."

"Was he the mayor too?" I asked.

Daniel nodded. "Yup. A Grant has always been the mayor, going back one hundred and twenty-five years."

"Wow. Always?"

"Always."

"How many Grants are here now?"

He shrugged. "Just me. I'm the last one."

Ha. I knew what *that* was like.

"And if you leave?" I asked.

He laughed. "Why would I ever leave?"

I gave him a small smile.

He pulled out a knife and a cutting board. "After Wilbur died, my great-great-grandmother Ruth Grant took over. She set up an illegal Prohibition bootlegging operation out of the basement of the house. The most prosperous years in Wakan history. They named a gin after her. We use it to stitch people up with fishhooks."

I laughed.

I eyed a few novelty woodworking pieces in the corner of the garage. There were three of them. One was a wall hanging of a horse, its mane flowing behind it, twisted into the knotted wood. There was a mirror with an intricate floral appliqué frame, hand-wrought. And a custom rocking chair. He'd etched an elaborate whimsical design into the headboard. It was breathtakingly beautiful. Works of art.

"Did you do these?" I asked, pointing at the small collection in the corner.

He glanced up from chopping carrots. "Yeah."

"Who are they for?"

"Just practice pieces."

"These are your *practice* pieces?" My *God*.

Daniel was an artist. It was like he brought the wood to life in his hands.

I traced the curve of a rose carved into the mirror frame. "How much do you sell these for?"

He shrugged. "I don't know. The materials aren't very expensive. That horse? The beam came from an old barn we were tearing down. Got it for free. It's mostly my time."

"Well, how much time did it take to do this one?" I pointed at the mirror.

He looked at it. "Couple of weeks? I don't know. I'd probably ask two hundred for it."

I scoffed. "You're undercharging."

He laughed like I'd told a joke.

"See the wood I used for the horse?" he said. "I liked it because of the color. The barn was a hundred, hundred and twenty years old. The ammonia from the cow's urine stains it over time. Darkens it." He nodded at it. "You see the ghosts? Those lighter patches on the horse's neck? That's where the metal brackets used to be. The ammonia didn't get to that part of the wood, so it's lighter." He pushed his chopped carrots into a pan. "I like working with things that have history. It gives it character. There'll never be another one exactly like it."

My face went soft. He *was* an artist.

I glanced over at him. He looked *really* handsome standing there in his black Grant House T-shirt, all bearded with his dimples flashing, a wall of tools hanging behind him. There was something infinitely sexy about a man who could build things.

And cook things. When he started to sauté the onions and garlic, I think I fell a little bit in love.

I came back over to the kitchenette and sat on the weight bench to watch him. Hunter put his face in my lap.

"Why don't you do the carpentry full-time?" I asked, petting the dog. "You're so good at it."

He shrugged over his frying pan. "Couldn't make a living out of it. The village is too small."

I smiled. "You could go bigger. Ship your pieces. I know people who would pay thousands of dollars for this stuff to furnish their cabins."

I could see by his smile that he took the compliment. I watched him add a jar of home-canned tomatoes to the pan.

"Do you cook the breakfasts?" I asked.

"I do. I've been trying to get you to stay for one. Looks like I'm finally getting what I want." He gave me a triumphant grin.

Both of us were smiling. We'd been smiling since the minute we were alone and allowed to do it.

"This was the best surprise," I said, almost to myself.

He beamed down at his pan. "You know, you can come whenever you want," he said. "I want you to."

"Whenever I want?" I teased. "I don't want to show up and you're not alone."

"I'll always be alone when you show up. I'm not seeing anyone else."

I didn't respond to this. It wasn't my business if he was seeing other people—even though the thought of it did bother me a little bit.

Was it weird that it bothered me? It should have been, right? I shook it off.

"Are you going to sneak into my room tonight?" I asked.

"I think it's better if you sneak into mine," he said, talking to his frying pan. "Your friend is sharing that bathroom. Plus, we can make more noise over here." He grinned.

"Why did you open the B & B? I thought you said it was closed for the season."

He went quiet for a long moment. "I had to. Amber—my mom—is selling the house."

I froze. *"What?"*

"She's selling it," he said. "To buy a bike shop in Florida. I have the summer to raise fifty thousand dollars for a down payment on the property so I can try to buy it. If I can't raise the money…" He paused. "I have to raise the money." He nodded at the garage. "I need to finish all this to sell at the swap meet. And I had to open the house early to convince her to wait."

I shook my head. "But…how can she do it? It's your family's house."

I couldn't even imagine if Royaume was being taken from my family.

Suddenly I could see the strain around his eyes. He must be totally overwhelmed. I looked around at the huge backlog of furniture. It was a warehouse full, and none of it was complete. There was no way he could do it all. Not while he was running the bed-and-breakfast at the same time.

"I'm so sorry, Daniel." I didn't know what else to say.

He just smiled. "It'll work out. This weekend helps. I got most of the rooms booked. And I get to see *you.*"

I stayed the whole night in Daniel's loft. I texted Gabby and Jessica and told them I was going to sleep so they wouldn't check on me when they got in. Then I locked my room and came back to the garage and slept with Daniel—well, our version of sleeping, which didn't involve much sleeping at all, actually.

When he got up at 5:45 to put coffee on in the house, I snuck back in with him and went to my room.

I loved spending time with him, just hanging out with him. It was so easy and fun.

He didn't feel like his age. Maybe he'd had to grow up fast, like I did.

Well, I'd grown up fast in some ways—and I hadn't in others. I was college bound by seventeen, but I didn't have a first kiss until I was twenty. I didn't lose my virginity until I was twenty-four. I didn't really get to do the teenager thing. Guess I was getting to do it now though, sneaking out of the house like a kid.

I met the girls in the dining room for breakfast at nine.

"Oh, my God," Gabby said from her seat at the table when I walked in. "You missed out. We had *so* much fun last night."

I poured myself a coffee from the station Daniel had set up on the buffet table against the wall. "Really?" *Me too.*

"Yeah, so we went to this VFW, which was kind of ratty, but it was the only thing that was open. This guy started hitting on us and he pulls out this guitar and sings 'More Than Words'—I died."

I choked on my coffee and spit it back into my mug. "Was it any good?" I asked, still laughing, wiping up my chin.

Jessica scoffed. "It was as bad as the food at that restaurant we ate at last night," she muttered. "What did *you* eat for dinner?"

I took a seat and shrugged. "The guy made me a sandwich."

He actually made me pasta Bolognese using tomatoes he'd grown and canned. It was amazing. I was having a very different weekend than they were…

Daniel came in balancing three plates on his tattooed fore-arms. We made split-second eye contact before we looked away from each other.

The chemistry between us was off the charts. He made my body react just by being in the room, and it occurred to me that this would be true even if we'd never touched each other. Even if I had been here on a couple's weekend with Neil and this was the first time I'd ever met him, I would have noticed it. It was like a pupil shrinking under a light, totally involuntary.

He started setting French toast in front of us.

God, he looked good. He was wearing an apron. His hair was sort of messy and looked effortlessly adorable. Just when I thought he couldn't get any cuter . . .

"How's your head?" Jessica asked me. "You look like you were up all night."

"I was," I said, glancing at Daniel just in time to see the corner of his lip twitch.

I didn't have makeup on. I never in a million years would have let Neil see me like this in the morning. But Daniel said he didn't mind, and I was too tired from last night to make the effort. Honestly, I really didn't think he cared. The man was a perpetual erection around me. If the way I looked in the morning turned him off, his penis certainly didn't get the memo.

Daniel cleared his throat from the end of the table. "Baked French toast with a splash of Madagascar bourbon vanilla, topped with macerated berries, served with candied maple bacon and fresh melon. Let me know if I can get you anything else." A smile and a flicker of eye contact with me and then he left the room.

We started eating.

"This is *so* good," Gabby said, moaning.

It *was* good. I really should have let him make me breakfast sooner. Wow.

I was beginning to think maybe I should start taking Daniel up on more of his offers. So far he hadn't disappointed me—in anything.

I heard a creak in the foyer, and Hunter came in. The front door must have been ajar. He trotted over to the table with a plush toy in his mouth and put his face in my lap.

I smiled. "Hey there."

I wiped my mouth with a napkin and reached down to pet his head.

Then the plush toy moved.

"Oh, my God!" I screamed, pushing away from the table.

I stared at the thing in his jaws in horror. "He...he has a squirrel!"

Gabby and Jessica practically fell over backward getting up. Daniel must have heard the noise, because he came running in from the kitchen.

Hunter backed into the mouth of the dining room, blinking at us innocently, like he didn't know what the big deal was.

The thing hung limp from his mouth. Then the tail twitched. Oh no, it was playing dead.

Daniel put his hands out. "Hunter... *don't move.*"

I swallowed, my back pressed against the buffet. "Maybe you can get him to go outside?" I whispered.

Daniel nodded. "Good idea," he said, his voice low.

He started slowly for the front door.

The squirrel began wiggling—Hunter flung it in the air.

Everyone shrieked.

He caught it again like a kid casually tossing a baseball and then shook it around until his ear was inside out, and then he went back to blinking at us.

We were all holding our breath, hostage.

Daniel got all the way to the foyer. He opened the door wide and pointed. "Hunter, *out*."

Hunter looked at him, confused. Then he dipped his head and very gently placed the animal at Daniel's feet. It immediately sprang to life and darted under the dining room table.

Complete chaos.

Screaming, chairs knocking over, broken glass.

Gabby, who had sat at the end against the wall and who was now effectively trapped by fallen chairs, climbed the table and scrambled on her hands and knees over plates of food to escape.

Hunter smiled around at the activity, looking proud of himself.

We burst outside, leaving Daniel and his dog in the house.

When we got out on the lawn, we stood there gasping. Jessica was clutching the front of her shirt like she was having a heart attack and Gabby had an entire piece of French toast stuck to her boob from the table army-crawl. It began to peel off, slowly, and then it landed on the grass with a plop.

Breathing hard, we stared at it sitting there.

And then we started to laugh.

Uncontrollable, soul-releasing laughter.

We were laughing so hard when Daniel came outside a few minutes later to release the thing, we were crying.

Hunter bounded down the stairs and bounced among us, tail wagging. He let out a long *rooooooooooo!* Then he ate the French toast.

I had to wipe tears off my cheeks.

Daniel came over to us, looking apologetic. "I'm sorry. He's got a soft mouth," he said, rubbing the back of his neck. "It's good for a hunting dog. Means they won't maul the birds they retrieve. It also means they don't kill the things they catch..."

Jessica howled. I don't think I'd ever heard her laugh so hard. She was always so serious.

Daniel put a thumb over his shoulder. "I can replate everything if you just give me a few minutes," he said, looking embarrassed.

Jessica nodded, wiping under her eyes. "Please do."

When Daniel went back into the house, Gabby shook her head. "This place is so getting one star. What a shit show." She laughed.

I sobered instantly. "What? You can't give it one star."

Jessica shook her head, still tittering. "I'm pretty sure live rodents at breakfast deserve one star, Ali."

"It was an accident," I said.

"Uh, that dog shouldn't be around people," Gabby said. "He's not trained."

"He's a *rescue*. He's still learning."

Gabby wrinkled her forehead. "How do *you* know?"

"The guy told me. Seriously. Do not give this place one star. You'll hurt his business."

Gabby scoffed. "So, like, an entire squirrel at breakfast deserves what? Some rave review?"

I shook my head. "No. You don't have to lie. Just don't rate it at all."

She crossed her arms. "If I treated patients the way this guy runs this B & B, I'd be sued for malpractice."

"It's not that serious, Gabby," I said. "We all laughed."

Jessica looked annoyed. "Ali, she had to climb across a *table*.

Her new Lululemon shirt is ruined. And that dog practically knocked you over yesterday. He should be locked up at the very least. It's extremely irresponsible."

An acorn dropped behind her onto the grass with a muffled thud.

"You don't think you're being a little hard on him?" I asked, looking back and forth between them. "One star for the *dog*?"

"Frankly, no, I don't," Jessica said, waving off a dragonfly. "I think it's warranted."

We stood there in a tense moment of silence.

They didn't know.

They didn't know Daniel wasn't nothing to me. His struggles were not some abstract idea, because *he* mattered to me. They didn't know because I couldn't—*wouldn't*—tell them.

If I did, I'd lend him my protection. They wouldn't write that review because me asking them not to would be enough. If I just said, *Look, this is the guy I've been seeing. Please don't.* They wouldn't.

But I couldn't do that. Because then I'd be giving Daniel to Neil. And that was worse.

I wiped under my eyes.

"Grace costs you nothing," I said. And I went back inside.

CHAPTER 19

DANIEL

I was in the dining room cleaning up the mess when Alexis came back into the house with Hunter behind her.

The dining room was destroyed. Fucking destroyed. There was a piece of French toast stuck to the wall, coffee on the Oriental rug under the table, orange juice splattered all over the hutch, broken glass.

"I think I'm going to have to set you guys up in the four-season porch," I said to her, shaking my head at the room. Thank God I always made enough for seconds.

Hunter pushed his face under Alexis's hand and pressed his body to her leg.

"I didn't like the present, Hunter," Alexis mumbled.

I looked down at his shaggy head. "I think my dog might be in love with you. And grounded," I muttered. "He's definitely grounded."

She laughed dryly.

I shook my head. "What is his problem? He does *not* listen. I can't even get him to sit half the time. I mean, I know hunting breeds are stubborn, but Jesus."

"He's deaf."

I stared at her. "What?"

"He's deaf, Daniel. Maybe not totally, but—mostly."

I blinked at her. "Wha—how do you know?"

She gave a one-shoulder shrug. "Watching? When you give him hand signals, he obeys. When you talk, he ignores you."

I looked down at my dog. "Hunter, sit."

He looked up at me with his blank face.

"Sit, Hunter," I said again.

Nothing.

I put an index finger up in the hand signal for sit.

Hunter sat.

"Oh, wow," I breathed. "This clears up so much," I said in wonder.

She laughed weakly.

I dragged a hand down my beard. "Probably from the shooting. They shoot over the dog's head. That's probably why they retired him, he can't hear."

"So he's a good boy after all," she said, somewhat tiredly.

"All dogs are good boys," I said. "Even this one." I took one more look at the dining room and blew a breath through my lips. "I'll have breakfast out again in fifteen minutes. Can you let them know?"

"Yeah. Are their rooms haunted?"

I laughed. "What?"

"Did you give them haunted rooms? If not, can we maybe do a seance? Summon some demons? Because I wouldn't be upset if a closet opened up on them and blood poured out."

"Are you mad at them?" I asked.

"I'm a little irritated with them, yeah."

"I hear Doug sang them 'More Than Words' last night," I said. "That's not enough punishment?"

"Nope."

"I heard what they said about Jane's," I said. "Doreen makes everything from scratch there. It's her grandmother's recipes. It sucks they didn't like it."

"I'm beginning to think they don't like anything," she mumbled.

I was laughing at this when we heard shrieks from outside. Alexis and I made split-second eye contact before I ran to the window and squinted at the yard. "What the hell…"

"What is it?" Alexis asked, coming up behind me.

"I think it's…*acorns*?"

Jessica and Gabby were running to the front door, their hands over their heads trying to block the onslaught. The oak trees lining the driveway were dropping acorns like hail—which was weird because they didn't do that until the fall…

I opened the front door to let them in, and as soon as they crossed the threshold, the deluge outside abruptly ceased.

"*Unbelievable*," Jessica said angrily.

She had red welts on her bare arms.

Gabby was pulling acorns from her hair.

Alexis blinked at them in shock. "What happened?"

"The fucking trees!" Jessica snapped.

I went outside and jogged down the stairs. I stopped under the first oak and picked up one of the projectiles.

Acorn.

So weird…I turned it around in my fingers. I looked up at the tree, shading my eyes. I didn't see any on the branches. Maybe they all fell? But they don't drop until September. And when they do, they sure as hell don't drop like this. Maybe a squirrel's nest got knocked over or something?

I turned around, looking at the mess. There must have been a thousand acorns on the lawn.

Alexis came outside a moment later, looking weary. "They're just going to go eat at Jane's and then rent bikes."

I blinked at her. "Oh. They don't want breakfast?"

"Not here," she said glumly.

My stomach dropped.

This wasn't how I wanted this weekend to go. Not for my guests, not for me, and especially not for Alexis. I wanted to impress her.

I dragged a hand through my hair. "I'm sorry. I don't know how today got so messed up."

"It's okay," she said, sliding her hands into her pockets.

"When will you be back?" I asked.

"I'm not going."

I wrinkled my forehead. "You're not going with your friends?"

"I'm not very happy with them right now. I'm going to stay and help you clean up."

I was happy I was getting time with her, but I shook my head. "You don't have to do that."

"I want to. I can do the sweeper thingy."

"The broom?" I looked at her, amused.

Her cheeks got a little pink. "Yeah. That's what I meant."

I studied her for a second. "Do you know how to sweep?"

She tucked her hair behind her ear and looked away from me. "I...I don't clean my own house, Daniel. I've never done it before."

"You've never cleaned?"

She looked embarrassed. "No. Not really. No."

I blinked at her.

"I mean, I load the dishwasher. I put clothes in the laundry basket—"

"Can you do laundry?"

She paused a moment before shaking her head.

I don't know why, but this made me feel about two hundred thousand times better.

She crossed her arms. "Don't make fun of me—"

"I'm not."

"You're smiling."

"I'm smiling because this entire weekend has made me feel like I suck at everything and it's nice to know that maybe you suck at things too."

She snorted. "Daniel, you're good at everything. Trust me."

"Yeah, well, sex stuff doesn't count."

"Uh, it actually does. And I'm not just talking about sex stuff. Your woodworking, your cooking."

Those things didn't really feel equal to a medical degree, but I'd take them. At this point I needed all the help I could get.

"You don't have to clean," I said. "Just hang out with me."

But she shook her head. "I *want* to help. Would you show me?"

I smiled. "Sure."

CHAPTER 20

ALEXIS

I spent the day helping Daniel with his chores, and it was *work*. We cleaned up the breakfast disaster, and then we had to go do the rooms. Make the beds, clean the bathrooms. I had never scrubbed a shower before. It was exhausting.

And he did this *every day*.

It gave me a whole new appreciation for my housekeeper.

Bri liked to say she could tell I'd never cried in a walk-in fridge before. I'd never worked retail or in a restaurant. She said it should be mandatory that everyone work at a fast-food place for six months because it changes you, and I think this is what she meant.

It made me think about every time I left a dirty makeup wipe on the counter, or I tossed my shoes on the floor and came back to them put away. I must seem so rude, I realized.

By the time Jessica and Gabby came back from their bike ride, I'd calmed down a little.

I went to dinner at Jane's with them. Daniel told me Liz wasn't working, thank God, so nobody there recognized me. And the food was good. I don't know what they were talking about. I liked it. Doreen was there, and she said they sourced their produce locally. The eggs and milk came from Doug's farm.

We came back after dinner and spent a few hours in the screened-in gazebo by the river, drinking wine and hanging out. It was Saturday, so Daniel was at the VFW calling bingo, and I didn't even get to see him around the house. I would rather have been there with him than here with Gabby and Jessica.

I still wasn't happy with either of them. But Gabby promised she wouldn't write a review, so at least Daniel was spared that.

I snuck back in to sleep with him after they finally went to bed at midnight. I woke up at 5:45 again when he did and went back to my room. And that was it. The weekend was over.

Our last breakfast Sunday morning was uneventful—and really good. Gabby asked for the recipe for the lingonberry crepes Daniel had made, and he gave her a laminated recipe card on Grant House cardstock that he already had printed and waiting.

He was an excellent host. I felt confident that despite the squirrel/acorn debacle, he'd adequately redeemed the Grant House in the eyes of my friends.

I didn't need any redemption from him. I was very happy with the service *I* got. All weekend. Seven times.

We were loading our bags in the car to go home, and I had the saddest feeling.

I didn't want to leave. I didn't want to go back to the real world and my crappy situation with Neil.

And the other thing. I didn't feel like I got enough time with Daniel.

I started thinking about when I would come again, and I

realized I was already canceling plans with other people in my head to make time to be here. I'd gone from being positive I was never going to see him again, to seeing him being the only thing I felt like doing.

Somewhere deep in the back of my brain, a warning signal flashed.

I was having more fun with him than I expected. I wanted to spend more time with him than I expected—and this wasn't a good thing. It felt good, but it wasn't.

I couldn't develop a dependency on someone I couldn't have long term. And Daniel I could *not* have long term.

Chemistry and things in common aside, Daniel would never work in my life. He was too young, too far away.

He was too different...

I knew this. But I was getting ahead of myself. All this was just the excitement of something new. These feelings would fizzle out. In a few months we'd get tired of each other, and this would run its course, and we'd both move on. I wasn't going to worry about it.

I dropped my bag in the trunk and came around to the side of the SUV where Gabby was leaning, looking at her screen.

She had TripAdvisor up. There was a one-star rating at the top of the page.

When she saw me, she tucked her phone into her purse.

"What are you doing?" I asked, crossing my arms.

"Nothing," she said quickly.

"Were you rating the Grant House?"

Jessica moaned, tossing her bag into the back seat. "Who cares?"

"She said she wouldn't," I snapped at her.

Gabby gave me a look. "Ali, people depend on my reviews. This is my honest experience."

I pressed my lips into a line.

"Look, I was gentle, okay? And I made sure to mention that he comped our stay—"

"Wait. He *what*?"

She shrugged. "He comped our stay."

I shook my head at her. *"Why?"*

She looked at me like I'd spoken the word in another language. "Uh, because I complained?"

"Why would you do that? He was perfectly polite to us."

She put a hand on her hip. "Come on, Ali. A dog *attacked* you. A dang squirrel was in the house. We didn't eat breakfast yesterday, and it was part of what we paid for. Jessica still has red marks on her arms from the acorns."

"You're holding him accountable for the damn trees?"

She crossed her arms. "Yeah. I am. If they drop acorns hard enough to hurt people, then they shouldn't be where guests are walking around. One of us could have lost an eye. He could have at least had signs up warning us about falling debris. What's with you?"

I let a shaky breath out through my nose.

I was furious.

I saw Daniel get up at 5:45 in the morning just to make sure we had coffee if we happened to be awake wandering the halls. I knew the cheese he put out for us every night came from Doug's farm to help keep him in business, and Daniel had purchased that for our appetizer hour, and now he was losing money on that because we didn't even pay for our stay.

Now not only was Daniel going to be dinged on his star rating, it had cost him money to host us. And he *needed* that money.

I hated that I'd come here with them. I felt ashamed by

association. Had they always been like this? Or was I just now starting to find it unacceptable?

Had *I* been like this once?

And the answer to that made me feel ashamed too.

I blew a calming breath through tight lips.

Gabby would never back down from this. The more I pushed her, the more she'd dig in. She was way too entitled.

But I had a different idea.

"Okay. You're right. It's your experience," I said. And then, "Hey, do you guys want to see something cool?" I asked.

Jessica looked at her watch and blew out an impatient breath. "Fine. But can we make it quick?"

I nodded. "Yeah. Come on. Follow me."

I walked them to the garage and held the door handle, turning to them. "I saw this yesterday while you were on your bike ride." I knocked and then peeked inside. Daniel was at his workbench. "Can I show them those freestyle projects you have?"

He blinked at me. "Sure."

I let them in and took them to the pieces he kept in the corner of the garage.

"Oh, wow..." Gabby breathed.

"Aren't these cool?" I asked. "He's a sixth-generation carpenter. His great-great-great-grandfather actually built the house we stayed in."

"Does he sell these?" Gabby asked.

I nodded. "Yup."

Jessica was examining the mirror. "This would be great in Marcus's office at the cabin. I didn't get him a birthday gift. How much?" she asked, looking over at Daniel.

"Three thousand," I said before he could answer. "I asked him yesterday. This one took over a hundred hours to make. The wood's—what did you say it was?" I asked him.

Daniel was blinking at me. "Black walnut?"

"Black walnut," I said, turning back to her. "It's one of a kind."

"I'll take it," Jessica said, like an afterthought. "Do you take Venmo?"

"Uh, yeah?" Daniel said, looking shocked.

I pointed to the horse. "I thought that one would be cool for the den at your house," I told Gabby. "This one is thirty-five hundred. It's hand-wrought from a beam that was in a hundred-year-old barn. See the color? The ammonia from the animal's urine stains the wood," I said, repeating what he had told me. "That's where the bracket used to be, this lighter spot?"

She crouched to look at it.

"Can he put it in the car?" she asked. "It looks heavy."

A text pinged to my cell phone as we drove out of Wakan a half hour later. I was in the middle of writing the Grant House a five-star review.

Daniel: WTH???

I smiled.

Me: I'm sorry they were like that. You shouldn't have comped their stay.

I could see him writing a text. The dots were bouncing.

Daniel: It was the right thing to do. Their visit wasn't up to my standard. It was customer service.

And then: They paid way too much for those pieces. You shouldn't have told them they cost so much.

I scoffed quietly. It was nothing for them. Just like it was nothing for me.

I'd played with a pig in a two-thousand-dollar dress. I stepped in dog poop in a shoe that cost as much as the weekend away for three that Daniel just comped, and I just left it there. It wasn't even worth my time to clean it. I didn't even *think* about these things. They were insignificant to me.

I was floating around in some universe that I was beginning to realize most people didn't live in. Daniel certainly didn't.

I didn't like how easy it was for someone like Gabby, in her position of privilege, to punch down. At *all*.

It was such an unfair power dynamic. She was like a kid wielding her one-star reviews like a toy, for fun. Only it wasn't a game. It was someone's livelihood.

And here was Daniel, doing what he felt was the right thing, refunding the whole weekend. He was in the worst position to be generous, yet he was. And she was in the best position to show grace, and she didn't. And doing it would have cost her nothing.

And *that* was the fundamental difference between them.

I typed my response.

Me: You deserved asshole tax. Trust me.

And then I paused, thinking about what I wanted to say.

Me: Know your worth, Daniel.

I wish it had always been as easy to know mine.

CHAPTER 21

DANIEL

Alexis hadn't been out to see me since last weekend when she came with her friends, but we talked every day for hours.

I liked her. I liked her so much, it wasn't even funny.

The sex was unreal, she was smart and beautiful, and I loved hanging out with her. I hadn't felt like this in such a long time, I couldn't even remember being this into someone. Maybe I never had been.

My entire life was now reduced to two things. Raising the money to buy the house and trying to get Alexis to come see me. I'd go see her if it wasn't for the first thing.

I was working myself to the bone.

When I wasn't dealing with guests or the house repairs I'd promised Amber, I was working in the garage on the pieces I was trying to finish. I was exhausted.

Today was the first day in a week that I was giving myself a day off, treating myself to a breakfast I didn't have to cook before I headed over to Doug's to help him with stuff on the farm. I should probably have just backed out and told him I had too much work to do at home—which I did. But I needed the change. And being outside and with my friends was a nice break, even if I'd be doing manual labor the whole time.

I was at Jane's in a booth waiting for the guys. I was a little early, so I called Alexis. She answered on the second ring.

"Daniel, I can't talk right now. I'm having an emergency." She sounded like she was crying.

I sat up. "Are you okay?"

She sniffed. "No. Not really. The power is out, so the coffeemaker won't work."

I barked out a laugh.

"This is not funny! It's been two hours and I have to go to work."

"Okay. This is serious. You should probably drink all the vodka before it goes bad."

"Daniel!"

I chuckled. "Okay, okay. I think I can help. Is your oven gas or electric?"

"I think it's gas."

"You *think*?"

"I don't coooook," she said miserably.

I grinned. "If it's gas, it should work, even if the power's out. You can boil water and use a French press if you have one."

"I only have a Keurig."

"Can you just get in the car and go to a coffee shop?"

"I tried. The garage door won't open. No power," she said, defeated. "I'm trapped."

The way she breathed the last word made me move the phone away from my mouth to laugh.

"Pull the emergency release," I said, smiling.

"There's an emergency release?"

I pinched the bridge of my nose, trying not to crack up. "There is. Go in there, and I'll tell you how to open it."

"This is how you die in the zombie apocalypse," she said with wonder. "I always thought it would be an infected zombie bite or exposure or something, but it's this. You get a caffeine headache on the first day and you lose your will to live and you just lie down and they eat you."

I laughed. "In the event of a zombie apocalypse, I promise I will not let you get eaten."

"How? You're not here."

"I'd come get you. I'd put together a recovery team. You're a doctor. You're a high-value acquisition. Doug bet me a hundred bucks I couldn't get the best Zompac squad, I need you."

She laughed weakly.

I heard a door open. "Okay, I'm in here."

"All right. You might need a ladder. Look for the motor. It's a small box on the ceiling in the middle of the garage. It's attached to a metal runner that pulls the door up. There's a little string hanging down from it. You see it?"

"Yeah."

"You pull that and then you can lift the door from the bottom and open it."

There was a quiet pause. "Daniel, you're my hero."

"Well, thank you. But I think the standard's a little low."

She paused. "I hate that I don't know things."

"How many bones are there in the human body?"

"Two hundred and six," she said without skipping a beat.

"Which one's your favorite?"

"I like the hyoid bone. It's basically free floating and no one talks about it." She sniffed. "It's very underrated."

I smiled. "Yeah, I think you're doing okay."

She laughed, and I heard the garage door open.

"Why is the power out?" I asked, nodding at Popeye shuffling in.

"I don't know."

"Is it the whole block?"

"Gabby and Jessica aren't home, so I don't know."

"Did you check the breaker?" I asked.

"What's that?"

I shook my head with a smile. God, this was so her. She was this conundrum of a woman. Completely remarkable in every way, doesn't know about breaker boxes or how to wash a load of whites or make a bed. I think I'd been cleaning since I was old enough to walk. One of Grandma's favorite pictures of me was me, three years old, holding a toilet bowl scrubber.

"There's probably an electrical panel in the garage," I said. "Go look for it."

"Okay, hold on."

"It's metal," I said, putting my coffee cup to my lips. "Probably gray. It'll have switches on it."

"Like a light switch thingy?"

"Did you find a light switch thingy?" I asked, amused.

"Yeah."

"Send me a picture of it."

I heard shuffling. Then a picture message came through. I zoomed in. "Your main breaker is flipped off."

She went silent on the other end for a long moment. "How does that happen?"

"It doesn't. If you overload one circuit a breaker might flip. But that would be one part of the house, not the whole thing."

"Soooo..."

"So someone probably switched it off. Did you have someone there working on the electrical or something?"

She went quiet again. "Yeah. It must have been them."

"Just flip it back. The power will come back on," I said.

I heard her flip the switch, and she made an excited little sound of relief. I smiled.

"So do I get to see you this week?" I asked.

I heard a car door slam. "I don't know."

My smile fell. I was about to push the subject, but I heard the restaurant door jingle. Brian and Doug were coming in.

"The guys just got here. I'll let you get your coffee and call you later."

We hung up right as they slid into the booth. "Hey."

Liz swung by and set menus in front of us. "Hey, guys. Coffee?"

They both nodded, and Brian smiled at her, a touch too brightly.

The way he looked at her made me look away from him, like I was intruding on a private moment.

Brian had been in love with Liz since we were kids. She didn't live here growing up. She only came for the summers. Brian looked forward to her visits the whole year. He'd be at my house so much in the summer that Grandma used to joke he was one of her honorary grandkids.

Then one summer we got a new sheriff—and Liz met *Jake*.

I watched Liz pour Brian a coffee. She had a brace on her little finger. My jaw tightened.

Jake was putting hands on her. *Again.*

He never did it in front of anyone. Whenever they were in public, he always put on some fucking show so everyone thought he was this doting husband. Such bullshit.

I almost knocked him out once after she came into the VFW with a split lip on St. Patrick's Day a few years back. He denied touching her, and I almost got myself arrested—and she was mad at *me* afterward. Didn't talk to me for weeks.

Sometimes when I saw this shit on her, I'd ask her anyway, even though I knew she wouldn't tell me. She'd just say this was a fall or a slammed door or something and she'd say it looking me dead in the eye. I hated it.

He cheated on her too, another thing nobody bothered to mention anymore because she never did anything about it, and it just upset her. He loved dipping into the tourists. I don't know why she put up with it. She could do so much better.

I looked away from her hand.

"How's the saving-up thing going?" Brian asked.

"Good," I said. "I haven't gone down to the swap meet yet, but I sold a few pieces to Alexis's friends. That helped."

That helped a *lot*.

Actually, I'd been thinking about that. Those ladies didn't even blink an eye. They just bought them, on the spot. Maybe Alexis was right, and I needed to cast a wider net. Get a website up, an Instagram page. Maybe put a few of the smaller pieces in some of the gift shops when they opened for the summer, see how they did.

Alexis made me want to be better.

If I'd never had to run the B & B, I think I'd be doing more with myself by now. Maybe I'd be practicing my carpentry full-time. I never got the chance to really explore it because my grandparents had died, and I'd had to change gears before I could figure out if I could make a go of it.

Maybe now I never would...

If I bought the house, I'd need to keep running it as a B & B to pay the mortgage. And not the way I'd been running it either. I'd have to be open year-round to cover that kind of payment.

I'd be an innkeeper for the rest of my life.

Not that being an innkeeper wasn't a good business. It's just not what I wanted to do. I don't think it was what I was *meant* to do.

All of this felt a little like selling my soul. Like letting the house go would destroy me, and so would keeping it.

Doug put his coffee to his lips. "What's up with the girlfriend?" he asked me.

"She's not my girlfriend," I mumbled.

She wasn't my girlfriend, because she didn't want to be my girlfriend. *I'd* jump at the chance to be Alexis's boyfriend in a hot second. But I knew it wasn't going to happen.

She never made me feel like I wasn't good enough for her, but she didn't have to. It was obvious. I'd accepted this with a resigned understanding of my position and decided that I wasn't going to dwell on it, especially because there was nothing I could do to change the situation. I couldn't snap my fingers and be a damn surgeon. I couldn't be anything other than what I was.

"Why isn't she your girlfriend?" Doug asked.

"I don't have anything to offer a woman like that."

Doug set his mug down. "Have you ever heard of penguin love stones?"

"What?"

"A penguin love stone. When a male likes a female, he finds a perfect stone and he brings it to her. If she likes it, she puts it in her nest and that's it. They're paired for life."

Brian watched Liz taking an order at another table but talked to us. "And your point?"

"My point is, the penguin's not picking her mate because he's the one who has the best rock. It might look that way, but she's not. She's taking the rock because the male she wants the most is offering it. Sometimes what you have to give is enough. Even if it's a rock instead of a diamond."

I let out a long breath. If only that were true.

We ate breakfast. Doug was in a good mood, which was nice. His depression always got better in the spring. More sunlight, more time outside, tourists starting to come back. He was thinking of putting in a wood-fired pizza oven at the farm to do pizza and wine pairings in the summer, bring in more business in addition to the petting zoo and barn weddings he did.

Brian listened to us talk and watched Liz. Every time she cleared a plate, he'd look at her brace and his jaw would flex. This shit with Jake was hard on all of us, but for Brian I think it was a special kind of hell.

When we were finishing up, my phone rang. I grinned. Alexis.

"I gotta take this," I said, sliding out of the booth.

I pushed through the door and swiped the Answer button when I got outside. "Hey. You get your coffee?" I smiled.

"Iced coffee tastes *soooo* much better when you're late for work," Alexis said, sounding like her old self again.

I laughed. "Glad I could help."

"I have to go in a second, but I wanted you to hear something. I'm going to put you on speaker but don't talk, okay?"

"Okay…"

"Someone's singing opera in the ER," she said.

I could hear the squeaky sound of shoes on a polished floor like she was walking me somewhere.

"Opera?"

"We've got a bachelorette party here. The bride has alcohol poisoning and her friends brought her in. The whole group is drunk. One of them is a soprano, and she's singing in the room. It's amazing. Ready?"

"Ready."

She put me on speaker, and I heard a door open. The voice of an angel drifted through the phone. "Ave Maria."

It was beautiful. Ethereal. It brought tears to my eyes, standing on this sidewalk. It felt like a gift, this unexpected beauty in the middle of a mundane morning.

Alexis tapped me into a different world. She was this incredible woman, working in a hospital two hours away, treating a patient whose friend was singing in Latin. Just in her normal routine, Alexis was living a life a thousand times more interesting and cultured than mine—and she wanted to include me in it.

This gesture made me grateful in a way I couldn't explain. She was giving me more of herself, even if it was just a peek into a moment of her day.

When it ended, Alexis whispered into the phone, "Gotta go." And she hung up.

I smiled, wiping at my eyes. I stood there, looking at my screen, with a grin on my face.

I wanted more.

I wanted to see her world with my own eyes, not just these glimpses behind the curtain. I wanted to be a part of it.

But it was by invite only. And I doubted she'd ever ask me.

I was getting ready to head back in when the phone rang again.

This time it was Amber. My good mood disintegrated. I let the phone ring three times before I reluctantly pressed it to my ear. "Yeah?"

"Hey. Um, so I didn't get the direct deposit this week?"

I scrubbed a hand down my face. "It hasn't even been seven days since I reopened the house. And I had to comp the stay for my guests last weekend."

"Uh, okay, why?"

"Just some dumb stuff. The trees dropped some acorns on them and—"

"Okay, Daniel? I don't care." Her voice was edgy. "You said I'd be getting money every week."

I blew out a calming breath. "The house is booked up through Sunday," I said carefully. "I can send you the money on Monday."

"How much?" she asked quickly.

I drew my brows down. "Is everything okay? You seem . . . tense."

Actually, she seemed wired. She seemed *high*.

Amber being high wasn't exactly a new development. She'd been doing better over the last few years though. But if she was getting back into drugs, I didn't like that she was doing it when the money for the house was dangling in front of her like a blank check.

"I'm fine," she said, a little too curtly. "I just need the money. If you can't get me money every week, the deal's off."

I nodded. "Okay. Last weekend was a one-off. It won't happen again."

"And don't be comping people. What's wrong with you?" she snapped.

I let this slide. No point in getting into it with her. Last weekend aside, I was very good at what I did for a living. I didn't need her advice *or* her criticisms. I didn't need anything from my mother and I never had.

There was no love lost between me and Amber. I didn't want to see anything happen to her—but I also knew there was nothing I could do about it if it did.

Amber's crises cycled. And she bit the hand that fed her, every time. If I offered to let her come dry out here, like Grandma always did, I'd live to regret it. I'd be more likely to find myself canceling missing checks and searching for family heirlooms at pawnshops in Rochester than I would be saving her from herself. So I had to do my best to save the house instead.

"I'll have the cash in the account Monday," I said.

"Fine."

She hung up on me.

I stood outside for a minute, staring at the mural on the side of the pharmacy. I wasn't getting six months. I'd be lucky if Amber gave me six weeks. The best I could do was hope for as much time as possible.

In a season, one way or another, my life would never be the same.

CHAPTER 22

ALEXIS

This was the second morning in a row that I woke up to Neil ruining my day. Yesterday he turned off the power in the house, and today he was in my kitchen.

He was sitting at the table, sipping an espresso, wearing his gray pants and white golf polo.

I wanted to scream.

"Good morning," he said, smiling at me. "I made the quiche you like." He nodded to the bar, where a slice of my favorite spinach and broccoli quiche sat with a glass of fresh-squeezed orange juice on a tray. There was a ramekin of mixed berries on the plate and a tiny vase with a single flower in it.

I loved that quiche. He made it on special occasions like my birthday.

He was doing the thing.

The thing he *always* did. He was trying to make nice and act like nothing had happened. Like his bad behavior was a cut movie scene that never took place. Like I was going to suddenly forget that he'd turned the power off to the house yesterday, or that he was living here against my will after subjecting me to years of emotional and mental abuse and I was just going to sit and have a casual and pleasant breakfast with him. In fact, he was probably banking on it.

Only I wasn't the same woman now.

I used to be so worn down from his mood swings and so desperate for any bit of kindness from him that I'd just give in. I'd just let it go, let him get away with it. I'd thank him for the flowers or act excited about the expensive vacation he'd booked instead of actually saying he was sorry. I'd eat the quiche.

Fuck the quiche.

I ignored him and went to the fridge to get my protein shake.

He was gone a lot. He was the chief of surgery, so he worked eighty-hour weeks plus on-call shifts. There were very few mornings I'd have to deal with this—but I *would* deal with it. Because I would be *damned* if Neil got my house.

He probably thought this little "I'm living here" stunt was going to make me fold like I always did when he bullied me.

But I was done being bullied. *Done.*

I'd had a long talk with my therapist about this situation. Neil wasn't a violent person—he was just a jerk. I had absolutely no fear for my safety with him being here, and if I had, I'd have given up the house, no matter how badly I wanted it. My therapist had been more concerned about whether I could handle the mental and emotional toll it would take to see it through.

And the answer was yes.

I don't think I could handle the toll it would take if I *didn't*.

Letting him get away with this felt like allowing myself to be victimized all over again.

He wanted me displaced and the home that I deserved and earned to be taken from me as some sick punishment for daring to not take him back. I would never give him the satisfaction.

Something in me had shifted in the last few weeks. It was like the more distance I got from this relationship, the stronger I became, and standing up to him was getting easier and easier. I was perfectly willing to put up with his presence and hold my ground in exchange for the chance to finally show him I could.

My attorney said we'd have to go to mediation for the house. When that didn't work, because it wouldn't, we'd end up in front of a judge. The house would have to be assessed, and I had to pull together financial records. Three to six months. I just needed to deal with this for three to six months and then it would be over either way. He'd get the house, or I would. But at least when it was done, I wouldn't have let him win, once again, without a fight.

I could feel Neil stare at my back from the breakfast nook. I needed to get a fridge for my room.

I heard him getting up. "Ali..."

"Don't," I snapped, shooting him a look.

He was leaning on his palms on the table. "If you refuse to speak to me, this is going to be a very long couple of months."

"It's going to be a long couple of months anyway. If you don't like it, *move*," I said, giving him his line back from the other day.

The doorbell rang, and I used it as my excuse to walk out of the kitchen.

When I opened the front door, it was Mom and Dad.

I blinked at them. "I didn't know you were coming over," I said as they came in.

My parents were in their seventies, but they had the stamina of fifty-year-olds. They'd both worked like machines right up to their retirement in March. Dad only retired because his eyes weren't as good as they had been, and it made surgery difficult. Mom had arthritis. Otherwise they probably would have worked until they dropped dead.

Dad was in a blue polo and white pants, his gray hair slicked back handsomely. Mom's outfit matched like they'd color coordinated, her gray hair swept into a white visor.

Dad kissed me on the cheek. "Golfing with Neil. Is he ready?"

"You're..." I shook my head. "Dad, Neil and I broke up," I said, following them into the living room.

Mom took the recliner and Dad sat on the sofa. "And?"

I crossed my arms. "And it's not appropriate for you to golf with my ex."

"Alexis, Neil and I were friends and colleagues long before he dated *you*," Dad said.

I licked my lips. "Dad. He *cheated* on me—"

He put up a hand. "I'm not going to get involved in your lovers' spat. Couples fight. You'll work it out—or you won't. But I won't get in the middle of it either way."

I blinked at him. "Well, it might interest you to know that he's living here against my wishes."

"It's his house as much as it's yours. And frankly, you should give it to him. You're the one who wants to end the relationship, and with the shifts he works, it's better for him to be close to the hospital. Unless you're planning on taking on a higher workload, I don't know how you can argue that you're more entitled to it."

I stood staring at him in shock.

Mom gave me one of those silent "resistance is futile, let it go" looks. I pressed my lips into a line.

Dad shook his head. "I just don't understand why you won't consider counseling. Relationships take work, Alexis. You don't leave the moment things become difficult."

Mom put her hand on his knee. "Cecil, I think we should let them sort things out on their own time, don't you? They're both so busy with work—"

"Which reminds me," Dad said, cutting her off, "I've been informed that Dr. Gibson is retiring in a few months, which means that chief of emergency medicine is going to be available. You'll run for this. We've both already made our recommendations to the board. Your mother and I have tolerated your lack of ambition for long enough. If all you wanted was to be a glorified paramedic, you should have saved us three hundred thousand dollars on med school."

I felt my heart rate pick up.

I licked my lips. "Just because I'm not a surgeon doesn't mean what I do isn't important," I said carefully.

But it was pointless. Because to my dad that's *exactly* what it meant.

Both my parents were surgeons. Dad had wanted me to go into neurosurgery. He would have preferred Derek had followed one of their specialties instead of plastics, but my brother proved early on that his field came with enough fame to placate Dad. But I didn't have that.

What I had was *Neil*.

Neil had leveled me up. Dad didn't like my field, but he dropped his neurosurgery campaign because Derek was there to carry the torch and *I* landed the chief of surgery. To him, dating Neil was an accomplishment in and of itself. But on my own I wasn't enough. Especially now.

It occurred to me that Neil would have made a much better Montgomery than I ever did. In fact, right now, I think Dad saw him as a son more than he saw me as a daughter.

In that moment I wished it was the truth—that Neil was Dad's son and I was just Neil's ex-girlfriend, some random, unimportant woman who could break up with him and go on with her life. It would have been so easy for the universe to arrange it that way.

But the universe doesn't care.

Neil breezed in, and I fought down the tears that were welling. There was no way he hadn't heard us from the other room.

"Cecil! Jennifer!" Neil said, beaming. "Ready to hit the holes?" He swung an invisible club.

I watched Dad light up. He pushed up on his knees and shook Neil's hand. Then he turned to me. "Alexis, we need to discuss your speech for the hospital's quasquicentennial. Meet us for lunch at the clubhouse at twelve-thirty."

I gawked at him. "Wha—*no*! I'm not having lunch with *him*!"

Dad pinned me with a glare. "Young lady—"

Neil put a hand on his shoulder. "Ali has a full day today, C. We'll catch up with her another time," he said.

I watched Dad immediately give up the crusade. If Neil was fine with it, Dad was fine with it.

The idea of Neil bailing me out of this situation only pissed me off more.

Dad gave me one more disapproving glance. Then he made for the door.

Mom stopped and hugged me. "You know how he is," she whispered. "He loves you very much and just wants to see you achieve what he knows you're capable of. I love you, sweetie." She kissed my cheek, patted my back, and left.

Neil waited behind, and when my parents were too far to hear, he leaned in, his voice low. "He's under a lot of stress, Ali. Your brother married some trashy pop star and moved out of the country. And he's taking our separation pretty hard. Go easy on him."

I blinked at him. "Dad told you about her? He signed an NDA."

"Of *course* he told me." He paused, giving me a look I couldn't decipher. "Can we talk later? Please?"

I pressed my lips into a line, my breath shaky.

He waited, but I didn't answer. I couldn't. Because if I had to speak, I was going to scream.

"I'll see you tonight," he said, obviously taking my silence for a yes.

And he left.

The second the door was closed, I lost it. Rage and indignation and hysteria bubbled out of me, and I breathed into my hands.

I hated this. I hated *everything*.

I hated that Derek left me. I hated that Dad had zero integrity. I hated that I was such a disappointment, that I'd never wanted to be a surgeon, that I found the idea of standing in an operating room for hours on end boring and tedious. I resented the entire culmination of my existence and everything that had led me here. I hated Dr. Charles Montgomery, the very first in my family line to work at Royaume Northwestern. I hated every Montgomery who played into the legacy, strengthening it so that I couldn't break it, because for all the good it did, all the lives I *knew* it saved, right now I wished to God it didn't exist.

But mostly I hated Neil. If he hadn't turned into such a horrible human being, I might be happy right now. I might have married him, and he would have taken my name and *he* could have been The One so I didn't have to. And then everyone would have had what they wanted. Because right now the only way everyone could have what they want was for me to decide to be miserable.

I felt instantly claustrophobic, like the walls of this house were shrink-wrapping around me. I couldn't breathe.

A primal urge to run pulsed through my body. I bolted for the garage door, and I knew exactly where I was going.

I wanted to see Daniel.

I wanted his muddy dog to jump on me and I wanted to play with a baby goat and I wanted to be in a place with warm, soft furniture and let someone easy and good hold me in a town that asked me for nothing.

I put on the mud boots that I'd left at the garage door and I got in my car without even grabbing my overnight bag.

I listened to Lola's fourth album the whole way there, cranked up to deafening. She must have been in the same head space as me when she made it because it was very "You Oughta Know" by Alanis Morissette—which was perfect, because it matched my fury.

I didn't call Daniel to let him know I was coming.

For one, I was a sniveling mess for most of the drive, and I didn't want to dump on him the second he picked up the phone. I needed to gather myself before I talked to him—or anyone.

But two? I wanted to just show up. I wanted to see if he was alone, see how he responded to me popping in unannounced.

It was irrational and childish. I had no claim on him at all. But he'd said he wasn't seeing anyone else, and I wanted to catch him in a lie. I almost *wanted* Daniel to let me down. I had to see if he was who he said he was, if he was honest. If I got there and he had some other woman at his place, at least I'd know who he was now instead of later like I had with Neil.

When I pulled into the driveway, Daniel was in the garden. I watched his head pop up and the grin spread across his face, and my mood instantly lifted. I got out of my car, and Hunter bounded over with Chloe running behind him in her pink pajamas. I caught the dog, laughing. He let out his signature *rooooooo!* while Daniel closed the space between us.

"You're here." He smiled over his dog.

"I am."

He didn't skip a beat. He gathered me into him and leaned down and kissed me, and it was like a part of my brain shut off. The part that was stressed and worried and angry.

He pulled away an inch and whispered against my lips. "You should call me before you come though."

All the parts switched back on.

I took a step back, dropping my hands from his chest. "Oh. Right. I'm sorry. I shouldn't just show up like this."

He smiled. "I love that you showed up like this. But at least give me a heads-up so I can shower." He gestured to his dirty clothes. "And so I can have food ready for you."

The relief must have shown on my face, because his brows drew down. "Why did you *think* I wanted you to call first?"

I didn't answer.

Realization moved across his expression. "Did you...did you think I was going to have a girl here or something? I told you I wasn't talking to anyone else."

I hugged my arms around myself. "That's none of my business—"

"I'm not seeing other people," he said.

The corner of my lip twitched.

Then his amused expression fell. "Are *you* seeing other people?"

I shook my head. "No."

He grinned. "Good." He leaned in to kiss me again, and I pulled my face back.

"If you wanted to see other people, that would be okay."

His smile fell. "Why would I want that?"

I tucked my hair behind my ear. "You know, we never really talked about this, Daniel. Maybe we should set rules."

He studied my expression. "Okay."

"So what rules do you want?" I asked.

"You really want to know?"

"Yes."

"I want to be your boyfriend."

It punched me right in the heart, and my stomach did a somersault. But my brain shot it down.

He wants to be my boyfriend? Why? I'm too old. Too old for him anyway. I live too far away, our lives are too different.

What did he want with *me*?

It was almost naïvely sweet. Like when a kid says they want to be an astronaut or a ballerina when they grow up. And then of course you get older and you end up doing something else that actually makes sense.

Maybe he just meant that he didn't want us sleeping with other people? That he wanted to be exclusive? *That* I could understand.

I realized, almost in that moment, that I really didn't want him to see other people either. Even the thought of him hugging someone else launched me into an internal fit of jealousy so sudden it shocked me.

If I'd shown up here and he'd been with another woman, it

would have devastated me. I didn't even realize it until *just* now. Looking at his open face, feeling his warm arms around me, something inside of me screamed MINE.

But it wasn't fair to make him mine. Because I could never be *his*.

A boyfriend came with expectations. He'd want to meet my family, be with me for holidays, my birthday, his birthday. He'd want to come to my house, know my friends. And I couldn't do any of those things. Ever. It felt unfair to let him decide not to date anyone else when this would never go anywhere.

"Daniel, I don't want a boyfriend right now," I said. "I don't have room in my life for that."

I thought I saw a flicker of disappointment cross his face, but he gave me a smile. "That's okay. We don't need titles. We can just agree that we're exclusive and not doing anything else but this right now. I don't have time for much more anyway."

I nodded. "Okay."

He smiled. "Okay."

I should have been happy that I was getting what I wanted— monogamy without any of the strings. But I somehow felt disappointed anyway.

He leaned in and kissed me, and all my thoughts on this evaporated.

He had my face in his rough hands, and I could taste something fruity on his tongue. He wanted to shower, but I was glad he didn't. He smelled like Daniel. Like a combination of the fresh earth he'd been digging in and the cedar of his workshop and clean sweat.

He started to pull away, but then seemed to decide he wasn't done, and he kissed me again.

Ugh, this boy. I wanted to climb into him, merge with his body.

Daniel transported me. Everything about being here and being with him was a break from reality. He was closing open tabs on a laptop in my brain one at a time until he was the only thing on the screen. I felt Neil, my dad, and Royaume Northwestern fade into oblivion at the edges of my mind, and then disappear with a blip.

It was amazing that someone so wrong for me had this ability. Despite the incompatibility of our lives, he had this effect on me. I wondered distantly if we'd known each other in a former life and we'd found each other again. If that's why he was so familiar...

Only this time I'd been born too soon and into a different level of a caste system that he couldn't scale. It made me a little sad.

This relationship would never expand. It would never take a deep breath and pull in those around us. It wouldn't fill its lungs with my people and my life.

It would just be this. Only this.

And it wouldn't last.

He broke away smiling. "I'm going to go get cleaned up. Then we'll go get something to eat. Do you want to give Chloe her bottle while I'm in the shower?"

I nodded against his mouth, breathless.

When he was ready, he didn't drive us to Jane's like I thought he would. He drove us to the little family-owned grocery store.

I realized on the drive that I was actually okay with the idea of eating at Jane's with Daniel, with everyone in the town there to see. Partly because it was my own fault that I didn't let him make other plans. But the other part was that even though I knew technically Daniel was just a guy I was having sex with, it had evolved into something less scandalous over the last few weeks. I guess it felt more like we were dating than just hooking up.

With a jingle, he opened the door of the grocery store for me. He waved at Brian, who was checking someone out, and then he turned to me. "Okay. You didn't give me any time to plan anything for your visit, so we're going to get creative. We're going to play a game."

I arched an eyebrow. "A game?"

"Yup. A *very* serious game. The rules are binding."

"Binding, huh?"

"Binding. Rule number one." He paused for dramatic effect. "Never get involved in a land war in Asia."

"Daniel!"

He was laughing. "I'm kidding!" He ticked off on his fingers. "No substitutions, no backing out, and you have to try *everything* we get. Those are the rules. Do you agree to the terms?"

I narrowed my eyes. "I don't know...I think I need more information."

He crossed his arms. "I can't tell you more about it unless you agree."

I smiled. He looked so cute with his fake serious face. "Okay. I agree."

He rubbed his hands together. "All right, this is how it works. We take turns wandering down each row with our arms out like this." He made a T, with his fingers pointing to either side of the aisle. "The person watching says 'stop' and the one with their arms out has to grab whatever they're pointing to. Whatever we end up with is what's for dinner."

I laughed. "Are you serious?"

"Dead serious. And you can't complain about it. It is what it is. We get three free-choice items at the end to try to pull the meal together. We can use stuff from home if we need to, as long as we're using everything we got from the game."

I smiled. "Okay. Let's do it."

"All right. First we start with the entertainment."

He grabbed a cart and took me to the aisle at the back of the store where they had magazines and art supplies. There was a bin of DVDs for $2.99.

"Are you ready?" he asked, standing next to the bin. "I'll go first."

"Ready."

He plunged his hand into the movies and started digging around. I let it go for about thirty seconds until I called it. "Stop!"

He pulled out the movie he had his hand on and looked at it. "*Ever After*. Drew Barrymore."

"*Yeeeess!* It's so good!"

He dropped it into the cart with a smile. "Your turn."

We went to the snack aisle, and I put my arms out.

He waited for a second. "Go!"

I started walking.

"Stop!" he called when I was in the middle.

I looked at my options on either side. "Honey mustard pretzels," I announced, wrinkling my nose as I grabbed the bag. "And peanut butter crackers. Not bad."

We did the meat aisle and ended up with chicken thighs. In the produce section we got leeks and a bag of red potatoes. In the dairy aisle we got heavy whipping cream. For dessert we ended up with red, white, and blue bomb pops from the freezer case. Daniel grabbed chicken stock, celery, and a baguette as our three free items.

It was so fun—and *simple*. It's exactly the kind of thing Daniel was good at.

He was so different from Neil. It was refreshing. Neil always went all out for our dates. But it was more for him, not me. Front-row tickets, exclusive restaurants—whatever looked best for his social media posts. After a while I got desensitized to it. It all lost its luster. Especially because he spent most of the dates looking at his phone or talking about himself.

God. How had I not seen it?

But then I knew how I didn't see it. Because I'd been raised by a man who valued prestige more than he valued things like integrity and honesty. This was normal to me.

My brother was such a better person than the example he'd been shown. Derek broke out of the cage we'd come up in. I wondered if Lola had done it, if she'd been the one to show him a different way.

I mean, he'd taken that volunteer work in part because it would look nice on his résumé. But in the end, he'd stayed because he knew he could do good.

This was counterintuitive to everything we'd been taught. This work wouldn't make Derek rich or advance his career. It wouldn't help Royaume or impress our father. In fact, it would do the opposite.

I had a welling sense of delayed pride over him. I don't think I'd truly processed what it meant that he stayed to do what he was doing. I'd been so blindsided by how it would affect my life that I hadn't considered the shift that had taken place inside of my brother.

And then I knew something else too. I knew why he hadn't brought Lola back with him. He didn't bring his wife home because there would be no point.

Dad would never accept her. Never. Just like he wouldn't accept someone like Daniel. So Derek didn't even bother. He'd protected his wife from the rejection and gave up *his* life instead.

It was such a beautiful and selfless thing—even if in doing it, he'd condemned *me*.

But I didn't fault him for it. I was happy that one of us got out. He'd given up his seat on the throne to marry a commoner. At least that's how my dad obviously saw it. Gave up all his riches.

But all that glitters is not gold...

We checked out and went back to the garage with our haul.

I slid onto a stool by the kitchenette, and Hunter plopped next to me. "So what are you going to make me?"

"*We* are going to make it," Daniel said, unbagging groceries.

"We? I can't cook."

"Well, I'm going to show you," he said, placing things on the counter. "Doing it together is part of the activity."

I looked at him dubiously.

He smiled. "Come here."

I got off the stool to stand next to him by the counter.

"We're making soup," he said.

"Soup?" I nodded at the pile. "Out of this stuff?"

"Soup is easy. You can make soup out of anything."

He went to the tiny cabinet he used as a pantry and pulled out flour and an onion. He got some garlic and a stick of butter from the fridge and lined everything up on the counter.

A dragonfly was in the garage. It landed on the rim of a pot on the tiny stove. Those things were everywhere here.

I watched Daniel pull out a cutting board and a knife. "You peel the potatoes and I'll chop the onion," he said.

But I didn't move, because I didn't know how to start.

He noticed me balking. "What?"

I licked my lips. "I don't know how to peel potatoes," I said. "I've never done it before."

He blinked at me. "You've never peeled a potato?"

"No. We had a chef...I didn't have to."

Neil loved to point it out when I didn't know how to do something that most people considered basic. But those weren't the kind of skills I was raised to believe were important. My parents prepared me for a very specific kind of life. I was trilingual. I had an MD from Stanford and a PhD from Berkeley. But I never learned how to do laundry. I didn't clean my own home. Before Daniel showed me, I didn't even know how.

I realized that this was one of the things Neil used to maintain control over me. Only *he* could take care of the house. How would I survive without him? I couldn't even cook.

I could order food from Grubhub or make a microwave dinner if I needed one. I could make a sandwich or a salad. But it was like Neil wanted me to have the illusion that I needed him, that I couldn't be alone. I had to be taken care of. I couldn't manage a house. I'd never eat that quiche again unless *he* made it for me.

I peered up at Daniel waiting for him to shame me for my lack of kitchen skills, like Neil always did. But he just shrugged. "Okay, let me show you."

I felt my face soften.

"How did you learn to cook?" I asked.

He smiled. "You have to know how to cook here. We can't always afford to go out to eat. Okay," he said, standing shoulder to shoulder with me after I washed my hands. "You're going to peel the potatoes, like this. When you're done peeling, you cube them. Like this." He took the knife and showed me. "We're cubing them so they cook faster. Since we're making soup we're taking the skins off, but I like to leave them on for mashed potatoes..."

As we went, he explained everything this way. Not just how to do it, but why. I liked this. It was the same way I trained my residents.

He was so patient—and standing as close to me as possible. It was really obvious and very, *very* distracting.

His fresh scent teased my nose, and I found myself leaning into it while I was supposed to be working.

He must have noticed, because he turned to look down at me and our faces were suddenly very close together—and then something happened inside of me that hadn't happened in a *very* long time.

I got *butterflies*.

"What?" he asked, smiling.

I swallowed hard and just blinked at him.

He nudged me. "What?"

I shrugged. "I don't know. I just find you distracting is all." I looked back at my cutting board, feeling a little shaken. Like something big had just happened that was completely out of my control.

I didn't get butterflies. I was too *old* for butterflies. Shouldn't I be completely beyond the age of crushes and puppy-dog love at this point?

I felt him smile, even though I wasn't looking at him. "Are you going to be able to focus on this task at hand, Doctor?" he teased, nuzzling his nose into my hair. "Because I'm going to need your undivided attention, and it seems like you're a little preoccupied," he whispered.

Butterflies *again*.

Oh, my God, no. I *wasn't* going to be able to focus.

I angled my head up and let him give me a kiss, feeling a little insecure about this new development.

He was so charming. And handsome. Devastatingly handsome. He was the kind of man who took my breath away—and it was because he was *good*. Kind and thoughtful and patient. Generous. And so *easy*. Nothing complex about him at all.

Neil was like a Russian nesting doll whose good qualities got smaller the more you uncovered him. But Daniel was the opposite. The more I knew, the better he became.

I liked that he took care of Popeye. And I understood why the town had declared him their mayor—not because he was a Grant, but because I had a feeling the Grants were a certain type of people. Diplomatic and well liked. And I knew this not because he told me, but because of the way other people treated him.

Liz spoke highly of him the day I met him. Brian spent two hours of his night sitting in a projection room at a closed drive-in just so Daniel could take me to a movie. Doreen called him because she knew he would go check on Pops. Then he drove Pops to the doctor all the way in Rochester after his fall, and installed that bar in his shower.

If you looked at the way the people around Neil treated him, you might come to the same conclusions, that he was well liked. Neil had a prominent seat at everyone's table. But the difference was, nobody *relied* on Neil like they did with Daniel. Any relationship that Neil had was based on a shallow connection of status signaling. Nobody ever needed anything from him other than the grace of his presence and his fake bravado.

If Neil was at your party, it meant you were important. You

were someone he wanted to be seen rubbing shoulders with. But if you ever had to rely on him, he'd let you down.

If Daniel was at your party, it meant you were a good person. It meant you were someone who had earned his affection. And I was starting to realize that his affection equaled a level of devotion that I don't think I'd ever known outside of maybe Bri and Derek. And it seemed to encompass a whole town. Like this cloak of loyalty was big enough for everyone.

And then I realized, almost with awe, that *I* must have somehow earned his affection too. He must like me, and not just in a sex way, or why else would he spend so much time on the phone talking to me and want me to be his girlfriend?

Huh.

I started chewing on the side of my lip as I peeled my potatoes.

I remember feeling so important when the chief of surgery took a liking to me. I think I was so dazzled by that and Neil's false charm that I didn't see the red flags waving in my face. I brushed it off when he was rude to our servers or his nurses didn't like him.

With Daniel it was the opposite. I was so dead set on being certain I couldn't be impressed with him, that it was almost startling to discover that I *was*.

His phone rang in his pocket, and he set his knife down to answer it.

"Seriously?" I gave him an arched eyebrow. "Your ringer is on? You call people *and* your ringer is up?" I teased.

He laughed. "How else will I know if someone's calling me? Isn't that what a ringer's for?"

He pulled his phone out. "It's Liz." He answered. "Hey, what's—" He stood there listening. His brows drew down. "She's here. Okay. Okay, hold on." He put the call on speaker.

"Alexis?" Liz said.

I looked at Daniel, confused. "Hi, Liz—"

"Okay, so Hannah's having her baby and they wanted to take her to the Mayo Clinic, but it started to go really fast and they couldn't get her in the car and—"

Screaming and then shattering glass.

"Can you guys come?" she asked, sounding panicked.

I nodded at Daniel, and we started running for the door.

Liz was panting. "We're on a video call with a labor nurse from the hospital. Doug's here trying to help, but Hannah won't let him touch her and the ambulance won't be here for forty more minutes and I don't think she's got forty minutes."

"Is she crowning?" I asked. "Can you see the head?" We were already jumping into Daniel's truck.

"I...I don't know. There's a lot of fluid. Blood and stuff. I think her water broke."

"Okay, we're on our way. Listen, I need you to boil some water and get me all the clean towels you can find. I need disposable gloves, scissors, and snack bag clamps. The ones that close your chip bag? Get a cup and fill it with rubbing alcohol and drop the clamps in there and have it waiting for me."

"Okay. Okay, yeah."

"I'm going to stay on the phone with you until we get there," I said calmly. "Don't panic."

Daniel was already on the street headed north. "Three minutes," he said.

When we pulled up in front of the house, it looked like half the town was there on the lawn. I could hear screaming and shouting from inside.

We ran through the living room and into the bedroom to chaos.

There were half a dozen people in the room. Liz was standing by the nightstand holding a phone to her ear and another one on video call. Doug was by the door, and a very pregnant Hannah was sitting up in the bed, sweaty and flushed.

Doug looked exasperated. "Hannah, just let me look!"

She shot him a glare. "Doug, I will hold this baby in until literally anyone who is not you shows up to deliver it. You are *not* seeing my vagina today. That is not how this ends!"

"I'm a medic, Hannah!"

"You don't deliver babies in the army!"

"I've delivered goats!"

"GET THE FUCK OUT!" She grabbed an alarm clock and hurled it across the room. Doug pivoted just in time, and it hit the wall next to him with a crash, raining shrapnel into an already mounting pile of broken objects.

Hannah clutched the blankets and screamed in pain.

Liz saw me. "The doctor's here!"

Doug looked over at me, relieved. "Thank fucking God." He smacked a box of disposable gloves into my hands. He glanced back to the patient. "Seeing your hoo-ha is not my idea of a good time either, Hannah!" He turned back to me. "I'm outta here. Call me if you need help," he mumbled, edging past me.

I washed my hands and forearms in the adjacent bathroom and then made my way to the bed, putting on gloves. "Hannah, I'm Dr. Alexis. Do you know how far apart your contractions are?"

She shook her head, her eyes squeezed shut.

I turned to Daniel. "I'm going to need everyone who isn't one of the parents to leave the room."

A worried-looking young woman sitting at the edge of the bed raised her hand. "I'm Hannah's wife."

"What's your name?" I asked.

"Emelia."

"Emelia, you stay. Liz, did you get me those things I asked for?"

She nodded and pointed to the towels. "The water is boiling. Doug already started it before you asked."

"Okay, I need you to boil the scissors for me for five minutes. Bring them to me as soon as they're done. Be careful, they'll be hot. Put them on a clean plate to cool."

She nodded quickly, handed the phone on the video call to Emelia, and left the room. When I heard the door click, I lifted the sheet. "I'm going to check your cervix, okay?"

Hannah opened one eye and nodded through a contraction with tight lips. I waited until it passed before I started my examination.

"Any complications with the pregnancy?" I asked.

Emelia shook her head. "No."

"Gestational diabetes? High blood pressure?"

"No. She's healthy. The baby is healthy," Emelia said, her eyes wide.

Hannah was ten centimeters and fully effaced.

"All right, Hannah? We're not going to have time for the ambulance," I said. "We're going to push on the next contraction."

But Hannah shook her head. "No. No no no no, this isn't how it's supposed to go. I have a birth plan. I have a...I'm supposed to have an epidural!"

"I know," I said calmly. "But what's important right now is getting the baby out safely. And since we don't have any way to monitor the baby, we can't wait. The baby could be in distress, and we need to get them out here with us so I can check on them, okay?"

She looked terrified, but she nodded.

"Where would you like Emelia, Hannah? Holding your hand? Or watching the birth?"

Hannah was crying. "I want her to watch."

I nodded. "Okay. Emelia, you can come stand here with me."

Emelia came around, still holding the phone on the video call with the triage nurse.

"Do you two know what you're having?" I asked conversationally.

Hannah shook her head.

I began tucking towels under her. "What names have you picked out?"

Emelia's voice shook. "Um, Kaleb if it's a boy, and Lily if it's a girl."

"Good names." I smiled. "You ready to meet Kaleb or Lily?"

Hannah nodded.

I saw her body tense with another contraction. "Okay, ready? Here we go. Big breath in and hold it, and we're pushing for ten seconds. One, two, three—good job—four, five, making good progress...seven, eight, nine. Gooood."

Hannah gasped with the pain.

"I know it hurts," I said. "But just think, now you'll know what it feels like for a man with a cold." Jessica's favorite delivery line.

They laughed, and the tension lifted a little.

She pushed with three more contractions before the baby's head came out.

The cord was wrapped around its neck.

"Hannah, I need you to try not to push and just pant for a few breaths," I said steadily.

My fingers worked to unloop it, but it was double wound and wrapped too tight. I couldn't reduce it.

The double loop around the neck had shortened the cord. I couldn't see what was going on inside or how much slack we had, but if it was short enough, when the baby came out the cord would pull tight like a noose cutting off the oxygen supply to the baby. I might not be able to get it off in time or clamp and cut it safely before delivery, especially without my medical instruments.

I needed to use a somersault maneuver to deliver the baby. I would have to push the baby's head toward Hannah's thigh instead of pulling the baby straight down. It would let the shoulders and the rest of the body be born in a somersault and keep the neck near the birth canal so that the cord wouldn't be stretched and further tightened.

All of this moved through my brain in a split second of calm. Years of experience and training and instinct took over. I had no monitors or nurses. I didn't even have heel rests. But I knew what to do.

I made confident eye contact with Hannah. "We're pushing one last time and we're going to make it a good one."

I started my countdown. My fingers angled the baby's shoulders expertly, and then in a rush of fluid and blood, I pivoted the baby into a perfect somersault delivery.

It was a girl. And my instincts had been right. The cord had just enough slack for the somersault. Not enough if I'd let her come straight out—and if I hadn't been here, that's how she would have come. Especially if Hannah wouldn't let Doug help her.

The cord would have pulled taut, and they might not have gotten it off in time. The baby could have had brain damage.

Cerebral palsy, epilepsy, intellectual or developmental disabilities. She might have died.

But she didn't because *I* was here.

This is why I did what I did.

In moments like this I knew I was doing what I was meant to do. Moments like this made me know that no matter what Dad said, there was honor in my specialty—even if there wasn't glory.

I quickly unwrapped the cord from the neck and placed the baby on Hannah's belly and started rubbing the baby's back. She cried. A good, strong cry.

I smiled. "Meet Lily."

The ambulance showed up fifteen minutes later. I got the medics up to speed and handed off the patient. When I came out of the room, the whole town was no longer on the lawn—they were in the living room. Daniel stood when he saw me, and everyone looked at me expectantly.

I smiled and put my hands up. "It's a girl."

The whole house erupted into cheering. I got hugs from about three dozen people before Daniel saved me.

He hustled me into a corner and slipped his arms around my waist, beaming down at me. "So you don't know how to peel potatoes, but you can deliver a baby?"

"What, like it's hard?"

He laughed and kissed me. And I didn't care that he did it in front of everyone either.

Hannah came out on a stretcher with a beaming Emelia next to her, and as soon as they were gone, the weirdest thing happened. The houseguests didn't leave. They mobilized. They poured into the bedroom and started stripping the bed, there was someone emptying the dishwasher, someone turned on a vacuum. The smell of Windex and Pine-Sol drifted up around us. The front door was still open, and I could see half a dozen people outside pulling weeds and mowing the lawn. Person after person streamed in with foil-covered casserole dishes, and someone was stationed in the kitchen, receiving them and putting them into the freezer.

"What are they doing?" I asked, looking around at the activity.

"They're doing what we do," Daniel said. "We take care of each other."

Something about it made me feel a little emotional. This was more than just a handful of their closest friends. This was a whole town. The whole town was here.

This wasn't just a community. This was a family.

Popeye shuffled up to us, holding a toolbox. Even he was helping.

"Hi. How you feeling?" I asked.

He looked at me with one eye squeezed shut. "Nifty coincidence you're here, wouldn't ya say?"

He didn't wait for me to answer. He gave Daniel a knowing nod and then hobbled off toward the garage, mumbling to himself.

"What was *that* about?" I asked, looking up at Daniel.

"Eh, he's got this theory about the town."

"What theory?"

He looked a little amused. "He says the town has a way of protecting itself. That it gets what it needs. He thinks you were here today because Hannah needed you."

I wrinkled my forehead thinking about it. "Huh. I wasn't actually planning on being here today."

"Oh, yeah? What changed your mind?"

My parents were playing golf with my ex?

"The weather was nice," I said instead. I tilted my head. "Hey, do you know how to make a quiche?"

He peered down at me. "Quiche? Yeah."

"Will you show me?"

He shrugged. "Sure. We can make one tonight and have it for breakfast."

I smiled. "I think I'm going to want you to show me a lot of things, Daniel. There's a lot I need to learn."

CHAPTER 23

DANIEL

We were lying in my bed, the morning after Hannah's baby came. It was eleven a.m. I had guests coming, but not until later today. Check-in wasn't until three o'clock, so I got to hang out with Alexis in my underwear until she left.

We were napping—we'd been up all night.

I snuggled into her, nuzzling my nose into her neck. She made a happy groaning noise and rolled over, and the second I had her lips in reach, I kissed her.

We were exclusive.

I couldn't stop smiling.

I knew being exclusive wasn't everything. It wasn't a title. It wasn't boyfriend, girlfriend. But it meant I wasn't competing with anyone else, not for her attention or her time. Maybe it meant she'd come down more—maybe she'd even ask me to visit her.

But most of all I was glad there was nobody else, because the idea of it made me feel fucking unhinged. I didn't realize how much of a relief it was until it was off the table. I don't think I allowed myself to think too much on the fact that she may be seeing other people because I didn't feel like I was in any position to ask her not to.

I had these visions of what kind of guys probably hit on her over there. Older, successful—rich. Driving expensive cars, taking her to places I could never afford in a million years. It felt impossible that I'd managed to get her to agree to this. But I wasn't gonna look a gift horse in the mouth. I was going to take it, say thank you, and *run*.

I heard a huffing noise, and we both looked over. Hunter had put his chin on the bed to look at us, his tail wagging. His lip was curled up around a single snaggle tooth, and his bushy eyebrows pivoted as he looked back and forth between us. This dog loved her.

Alexis laughed, smiling up at me. "Did you know that dogs developed eyebrow muscles to better manipulate us?"

I propped myself on my elbow. "Really?"

"Yup. Wolves don't have them. Dogs that had more expressive faces were more likely to connect with their owners. So they evolved." She nodded sideways. "To this."

Hunter backed up and let out a long *roooooooo!*

I laughed and slid a hand down the back of her thigh to wrap her leg around my waist. She took it one step further and rolled on top of me, straddling me. The shirt I'd loaned her was pushed up around her hips. She put her hands on my bare chest and lowered to kiss me, her hair falling around my face in a curtain.

There were a million other things I should have been doing. Working on the unfinished pieces in the garage, getting the house ready for guests, repairing the loose step by the four-season porch—I didn't give a shit about any of it. I'd work harder and faster to make up for the lost time, I'd take the hit, because this was worth it. It was more than worth it.

I was so proud for everyone in town to see me with her yesterday. I was proud of what she did with Lily—I was proud to even know her.

I don't think she realizes how exceptional she is. I got the sense nobody tells her, which is weird.

She rolled her hips against the hard-on she was causing. Our breath picked up and our kiss deepened. In one fluid movement, I rolled her onto her back and slipped a hand into the top of her lace underwear. She was wet, and the thought that she was wet for *me* made my dick even harder than it already was.

Damn, she turned me on.

I circled two fingers around the knot of nerves between her legs, and her breath shuddered at the caress.

She bit her lip. "How do you *do* that?" she breathed.

"Do what?" I asked, my voice husky.

"Know how to touch me."

"I pay attention to you," I said, kissing her collarbone gently. "How you feel matters to me."

Something changed in the set of her body. I brought my face up to see what it was. There was something in her expression I couldn't read—and maybe she didn't want me to read it, because she pulled me down on top of her and kissed me.

I was glad I was going to have the shirt she was wearing after she went home. Something that had her perfume on it, smelled like her.

When she left, the only proof I ever had that she'd been here, or that she even existed at all, was the ache I was starting to feel when she was gone.

CHAPTER 24

ALEXIS

It was early May, a few days after I'd delivered a baby in Wakan, and Mom and I were celebrating Mother's Day.

She was on call so much when I was growing up that celebrating on the actual day was almost never possible, so we'd started the tradition of doing it before the holiday. Today we went to the Mad Hatter Tea House in Anoka. It was a historic home on the Rum River that reminded me a lot of the Grant House, actually. It was built by a doctor in 1857. Going there was one of my favorite things to do with Mom.

She was better when Dad wasn't around. More... *her*.

She had on a white lace dress with a brimmed hat that had white feathers on it. She wore my grandmother's pearls and elbow-length satin gloves. Her makeup was delicate and natural. She looked like she belonged to a different time.

Mom was elegant, always perfectly put together. She made it seem effortless, though I know it wasn't.

Mom had been personally responsible for the continued success of Royaume over the last forty years. She and Dad were a power couple.

He made the medical journals and posed on the covers of magazines, and Mom brought in the money and the talent. She charmed donors and doctors alike, bringing in gifted physicians from all over the world.

And *these* were the shoes I had to fill.

I couldn't be Dad. And I couldn't imagine ever being Mom either. I didn't know how.

I was struggling with what I was going to do in my new role.

Derek's path had been obvious. He was a little of everything. One part both my parents. Charming and charismatic, driven and successful. He would have probably ended up with a reality TV show on TLC or something. Then he would have used his fame to attract donors and continue to elevate the hospital.

I had no idea what *my* thing was going to be. I hated networking. My field didn't really allow for notoriety. I couldn't stand the idea of being on television.

I'd have the hospital's resources at my fingertips. I could start a clinical trial or get behind some other initiative. The board would approve anything I wanted. But what? What was I passionate about? I didn't really know.

And it terrified me.

I was afraid I was going to drop this ball so completely it would shatter, and I'd never be able to put it back together again.

The server set down a teapot with the house orange bergamot in it. A few minutes later our three-level tray arrived with tiny sandwiches and petit fours.

I put a sugar cube into my floral teacup. "So, how are you enjoying retirement?" I asked Mom.

She sighed. "I'm not. I miss working. I'm so happy I get to help you prepare for the gala, just to have something to do."

Mom was going to start training me for the speech I had to

give at the event. Public speaking wasn't my thing either, but I'd have to do it nonetheless.

She put jam on a scone. "So tell me, what have you been up to?"

I stirred my tea. "Nothing."

I hated that I couldn't tell her about Daniel. I hated it.

While Mom and I had waited for our table, we'd wandered upstairs to the gift shop, and I'd bought a whole bag of things for him. Scone mixes and homemade lemon curd and six different kinds of loose tea. Mom asked me who it was for, and I had to lie and say it was for Bri.

Mom was squarely Team Neil. And even if she wasn't, she'd tell Dad anything I shared with her, and then I'd hear it from him. Not that there was anything to tell. Daniel wasn't going to be anything serious. But I didn't like that there were entire parts of my life I felt I couldn't talk to her about.

But wasn't that true even when I was with Neil?

I never told them what Neil did beyond the cheating. It was weird, but I got the sense they'd blame me for it. Like Neil was so far up on their pedestal, not even emotional abuse could knock him down.

I changed the subject. "So have you talked to Derek?"

She paused. "I haven't spoken to your brother since he left." There was something tight about her voice. "How are you?" she asked. "I know this has been a lot of change for you. Derek leaving and Neil."

And Dad.

He hung there in the silence.

Sometimes I thought Neil and Dad were so much alike. The same drive, the same demanding type-A personality. It's probably why they got along so well.

"Any updates on the chief position?" she asked.

"Not yet," I said. "I haven't seen Gibson yet," I added.

I know Dad had basically informed me that I'd be taking

this job, whether I wanted it or not. But fortunately I actually *did* want it. I'd always wanted it. If I hadn't been with Neil, I'd probably be chief already. It had come up a few times over the years, and he always found a way to talk me out of it.

I don't think he *wanted* me to advance. Like it made him feel threatened that I might end up his equal in any way. I think he liked the trophy aspect of having a Montgomery for a girlfriend, as long as I stayed beneath him.

It was funny that the very thing Dad was upset about—my lack of ambition—was brought on by the same man he was demanding I reconcile with.

"I think you'd make an excellent chief, Alexis." Mom put a hand over mine. "I know how overwhelming all this is, but you'll find your stride. There's so much you can do at Royaume, especially in a position of leadership. You will never find this same influence anywhere else. You will never be able to change the world the way you can here. I can't wait to see what you do with it."

I smiled a little.

That was the difference between Mom and Dad. Dad didn't want me to embarrass him. He wanted to be able to brag about me and my accomplishments at dinner parties.

Mom wanted me to be *effective*.

She wanted to help people. And you know what? So did I.

I didn't want it. I didn't sign up for it. But Mom was right. I really could do amazing things here.

I just had to figure out what those things were going to be.

Two days later Bri found me in the supply closet by the chief's office. "What are you doing?" she asked, peering over my shoulder in the doorway.

I surveyed a shelf of baby formula. "Gibson said I could have whatever I want out of the free sample stash. I think I need a trauma kit for my car."

"For what?"

I picked up a can of Enfamil and started reading the label. "I keep going on medical calls in Wakan. I delivered a baby last week, and I didn't even have PPE."

"You delivered a baby," she deadpanned.

"Yeah. With a double nuchal cord." I nodded at a machine gathering dust on a shelf. "Do you think Gibson would let me have that portable EKG?"

She shrugged. "I don't see why not. A rep gave us that two years ago to test in the ambulances. We're not using it, and they don't want it back." She peered at the pile I had started. "What else you got?"

"Gauze, Kerlix wrap, Ace bandages, butterflies, liquid stitch, needles, syringes, lidocaine—you know they're stitching each other up with a fishhook over there?"

She scoffed. "Probably using Krazy Glue too."

I paused, holding a C-collar. "I bet they *are*..."

She started pulling things. "So what are you doing tonight? Want to have dinner?"

"I can't. I'm having dinner with my parents. They want to talk about the quasquicentennial."

She grabbed a box of instant ice packs. "How about dinner tomorrow then? Or are you going to that thing at Gabby's?"

I shook my head. "I'm not really hanging out with them right now."

"Why? Because of the TripAdvisor thing?"

I shrugged, tossing a few eye shields into the keep pile. "That.

And I don't know. I just don't think I have as much in common with them as I thought I did. But I can't go tomorrow either. I think I'm going to Daniel's."

I was definitely going to Daniel's.

I'd stolen a different hoodie on my way out the other day. This one was from Cabela's. It was gray and it had deer antlers on the front. Daniel had a cherry ChapStick in the pocket that tasted like his mouth. It was like a tiny bonus prize, and I loved it.

I'd turned the thermostat down to freezing last night just so I could sleep in it. I'd lain in bed wearing it, talking to him on the phone until almost midnight. Even thinking about it made me smile.

"So I took a page out of your dating playbook this week," Bri said. "Went on a Tinder date with a twenty-six-year-old."

I arched an eyebrow. "And?"

"And the guy's entire apartment was a TV, an Xbox, and a recliner parked in front of it. His mattress was on the floor. He only had one plate."

I laughed.

"Does Daniel have more than one plate? Because I feel like he's a more than one plate kind of guy."

I grinned at the shelves. "He has lots of plates. Nice ones, actually. Antiques."

"I bet he folds towels the right way too. A mythical creature."

I laughed. "Did you sleep with him? The twenty-six-year-old?"

"No. I refuse to have sex with someone who doesn't have a head-board. I'm not that desperate—yet. My vagina has officially been closed so long I'm afraid a Spirit Halloween is going to move in."

I laughed so hard I started to choke on my spit.

She grabbed a box and tapped a finger on it. "Take some SAM

Splints in case you get a broken bone. Burn sheets. Do you have a pulse ox? Blood pressure cuff?"

"No."

"I'll get you one. And get a nitroglycerin case. You're gonna need some aspirin, Benadryl, anti-nausea pills, epinephrine, atropine—this is fun! It's like apocalypse prepping."

I laughed. "They don't have a clinic out there. From what Daniel tells me they don't drive into town until something is literally falling off their body."

"No wonder they're hitting you up when you're over there."

I nodded my head at the shelves. "Yeah. I just figure if it's going to keep happening, I should probably have stuff in the car."

"So you're still going down there, huh?"

I shrugged, looking at the gauze. "Yeah."

My cell phone vibrated, and I pulled it out of my pocket. Daniel. A picture of a duck and the caption *Duck Norris*. I laughed. He must be at Doug's.

"Was that him?" she asked.

I smiled up at her. "Yeah."

"What's he texting you?"

I gave a one-shoulder shrug. Then my phone pinged again, and a selfie of him holding Chloe came through.

My heart *melted*.

His hazel eyes were twinkling. He had on a gray T-shirt and a radiant smile. Chloe was nibbling his beard. I had to clutch a hand over my chest.

I could almost smell his fresh scent through the screen. I could picture wrapping my arms around him and nuzzling his Adam's apple, and he'd hug me in that warm, easy way he had. Heat dropped to my core just thinking about it.

I saved the photo to an album called Daniel, and I had the most peculiar urge to make the picture my screensaver.

"What?" she asked, watching me.

"Nothing," I said, smiling.

Bri shook her head at me. "Oh, my God...you're *falling* for him."

My head jerked up at her. "What? No."

She crossed her arms. "You so are."

"No. No, it's just a fling." I waved her off.

"Like hell it is."

I put my phone to my chest. "I am *not* falling for him. It is a sex thing."

"A sex thing is a sex thing. You don't text him and smile all giddy over your phone. You have the sex and you leave and then you don't text him again until you need to see if his penis is available. What's he sending you? Is it a dick pic? Because if it isn't a dick pic, then you're off topic."

"What, we can't talk about anything else that isn't sex related?"

She put her hand out. "Let me see your phone."

"What? No!"

"Alexis, let me see your *phone*."

We had a silent standoff. Then I smacked it into her hand. She stood there, looking at it. She arched an eyebrow at me. "This is him?"

"Yeah."

She groaned. "Oh, for fuck's sake."

I started chewing my thumb. "What?"

She glanced at me. "He's cute," she said, like this was a disappointment.

"Yeah. So."

"So cute isn't good. You get attached to cute."

She scrolled on and then looked up and pinned me with a stare. "This is a *duck* pic."

"And?"

"Where are the dick pics?"

I crossed my arms. "He doesn't send me those. And if he did, I wouldn't let you see them."

She thumbed to my call log, and her eyes narrowed at my screen. "You talked to him for three hours last night? On the phone?!"

I snatched my cell. "Give me that back."

She put her hands on her hips. "You *like* him. You are *dating* him."

"It takes two hours to get to Wakan," I said defensively. "When I go down there, we have to do other stuff. It can't just be all sex."

She gawked at me. "You are standing here, *lying* to your best friend—I have known you for *ten years*. It is all over your damn face." She waved a hand in front of my nose. "You're packing a trauma kit for the car because that's how much time you plan to spend there, and you're trying to tell me this is just a sex thing?"

I went back to looking at bandages so I wouldn't have to look at her. "Maybe I do like him. A little." I shrugged. "He's sweet."

And generous, and funny, and attentive...

She was shaking her head at the side of my face. "You know this can't be a thing, right? Your dad would disown you."

I scoffed. "He's ready to disown me anyway for not getting back with Neil. You know what Neil did last week?" I looked at her. "He turned off the power before he left for work."

"He did *what*?"

"Yeah. I thought it was a power outage."

"Why the hell did he do that? Just to be a dick?"

"Yup. He probably thought I'd call and ask him for help. It's this super passive aggressive 'you need me' thing. He's pissed because he thought we were going to talk the other day and I went to Daniel's instead. He texted me all night, asking where I was. It was like this roller-coaster ride of him getting all pissed off because I didn't show, and then a series of apologies and then he was pissed off again because I didn't reply. He's been sulking around all grouchy. Slamming doors and—" I rubbed my eyebrow. "I cannot *wait* for this to be over."

"Does Neil know about Daniel?"

I shook my head. "No. Hell no. I tell him I'm at your house."

"Good. He's too shady to know what you're up to. Don't ever let him know. If this asshat turns the power off just to get your attention I don't even wanna know what he'd do to your fuck buddy. Does Daniel know about him?"

"He knows enough."

"And what does he say?"

I shrugged, picking up an oxygen canister. "We don't really talk about it. I don't need to bring Neil with me to Wakan. I go there to *not* think about him." I rolled my eyes. "You know Neil made me a quiche the other day—"

"Ewwww, did you eat it?"

"No. No way." I made a face. "But he left it there in the kitchen. It's growing mold."

"Uh, so throw it away?"

"He put it there, *he* can throw it away." I set the oxygen canister down with a clink. "I can't *stand* being home with him.

That's why I go to Daniel's a lot. It just gets me out of the house. I'm not falling for him."

She looked unconvinced. "Uh-huh."

"What? I know this can't go anywhere."

She cocked her head. "Well, maybe you should stop it then."

I blinked at her. "What?"

"Stop seeing him."

I paused for a moment. "Why?"

"Because I know you, Ali. And no matter what you're telling yourself, I see what's happening. You're just setting yourself up to be hurt. You're setting *him* up to be hurt."

"I've already told him I don't want a boyfriend. He's okay with it. We're just having fun."

She looked almost sorry for me. "Ali, I know Neil messed you up, so this is hard for you to believe, but you are an amazing woman. And there's no way this guy can't have feelings for you, because he's going to see that. So either you're gonna tell your family and Royaume Northwestern to go screw themselves while you move to the middle of nowhere to be with him, or you're going to get your heart broken."

I paused. "I'm not moving. I can't."

"Can he move here?" she asked.

I shook my head. "His whole life is that town. And he's trying to buy his family's house."

She nodded. "Okay. So let's talk through this. This dating goes on. You two fall in love. He can't move here, and even if he did, your dad would never accept him, and your mom never disagrees with your dad. Derek would have been nice to him, but he's not here. Neil would take a jab at him every chance he gets. You think Gabby and Jessica and their uptight husbands are gonna welcome him into the fold? They're not. So he stays where he is, and you, what? See him once a week for the rest of your life? You can't live with him. Can't commute four hours a day, can't change hospitals. So what happens when he wants to get married? Or have kids? You gonna do that with him? What's the plan?"

I licked my lips. "I don't know."

She nodded. "Right. You don't know. See, this is what I mean. You keep seeing him and you're gonna end up more messed up than after Neil. This was supposed to be a fling. No feelings. You hooked up with this guy *because* he was someone you couldn't catch feelings for. And now you are, and you need to call it off before you can't anymore."

I swallowed. The thought of breaking things off with Daniel felt...it felt like the only thing that was making me happy was about to end.

But I guess it didn't matter, because I wasn't going to have time for him much longer. Because this morning I'd officially put in my bid for the chief position.

I sighed. "It's going to have to end soon anyway. I'm running for chief."

"Seriously?"

"Gibson is leaving in August. It hasn't been announced yet, Dad told me."

She grinned. "That's awesome! You get to be my boss! I'll get all the days off I want!"

I laughed a little.

"Man, you'd be *perfect* for that job," she said. "That's a lot of work though."

"I know. But I'm excited. I think it's going to be good for me. I'll have more influence with the board. I can get more done."

"Your dad might finally shut up."

I snorted. "God, I hope so."

That alone might actually make it worth it.

I was in a down mood after work. Neil made it a point to slink around the ER. I ignored him. But most of all, I couldn't stop thinking about what Bri said, that I should break it off with Daniel.

The truth was, I think I *was* starting to get attached to him. And not just in a sexual way.

I had too many thoughts about this. None of them good.

Even if the distance and the age gap and social canyon weren't a thing, was it smart to nose-dive into another relationship three months after the last one? Aren't you supposed to be single for a while after a breakup? Find yourself or something? What would it say about me if I jumped right into another serious relationship? That I was codependent? Couldn't be alone?

Maybe I *should* be alone.

I was in no position to be with someone right now.

Bri was right. If I was getting attached, I probably should cut the cord now.

But the thought of doing it made me feel like I couldn't breathe.

The idea of not seeing Daniel ever again was so upsetting, I couldn't even think about it. Which only made me feel panicky because it made me more sure that I *was* actually attached to him, which sent me down a rabbit hole of wondering if he was attached to *me*.

I mean, he wanted me to be his girlfriend. But was that attachment? Was it *feelings*? Or did he just not want us to have sex with anyone else?

Part of me hoped he wasn't attached. Why have us both get hurt when it ended?

But the other part of me hoped he liked me back. The other part of me was *desperate* for him to like me back. Because the only thing more terrifying than never seeing him again was for this to be one-sided.

Oh, my God. I *was* falling for him.

I was. I *totally* was.

UGH.

I didn't have time to think about this. I had dinner with my parents tonight, and my brain could only deal with so much. I wasn't looking forward to seeing Dad. The only good thing about it was I would get to tell him about the chief position and maybe he'd lay off me a little after.

I took a shower and was sitting at my vanity doing my makeup when the phone rang. Daniel.

"Hey," I said, smiling.

"What are you doing?"

"Sitting in a robe in my bathroom getting ready for dinner with my parents."

"*Soooooo* you're naked?" I heard him grin.

"I have a robe on."

"*Soooo* you're naked under the robe?"

I smiled. "*Yeeees.*"

"Send me a picture."

I arched an eyebrow. "You want a picture?"

"Yeah, why not?"

I grinned and got up and went over to the bed. "I'll send you one if you send me one," I said, sliding onto the mattress.

"I'm not really in a place to take a picture right now," he said.

"Send me one later."

"Okay. And what kind of picture do you want? I'm going to need to hear you say the words 'send me a dick pic, Daniel' for consent reasons."

I laughed. "Send me a dick pic."

"One dick pic, coming up."

"Awwww, just one?"

I could tell he was smiling.

"Do you want to tell me what kind of pictures *you* want?" I asked. "For consent reasons?"

"With you I consent to everything."

I snorted.

"You know, for the record, I wish I was there and didn't need the picture at all..." he said.

I gave the phone a wry grin. "And what would you do to me if you were here?"

"Hmmmm. Let's see," he said, his voice low. "First I'd push you down on the bed. Then I'd slide over you and kiss you from your neck up."

I made a low moan in my throat. "I like that..."

"I'd take my hand and press it to your cheek and look you in the eye. Then I'd tell you that you're the most beautiful woman I've ever seen. That I think you're brilliant and kind and that seeing you is the highlight of my entire week. That when you're on your way, I'm already dreading you leaving and when I'm with you I'm happy."

I blinked into the bedroom. I couldn't breathe. "Daniel..."

"I'm sorry," he said softly. "I know that's not foreplay."

I shook my head. "Yes," I said quietly. "It is."

I could tell he was smiling. "Gotta go. Need to put out appetizers." He paused. "I miss you."

It punched me in the heart. He'd never said that to me before. This was another level, unlocked.

There was I miss you. I love you. Boyfriend, girlfriend, meet the family, live together, engaged.

Married...

But we'd never reach most of those levels. We'd never even come close.

I couldn't even picture his truck parked in the driveway of my house. My homeowners' association would probably give me a ticket.

For the first time in my life, I was in a situation where I knew I was making a terrible mistake. I was careening toward certain death at terminal velocity. But I couldn't *not* do it. I knew continuing this thing with Daniel was pointless. There was no happy ending here. But I missed him. He missed me. And I wanted him to know it. At least tonight.

"I miss you too."

CHAPTER 25

DANIEL

Alexis sent me a picture of her from the neck down. Black silk robe, open in the front, lacy black underwear.

I practically ran back to my garage.

I'd never taken a dick pic before. I was getting ready when my phone rang. Doug.

"Hey, I can't talk right now, I'm right in the middle of something," I said.

"What are you in the middle of?"

"I'm... I'm taking a picture for Alexis."

Silence.

"I'm coming over."

"What? No. Don't come over."

I heard his screen door slam.

"I'm serious, Doug, I don't need you."

"Let me guess. You're taking a top-down shot, using the flash, standing in your shitty garage bathroom, you can see your feet in the picture and you're wearing socks."

I looked down.

Shit.

I heard his engine turn over. "That's what I thought. Don't do anything until I get there."

"Doug—"

"DON'T DO ANYTHING UNTIL I GET THERE."

He hung up on me.

Fifteen minutes later Doug walked in. He had a ring light.

"No." I shook my head. "I'm not using that shit."

He walked past me into my workshop. "She's going to show this to her friends. You want to send her a shitty dick pic? That's what you want?"

I followed him over to my workbench. "She's not showing it to her friends."

"Daniel?" A female voice came out of Doug's phone on speaker. "It's Liz. She's definitely going to show it to her friends."

I threw up my hands. "What the hell?! You called Liz?"

He shrugged. "I had to borrow her ring light."

I could hear her laughing, and I pinched the bridge of my nose. "This is so embarrassing," I whispered.

"What's embarrassing is sending a dick pic that all her friends make fun of. This is fucking important," he said, shoving his phone with Liz on speaker into my hand. "Literally everyone she knows is about to see the goods, you can't mess this up."

I shook my head. "You're not helping me take this picture."

He looked at me like I was speaking in tongues. "I'm not taking your damn dick pic. I'm setting you up, giving you all the tools, and *you're* taking it."

Liz came over the line. "Okay, so listen, there is an art to this."

I lolled my head back and stared at the ceiling.

"You need to hold it," Liz said. "Don't just let it hang there by itself all lonely."

"Grip it by the base," Doug said, miming it with his hand. "But don't do that thing where you squeeze your balls to make it look bigger. She's seen it, she already knows."

I snorted.

"Don't get a close-up. It's way too aggressive," Liz said. "Try and get your abs in there, maybe a little thigh or some side butt. Women like that. Double-check the background. No dirty laundry or a TV on. Do not, under any circumstances, take this pic wearing only a shirt. It's extremely creepy. You can be wearing pants or boxers sort of pulled down, but no shirt. And don't put a ruler next to it."

I scoffed. "Men put a ruler by it?"

"All. The. TIME," she said.

Doug shook his head. "Rookie shit. And manscape," he said, setting up the light. "It'll make it look bigger."

I blew out a breath. "Anything else?" I asked reluctantly.

Doug was standing back with one eye closed, his hands in front of him, framing a section of my tool wall. "I think here's good. Manly. She sees the tools in the background, makes her think of getting nailed."

Liz laughed through the phone. "I'm hanging up now. Good luck!" And then from the background, "GOOD LUCK!"

She was at the bar. With everyone.

I put my face into my hand.

It took me twenty minutes, but I got the picture and sent it to Alexis. She called me five minutes later, whispering.

"I got this in the middle of dinner with my parents."

"Oh, shit—"

"No, so far it's been the highlight of the whole night," she whispered.

I laughed. "Where are you?"

"In the bathroom."

I leaned back in my seat and stretched. "You should bring them down."

"Who?"

"Your parents."

She went silent on the other end.

"You wouldn't want to meet my parents," she said. "Trust me."

There was something "end of discussion" about her tone. I let it go.

"So when do I get to see you?" I asked.

"I can come down tomorrow after work."

I grinned. "Okay. Do you mind if we go out to eat?"

"You want to take me out?"

"There's a thing at the VFW. It's not anything fancy. Just a spaghetti dinner. Liz and everyone will be there. If you're not comfortable with that we can skip it."

"I like spaghetti," she said. "Sounds like fun."

I moved the phone away from my mouth like she could hear my grin. "Okay, it's a date," I said. "Hey, didn't you say once you were a picky eater?"

"Yeah. I am."

"You eat everything I give you."

She laughed a little. "I like everything you give me. I don't like bar food. Fried stuff."

"So if I'd tried to make you some hot wings or something, you wouldn't have come home with me that night? It was nothing but the thin promise of a grilled cheese that tipped the scales?"

"I would have gone home with you that night, no matter what you were making."

"Because of the baby goat?"

"No. Because of you." I could hear the smile in her voice. "Gotta go."

I couldn't get the grin off my face. I hung up with her, beaming.

She didn't tell me it wasn't a date—which meant it *was*. She was coming out with me in public tomorrow, hanging out with my friends. She also told me she missed me earlier.

I'd been afraid to hope that this might not be one-sided. It felt impossible that I could interest a woman like Alexis in any way that was more than just sex. But now I dared to hope.

The progress was slow, but it was there. Tiny victories on my part. She was letting me in.

I didn't think she'd actually let me meet her parents, but I threw these things at her to see what would stick anyway. The worst she could say was no—and sometimes she said *yes*.

She'd said yes to being exclusive. She'd said yes to spaghetti with my friends—which I'd sandbagged a bit. It was a little more than just a casual dinner. But everyone wanted it to be a surprise, and I wasn't going to ruin it.

I felt like if I could keep getting closer, maybe a miracle could happen.

Maybe one day there would only be yes.

CHAPTER 26

ALEXIS

I hung up with Daniel, touched up my lipstick, and went back out to dinner with my parents.

We'd just ordered, and our drinks had arrived while I was gone. We were at Sycamore in Minneapolis. It was a high-end steak place that looked like the inside of first class on the *Titanic*. It was dimly lit, with crisp linen tablecloths and stately paintings of important white men on the walls.

That always annoyed me, that the white men got the stately paintings. Even at Royaume, the hallways were lined with them. All the men throughout the history of the hospital who'd made significant contributions. Mostly from the Montgomery family, but still.

I was going to request stately paintings of all the marginalized people who had contributed to the hospital's success over the last hundred and twenty-five years.

I'd been thinking a lot about what I wanted my contribution to Royaume to be. Maybe I'd start a weekly free clinic for low-income patients, get some donors to contribute to new programs for financial aid.

These last things had never felt as important to me as they did now.

Every time a patient came to the ER in their own car because they couldn't afford the ambulance ride or they put off care until they were in such bad shape it was an emergency room visit, I thought about Daniel.

Most people in Wakan were barely making it as it was, and a hospital stay would ruin them.

I always tried to help my patients when they couldn't afford care.

Last week a man came in with a simple perforated eardrum, and I saw him in the waiting room and wrote him a prescription without checking him in so he wouldn't be billed for an ER trip. When I could, I coded procedures so they fell under a wellness visit or I sent a patient to their primary care physician where it would be cheaper instead of giving them a treatment that could wait. But I was starting to feel like it wasn't enough. I was starting to feel like I could be doing more. And now I was in a position to.

There were definitely perks to being a Montgomery. Maybe I should start to use them.

Mom and Dad stopped talking as I slid into my seat and put my napkin in my lap. Dad leveled his eyes on me. "So what was this announcement you wanted to make?"

Mom waited patiently.

I'd been the one who'd made this dinner date. They'd been wanting to talk to me about the quasquicentennial, and I'd been turning down all their invitations to do it, mostly because they all included Neil. So I'd booked the reservation myself and told them we could talk about the event over dinner, and I added that I had something I wanted to tell them.

I smiled. "I've put my bid in for chief."

Dad's brows drew down. "Of course you've put your bid in for chief, I expressly told you to do so. What kind of announcement is that? What about Neil?" he asked, looking confused.

"What about him?" I asked, looking back and forth between them.

"You're not getting back with Neil?" Mom said, her eyes darting nervously to Dad.

"What? No..."

"Oh, for Christ's sake, Alexis," Dad said. "What was the point of this dinner?"

I blinked at him. "I...I thought you'd be happy. About the chief thing. You wanted me to run. I'm officially running."

"Bringing us here to tell us you're doing what you should have been doing in the first place is not worthy of a dinner announcement," he said.

Mom licked her lips. "Sweetheart, we were under the impression that you were getting back with Neil."

I pressed my lips together and let out a slow, patient breath through my nose. "Mom? Dad?" I put my hands on the table. "I am *never* getting back with Neil."

"Why the hell not?" Dad snapped.

It was so loud, people from other tables turned to look at us. I gawked at him in shock.

He pointed a finger at me. "You've given that relationship about as much effort as you've given your career. You've done the bare minimum, and you wonder why it isn't successful."

Mom put a hand on his shoulder. "Cecil..."

"No, Jennifer, she needs to hear this."

His face was red.

"That man deserves your *respect*. You don't even return his text messages. He's made every attempt possible to make amends with you—and if you don't want to make them, that's your business. But until you've exhausted couple's counseling, do not sit here and act like you're not part of the problem."

I felt my face growing hot. "Dad, he was *abusive*—"

"Did he hit you?" Dad asked. "Call you names?"

A lump was forming in my throat. "No—"

"Did that man ever lay a *finger* on you?"

I felt tears welling in my eyes. "No." I swallowed. "He was mean, Dad. He's *still* mean. He acts differently when you're not there—"

"He's probably just frustrated with you, and frankly I don't blame him. Honestly, I don't know what we did to deserve children like this. I really don't."

Mom was rubbing his shoulder. "Let's just calm down—"

"We coddled them, Jennifer. They've never had to work for anything. Lazy."

My mouth fell open. "I was *valedictorian*. I graduated first of my class at Stanford. I've worked my ass off to get—"

Dad jabbed a finger at me. "Don't you *dare* take that language with me, young lady. I have had about enough of this back talk from you. So help me, Alexis, I will cut you off like I've cut off your brother. I have zero tolerance for this disrespect."

I blinked at him. "What do you mean you've cut off my brother…"

"Your brother has made his choice," Dad said. "He's not welcome in our home until he's rid himself of this woman he's run off with."

I gaped at him. "That woman is his *wife*!"

Dad's nostrils flared. "That's no daughter-in-law of mine. And you'll be careful to remember that. This family isn't some greasy diner that you can stumble into with some tattooed junkie you've picked up. I will not have our name associated with—whatever the hell she is."

Mom couldn't even look me in the eye.

I shook my head, incredulous. "You're disowning your own son because you don't like his wife," I said slowly. "Who you've never even *met*."

He leaned forward. "I don't need to meet her. Her reputation precedes her. She has a goddamn sex tape, for Christ's sake."

The unfairness of this made my jaw go tight. Lola Simone's sex tape was no different than the pictures Daniel and I had just sent to each other.

"She trusted someone, and they betrayed her," I said. "That's not her fault."

"I would rather go to my grave never breathing another word to your brother than acknowledge the embarrassment he's invited into this family. He owes every single one of us an apology. Marriage should be dignified. *Neil* is dignified. You may not have been married to him legally, but you were married to him in practice and you better damn well start to act like it."

The server came to the table with our food, and Dad stopped talking and sat back in his seat with a clenched jaw. We sat there, silent, as plates were placed in front of us.

When the server was gone, Dad began eating, cutting his steak angrily, like he'd given up getting through to me and just wanted to get dinner over with so he could leave.

It took everything I had in me to muscle down the urge to cry.

Mom picked up a fork and just hovered it over her plate, staring at it. I recognized that look. I'd worn it myself. It's the look you have when you're too tired to carry on the fight.

It's the way you feel before you accept the quiche.

I got up and fled to the bathroom. A few moments later Mom came in behind me.

I went into a stall and ripped a piece of toilet paper off the roll. "How could you let him do this to Derek?" I wiped at my eyes. "That's your *son*."

"And what could *I* do about it, Alexis?" She threw up her hands. "Your father is your father. I'd have more luck moving mountains than moving that man. And your brother knew *exactly* what he was doing. He knew your father would never approve, that's why he got married in secret. You can blame me all you want, but your brother is a grown man, and he made his own choices knowing very well what the consequences would be."

Mom turned slowly and dropped onto a tufted chair in the corner of the bathroom like her body weighed a million pounds.

"I am a seventy-three-year-old woman, and I am *tired*. I love your father. He is brilliant and wonderful in so many ways, but he is a difficult man, and that's *never* going to change. You take him as he is, or you get nothing at all. Your brother picked nothing—but he *did* pick."

I sniffed and looked away from her.

"Alexis, your father has lost everything that matters to him in the last two months," she said. "His career is done, and his vision is going. The future of the legacy is uncertain, Derek is gone, you left Neil. He's almost eighty years old, and his entire life is out of his control."

I squeezed my eyes shut and leaned on the sink.

"He's an old man. I don't know how much more time we'll have with him. Try and meet him somewhere in the middle," she begged. *"Please.* What's a few counseling sessions with Neil? You can't know if it's salvageable unless you try to salvage it. And if it doesn't work out, it doesn't work out."

I opened my eyes and stared at her, incredulous. "Did you not just hear me say that he was abusive?"

She threw up her hands. "What is going to happen with a therapist sitting there watching? For heaven's sake, maybe Neil will learn something. It's only one hour a week. Give your father what he wants, so he can get over it and move *on.* Show him that you respect his opinion. He needs that right now."

I swallowed the lump in my throat. She wasn't asking me to do this for Dad. She was asking for herself. Because Dad would be unbearable if I didn't. He probably already was.

I couldn't even respond. There was no point. She was right. My father was my father.

Derek...

He would never be at Thanksgiving again. He wouldn't be at Christmas. He wouldn't be at our parents' birthday parties. He'd probably never even see the house he grew up in again.

I didn't for one second doubt my dad's ability to hold on to his hate until the bitter end. He'd had a petty falling-out with his sister fifty years ago and he'd never spoken to her again. Not even on her deathbed.

My heart broke for my brother and my mom. And it broke for me too.

I don't think I'd truly, truly processed the impossibility of me and Daniel until just now. Not really. I knew fundamentally that it could never work. The distance alone. But now the incompatibility of our lives glared from every angle. From above, below, and beyond.

Daniel wanted to meet my parents, like any boyfriend would. But Daniel could never be at a table with my parents. Not in a million years.

My dad wouldn't just dislike him. He'd *forbid* me to be with him. And Mom was too weak to disagree.

Daniel would be my Lola. He couldn't be my date to the quasquicentennial. He couldn't come to a family barbeque or the birthday brunch they did for me every year.

Dad couldn't even know he existed. Dad would never be happy with anyone who wasn't *Neil.*

I wasn't even allowed to be alone. Me choosing to be alone instead of with Neil was an insult to his injury.

Daniel would be under constant attack the second he stepped into my world. And this dinner just proved it. It was hard enough for *me* to be a part of it, and *I* belonged here.

So what was the point in dragging it on with Daniel? Getting more attached? What was the point in saying *I miss you,* like that mattered at all in the long run? Bri was right. I should set him free. Let him find someone else who could be with him the way he deserved. Someone whose parents would be happy to meet him—because these things mattered. They mattered to him and they mattered to me too.

Daniel was wonderful. He just wasn't wonderful for *me.*

I didn't want to go home after dinner. I felt like Neil knew I'd been ambushed and a second ambush was waiting for me when I walked in the house, like he and my dad would have coordinated their attacks.

So I went to Bri's.

When she opened the door, she opened it talking, even though I hadn't told her I was coming.

"Uh, I was just texting you, because what the hell is *this*?"

She held out her phone with a photo of a tabloid magazine on the screen. A picture of Lola Simone and my brother was on the cover with the headline "Secret wedding!"

Well, I guess that's why Dad was so triggered at dinner…

I rolled my eyes. "At least they used a good picture of him," I mumbled. "He'll be happy."

I edged past her into her living room.

"So it's true?" she asked. "Was this the NDA thing?"

"Yup," I said tiredly, flopping onto her sofa.

She looked at the cover again. "Damn. No wonder he fled the country. Your dad probably has a hit out on him. Or *her*."

It didn't even surprise me the story got leaked. With the way Dad had been throwing the Lola news around, it was only a matter of time. At least the happy couple had gotten a few weeks of privacy before it hit the gossip mags.

She tossed her phone on the sofa and sat next to it. "So why are you here? I guess the dinner didn't go well?"

I squeezed my eyes shut. "My dad disowned Derek."

She blinked at the side of my face. "Like, actually?"

I let out a long breath. "Like in every sense of the word. Derek's dead to him."

She sat back into the sofa. "Wow," she breathed. "That's so medieval."

"And I think I have to go to couple's counseling with Neil."

"Eww, *why*?!" She looked horrified.

"Because if I don't, Dad'll never let it go."

She scoffed. "He'll never let it go anyway. Nothing short of getting back with Neil is going to be good enough. Your dad will just keep moving the goalpost. It'll be all 'well, you didn't go long enough' or 'you didn't take it seriously enough.' Your dad's a monster. Why don't you just tell him no?"

"I can't. It'll just make it worse for Mom."

It would make it worse for *me*.

"And? Did it ever occur to you that your dad is just as emotionally abusive as Neil? That maybe you learned to put up with Neil because from the earliest age you were taught that to be loved you had to placate an asshole?"

"He's my dad, Bri."

I shook my head, staring wearily into the room. "Imagine never seeing your parents again because you fell in love with someone," I said quietly.

"Do you think Derek knew this would happen?" she asked.

I nodded. "I do. I think he married Lola knowing *exactly* what he might be giving up." I let out a breath. "I think you're right. I need to stop seeing Daniel."

She studied me. "Are you okay?"

I shook my head. "No. Not really."

We sat in silence for a minute.

"I don't really know what to say to you right now to make you feel better," she said. "All my ideas are scary."

I snorted.

"I'm serious. I'm a wartime consigliere. All I have for you are detailed revenge plots and alibis. But I'm telling you right now, if we kill Neil, you're the one digging the hole. I'll lie for you in court, I'll help you move the body, but I did not put myself through med school to dig."

I laughed dryly.

"By the way," I said, "Daniel finally sent me a dick pic. A really good one."

"*Ooooooh*, can I see it?"

"No, definitely not."

She jabbed a finger at me. "See?! You *do* like him! That was a test and you failed!"

"How did I—because I won't show you a penis sent to me in *trust*?"

"Dick pics are community property unless you're staking a claim on the guy who owns it. You've got a little flag that you just planted on Daniel's peen, it's waving in the breeze and it says *Ali* on it."

I was laughing now.

"You can see *alllll* my dick pics. Those boys throw 'em around like 'And you get a penis, and you get a penis, and YOU get a penis!'"

I choked and we both laughed for a minute.

Then I sighed. "Why is everything so hard?"

"Because you have too many fucks to give."

"Ha-ha."

"No, I'm serious. Give up some of your fucks and see how much easier things are. You're just spending all your time trying to please everyone else, and it's making you miserable."

I shook my head. "How am I supposed to not care if my parents ever speak to me again? Or if my dad thinks I'm a complete waste of his DNA? I'm already the weakest link in Montgomery history. I *have* to give a fuck. I have no choice."

She shook her head. "Imagine being a whole-ass *doctor* and having your family be like, 'why are you so disappointing?'"

I blew out a tight breath. "I mean, it's not like Daniel was going to work out anyway. Everything you said earlier was true. *I* can't move, *he* can't move. My dad is just the icing on the cake. Ending it was inevitable. I just don't understand why ending something that hopeless feels so shitty."

"Because it's not on your terms. None of this is."

I wiped under my eyes.

She scoffed. "You're gonna *hate* sitting in couple's counseling with Neil."

I groaned. "A thousand dollars says he has the therapist completely fooled."

"You should make him go to yours. That way she can call bullshit."

I picked my head up and looked at her. "You know what? That's actually genius." I smiled. "I just got an idea."

She grinned. "What?"

I pulled out my phone and dialed Neil.

He picked up on the first ring. "Ali?"

It annoyed me how much hope was in his voice.

"Hi, Neil. We're going to do a little trust exercise."

"Okay..." he said.

"For the next four months you're going to see a therapist. *My* therapist. You. By yourself. You're going to tell my parents that I'm going with you—"

"Why would I—"

"Shhhhh! I'm talking and you're listening. I'm going to give her permission to talk to you about anything I've talked to her about, so you'll have all the insight you need into why we're not together. You will tell my parents that we're in couple's counseling. And at the end of the sixteen weeks, provided you haven't thrown me under the bus to Dad and you've gone to all sixteen sessions—and I will need *proof* that you've gone to these sessions—I will agree to start going to therapy with you."

He was silent on the other end.

"You want me back so badly, this is your big chance. And it's also my final offer."

More silence.

"Okay," he said. "Yes, I agree. Thank you."

"Fine."

I hung up on him.

Bri was looking at me with wide eyes. "WOW. Maybe *you're* the wartime consigliere." She shook her head. "I can't believe he agreed to it."

"He had to. He's lost control. His other strategies aren't working," I said.

"Do you think he'll actually do it?" she asked.

"I have no idea. I'm leaning toward no."

"And if he does?"

I shrugged. "Then Mom and I get a four-month mental health break? And then I end up doing what I think I'm going to end up having to do anyway, which is to pretend to work on our relationship?"

She let out a resigned sigh. "Oh, Ali."

"It'll be good for him if he goes," I said. "He needs therapy."

"What he needs is Jesus."

I laughed. Then my smile fell.

"You know what's weird? Daniel is only twenty-eight and he has his life figured out. Shouldn't *I* have my life figured out by now? I should, right?"

"I bet his life isn't figured out either. Nobody's is. I thought mine was, and look how *that* turned out."

I peered over at her. She was looking at her hand, twisting a ring around her pinky finger.

"Are you doing okay?" I asked.

She shrugged. "Define okay. Benny's getting worse. I can't do anything to help him. My marriage has failed, and I can't even find a guy decent enough to have casual sex with. I'm bored and alone all the time, living in my mom's crappy house."

She went quiet for a moment. "I just want one of us to be happy. Why can't we be happy?"

I sighed. "What does happy even look like, Bri? I fall in line and do what's expected of me, give up Daniel, but I get to keep my family? Or I give it all up, become the shame of the Montgomery legacy, lose my dad, devastate my mom, but I get the boy I like? Which one is happy?"

She shrugged. "It's easy. It's whichever one you can't live without." She looked at me earnestly. "But I'll be there for either scenario. I'll always be there."

I studied her face gratefully.

Bri was amazing. She didn't deserve what happened with her ex or what was happening with her brother. She deserved everything and more.

"Maybe we should both quit Royaume," I said.

She laughed. "Quit men too. Move in together and start a YouTube channel where we day drink and rate bread."

I laughed and leaned over and hugged her. "I love you," I whispered.

"I love you too," she said with her chin over my shoulder. "But I'm still not digging the hole."

CHAPTER 27

ALEXIS

When I'd seen Neil this morning in the kitchen, he tried to do the thing where he puts a tender knuckle to my cheek, like my counseling offer was some meaningful moment of forgiveness from me. I smacked his hand off me and grabbed the Keurig from the kitchen, marched it to my bedroom, and locked the door.

I had to come back down a minute later to shove coffee pods into the pockets of my robe, so the gesture lost a little momentum, but I think the message was pretty clear. If he wanted to talk, he could talk to me in four months after he'd jumped through all my hoops—which I half expected him to not do. But at least it would get Dad off my back long enough for me to breathe.

Now it was almost seven o'clock and dark already, and I was twenty minutes away from Wakan.

I'd lost a patient today.

I lost patients all the time. It was the nature of the work I did. But this one bothered me more than usual.

I felt eerily numb afterward, like I'd officially hit my capacity to process crappy things. The dinner with my parents, Derek's disown-ment, deciding to end it with Daniel—it was all too much. I hoped the emotional disconnect lasted. I just wanted to get through my last night with Daniel in one piece and ugly cry when I got home.

I listened to Lola's fifth album on the way down. It was sad. The whole thing reminded me of Jewel's song "Foolish Games." Made me wonder what Lola had been going through when she wrote it.

Sometimes I tried to line up her albums with what I could find about her online. There was a rumor she had been dating one of her backup dancers around the time she recorded this. Maybe it had to do with him.

I think Lola had a hard life. I hoped it was easier with my brother in it. I bet it was. No—I *knew* it was. Because I knew how much my brother must love her, and when my brother loved someone, he did it with all of himself.

I hadn't talked to Derek since he left. There was a twelve-hour time difference with Cambodia, and he was in a rural part of the country where phone access was hard. But I could feel my brother, and I knew he could feel me. I was sending him and his wife so much love.

If Derek said Lola was worthy, she was. Simple as that. His word was all I needed. I wished it was that way for our dad, that I could just show up with someone like Daniel and Dad would know immediately that he must be exceptional if I've brought him home.

But my father didn't measure people that way.

It was funny that someone as horrible as Neil could have Dad's respect, and someone as good as Daniel never would. All because Daniel didn't have the right education or job or family.

My brother was a cautionary tale. Not about disobeying my

father. But about falling in love with someone he didn't approve of, that made disobeying him necessary.

When I got to the Grant House, Daniel was waiting for me outside like he always did. He didn't have Chloe. She'd gone back to the farm yesterday since she was off the bottle.

Change was inevitable. Only today it made me deeply, deeply sad.

I sat in my car for a moment longer than usual just to take it in—because it was the last time Daniel and Hunter would be waiting for me.

When I got out, Hunter plowed into me, then Daniel came at me with the same energy, wrapping me in one of his big bear hugs. They were both always so excited to see me.

Neil had never greeted me like this. Maybe it was a maturity thing. I remembered what Bri said about men being puppies at this age, and it felt true. Daniel had this pure happiness about him every time I showed up.

I closed my eyes and breathed in and just melted into his kiss.

He pulled away enough to look at me. "You ready for dinner?" he asked. "I thought we could walk over. It's a nice night."

I peered up at his smiling face and sniffled. "Yeah. Let's walk."

He tilted his head. "What's wrong?"

I shook my head. "Nothing."

He peered at me, his warm hazel eyes looking into my soul. "It doesn't feel like nothing."

"I lost a patient today."

His handsome brows drew down. "What happened?"

I paused a moment. "It was a seventeen-year-old. His kayak flipped. No life jacket."

Daniel studied me wordlessly.

"You know what's so dangerous about drowning?" I said, looking up at him. "It's silent. So unless someone's paying close attention to you, no one saves you."

He brushed my hair off my forehead. "I see you. I would save you if you were drowning."

It was sweet, but he wouldn't. Because I wasn't drowning here with him. I was drowning two hours away from here, alone.

"Let's go eat," I said, changing the subject.

He nodded. "Okay. Let me just put Hunter inside, and we'll get going."

A few minutes later we turned onto the bike trail that went to Main Street, and Daniel threaded his fingers in mine.

"So how was your day?" I asked, wanting to talk about anything that wasn't me.

"Well, let's see," he said, talking to the trail ahead of us. "Hunter ate a ChapStick. Kevin Bacon got out again. This time, he let himself into the pharmacy and ate all the candy bars by the register. Scared the crap out of Mrs. Pearson."

I laughed weakly. "Doug isn't going to eat him, is he?"

He shook his head. "No. Doug's a vegetarian."

I wrinkled my forehead. "Really?"

"Yup. Doesn't drink either. Kevin Bacon has a long life of frightening the villagers ahead of him."

I laughed.

"Then I spent some time down by the river," he said.

"Swimming?"

"No. Too cold still. I was looking for something for you, actually," he said, letting go of my hand to dig in his pocket.

He pulled out something and put it in my palm. It was a rock about the size of a walnut, smooth and gray.

"It's shaped like a heart," he said. "Took me two hours to find it."

My heart disintegrated. It broke from the inside out and crumbled in my chest.

I loved it. I loved it more than I'd ever loved anything.

It wasn't flashy. It cost him nothing but his time—but that was the gift. Daniel didn't *have* time. That was his most valuable commodity right now, and he'd given it to find me this?

It made my chin quiver. It felt like the sweetest thing anyone had ever done for me, which was ridiculous because it was just a rock.

When I didn't say anything, he spoke. "I'm sorry. It's dumb. I thought you might—"

"I love it so much. I love it so much I don't even know what to say." I blinked up at him with tears in my eyes.

He looked almost hopeful. "You like it? Really?"

"I love it. Thank you."

This gentle, thoughtful, sweet boy.

I reached up and hugged him, and he folded around me like he always did. Only there was something almost rooted about his arms this time, like he was trying to keep me from drifting off.

Or sinking.

I was always going to keep this gift. Even if I married someone else. I would keep it until the day I died.

I had an eerie premonition of relatives going through my belongings after my funeral, just like we'd done a few weeks ago for Aunt Lil. They'd find this rock and wonder why it was in the single shoebox I'd taken with me to the retirement home.

I wondered how many of the little trinkets I'd found in Aunt Lil's box were like this. The remnants of small moments in her life that stayed with her forever. Proof of a thumbprint on her soul.

It's amazing how someone can touch you, even if you only know them for a moment in time. How they can change you, alter you indelibly.

Daniel had altered me. I was already better for knowing him. Which made leaving him all the more bitter.

I pulled away and wiped at my eyes, and Daniel looked at me gently before taking my hand again.

When we got to the VFW, there was a sign out front that said CLOSED FOR PRIVATE PARTY. Daniel stopped me at the door. "Okay, so I need to warn you about something."

"What?"

"I wasn't totally honest getting you here. They wanted me to keep it a secret. There's a little thing in there for you."

I pulled my face back. "What thing?"

He didn't answer me. He just opened the door and led me inside.

The place was packed. It looked like standing room only. And when they saw me come in, everyone started to cheer and clap.

A big sign hung over the bar: THANK YOU, DR. ALEXIS.

I blinked at the room with my hands over my mouth. "Daniel, what *is* this?"

Liz, Doreen, Doug, Pops—everyone was here.

Then Emelia and Hannah cut through the crowd. Hannah had the baby in her arms, and I knew instantly what this was about.

Daniel leaned down and whispered in my ear. "Something about the cord was wrapped around the baby's neck? Emelia had a nurse on a video call through the delivery. She said you saved Lily."

I started to tear up.

I got thanked often in my line of work. But never by an entire town.

Hannah smiled at me as she approached, and hands were slapping me on the back and people were grinning at me and clapping.

It filled me up. It was like all the things my dad and Neil drained out of me, these people tried to put back. They dropped love and appreciation and acknowledgment into my empty well, one smile and thank-you at a time.

"We just wanted to say thank you," Hannah said, smiling. "Lily might not be here if you didn't come."

I wiped under my eyes. "It was my pleasure to be here."

"Do you want to hold her?" Emelia asked.

I sniffed and nodded. "Can I?"

Hannah leaned in and put the baby in my arms. I pulled the blanket down and looked her over. She was perfect.

I rubbed a knuckle on her little pink cheek. She was almost two weeks old now. She'd probably be getting her first shots soon, and her belly button scab was getting ready to fall off. She was bigger.

This was the one negative side of working in emergency services. Most patients—with the exception of repeat offenders like Nunchuck Guy—were in and out and I never saw them again. I never knew how they did, if they got better, if they got worse. My job was to get them stable and process them to the doctor they needed to see to get well.

Sometimes I did wish I got to see my patients again and again. To see them grow up, stay with them through their lives and witness the changes.

"Are you nursing?" I asked Hannah, talking to her but smiling at the baby. "I brought you some formula if you need it."

"I am nursing," Hannah said. Then she lowered her voice. "Actually, I was wondering if I could talk to you about that. My boob really hurts and it's kinda warm?" She tugged at her bra strap uncomfortably.

I smiled. "I can have a look at it."

Hannah looked relieved. "Thanks."

I handed Lily back to her mommies, and Daniel took me to a table with Doug at it. The music started playing, and the party got started. It was a buffet spaghetti dinner, and Doreen had made a huge chocolate sheet cake with *Thank You, Dr. Alexis* on it. Daniel sat next to me and held my hand on the seat between us.

I felt so... *loved*.

By *all* of them.

I'd had dinner with my own parents last night and I didn't feel this loved. They made me feel like crap, actually.

Someone brought me a heaping serving of spaghetti and a salad. Daniel got me a glass of wine and kissed me on the side of the head when he sat back down. The room was alive with laughing and forks clinking on plates, friendly faces looking my way and beaming.

Jake was in the bar. He was wearing his uniform and laughing a little too loud with someone over by the pool table. Something about him rubbed me the wrong way, but I couldn't put my finger on it.

Doug leaned in while I was watching Jake. "Can I ask you a question?"

I wiped my mouth with a napkin. "Sure."

"What happened with the delivery?" he asked. "They said the cord was wrapped around her neck and you delivered her right. How did you do it?"

"I somersaulted the baby to keep the cord from tightening."

"Will you show me? How you did it?" he asked.

"You want me to show you?"

"Yeah. I don't like that I could have messed that up. If it happens again, I want to know how to do it."

I nodded. "Okay. Sure. Oh, which reminds me, I have a stitch kit I want to give you."

He lit up. "Really? A kit?"

"Yeah. No more fishhooks and gin."

Daniel laughed and picked up my hand and kissed it.

Liz made her way over with a Coke for Doug. "Another wine?" she asked me.

"No, I'm good. Thank you." I smiled.

Daniel nodded at the empty seat next to Doug. "Sit with us."

"Can't, I'm on shift," she said. "Where's Brian?" she asked, looking around.

"On a date," Doug said. "Rochester."

Liz's smile instantly fell. "Oh."

Daniel looked at his watch. "He should have been back already. Must be going well."

"Right," Liz said, looking away from us. "Well, let me know if you guys need anything else." Her voice had gone flat.

I watched her walk back to the bar. The guys didn't seem to notice the shift.

"Did Liz and Brian ever date?" I asked.

Doug scoffed. "Nah. He's not her type. She likes assholes," he said, talking into his soda.

I watched her wiping down the bar, her smile gone.

"Nobody likes assholes," I said quietly. "Sometimes that's just what you think you deserve."

After dinner, I showed Doug how to somersault a delivery using a rolled-up sweater baby with a phone charger wrapped around it. Then I did a breast exam in the bathroom and prescribed Hannah antibiotics. "Prescribed" being me telling Hal, the pharmacist, who was eating a slice of cake at the next table, what she needed and him walking across the street to open the pharmacy to give it to her.

When I finished, I went looking for Daniel and spotted him leaning on the bar talking to Liz. I stopped and watched him for a moment from across the room.

This was the place I met him. *Really* met him. I was sitting on that stool. He was standing in the same spot. Only *everything* was different now.

This place didn't look tired and old to me anymore. I didn't even notice the worn seats and the mismatched chairs. This bar was the heart of this community, I realized. It was where they celebrated and gathered. And it was where I learned his name. Touched him for the first time. Even the way the place smelled made me feel nostalgic now.

And Daniel wasn't just some random guy in a bar anymore.

He had become the brightest light in my life, what I looked forward to every day. The man who spent two hours down by a river trying to find me the perfect rock.

He *saw* me. And I believed him when he said he wouldn't let me drown.

My heart tugged.

And tomorrow morning, I would drive out of this town and never come back. I wasn't going to see him again. Any of them.

Daniel turned and looked for me, and when his gaze met mine, he lit up. One of his adorable, dimpled grins, his hazel eyes creasing at the corners.

My heart cracked right down the middle.

He pushed off the bar, closed the distance between us, and slipped his arms around my waist. I was so proud to be the woman here with him tonight. To be his date, the one he chose. It was an honor. Not because he was the mayor or the most handsome guy in the room but because he was the *best person* in the room.

"Ready to go home?" he asked.

I had to muscle down the lump in my throat.

No. I wasn't ready to go home. But I'd have to.

We said good-bye to everyone and started the walk back.

Before we left, Daniel had walked me around the VFW, showing me the yellowing articles framed on the walls with stories of his family's contributions to the town. There was the Spanish flu save and the Prohibition story he'd already told me about. Then there was a newspaper clipping, printed by the *Wakan Gazette*, about Daniel's great-grandfather John, who started a human chain to lead children out of the schoolhouse to safety during the deadly 1940 Armistice Day Blizzard. His wife, Helen Grant, used the Grant House's large wood-fired oven and baked off a hundred loaves of bread and sent it with her husband via sleigh along with medical supplies and firewood to every house in town. Neither of them slept for three days. Survivors recounted tears of joy as John arrived with the care packages. Wakan didn't lose one person.

There was an article about Daniel's grandfather William, who came to the rescue in 1975 when a fast-moving wildfire threatened to burn down the town. He coordinated a response team and worked through the night to create a firebreak that saved the town before the blaze reached Wakan. Linda, Daniel's grandmother, took charge of the evacuation efforts and ensured everyone made it to safety. The Grants were the last people to leave.

After the F2 tornado of 1991, William and Linda Grant set up a generator and a soup kitchen in the VFW to make sure everyone was fed during the cleanup. Then they advocated and won when the county wanted to divert the highway in a move that would have decimated the summer tourism. They kept the town clean and proud and safe. They were Wakan's first and last line of defense, in all things.

There was story after story.

The Grants were groundskeepers, I realized. Humble royalty. They tended to Wakan and its people with the same care that Daniel tended his garden and his house. It was bred into him, like medicine was bred into me. His kingdom was smaller and his legacy was different, but he was tied to his birthright just like I was tied to mine.

It was funny to think that for the last hundred and twenty-five years our two families had existed at the same time, doing the same things they were doing now. The Grants gave their lives to Wakan and the Montgomerys gave theirs to Royaume.

I bet abandoning his calling never once crossed Daniel's mind.

I felt guilty wishing I wasn't who I was. I knew the importance of the Montgomery legacy. I knew what I could do with it, how many people it saved, and how much difference it made in the lives of those it served. But I wished it wasn't mine. I wished it belonged to someone who knew how to use it. I didn't, and so I couldn't honor it the way I knew I should.

Everyone would be waiting for me to become something exceptional, do something huge, make my mark. And I had no idea how.

I had a feeling I never would.

"Hey, you want to see something?" Daniel asked, breaking into my thoughts.

"Sure."

We cut through the park next to the river and stopped at

a statue of a man in the middle of the square. Daniel nodded up to it. "This is my great-great-great-grandfather. He founded the town."

I looked up at the regal bronze figure. The plaque under it said JOSEPH GRANT.

The resemblance to Daniel was eerily strong. The same kind eyes and steady gaze.

Daniel stood there, peering up at it, and I studied the side of his face.

Daniel had to be here when the town needed him. Eventually, he would be needed, just like all the Grants before him. Because hardship was inevitable, and nobody cared more for Wakan than this family. That's why they'd always risen to the occasion. And that's why one always had to be here.

He had to be here. And he had to be in that house.

I knew in my soul that's part of what gave him strength to do what he had to do. A Montgomery working in any other hospital would still be a Montgomery, but it weakened us, made our influence thinner. I had to be at Royaume, and he *had* to be within Grant House.

I was talking before I even had a chance to think about what I was saying. "If you need the money, I can loan it to you," I said.

He turned to me and drew his brows down. "What?"

"The fifty thousand dollars. I can loan it to you."

He blinked at me. "You have that kind of money?" he asked.

I nodded. "Yeah. I do."

And it wouldn't be a loan. It would be a gift. A parting gift.

If he knew I didn't want it back, he wouldn't accept it. He was too honorable. But I wanted to do this for him.

Maybe *this* was the reason I'd driven through this town all those weeks ago. The reason a raccoon ran my car off the road and a handsome stranger had rescued me. Maybe Popeye was right about the town getting what it needed. And it needed Daniel. I couldn't stand to see him lose his castle, and I could make sure he didn't. I was probably the only person here who could.

But he shook his head. "Alexis, I appreciate the offer. I really do. But I can't."

"Why? You're working so hard. I have the money. Let me help you."

He let out a long breath and looked away from me. When his eyes came back to mine, they were steady. "You're not a bank, Alexis." He closed the gap between us and slipped his arms around my waist. "But thank you for offering. It means a lot that you did."

I shook my head. "There were people who helped me to get to where I am, and now I can help you. I wish you would let me."

But his face was resolved.

I pressed my lips together. "Promise me if you can't raise the money that you'll let me loan it to you. Don't lose your house."

He let out a resigned breath. Then he nodded. "Okay. I promise."

But I knew he wouldn't. He wouldn't because he wouldn't take anything from me if we weren't together.

And after today we wouldn't be.

He hugged me. Then he started laughing a little.

I pulled away. "What?"

He shook his head. "It's nothing. It's just I offered you a rock and you offered me fifty thousand dollars."

I snorted.

"Come on." He chuckled.

He threaded his hand in mine, and we strolled out of the park onto the moonlit bike trail leading to the Grant House.

The night was beautiful. The walk was lined with apple trees in full blossom. White flowers in the thousands arched over the path and ensconced us in their light fragrance. It was gorgeous and surreal. We made our way slowly, looking up, our hands clasped between us.

Daniel stopped. "Hey, look at that."

He nodded to a break in the trees at the full moon, framed between cloudy apple branches. It looked bigger than usual. Closer. I stared up at it, and a warm breeze rolled through the canopy and loosened a snowstorm of petals that drifted down around us.

It was like the universe had dipped a snow globe. Only the petals didn't fall. They floated like dust motes. Flower fairies, twinkling in the moonlight.

"Do you see this?" I said with wonder.

Daniel was looking around, his mouth open. "It's like . . . magic."

It was gentle and ethereal and soft, and they hovered around us, moving in slow motion. Daniel put up a finger to touch one, and the disturbed air swirled the petals like snowflakes in a flurry.

"Have you ever seen anything so perfectly beautiful?" I breathed.

I turned to Daniel. But he wasn't watching the petals anymore. He was looking at me. "Yes . . ." he said quietly, holding my eyes. "You."

Then he slipped warm hands onto my cheeks, and in front of the moon and the heavens and the magic that was swirling around us, he kissed me.

The world stopped turning.

We were suspended in frozen animation. A moment so perfect it couldn't be real.

And I realized then that it was too late.

I was in too deep. The time to walk away had ended. I think it was over the moment it began.

Wakan and Daniel were planted inside of me and they were growing there, like a garden bursting into life. Roots plunging and anchoring me, vines twisting and flowers pushing from the earth and blooming in my soul, filling me up.

And I never wanted to leave.

Forget wanting to end things. I couldn't even picture getting in my car tomorrow to drive home. Everything that wasn't this felt hollow and meaningless. I couldn't be the one to end it.

It would have to be him.

I'd have to tell him that this was a dead end and let him decide if he wanted to stay the course. I decided this all in a split second of Daniel's lips on my mouth, *everything* changed.

He broke away from the kiss, breathless, and looked at me with his hazel eyes. He licked his lips, and his mouth parted like he was about to say something—and then screeching wheels snapped us out of the moment. A police cruiser had skidded to a halt at the end of the block diagonal from us.

The petals turned to stones and they fell.

Liz was in the passenger seat. Jake had the back of her head by the hair.

My stomach plummeted.

We watched in horror as he shoved her sideways by the nape of her neck, flung his door open, and stormed around to the passenger side of the car. He yanked her out by the arm, and she fell hard on her knees. "Fucking walk home," he growled, jerking her up to her feet and dragging her to the side of the road.

He pushed her into the curb and left her there.

It was over in less than thirty seconds, and by the time he was peeling out, we were already running.

Daniel flew to her side. "Liz!" He gathered her up as the sound of wheels on asphalt faded into the distance.

She trembled almost uncontrollably, choking on her sobs.

"Let me have a look," I said, crouching in front of her.

Daniel shook his head. "Jesus Christ, Liz. He's gonna fucking kill you." His voice cracked.

"He's done this before?" I asked.

Liz couldn't answer. She was trying to catch her breath. But Daniel made eye contact with me and gave me a look that told me everything I needed to know.

Of course Jake had done this before.

Before Neil I hadn't known about the kind of abuse that could be whispered. But I knew about *this*.

I saw this all the time. Every day. It came in and out of my ER. And sometimes the ambulances didn't bring patients. They brought bodies.

I gave Liz a quick once-over. She had road rash on her knees and a little gravel in the palms of her hands. I flexed her wrists for pain. She didn't have any. I needed to get her home to clean her wounds.

"Daniel, I need to get her back to your house. Should we pick up her car?"

"She doesn't have one." Daniel stood and dragged a hand through his hair. "I'm calling the police in Rochester."

Liz snapped out of her hysteria in a split second. "No! Daniel, you can't!"

He shook his head at her. "Liz, *enough*. He's never gonna stop, we have to do something."

She looked panicked. "I just need to go home. He didn't do anything. He was mad, but he didn't do anything."

I dipped my head to look her in the eye. "Liz, you're bleeding. We were here for the whole thing. We can tell them what we saw."

She looked at me, her eyes wide. "I fell. I fell getting out of the car. That's all. He didn't hit me. I just fell out of the car when he was helping me out."

I wanted to put my face in my hands.

"Is there anywhere for you to go?" I whispered.

Her chest was rising and falling like she was riding the edge of hysteria. "No," she said. "He would find me."

We walked Liz back to Grant House. I cleaned her up and checked her over more thoroughly. She had fading bruises on her left arm in the shape of a handprint. Probably from a week or so ago. A healing cut on her neck. One of Doug's fishhook sutures? She must have been pretty desperate to let him sew her up in such a sensitive area without lidocaine. But going to an urgent care would mean questions and a paper trail.

I didn't even need to see one to know what an X-ray would show me. Healed fractures. Bones set wrong or not at all because she was afraid to go to the ER—or Jake was. He wouldn't want there to be evidence.

I gave her some Advil and we put her in the living room with some ice packs for her knees. Then we went to make her some tea.

As soon as we were alone in the kitchen, Daniel wiped a hand down his mouth. "We need to call the police."

"Are there cameras on that street corner?" I whispered. "Does Jake wear a body cam?"

He shook his head. "No…"

I pressed my lips into a line. "She's not going to be a willing participant, Daniel. You call the police and you know what she's going to tell them? That she *fell*. That he never touched her. It'll be our word against hers."

I could see by his defeated expression that he knew I was right. He shook his head. "He's going to kill her. This shit's been going on for years. It's only getting worse. She won't let us help her, she won't go to the police. She fucking defends him, like she deserves it," he whispered. "Why the hell is she like this?"

"She has battered women's syndrome. It's a cycle of abuse, and it's going to be very hard for her to break, especially with her circumstances. Jake has all the power," I said quietly. "He's made sure of it. She doesn't have a car or anywhere to go. He probably keeps all the money. She may think the police won't do anything because he's a sheriff. And she might even be right about that."

I looked him in the eye. "Believe me when I tell you that there's nothing you can say to her to make her leave if she's not ready. If you force her into going, she'll only come back, and when she comes back, it'll be worse. And if he catches her leaving…" I shook my head. "The most dangerous time in an abusive relationship is when you leave, because when you do, the abuser has lost control."

He studied me. "What do we do?" he asked.

"Give her a way to escape. Money, a car, a place to go. So when she's ready to leave, she can really leave."

He nodded. "Okay. Okay, I can do that."

"We need to get her a cell phone. One Jake doesn't know she has, so she can Google resources, look for an apartment or a lawyer. She can keep it in the safe at work. He cannot know we're helping her. If he thinks anyone else is involved, he'll make her cut ties. He might make her quit her job so he can further isolate her, alienate her from her friends. We can help her, Daniel. We can set her up and give her all the tools. But we can't save her unless she's ready to save herself."

But I could tell from the look in his eyes that she wasn't.

And he didn't know if she ever would be.

I drove Liz home. Neither of us wanted to take her, but when we refused to drive her, she started to walk, and she was in pain. I got the sense she needed to talk and would be more open with me than Daniel, so I didn't let him come.

Liz and I pulled up in front of her tiny house. The lights were off, and the cruiser wasn't in the driveway. She said Jake worked until midnight, so we weren't expecting him.

"Can we just park for a second?" she asked. "I'm not ready to go in there. I just need a few more minutes."

She was calmer now. She'd cleaned up her face and stopped crying, but she was still visibly shaken. "I need to smoke."

We went outside and sat on the curb.

I knew Jake wasn't coming, and he'd likely maintain his good guy façade in front of me even if he did, but I kept checking the street for police lights anyway. It was the first time in my life I was actually scared of seeing them.

Liz pulled out a smashed-in pack of Marlboros from her jacket pocket. She must have fallen on it. When she opened it, loose tobacco spilled out. She picked through it until she found the least damaged cigarette, put it to her lips, and lit it with shaking hands. "I don't normally smoke," she said. "Carl left them on the bar. Now I can't stop."

Picking up unhealthy habits to cope with abuse wasn't unusual. I'd done it myself. I did it every time I woke up before Neil to put makeup on. I couldn't even imagine what else I would have done to escape my reality if I hadn't escaped it in person.

Liz stared out into the night. "He dragged me out of the VFW parking lot," she said.

"What happened?"

She blew smoke, holding her elbow by the hand. "It was dumb. It's always dumb." She sniffed. "It was about Brian."

"Brian?"

"He just...he has this thing with Brian. It's this stupid thing, and he can't let it go."

"What thing?"

She took a long drag on her cigarette and blew it out shakily. "We kissed once, when we were fifteen? Me and Brian?" She looked over at me and chewed nervously on the side of her thumb. "Spin the bottle. But you'd think we had some steamy affair by the way Jake acts." She ashed her cigarette. "After you guys left, I said something about him being smart to open the drive-in to supplement his income, and it went from there."

I licked my lips. "Liz, I want to tell you something. Something I wish people would have told me once."

She looked over at me, waiting.

I held her eyes. "I believe you. I can handle anything you need to tell me. You don't need to protect me from the truth and I'm here to help you in any way I can. It's not your fault. And you *don't* deserve it."

I saw the words crash over her. Her chin quivered.

There was so much power in those words, I realized. I wondered how much sooner I would have found the strength to leave if someone had been saying those things to me when I needed to hear it—and I'd believed them.

I went on. "When you're ready to leave, we will help you."

She sat quiet for a moment. "I can't," she whispered. "There's no way."

"I know it feels like that. Trust me, I do. But you can, and you will. Start taking the steps now."

I dipped my head to look at her. "Are you on birth control?"

He'd get her pregnant to trap her. Make her more dependent on him. And she'd never be in more physical danger than she would be when pregnant.

She shook her head. "No. He won't let me." She sniffed. "I asked Hal if he could get me the pill, but he said he can't do it without a prescription. That if Jake found out he'd get his license revoked. I can't get away for three hours to see a doctor in Rochester. Jake always goes with me, and he never lets me go in alone. Every month I pray for my period—"

"I can prescribe something for you."

She let out a shaky breath through her nose. "Thank you."

"Liz, I'd like your permission to file a police report."

She jerked away from me. "What? No!"

"Yes. You should have something on record. You don't need to have anything to do with it. You can say you didn't know."

She shook her head at me, incredulous. "And what do you think this is going to accomplish?"

"They'll investigate—"

"And then what?" she snapped. "He's gets fired and gets twenty-four hours in jail before they let him out again? And now I'm more fucked than I already am? He'll blame *me*. I already work two jobs, we barely pay the bills, and at least when he's at work I get a break. *Don't*."

Her eyes begged me.

"Please," she said. "I know he'll apologize. I know he feels bad. He always regrets it. Promise me you won't, Alexis."

I looked at her, my eyes sad.

If I filed a report against her wishes, she would never come to me with another injury. She wouldn't feel safe going to anyone. And she was right. Jake would blame her for the investigation, even if she had nothing to do with it.

Jake was like Neil. He couldn't accept responsibility for himself. It would make things worse for her, and there would be no resolution anyway if she wasn't going to cooperate. But the idea of not calling the police made me feel like an accomplice to his crime. I didn't want to be a bystander to this, and I didn't know what to do.

"Okay," I said. "I won't call. But I'd like your permission to document everything that I saw. Let me take pictures of your injuries. And I want you to write down what he's done."

"No—"

I put up a hand. "I won't give it to anyone. I promise. But you need to have this. You might want it one day. We document tonight and then I want you to keep a diary of anything he does from this point on. *Anything.* If he punches a wall or breaks something, take a picture if your phone is safe and send it to me. Then delete it. If he makes a threat, you write it down. He hurts you, you write it down. And write down anything else that you remember, as far back as you can. You can leave it at Daniel's, we'll keep it safe. It could help you in court."

She studied me for a moment, like she was deciding if she could trust me.

"Okay," she said reluctantly. "I'll do it."

We sat there quietly for a few minutes while she smoked. Then she stubbed out her cigarette and put her chin on her knees.

"What about your family?" I asked. "Do they know?"

She laughed dryly. "They wouldn't even believe it if I told them. They love him. Every time we go home, he brings my mom flowers. Fixes the hot rod with my dad." She paused for a moment and wiped her cheek. "I wasn't always like this, you know. I didn't grow up seeing this. I know they say if you see abuse it makes you more likely to accept it, but my parents were in love. My dad didn't even spank us. All my sisters are in good marriages. My brother doesn't do this. It's so embarrassing. I feel like such a failure." She choked on the last word. "Like if they knew, they'd think I brought it on myself or something, because why else would Jake lose it on me?"

"Yeah, well. I know about that," I said quietly.

She looked over at me. "Your boyfriend hit you?"

"He was emotionally abusive. He still is."

She shook her head. "But... but you're so *smart*..."

I scoffed. As if smart has anything to do with it.

I dragged a loose hair on my cheek with a finger and stared out into the street. "I saw this documentary on a tsunami once," I said. "When it's coming, it pulls the water away from the beach. Pulls it lower than sea level so the ocean floor is exposed. You can see all the sand and shells and coral, so people go in to look at it. And then the tidal wave comes, and it's too late to run. It already has you."

I looked her in the eye. "They lure you in. They make you feel like you're the best thing to ever happen to them, like you're the most special woman in the world—like you're seeing something rare. But that's the trap. It's how they get you close enough to drown you. And Liz? Nobody can save you until you're ready to save yourself."

CHAPTER 28

DANIEL

I waited for her on the porch. When her headlights turned in to the driveway, I jogged down the steps to meet her.

She looked exhausted as she climbed out of the car in the light of the flood lamp.

"She's home," she said, standing with me in front of her car. The engine ticked and heat came off the grille, radiating into my legs. "We sat on the curb until she was calm enough to go back inside. She let me take some pictures of the injuries, but she still won't let me call the police."

I reached out and put a hand on her arm. "Are you okay?"

"I'm fine." She hugged her arms around herself. "Daniel, we need to talk."

My stomach dropped.

"Okay. About what?"

"Let's go inside. Talk in your room."

I followed her up the spiral staircase to my loft, my heart pounding. This wasn't good. I knew it wasn't good. Nothing good ever comes out of "we need to talk."

When we got inside, she sat on the bed, and I took the spot next to her. "What's wrong?" I asked.

It took her a moment to begin. "Daniel, when we started this, it was just a sex thing for me."

I waited. It looked like she was struggling.

"That's not what this is for me anymore."

I would have smiled at this except she looked so serious.

She licked her lips. "Is this still just a sex thing for you?"

I shook my head. "No. Definitely not."

She held my eyes, but she didn't smile. My mouth was dry. I didn't like where this was going.

"Daniel, I came here today planning to tell you that I can't come see you anymore."

My heart plummeted. *No . . .*

"But I can't do it. So I need to be really honest with you so you can have the final say in what's going to happen."

I nodded. "Okay."

"I'm applying for a new job. If I get it, I'll be working eighty hours a week. I'm already not in the greatest place to have any kind of relationship. If I get this job, it'll be worse. And even if I don't get the job, I'm not sure continuing to see each other is a good idea for either of us."

I shook my head. "Why?"

She looked away from me. "I don't see us having a future." Her eyes came back to mine.

My heart cracked.

"I'm sorry," she said. "But I have to be honest with you about that. And that's a problem because I'm starting to have feelings for you. So my instinct is to break things off because that's what's fair to you—"

"Why don't you let *me* decide what's fair for me?" I said.

She sucked her lips together. "Daniel, if we keep seeing each other, it will be temporary. It won't lead anywhere, and it won't last."

"I don't care."

I said it before I could even think about it. But it was true. I didn't care. If the choice was her walking out of my life tonight and never seeing her again, or getting more time with her, no matter how short that time might be, I wanted the time. I *needed* it.

She studied my face, and I knew she was deciding for me anyway, even though she'd given me the choice.

"Look," I said. "I'm a big boy. And I acknowledge and appreciate everything you're telling me. But I'd like to keep seeing you."

She went quiet for a long moment. I felt the teetering. Like this could go either way. I held my breath.

"Okay," she said finally.

"Why?" I asked.

"Why what?"

"Why don't you see a future with me?"

It was one of those questions that you don't really want the answer to. She was being brutally honest with me, and I knew she wouldn't sugarcoat this either. But I had to know.

"Our lives don't fit," she said simply. "They just don't."

She didn't need to elaborate. I knew what she meant. We lived too far apart. She couldn't work here, and I couldn't move. I was too young for her...

At this point I wasn't even sure it was the age thing that was the actual problem. I don't think that had been an issue for her in a while. It was that I hadn't lived long enough to figure my life out yet.

She had almost a decade head start, and even then I'd never achieve the things she had professionally or financially. But if I were older, maybe it would have closed the gap a little.

If I could snap my fingers and fast-forward a decade or two, I would. I'd lose all that time if it would make the difference.

Maybe I'd be a successful carpenter in twenty years. I might own the property and have a business selling my woodworking. Have an innkeeper working for me to take care of the guests. Or maybe I'd be living in the house and not in the dusty garage she had to sleep in to be with me.

But as it stood? I couldn't even afford to take her on a trip or buy her something nice. I'd met her friends. I couldn't imagine hanging out with them, let alone their husbands. I had nothing in common with those people.

But the funny thing was, even though I didn't fit into her life, she fit into *mine*.

When she was in Wakan, she was my girlfriend. She didn't want the title, but it didn't matter. It was what it was.

But when she was back in her own world, *I* wasn't her boyfriend. I don't think I even existed for her outside of this place. And I didn't know how to change that—and neither did she.

I felt desperate all of a sudden. Like a clock had begun ticking. An expiration date had been set on this thing between us, and she was right—it wasn't a sex thing. Not even close. I'm not sure it ever really had been.

A small part of me hoped I could change her mind. If I was good enough to her, if I made her happy enough, maybe she'd reconsider. Maybe even if she got that job, we could figure it out. We could make it work.

But the realistic side of me knew none of those things were going to happen. There wasn't going to be a save.

All I could do was give her what I could. And that wasn't enough. She had a whole different life in a whole different world, and she'd only ever been here to visit. It was the reality of this situation. I'd always been on borrowed time with her. And I think I'd always known it.

I had to be in this with my eyes wide open. I had to sign up to be hurt when the time came for this to end. Because it *would* end. She'd made that clear.

"I'm in," I said. "When it's over, it's over."

But I knew even then, it wouldn't be. I suspected it would never really be over.

At least not for me.

CHAPTER 29

ALEXIS

I spent four months with Daniel. Four amazing, incredible months.

It was August now, twelve weeks since we'd had our talk. The tourists were back, and I'd watched them breathe life into Daniel's town.

The ice-cream and fudge shops were open, the pizza place and Mexican restaurant were back and had an hour wait every night, and the RV park was packed. The Grant House was booked seven days a week, and I helped Daniel with it while I was there. He usually wouldn't let me get up to put the coffee on. He wanted me to sleep. But I spent the rest of the day doing what he did. Making beds, checking in guests, helping prepare breakfast.

I hated to admit it, but now that I helped Daniel, I understood what Neil had meant about me not knowing how to run a house. It was a *lot*. Repairs, maintenance, landscaping, cleaning. Even if these things were being delegated, they were a ton of work.

I'd been so shielded and privileged growing up. We'd had a

property manager who dealt with it all, and then Neil had done it when we moved in together. Even in my ER, my nurses did all the dirty work for me. But I was learning. And it was changing how I saw the world around me and how I wanted to be seen.

I didn't like that others had to take care of me. I wanted to know how to take care of myself. I wanted to pull my weight and learn to be self-reliant so that when I did depend on someone, it was by choice and not necessity. And it was Daniel who was teaching me how.

Daniel empowered me instead of stripping me. Lifted me up instead of keeping me low.

Daniel gave me everything he knew. He kept nothing for himself, the way Neil always did. Daniel gave his knowledge freely and happily, even though it lessened any advantage he might have had over me—and in doing it he weakened the last bit of hold Neil had, even if all Daniel did was show me I was capable of anything I needed to do.

It was Tuesday, and I was at home. I usually worked days, but I'd covered a shift for Bri last night and I didn't get in until midnight. I didn't want to get to Wakan at two a.m. so I decided to sleep here and drive over in the morning.

I *loved* being at Grant House.

It was warm and lived in. It felt almost alive somehow. Every single thing in those walls had a story. It was color and depth and crackling fireplaces and quiet nooks. A creaking step that felt like a gentle sigh under my feet. Ancient ferns and hand-wrought crown molding, the hundreds of delicate stained-glass butterflies on the window on the landing, black-and-white pictures of strangers that felt familiar now.

My blood pressure was lower in Wakan. It was like a finger pressed to my lips with a long *shhhhhh*. And Daniel was a gentle hammock, rocking. Everything about them was centering and calm.

And I'd fallen in love with them both.

I wish I'd never met him.

Letting Daniel go was going to be the hardest thing I've ever done.

I felt like I was swimming out to sea with him, getting farther and farther from shore, and I'd saved no energy for the swim back.

I'd made an Olympic sport out of avoiding Neil. It was almost possible to pretend he didn't live in my house. The only reminder I got was my dad occasionally showing up unannounced—not to see *me*, of course. To have drinks with my ex. To golf with my ex. To go on boat cruises with my ex. I was invited—as long as I was okay hanging out with Neil.

I wasn't.

I made excuses and Neil didn't push it, so my dad didn't care that I didn't go. Other than that, Dad had been quite pleasant the last few months. With me vying for chief and him thinking Neil and I were in counseling, I was his little princess again. Mom looked like a thousand-pound weight had been lifted off her chest, probably because Dad was back to being the better version of himself.

It was amazing how lovable and agreeable he could be when you were doing what he wanted.

What *I* wanted was to be in Wakan.

The only time I'd spent in Minneapolis these last few months outside of work was the once-a-week coaching session I had with Mom to practice my speech for the quasquicentennial. She'd written it. Not a word of it was mine—which was fine, since I had no idea what I'd even say if it was.

I'd completely stopped going to therapy, just to give the hour to Daniel instead. I didn't have enough of them to spare. I used up most of my vacation time to give me extra days with him. I even stayed for a ten-day stretch back in July. Didn't go home once. Told my parents I was on a yoga retreat.

If Wakan had been closer, I'd have gone there just to spend the night. I'd have gone there on my lunch break. But one thing I'd discovered over the last few months was that the second the tourists came back, the traffic started. Road work, a fender bender—any little thing backed up the roads. One day it had taken me *four hours* to get to Daniel's.

It was like the universe just wanted to reiterate how unsustainable all of this was.

But still, I made the trip as often as I could. And the town didn't seem to mind, because Daniel's garage had turned into a minute clinic over the last twelve weeks.

Ear infections, bladder infections, poison ivy, sprained ankles, burns. If I had what I needed to treat them, I did. So far, I'd only had to send one person to Rochester. And I'd been showing Doug how to do things. He was going to treat them anyway. At least if I gave him some instruction, the outcome would be better. He was a very good student. And counterintuitive to the rest of what I knew about Doug, his bedside manner was remarkably good. I'd actually suggested he go into nursing last week.

Anyway, it was good someone would be there to pick up the torch once I was gone. Because in a few days, I *would* be gone. The board was voting on the chief position tomorrow, and after that, my training would begin. Then a few weeks after that, I had the court date for the final determination on who got the house.

And I'd have to break up with Daniel.

I was doing my best not to think about it and failing miserably. The vote would be the beginning of the end. The first domino to fall.

Everything was about to change.

It was eight a.m. I was under the sink, fixing the garbage disposal, when Neil came in.

"Oh. You're here," he said, sounding surprised.

He *should* be surprised. It had been weeks since I'd run into him at home.

I didn't answer.

"What are you doing?" he asked.

I adjusted my headlamp. "Sticking a hex-head Allen wrench in the breaker socket at the bottom of the garbage disposal. I need to get the flywheel to turn to free the jammed impeller blades." I gave it a crank. "*Annnnd* done."

I scooted out from under the sink and stood, flicking on the disposal. It ran. I cocked my head at him.

Neil blinked at me. "How do you know how to do that?"

The question made me think of all the times I'd asked him the same thing, and he'd given me some snide comment about not having the time or the crayons to explain it to me.

I took off my headlamp. "The things I'm capable of would shock you, Neil."

The buzzer went off on the oven, and I put on mitts and pulled out what I was baking. A surprise for Daniel. I set the quiche on the stovetop to cool. "Spinach and broccoli. My favorite."

His jaw dropped.

Daniel had shown me how to fix the garbage disposal last month. He'd also shown me how to change a tire and put in a car battery and putty a wall. He taught me how to use an iron to get the cloudy white spots off a wood table and how to lift wax out of a carpet. I knew how to roast a chicken and make strawberry jam and compost for the garden. I knew white vinegar got smells out of clothes and how to make a campfire and what poison ivy plants looked like. I could replace a doorknob and install a bolt lock—and I did this on my own bedroom to keep Neil from poking around in there when I wasn't home.

Neil was watching his power over me dissipate like steam from a shower. I hoped it made his brain explode.

Neil cleared his throat. "I'm glad I caught you. I wanted to talk to you about something."

"Nope. I'll talk to you when we start our therapy sessions. That's more than enough." I started to walk out of the kitchen.

He spoke to my back. "Did you rehire Maria?"

I stopped in the doorway and groaned internally. He'd fired our housekeeper last week. "Yes," I said, turning to him with my arms crossed.

"Why? She broke half the coffee mugs."

"She tripped carrying a tray of them up from your room. It was an accident, and she hurt herself. She has a contusion on her shin the size of a lemon. You added insult to injury by firing her."

"That was my favorite mug in there," he said, looking wounded.

I squeezed my eyes shut and rallied my patience before opening them again. "Neil, grace costs you nothing—and God knows I've given *you* enough of it over the years."

I turned for my room. "If you don't want her, get a different person for your floor of the house. I'm keeping her."

"Ali—"

"What?!"

"I've been going to therapy like you asked." His voice was hopeful.

I knew he'd been going. He'd been emailing me the weekly invoices. He was on week twelve of the sixteen-week ultimatum I'd given him. *And* he'd gone to some intensive four-day weekend therapy retreat thing last month too, which was weird. He missed Philip's birthday because of it. He also hadn't told my parents I wasn't going with him. He was keeping all his promises, which was not only surprising but also annoying, because it meant I would have to keep mine.

"I only have four more sessions," he said. "Then we can go together."

"Yeah. Fine. Whatever." I went up the stairs to my room and locked the door.

I'd made a deal with the devil, and it was almost time to pay. It was almost time to pay for all of it.

By next month I'd probably be chief of emergency medicine. I'd either be the sole owner of this house or I'd be moving out, Daniel and I would be over, and Neil and I would be in couple's counseling. The only good part of any of this was that I might get the house. But besides that, I had more to dread than to look forward to.

I took a shower, grabbed my quiche, and headed to Wakan. I got there just in time to help Daniel with chores.

Check-out of the Grant House was eleven a.m. If we cleaned the rooms fast enough, we got done by noon. The new guests didn't arrive until three o'clock, so we got three whole hours to go do stuff. We'd go to lunch or take a bike ride or walk around. We went to the antique store and browsed, one of our favorite things. Sometimes we'd just curl up together on the four-season porch and read.

Today we were floating down the river on tubes with Doug, Brian, and Liz.

We packed a cooler with drinks, put on a tiny Bluetooth radio, tied our tubes together, and went drifting.

Brian, Liz, and Doug had broken off and were behind us, upriver a few yards. Daniel and I were alone, holding hands.

"It's so beautiful here," I said, tipping my head back to look at the branches arching over the river.

"You should see it in the autumn. All the beauty falling down around you."

"I've never done anything like this," I said quietly. "It's so relaxing."

"Never been to a drive-in, never floated down a river," he said, smiling. "What kind of stuff did you *do* as a kid?"

I shrugged. "We summered in New England usually."

He laughed. "Why does this not surprise me?"

I smiled. "Hey, don't make fun of me."

"Did you have a governess?"

I flicked water on him. "It was an au pair, actually, and it sounds fancier than it is."

"Uh-huh."

"Hey, I don't hold your childhood against you," I teased.

"Maybe you should try it. You like holding things against me."

He leaned over, slipped fingers into the back of my hair and kissed me, and the whole world disappeared around us. It was always like this, the complete and total submersion into Daniel. It got me every time.

Doug made a sharp whistling noise from behind us. "Hey! Keep it clean!"

We laughed and sat back into our tubes.

I looked at Daniel. He was so handsome. He had on dark blue swim trunks and sunglasses, his tattooed forearms popping against the black tube. His body was defined and toned, his hair wet and slicked back.

He got hit on a lot. A *lot*.

I saw girls look at him all the time. Even when he was checking in guests, he'd get smiles that I knew were more than just smiles.

I wondered how fast he'd move on once I was gone. A few weeks? A month?

It was like he was reading my mind.

"So the hospital vote is tomorrow, right?" he asked.

I nodded. "Yeah. At six."

"And then what happens?"

I raised my foot out of the water and let droplets drip into the river off my toes. "And then if I get it, I'll start my new job a few days after that."

He went quiet for a moment. "You said eighty hours a week, right?"

"Maybe more."

Even with his sunglasses on, I could still see the light fading from his eyes. Or maybe it was the light fading from mine.

We were nearing the end.

There were two ways we could do it. Break things off cleanly and just stop talking—or let it die a slow and painful death.

We'd put it on life support, try to keep things going, and it would delay the inevitable. His texts would go unanswered because I'd be too busy to reply. I'd make plans to go see him once or twice a month and then end up canceling when I got called in. We'd try to talk, but I'd be too tired. I'd get invited to holidays and celebrations with parents who wouldn't have him, so he couldn't come.

Then maybe he'd meet another woman. And he'd tell me this. And *then* it would be over.

Eventually everything good we had would be strained and faded. And I would have wasted yet more of his time. So I was planning on a quick, clean break. After all, those were the ones that healed fastest, right?

I gazed out over the river. Dragonflies darted around. I could smell freshly cut grass and some kind of flower. Cicadas were buzzing. The leaves on the maples were dark green, and the days were long and warm and bright. I wondered what this place looked like in the fall and winter.

I wondered what Daniel looked like in those seasons too. But I wouldn't be here to find out.

I'd been listening to Lola's eleventh and last album on repeat, the one she made before she got sober and started producing. She must have been going through something similar when she wrote it because it was all about lost love. Songs about being torn apart and heartbroken. She had a bonus track at the end. A cover of "Love Song" by The Cure. This crooning, sad, slow rendition that made my heart feel like it was crying.

You could feel Lola through her music, like her emotions streamed out of her voice. She was so raw and vulnerable, and I knew, even without meeting her, how remarkable she was. I knew why Derek fell in love with her.

"Why didn't you ever marry him?" Daniel asked out of no-where, breaking into my thoughts.

"Huh?" I looked over at him. He was peering at me from his tube.

"Your ex. The surgeon."

I blew a long breath. "Well, at first he didn't want to get

married. He'd been married once before, and he didn't want to do it again. Then he did start talking about it, and I didn't want to marry him."

"Why?"

I shrugged. "The relationship wasn't good at that point. I think he just wanted to marry me to keep me. He could tell I was unhappy."

I hadn't told Daniel much about Neil. He didn't even know Neil was living in my basement. There was no point in getting into it. This relationship was temporary anyway. Daniel wasn't my boyfriend, and Neil was less than a roommate and more of a squatter living in a different apartment in the same building, as far as I was concerned.

"Do you want to get married?" he asked.

I nodded. "Yeah."

"Kids?"

"I'd like to have kids. Do you? Want to get married and have kids?"

"Yes."

He was looking at me through his sunglasses, so I couldn't really see the expression on his face.

It occurred to me that we were talking about things that the two of us would do with someone else one day. If I ever did find a suitable man who my dad wouldn't hate, I'd have to fast-track everything. Married quick, kids quick. My biological clock was ticking. I might even have difficulty getting pregnant if I started right now, today. At thirty-seven, I was already considered of an "advanced maternal age." Even thinking those words made me feel ancient.

Daniel wouldn't have a hard time at all finding someone to

marry and have kids with. He had his whole life ahead of him. He could find some twenty-five-year-old who he could take his time with. Wait a few years to start having a family.

We sat there, quietly looking at each other, holding hands.

Daniel.

What a great daddy he'd be. And a good husband. So good. And he was *so* gifted.

I'd been watching him finish these woodworking pieces for the last three months, and I was completely in awe of him. There was magic in his hands. He could see a piece of wood and transform it into something that felt like what it was always meant to be. I'd watched him create stunning one-of-a-kind headboards, a gorgeous lightning strike–inspired tabletop that he hollowed out in the middle and then charred along the edges before he filled the center with resin so the crack was flat and clear. He had this twisted, gnarled stump that Doug gave him that I would have thought was nothing but firewood, and he used it as the base for a coffee table where he inlaid different wood to create a mosaic pattern. He was starting to get noticed on Instagram too, now that I'd taught him how to use hashtags. His last post had over two thousand likes.

There was a bittersweet feeling knowing that I'd never see Daniel become the rest of himself. He was just starting to turn into the man he'd become, and I wanted to be there for it. I wanted to help him and support him.

But I wouldn't get to.

Everything about this made my heart hurt.

I had the weirdest urge to climb onto his tube and let him hold me. But it would be too heavy. The tube would sink. We'd end up underwater.

Liz shrieked from behind us and Doug let out a loud laugh. We looked just in time to see Brian splash them, and Daniel and I smiled at the trio.

"How long have they lived here?" I asked, nodding at his friends.

The fingers on his free hands trailed in the water, making little wakes. "My whole life. Liz grew up in South Dakota, but she came here every summer with our cousin Josh and all his sisters. The guys were born here. We grew up together. Literally. They were even with me the day my grandparents died."

"How did they die?"

He peered out over the river. "Grandpa had a heart attack, and Grandma went later that day."

"The same day?"

"Yeah. It didn't really surprise anyone. I always knew it would happen that way. They were inseparable." He looked at me. "Neither one could live without the other."

I looked away from him, back at the slowly passing shoreline.

"You know, you really can die of a broken heart," I said somewhat absently. "I see it all the time. Stress-induced cardio-myopathy. It's a real thing."

He paused for a long moment. "I know."

We rounded an elbow in the river, and the sun slipped behind a cloud. It got instantly dark. A hard wind rustled the trees, and I shivered a bit. "It's not supposed to rain today, right?"

Daniel looked at the sky and shook his head. "No."

"It looks like it is…"

An enormous thundercloud seemed to have come out of no-where. And then we saw the figure standing on the bluff.

Jake.

He was in front of the hood of his cruiser, five or six yards away and twenty feet up, his arms crossed. Just...watching. It gave me chills.

I looked back at Liz, and she'd gone completely frozen. I instantly knew why. Because she was tethered to *Brian's* tube.

Daniel seemed to realize it too. He looked at me, his expression serious.

Liz put on a bright smile to wave at her husband. The same one she'd put on the day I met her when Jake came into the VFW to return her sweater—only now I saw that for what it was.

It was Jake showing up at her work, just to remind her that he could, at any time. Jake reminding her that he was watching, just like he was reminding her now. And Liz, putting on the mask she wore for the public.

So similar to the one I'd worn for Neil...

"Hi, babe!" Liz called, waving at him, but I could hear the forced cheer.

Jake just stood there, glowering down at her.

As far as I knew, Jake hadn't hit her again since the last time.

I asked her almost every time I saw her. She said things were fine. But I didn't think she would tell me if they weren't. Not unless she was injured enough to need me.

They had probably been on the upswing of their abuse cycle these last few months. The honeymoon part right after a bad episode where he'd be on his best behavior and shower her with gifts and affection. Whatever was Jake's equivalent of Neil's quiche. But by the look on his face now, that was coming to an end...

We drifted in front of him, slow and vulnerable.

Like sitting ducks.

A voice crackled over Jake's shoulder mic. He leaned into it and said something. Then he turned and got in his cruiser and drove off.

The clouds parted, and the sun poured back over the river. It wasn't until they suddenly reappeared that I realized all the dragonflies had vanished.

I looked over at Liz, and she'd gone sheet white.

"I'm going to talk to her," I said.

Daniel nodded and let go of my hand, and as if we all knew what was happening, all five of our tubes split apart and reconfigured, me alone with Liz and the boys downriver.

I paddled with my hands over to her. "Liz?"

She looked shaken.

"Liz? Are you okay?"

She didn't answer.

"Do you want me to take you somewhere—"

She shook her head. "No. It'll be okay," she said quickly.

"Liz—"

"It's fine. He'll calm down. I work until midnight. By the time I get off he'll be calm."

I eyed her. "I can take you someplace, Liz. Any of us can."

A dragonfly landed on her knee, and she stared at it wearily.

"If I'm lucky, maybe he'll get tired of me," she said quietly. "He'll find someone else and just leave me, and I can be done." She paused for a long moment. "If I leave, I'll never be able to come back here. He'll kill me. I'll spend the rest of my life hiding, and I'll never see Wakan again."

There was the tiniest, almost imperceptible glance at Brian when she said this.

My heart broke for her.

No matter what she did, Jake would win. Neil was still winning too, in a hundred different ways.

Sometimes it feels like the bad guys always do.

CHAPTER 30

DANIEL

We pulled up to the Grant House in my truck, still wet from our trip down the river. Hunter was loose.

"Did you leave him out?" Alexis asked, braiding her wet red hair over her shoulder.

I looked at her a moment longer than I needed to, thinking how beautiful she was. I couldn't stop thinking it every time I looked at her. She made me feel like I must have done something right in a past life to get the privilege of being with her.

Even if it was only for now.

"No," I said, peering back out through the windshield at my rogue dog. "Great. Now he opens doors."

She laughed and got out, and Hunter ran around to meet her like he always did. We'd gotten him to stop jumping, so that was good, but he still preferred Alexis to me, hands down.

I turned off the engine and stepped out of the driver's side. Then the smell hit me.

"Uhhhhh...Daniel?" Alexis said, wrinkling her nose. "I think he got skunked."

He *definitely* got skunked.

I could practically see green stench waves wafting up from his head. He sat, smiling back and forth between us, looking proud of himself.

"Jesus, Hunter." I breathed into my elbow.

"We need hydrogen peroxide, baking soda, and dishwashing soap," she said, shaking her head at him.

"How do you know?" I gagged.

"We get skunked patients in the ER."

"You wash skunked patients?"

She shook her head. "No, my nurses do it." She pulled back his eyelids. "It can cause ocular swelling if they get it in the face. He seems okay. I can wash him. I've already got it on my hands."

I had to smile a little. A few months ago, this woman hadn't known how to sweep. She didn't scrub toilets or clean the kitchen. Now she was washing skunk off my dog? It made me feel oddly proud of her for some reason.

"I'll help," I said.

She grabbed him by the collar. "Are you sure? No point in both of us getting gross."

"I'm sure."

I didn't want to lose time with her. Not even to this.

The sand in the hourglass was running out.

They were voting on her new job tomorrow. If she got it, which she seemed to think she would, that was it.

She'd given me three more months. I was grateful for it. But at the same time, I knew it might have been better to let her leave that day after the spaghetti dinner and never see her again. Because while it would have hurt me, it didn't have the power yet to kill me.

Now it did.

I was in love with her.

I couldn't even breathe thinking about this being over. It woke me up at night, made me feel for her next to me to be sure she was still there. I wanted her to stay so badly, I didn't know what to do. I felt desperate. I wished I had a genie in a bottle or a fairy godmother, someone to grant just one wish. Just *one*.

But as it stood, there was nothing to be done.

A lot had changed in the last three months. Amber hadn't called to ask me for money or to let me know the deal was off. I called her last week just to check in, and she sounded good. My guess was she'd come out of whatever self-destructive slide she was on the last time I talked to her and she was doing okay—for now.

I'd cleared out most of the backlog in the garage and sold it at the swap meet. Made eight thousand dollars, so not bad. I'd been focusing more on my freelance pieces than anything. Alexis liked them.

She'd started an Instagram and an Etsy store for me, and I'd been using it. I shipped a headboard to an interior designer in Maine last week, made two thousand dollars on that one item. It was looking like I could raise the money in time. I was almost halfway there, and I had half a dozen projects in the works and the house was rented out straight through October—but what happened with Alexis would determine everything in the end.

I'd decided. I'd give up my life here to be where she was if she'd have me. I'd give up my house and this town and all the people in it. If she was at the hospital eighty hours a week, I could be there when she left and be there when she came home. Make her breakfast, take her lunch, take her dinner. I could pick up the slack. She wouldn't have to do anything, it could be all me this time—I'd go to her. It didn't have to end.

We'd gotten so close after the last three months. We were comfortable with each other now. She'd walk around my room naked, looking at the little wood carvings I had on my windowsill or flipping through one of my books. Pee with the door open. We didn't use condoms anymore. She had an IUD, but knowing that barrier had come down between us, that we had that extra layer of trust...

All these little things were everything. At least they were to me.

But she still talked like the end was still going to be the end. She was always trying to remind me it was coming, like she wanted to manage my expectations. She wouldn't leave anything here. Not even a toothbrush. She wouldn't take the drawer I offered her or the key I'd tried to give her. Every time she left, all of her did. And it always made me feel like this time could be the last time, because there was nothing here for her to come back for.

There were times when we were together and I knew I made her happy, and I told myself that meant I might have a chance. And then something would happen to remind me how extraordinary she was and how she had a different life she needed to go live, and I'd feel hopeless.

I'd hear her talking to some other doctor on the phone, saying things that I couldn't even begin to understand. She was so damn smart. She learned things like it was nothing. I could show her a recipe and she could make it again from memory, remember all the measurements and ingredients, just from seeing it once. There was the time a day laborer from a nearby farm came to see her with an infected cuticle, and Alexis started speaking Spanish. Just rolled right into another language I didn't even know she spoke. When I asked her about it, she said she was fluent in sign language too. I couldn't believe it. I just stared at her.

Sometimes it felt like she belonged to a different world.

Literally. Like wherever she came from was so out of the ordinary, I couldn't even imagine it.

I'd never been farther than Rochester—well, once I went to visit my cousin Josh back when he was still living in South Dakota, but that was it. And his town wasn't much bigger than mine. I'd never even been on a plane before. I had no idea what living in a big city was like.

Alexis would bring me things sometimes, food from places over where she lived.

When I was a kid Grandpa would get me a Happy Meal every time we went into Rochester for the hardware store or the dentist. Most people take stuff like that for granted, but McDonald's was a treat for us here, a big deal. Hell, it still was.

But the stuff Alexis brought me was something else. It was like wherever she came from, nothing was average. She brought these rainbow macarons from some French bakery in Minneapolis, wrapped in red ribbon and brushed in gold leaf. Handmade chocolates from an artisan chocolatier with apricots inside of them. These fancy donuts with bacon on them, soft colorful cupcakes from Nadia Cakes. Most of it was too nice to eat. I didn't even want to touch it. It was like the little rose-shaped soaps Grandma used to keep in a bowl in the downstairs bathroom that nobody was allowed to use to wash their hands.

Stuff like this—her Mercedes, her designer clothes, opera singers in her ER—all of it served to remind me that she belonged to somewhere else, some universe a million miles from mine.

She'd told me what hospital she worked in. I Googled it. It was the second largest hospital in Minnesota after the Mayo Clinic. It was the third best training hospital in the nation, a level-one trauma center. I found a documentary about her family, a two-hour show on the History Channel. Her dad was this world-renowned cardiovascular surgeon. He pioneered the Montgomery Method, some fancy way to do heart surgery. Her mom was a huge philanthropist and a spinal surgeon to boot, and her brother was a famous plastic surgeon.

Alexis was part of some elite medical legacy that I couldn't even begin to understand. But every single time she showed up she still slid into my life like she belonged here anyway. Every single time it made it that much harder to let her leave and go back to where she came from. And when she did, it gave me a sinking sense of hopelessness, because how could I and this place compete with whatever that was out there?

She said she didn't see a future with us. That our lives didn't fit. I knew there were things I could never give her. At best, I had about as much to offer as my damn dog—companionship and entertainment. I couldn't talk to her about the stuff her ex probably did, I couldn't make the money she made or buy her expensive gifts or take her on vacations.

But I could love her better than anyone ever could for the rest of her life. *That*, I knew. And if there was even a fraction of a chance that might be enough, I was going to take it.

I didn't have time to play it cool or let things happen slowly. I had to make my argument now. I was going to talk to her about the way I was feeling, I was going to ask her to let me try and make this work.

We took Hunter back behind the garage and spent the next half an hour washing my stupid dog. We locked him in the kennel to dry off and then went to take a shower.

She stripped in the bathroom, and I watched her as I got undressed next to her.

"I hope he learned his lesson," she said, stepping under the water.

"You know he didn't."

She laughed.

Last week he'd gotten porcupine needles in his nose. Alexis had to sedate him and take them out with pliers. This wouldn't have been noteworthy except that he'd done the exact same thing the week before that and clearly learned nothing about sniffing porcupines.

I couldn't say I could really fault him for chasing down things that could hurt him. I couldn't stop doing it either.

We'd already hosed ourselves down using the same stuff we'd cleaned Hunter with, so this was just a quick shower to wash our hair.

She stood under the water rinsing out the shampoo, and I wrapped my arms around her from behind and kissed the side of her neck.

My body reacted to her. Everything in me reacted to her, all the time.

When she called, my mood lifted. When I saw her coming down the driveway, my heart would pound. When she was here, I slept better. When she was gone, I was sad. She felt like the sun. Like she was the reason for everything. Like I'd always been waiting for her to get closer and bring me to life.

I pressed my hard-on into her, and she leaned into my chest. "Don't you want to wait until we get out?"

I shook my head. "No."

She laughed and turned around to kiss me. "Let's rinse and get in bed," she whispered. "We have another hour until check-in."

We toweled off and barely made it to the mattress. I slid over her body, both of us still damp.

I pulled the blankets over us and caged her under me, warming her up. She nuzzled my Adam's apple with her nose and wrapped her arms around my neck, and I felt like my entire universe was here in this bed, like everything that mattered was somehow right here in this dusty garage in this tiny town in the middle of nowhere.

Nothing could convince me this woman wasn't made for me to love. I think my soul recognized hers the second I laid eyes on her. Our bodies knew it the very first night.

The power she had over me terrified me. But it also gave me clarity.

There is a peace in knowing the one thing you can't live without. It simplifies all things. There was her, and then there was everything and everyone else. And only she really mattered. It was easy to know it.

I just wished she knew it too.

I hovered over her, kissing her softly. I brushed her wet hair off her forehead, and she gazed up at me with those beautiful brown eyes, smiling, and I couldn't not say it. It came out like an exhale, like something that was always there, only now I was finally giving it a name and breathing it into the universe and acknowledging that it existed.

"I love you," I whispered.

And then *everything* changed.

CHAPTER 31

ALEXIS

The words drained me like a plug being pulled from a basin. I wiggled away from him and sat up against his headboard. "Why did you just say that to me?"

He sat back in the bed. "What?"

"That you love me. Why did you say it?"

"Because I feel it?"

"You *can't* feel it."

He looked amused. "Well, I do. And it's not a big deal. If you're not there yet, it's fine."

But it wasn't fine.

"What are you doing?" I said. "We're not doing this."

"Doing what?"

"This!" I gestured between us.

"Alexis—"

I shook my head. "No. We talked about this. You knew this wasn't going to be a relationship. You knew this wasn't going to last. I get the job tomorrow. It ends after that, so why throw that word around? What is the point?"

He blinked at me. "The point is that I'm in love with you."

My jaw set. "No."

I got off the bed and started putting my clothes on.

"Are you leaving?" he asked, disbelief in his voice.

"Yes."

"Because I told you I love you—"

"No. Because you *think* you do. And you shouldn't." I pulled on my yoga pants. "I should have ended this months ago. I should have gone with my gut." I pulled a shirt over my tangled wet hair.

Daniel was off the bed, jumping into jeans. "Alexis..."

I grabbed my bag and walked out of the room.

"Alexis!"

I ignored him.

I came out into the sunlight to my car, and Daniel followed close on my heels. "Hey!"

"Daniel, this discussion is over."

"We haven't even had a discussion. How can it be over?" he said to my back.

I chirped off my alarm.

"Stop!" He grabbed my wrist.

I whirled on him and yanked my arm down. "No! You knew this was a temporary situation. You *knew* this wasn't going to have a happy ending."

He dragged a hand through his hair. "Look, I didn't plan this either, but it's happening now, and I can't pretend that it's not."

"It's *not*. Our lives don't *work*," I said. "They don't work together."

He shook his head. "How do you know? You've never even *tried* to make them work. You won't let me meet your friends or your family. I can't know where you live. Give me a chance. Let me try. I can come to you. I can do everything."

I shook my head. "And how are you going to do everything, Daniel? When you have to be *here* to run this house."

"I won't buy it. I'll move to Minneapolis to be near you."

My heart *broke*. The declaration pushed the air right out of my lungs.

"I'll get an apartment if you don't want to live with me," he said. "I'll get a job over there."

I let out a puff of air. "Daniel, you can't leave Wakan. They need you. You love it here—"

"I love you more. If you think I want any of this without you in it, you don't know *anything* about me." His golden-green eyes held mine. "I can't lose you. I won't. The job doesn't have to end what we have. I won't let it."

I stood there, anguished. "It's not even the job, Daniel. That's just the logistics. It's my *life*. My life isn't compatible with your life."

He threw up his hands. "What the hell is the problem? Make me understand it. We're great together. What is this big, horrible thing that you think I can't handle or we can't figure out? I'm your damn boyfriend, talk to me."

"You are *not* my boyfriend."

I watched the words hit him like a smack.

"If I'm not your boyfriend, what the hell am I, Alexis?"

I didn't answer.

"What am I? Nothing? Some fucking booty call? Really? That's what you want to pretend this is?"

Tears pricked my eyes. "This could never work, Daniel. Not the way you want it to—"

"Why?"

"Our lives are just too different. We don't fit. You don't know what I come from, the people I'm around, the things they expect of me—the way they *are*. I don't know how to let you into my world," I said hopelessly. "It feels more humane not to."

He put his hands on my arms. "Look me in the eye and tell me that you don't love me. I want to hear you say that you don't love me back. You say it and I'll let you leave."

My chin quivered. "I can't say it. Because I do love you. And *that* is the fucking problem." Tears spilled down my cheeks.

His eyes moved back and forth between mine. "If you want something badly enough, Alexis, nothing else matters."

I shook my head. "That's not true," I whispered. "Everything matters. All the time."

His sad eyes held mine, and I felt like I was going to crumble into dust.

"It's over, Daniel."

The words made him blow out a shaky breath.

I turned for the car, and his hands dropped away from me.

Then a crack of lightning came out of nowhere.

Daniel grabbed me in a split second and pulled me into him, putting his back to the strike as it hit the oak by the entrance. An enormous branch broke off and fell across the driveway.

I stood there, my cheek pressed to Daniel's pounding chest.

"Did you see that?" he breathed.

I couldn't even respond. It was like paddles had just shocked me back to life. I was instantly sobered.

"There's not even thunder," he said. "There's not even *clouds*."

I peered around him.

The branch sat smoking in the driveway. I looked up at the sky. Nothing but blue. "What in the world?" I whispered.

Then I pushed off him. "Go get your chain saw and move it. I'm still leaving."

He shook his head. "No. No way."

"What do you mean no way? I need to get out."

His eyes were wide. "I'm not messing with that. That was God."

"That was not—" I let a calming breath out through my nose. "Daniel, I do not believe that God had nothing better to do today than trap me in your driveway. I do not believe in cosmic interventions, I don't believe in magic; that was a completely explainable weather phenomenon. You need to move that branch so I can leave."

Then a loud crack of thunder rolled, the heavens opened up, and rain poured over us. Sheets and *sheets* of rain.

Rain. Without clouds.

I stood there, getting drenched, and Daniel crossed his arms in the downpour, looking amused. "The universe doesn't want you to leave," he shouted. "In fact, I'm going to say the universe wants you to go back inside."

"Arrrrrg!" I stomped to the garage in the mud.

I got into the door, and the second I did, I heard the deluge outside stop. Daniel came in after me and wrapped his arms around me from behind. It immediately de-escalated me, a robot powering down. I lost all the energy to fight him.

He stood there, holding me, his body curved around mine like it was made to fit me, and I felt like I was pressed against my other half. But he *couldn't* be my other half, because if he was, wouldn't we be made from the same thing? Why would we be as different as we were perfect for each other?

"I love you," he whispered. "We are *together*. This isn't over. And even if you leave, it won't be over because you'll take the love with you and it'll bring you back."

He turned me, and I looked up at him, completely helpless. But it was okay that I was helpless because he'd never hurt me like Neil did. He'd never do anything but what he does for all the people in his life. He'd be devoted to me and cherish me and take care of me.

And he was right. I couldn't escape this.

Love follows you. It goes where you go. It doesn't know about social divides or distance or common sense. It doesn't even stop when the person you love dies. It does what it wants.

Even if what you want is to not be in love.

CHAPTER 32

ALEXIS

He was my boyfriend.

We were in love.

And it didn't change a thing. Not really.

I still couldn't introduce him to my parents or my friends. The job was still going to take me away from him. He still had to live in Wakan, and I had to live in Minneapolis. I absolutely refused to let him move. We went around about it for hours last night until he finally gave up.

I wouldn't let him sacrifice his life to try to salvage something that wouldn't work out anyway. What did it matter if he lived in Minneapolis if I wasn't going to be home six days a week?

He had to stay in Wakan. Daniel's legacy was just as important as mine. Maybe more.

It felt like Wakan would cease to exist if it didn't have a Grant in it. Like it would be instantly diluted and thin, like Daniel held it together somehow, just by being there.

I couldn't even express how much it meant that he was willing to leave that all behind for me. But I also couldn't let him do it. Not for something as doomed as us.

So all we'd done was opt for the life-support version of the end instead of the clean break.

But he wanted to see if he could save our relationship, and I loved him too much to do the right thing and say no to it entirely. So I didn't.

I couldn't.

Daniel woke up early and moved the branch so I could leave for work. I drove back to the Twin Cities in time for my shift, feeling mentally and emotionally exhausted.

The vote was today. They'd announce the results at six o'clock.

I worked the morning, then headed upstairs to cast my ballot and went straight to the ER to the nurses' station to wait. Bri was there, charting her patients. She was off at six o'clock like me, but she'd stuck around for the announcement. It was 6:05 when Mom and Dad showed up with Neil, Gabby, and Jessica. They came in through the automatic doors and were still half a hallway away, but the results were on Dad's face.

I got it.

"Congratulations," Bri said, leaning in to hug me. "I voted for you twice."

I laughed, and she let me go. "Call me when you're ready to go celebrate. I'll leave you to the brute squad," she said, nodding at my family. Then she got up and left.

Dad approached the nurses' station. "You did it! We have another chief in the family. Well done."

I was oddly unexcited for some reason. Like it was happening to someone else.

I forced a smile and came around the nurses' station so Gabby,

Jessica, and Mom could give me hugs. Neil gave me a head nod of approval. "Congratulations."

"What time are you off, princess?" Dad asked. "We can go catch dinner."

"I'm off now actu—"

Gabby gasped next to me. "Oh. My. *God*…"

I wrinkled my forehead and turned around to see what she was gaping at, and my heart *sank*.

Daniel was walking toward me with flowers.

I was rendered completely mute. My mouth opened and closed, but no words came out.

"Isn't that the squirrel guy?" Gabby asked from behind me.

Jessica didn't take as long to catch on. "Oh, Ali…"

My ears started to ring. No. No no no no no no no, this wasn't happening.

Daniel closed the gap between us, beaming. "Hey."

I processed him in split-second clips of horror. He'd trimmed his beard down, and it somehow managed to make him look even younger than he was. He was in a faded T-shirt, and his tattoos were showing. All of them. He had on jeans and his leather bracelet, and his boots were muddy. Normally none of this even remotely bothered me. In fact, I *liked* how he looked. That was one of my favorite shirts, probably why he wore it. But I did not like this in the context of this situation. In the context of this situation, this was my worst nightmare.

He glanced at my parents, Neil. Then he nodded at Gabby and Jessica. "Hi. Nice to see you again." He looked a little surprised to see them here, which made sense, since I'd never mentioned they worked with me.

"What are you doing here?" I breathed.

He smiled. "I thought I'd surprise you. Take you to dinner."

My dad looked him up and down. "Alexis, who is this?"

I swallowed. "I ... "

Daniel put a hand out. "Daniel Grant."

Dad didn't shake his hand. He looked at it like it was dirty.

And then, in some weird alternate universe move, Neil stepped in. "Neil. Nice to meet you."

He shook Daniel's hand, and pure panic ripped through me.

"I'm sorry, who are you to her?" Mom asked, looking confused.

"Um," I licked my lips. "He's my—"

Daniel looked at me, his eyes telling me he was starting to read the room, and for a split second I seriously considered lying. Saying *anything* other than the truth. My trainer. My friend. An old acquaintance who just happened to show up with flowers to take me to dinner. And then I grasped for what answer would give him the most protection from this situation. I knew it wasn't boyfriend, but his eyes had begun to search mine, and I realized that he wouldn't understand. He wouldn't forgive me for this again, like he had when I did it with Jessica and Gabby. So I said it. I had to.

"He's my boyfriend."

Nobody said a word. Then Dad began to laugh. It was the maniacal laugh of a Disney villain, and I felt the whole room closing in around me.

"Your boyfriend?" Dad said, looking back and forth between us, amused. He nodded at my ex. "Did she tell you she's living with Neil?"

I watched Daniel blink in shock.

"Cecil, it's really not like that—" Neil said in a tone that was surprisingly stoic.

Dad laughed. "You've been in couple's counseling for the last three months, so I'd say it's like that, wouldn't you?"

Neil pressed his lips into a line, but to his credit he didn't say anything else.

Dad shook his head, looking positively titillated. "First your brother marries Lola Simone, and now *this*?" He practically howled.

Daniel looked at me and gave me a smile that didn't reach his eyes. "Call me when you get off." He handed me the flowers, kissed me on the cheek, and left.

I was going to have a panic attack. I could feel my breathing becoming labored.

Everyone's eyes were on me.

"Ali, you can't be serious…" Jessica said.

Gabby was practically gyrating, smiling like she couldn't wait to tell Philip. Mom had a hand over her mouth, probably realizing how bad the fallout would be for both of us once Dad let this sink in. But for the moment? Dad didn't even look mad. He looked *entertained*.

It occurred to me that the idea of Daniel was so ridiculous to Dad, he wasn't even a threat. This was a joke to him, like the whole thing was too absurd to even take it seriously.

"So has he asked you for money yet?" Dad asked, still chuckling.

"What?" I breathed.

"*Money*," Dad said. "Has he asked for it?"

"No!"

"But let me guess. You've offered it, right? It felt like your idea?" Dad looked amused.

I was too out of breath to answer him. He took my silence for a yes. And it *was* a yes, but it wasn't like that.

Mom looked whiplashed. "Alexis…"

Jessica was shaking her head. Gabby was texting into her phone a million words a minute, and Neil looked almost sorry for me for some reason. I couldn't take it.

I dropped the flowers on the nurses' station and ran after Daniel.

By the time I caught up with him, he was halfway into the parking lot. "Daniel!"

He kept walking.

I sprinted the last few feet and grabbed his arm. "Daniel, *please!*"

He turned to me, his eyes red. "You *live* with him? You're in couple's counseling? This whole fucking time?"

"It's not like that," I gasped. "He refuses to leave. He sleeps in the basement. We're not in counseling, we lied about it—"

He shook his head. "You never told me. You let me get blindsided—"

I was riding the edge of hysteria. "I didn't ask you to come! Why didn't you call?"

"You had that vote today. I wanted to support you, to be there for you, like your boyfriend *should*. What did you think I meant when I said I wanted to try? This is me trying, you *agreed* to this—"

"You shouldn't have shown up like that—"

"Why?" He threw his hands up. "You show up like that all the time. Everyone knows I'm with you, all my friends, all my family. You say you love me, but those people in there didn't even know I *exist*."

"Daniel—"

"Gabby and Jessica still don't know about us? After four months?"

"I told you, they know I'm seeing someone—"

"But just not *me*."

He shook his head at me, and the look on his face made my heart break. "Am I really that fucking embarrassing for you?"

When I didn't answer, he turned and started for his truck. I didn't chase him. I couldn't.

I was drowning and I couldn't breathe.

CHAPTER 33

DANIEL

I got in my truck and sat there, too shaken to drive.

She'd been living with someone else. This whole fucking time. That George Clooney guy who shook my hand, was he the surgeon? The ex?

That was the ex?

I understood now in full color what she meant when she said our lives didn't fit. Because if this kind of guy was what her people were used to, I never stood a damn chance.

And why the hell did he shake my hand?

I didn't think she was cheating on me. But how could she not tell me that guy was living in her house? And her brother was married to Lola Simone? She never thought to casually mention that her sister-in-law was one of the biggest rock stars on the planet? What *else* hadn't she told me? Where the hell did her friends think she went every weekend? Where did that Neil guy think she went? If she needed to lie to them, fine, but she didn't need to lie to *me*.

I knew there was more to this, but my brain couldn't work through it. My thoughts kept jumping around the whole awkward, horrible encounter, from the blank looks on Gabby's and Jessica's faces to the guy who was fucking laughing. And the worst thing of all was I think that was her dad. I recognized him from the History Channel documentary.

I didn't show up there to meet her family and friends. I wouldn't do that without her permission. I was just trying to prove to her I meant what I said. I'd put in the effort, make this work. It didn't even occur to me that everyone else would have the same idea and be there to congratulate her. I didn't know she worked with Gabby and Jessica or her ex because she'd never told me. Apparently she didn't tell me *anything*.

I felt betrayed, and it wasn't even rational because what else did I expect? She said she didn't see a future with us. She'd been very clear with me on that. She'd planned on ending it, up until last night, so I don't know why any of this surprised me. But to see it with my own eyes was something else.

How could we be in love and mean so much to each other if nobody in her world even knew who I was?

All of this just solidified what I already knew. I really *didn't* exist for her outside of Wakan. She had a whole different life, one I had nothing to do with, and she had no intention of including me in.

I was shaking too much to drive, so I sat there, trying to calm down.

Then I heard a tap at my window. A brown-haired woman in black scrubs stood there, eyeing me.

"Are you Daniel?" she said through the glass.

I blinked at her. Then I rolled down the window. "You know me?"

"Yeah, I'm Bri. I'm Alexis's best friend. I thought that was you. She didn't tell me you were coming today."

"I . . ." I cleared my throat and started again. "I surprised her."

Her eyes got big. "Oh. And what was *that* like?"

I shook my head. "Not good."

"Nope. It wouldn't be. Mind if I sit?" She nodded to the passenger seat.

"Sure."

She came around the back of the truck and let herself in. She slammed the door and pivoted to look at me. "Tell me what happened."

I dragged a hand down my beard. "I came to bring her flowers. She had that chief thing today. I found out she's living with some guy—"

"Neil?" She scoffed. "That guy's a dick. First of all, she's living with Neil like you live with cockroaches. She hates it, it grosses her out, and she doesn't tell anyone because it's embarrassing. They co-own the property. He won't leave. He wants the house, so he's squatting there like a hobo against her wishes. They're going to court for it in a few weeks and then one of them will move out. Next."

I swallowed. Okay. That was good. That was something.

"Gabby and Jessica were there—"

"The wicked stepsisters. I hate those bitches. Ali hasn't hung out with them in months. She didn't like how they treated you that one weekend. They don't matter. Next."

"There was some older guy and an older woman. Gray hair. Serious. He wouldn't shake my hand."

She sucked air through her teeth. "Those were her parents. Wow, you went through a portal right into the seventh level of hell."

I laughed, even though it wasn't funny.

"Look, I don't know what all was said and done when you walked in there, but I'm gonna tell you this. None of it was her fault. Her brother, Derek? He moved out of the country to avoid introducing his wife to those people. This is not a you thing, it's a them thing. If I know Ali, she's probably freaking out right now."

I felt my blood pressure going down. "Okay." I tilted my head. "Is her brother really married to Lola Simone?"

"Yup. She never talked to you about Derek?"

"She did. She told me all about him and that he was married. She just didn't tell me who his wife was, she just called her Nikki."

"She didn't even tell *me* until I saw it in the tabloids, and I've known her and Derek for ten years. She's trustworthy and she keeps promises and she'd respect their privacy, even to you. She's good like that."

I puffed air from my cheeks. Well, I guess I couldn't really be mad at her for doing the right thing.

Bri looked me in the eye. "Look, I know all about you. She tells me. I've seen everything but the dick pics. And I'm the only one who matters. Trust me."

I let out a shaky breath. "Okay." I nodded. "All right."

Then my cell phone pinged. I pulled it out. It was Alexis.

"Is that her?" Bri asked.

"Yeah. She sent me an address."

"Chateau de Chambord Street?"

I nodded. "Yes."

"That's her house." She put her hand on the door. "Well, you better head over there. Don't worry, Neil works until nine. I always check his schedule. I like to spray a little vinegar into his locker while he's on shift. Let him go home smelling like a salad."

I laughed. "Thank you."

She shook her head. "Don't thank me. Good luck, Daniel. I think you're going to need it."

I took the ten-minute drive to the address she sent me. As I wound through the streets, the houses got bigger and bigger and farther apart.

When I pulled up to the address she'd texted me, I stared up in disbelief.

Her house was a mansion. And not the way the Grant House was a mansion. This was the kind of place you saw on TV when you watched shows about celebrities. You could fit half of Wakan's Main Street on the lawn.

She lived here?

I mean, I knew she had money. She'd offered me fifty thousand dollars like it was nothing. But I didn't think she had *this* kind of money. I couldn't even afford to pay the water bill on a place like this.

I got out of my truck, feeling unsure I should even leave it parked in the driveway. It looked like a clod of dirt dropped on a white linen tablecloth.

Alexis opened the front door before I knocked. She was still in her scrubs, and she'd been crying. She stepped aside without saying a word to let me in, and I peered around quietly.

It was cavernous. And *cold*.

Everything was gray, like a filter was over it. The floors were white marble and the ceilings were vaulted, which only made the room seem more hollow. Like an ice cave.

She sniffed. "This is where I live." She said it like an apology.

She led me through the house silently. Our footsteps echoed as we passed an enormous living room with white sofas, a shiny black piano, muted Oriental rugs, expensive-looking paintings. There was a dining room with a table that could seat twenty and a huge crystal chandelier over it. Then a humongous kitchen, one she hadn't even known how to use until a few months ago.

I remembered her calling me when the power was out and her telling me the stove was gas. I scoffed looking at it now. It was a *huge* Viking range, nine burners, double oven, a wall-mounted pot filler over it. Here I was thinking I was talking to her about a regular old oven and it was *this*. It was almost comical.

There were more bathrooms than I could count. Hallways bigger than my loft with marble tables that had fresh flower arrangements the size of my dog sitting on them. A library with twenty-foot-tall bookshelves and a sliding ladder. At one point we saw a maid. She looked at me like I confused her, like maybe I was a new employee or something.

We moved through an office that overlooked a lake out back. There were awards and diplomas hanging. Hers and Neil's. So many between them, they covered half a wall. PhDs: Yale for him, Stanford and Berkeley for her. There was a pool with a waterfall through the French doors, and I remembered all the times Alexis sat out there to talk to me. Me sitting in my dusty, shitty garage where I made her sleep, and her in this place, like a palace.

I felt almost catfished. It was ridiculous, but I did. Like she hadn't been fully honest about who she was. But in truth, she *had* been honest. It was just that my imagination had failed me.

You fill in blanks. You take the information given to you and you make assumptions that complete the picture in your mind. I realized now that all my pictures had been drastically wrong. She was a hundred times higher up than I'd ever allowed myself to imagine. I couldn't even grasp this kind of wealth.

When I'd seen her at the hospital earlier, even that had been a small reality check. I knew she was a doctor. I'd seen her treat patients. But it was different seeing her actually there, wearing scrubs and standing in an ER, a doctor's name tag hanging off her pocket. I wasn't fully prepared for that, even with all the lead-up to it, and I *definitely* wasn't prepared for this.

I got now why she didn't know how to clean or cook—I *really* got it. Because someone who could live like this had people running their lives for them. People like *me*.

Now I understood even more what I must have looked like to her friends and family, why they reacted the way they did. Especially now that I'd seen her ex. I was everything opposite of that guy. How did someone like me fit? I was uncomfortable even being in this house. I couldn't imagine being with her here, cooking in that kitchen, even sitting in the living room. I felt the way the truck looked parked in the driveway. Out of place and like I didn't belong.

She took me up a grand, twisting staircase that made the one at home look small in comparison. Three more guest rooms, more bathrooms, and finally a room with a dead bolt on the door. She unlocked it and stood back while I went inside.

It was the master bedroom.

I looked around, not saying a word. It was bright and warm, like it wasn't a part of the rest of the house. A king-size bed sat in the middle of it. There were plush chairs and a rose-colored bedspread. A framed photograph of a girl in a field of poppies. There was a small fridge pushed against the wall with a microwave on top and a Keurig. It was the only room that felt like the woman she was in Wakan.

It was the only place where I finally saw *us*.

She had knickknacks on her nightstand. Small treasures. Little things I'd made her, a raccoon I'd carved from wood, just something funny I'd whittled out in an hour. There was a jar of the strawberry jam we'd made a few weeks ago, one of my hoodies tossed over a chair.

The heart-shaped rock.

Souvenirs.

This was why she wanted me to see her house. It was worth a million words of explanation.

For the first time she came full circle for me. I finally saw all of her. She came together like a puzzle that had been missing pieces. It was like she was two different people.

And then I realized she *was*.

Who she was with me was who she was on vacation. Who she was in Wakan wasn't real life.

This was her real life.

And I knew before she even said anything that she wasn't going to ask me to be a part of it.

She sniffed, and she looked like she might start crying again. "My dad wants me to get back with Neil," she said. "He loves him and won't accept our breakup. Neil's forcing me to live with him because he wants the house in the separation—and he wants me back," she added. "I can't leave my job to be with you because if I do I'll break a hundred-and-twenty-five-year family legacy. And if you come here to be with me, you'll lose your house and my parents won't ever speak to me again."

She pressed her lips together like she was trying not to sob. "So that's where we are. I'm sorry, Daniel…"

I felt my throat get tight, and I forced myself to say the words I already knew the answer to. "Are you breaking up with me?" I asked, my voice thick.

She looked anguished. "We knew it wasn't going to last. We got more time than I thought we would, and I'm so grateful for it." Her voice cracked on the last word.

I felt like my heart was being crushed in my chest. And I didn't even have anything to say because this wasn't on me. I'd leave my life to be here if she wanted that. I'd learn to get used to all...*this*. I'd deal with it, because if the alternative was being without her, I could never choose it. But this wasn't *my* choice. It wasn't up to me to decide for her to be disowned or whatever the hell her parents would do.

And what a fucked-up thing to even put on someone. What kind of people were these?

But then I already knew.

For the first time I *truly* saw what she was trying to make me understand every time she told me this wouldn't work out.

It wasn't just a money gap or an age gap or even a social gap between us. It was everything. Her entire family conspiring against us. Her friends. Logistics. Fate. A thousand qualifiers that I'd never have, things that would have had to have happened at birth, generations ago, to help me now. A well-connected family, a better education, a more important place than Wakan.

All we had was our love for each other. That's all we had.

None of the other parts worked or fit or made sense.

But I didn't need it to make sense, because for me the love was everything, it was all I needed.

But it wasn't enough for *her*.

People don't stay in Wakan. They come and they have a

magical time, and then they go back to their real lives. I'd fallen in love with a tourist. Because that's what she was.

And the vacation was over.

My eyes were tearing up. "Alexis, please. Come home with me. Or let me stay. Don't make me leave you…"

Her chin quivered, and she looked away from me.

"Please don't do this," I whispered.

I swallowed down the lump in my throat. "One day you're going to realize the mistake you're making. Please, Alexis. Realize it now."

She wouldn't. She didn't. She made me leave five minutes later.

CHAPTER 34

ALEXIS

Every day since I broke up with Daniel a month ago, I went through the motions like a robot.

I woke up, took a shower, went to work. On my infrequent days off, I slept. All day. And my dreams were worse than reality.

I dreamed of Daniel mostly. Of Wakan and the Grant House, running through the rooms, looking for him. And when I woke up, I'd feel around for a second to find him, only to remember he wasn't there and never would be again.

I was always tired now. And my brain was misfiring.

I couldn't remember the stained glass on the landing. It was the oddest thing. It was just gone from my memory, like Wakan had decided to keep it when I left. Was it a garden? Or deer in a meadow? Or a mosaic? It bothered me so much, I went to TripAdvisor to see if anyone had posted pictures, and there wasn't a single one. One of the most beautiful things in the house, and nobody had taken a photo? The only one I found of it was a black-and-white of the staircase on a website about historic Minnesota homes. It was taken the year the house was built. But the window was completely black. Like the camera had malfunctioned.

My mind reached uselessly for the memory and then finally gave up. It was something that only belonged to Wakan. And you couldn't have it once you left.

Not even in your dreams.

I took my dressing-down by Dad for the Daniel thing with so little emotion, he lost interest and gave up on lecturing me. I was like a catatonic patient. A zombie.

I didn't respond to Gabby and Jessica's texts. I didn't take Bri up on her offers to go to dinner or come over. I just buried myself in work, kept moving so none of what happened would catch up with me and pin me down.

Mom stopped by a few days after the scene at the hospital. She was hurt I hadn't told her about Daniel. Then she begged me to apologize to Dad for lying about trying to work it out with Neil.

What he needed an apology for, I couldn't understand. He was the only one getting everything he wanted.

I wondered, looking at her, if Dad had lured her in once like Neil did to me. If he made her feel like the most special woman in the world, pretended to be someone different, dangled the Montgomery legacy that she valued so much—and by the time he showed her who he really was, it was too late. And even without asking her, I knew that's the way it was.

The day after tomorrow was the quasquicentennial. It was my chance to network with the board and important investors for the hospital. It was the first time that I'd be operating as a Montgomery in an official capacity, stepping into the role I'd seen Mom play my entire life.

I should have been looking forward to it. Not the party or

the schmoozing part, but the beginning of my ability to make a difference. And I couldn't even muster the energy to care about it. It felt completely meaningless to me. Everything did.

This is what depression felt like.

I thought it had been bad back when I was with Neil. But this was a darkness I'd never experienced before. My body felt atrophied, like the simple act of getting up was a feat.

Nothing made me smile. None of the things I typically loved appealed to me. And it occurred to me that I had drowned. I didn't save myself. And now I was just floating, weightless, dead inside.

I wondered when it would get better—when doing the right thing would start to feel like the right thing. I didn't just end this for me, I did it for Daniel. So he wouldn't leave his life. So he wouldn't be subjected to the things that my friends and family would put him through, no matter how much I would try to shield him from it if he was here.

If this was the best thing for both of us, why was it so, so hard?

I got off even later than usual. There had been a mass casualty situation at work, a multi-car pileup. A seven-year-old had died, and I'd had to tell the family.

It was one of those days when I wished even more than usual that I could go be in Wakan with Daniel. That I could lie in bed with him, whispering in the dark, letting him brush the hair off my forehead and kiss me. Feel the rumbling in his chest while he told me that it was going to be okay. He'd make sure I ate, even though I wouldn't want to. Put me in one of his T-shirts while he'd cook me dinner, and Hunter would have his chin in my lap.

But I would never feel that safe and cared for again. I wouldn't find that kind of love a second time. I wouldn't even try. I knew how lucky I was to even have had it once.

I would be single for the rest of my life. No kids, no marriage. I didn't want it with anyone else. I would be my career now. I would finally be what Dad wanted. Nothing but a Montgomery—and a good one too. One without any distractions.

And the legacy would die with me.

Derek wouldn't be back, and I would never have an heir. In their lack of foresight, my parents had effectively set into motion the destruction of the one thing they cared most about.

I think they still thought I'd get back with Neil. Marry him, have children who'd grow up under the same abusive dynamic I had, with a narcissistic, controlling father and a mother too worn down to protect them.

It would never happen.

This was the price of their prejudice.

Grace would have cost them nothing.

I walked into my dark bedroom and dropped my bag on the floor. I peered around tiredly.

I hadn't moved any of Daniel's things. The heart-shaped rock was where I'd left it. The last hoodie I'd stolen from him was still draped over my chair. I stood there now, staring at it.

It would still smell like him. I could put it on and climb into bed and imagine that he was holding me.

And then I wondered if he was holding someone else. Seeing other people already. Trying to move on like he should. I pictured Doug dragging him to bars, getting him on a dating app.

Maybe some other girl was wearing his hoodies now.

It kicked the legs right out from under me.

Most days I was strong. I was able to live with the choices I had made. The choices I was forced to make. I could fight the urge to call him and hear his voice. I could stay away.

But not today.

CHAPTER 35

DANIEL

I felt like a different person.

Like I'd aged a century since the last time I saw her. I felt more like Pops than myself. I was bitter and sick of everything. And every day I got worse instead of better.

Losing Alexis would alter me forever. Like the rings in a tree, you could open me up fifty years from now and see when it happened, see the damage. I was ruined. I'd never be as good ever again.

I didn't laugh anymore. I didn't want to see anyone. Doug and Brian circled me constantly, but I was a bear to be around. I felt bad about it, so I stopped answering the door when they came over.

The only good thing that had happened since Alexis left me was that I'd raised the money for the house. The sale had just been finalized two days ago.

I'd put up the last of my custom pieces for twice what Alexis had charged her friends. Three times as much, four times as much. Because I didn't care. I didn't care if people bought them. I didn't care if they didn't. I didn't even care if I saved the house. And the funny thing was, the higher I priced them, the more people seemed to want them. They just paid it. So I raised the money and became a successful carpenter overnight, a home-owner. And the victory was so hollow, I didn't even care that I'd done it, because I didn't want any of it without her.

She was the one. I'd had four months to make her know it too, and I'd failed. Now I would live with that failure for the rest of my life.

I didn't need to keep running Grant House as a B & B, now that I was making so much with my carpentry. And that was good, because I couldn't stand to step foot in it. Not without her. I couldn't look at the snow-covered landscape on the stained glass on the landing or the roses on the banister or the mosaic around the fireplace because it was where I'd fallen in love with her, and that was so painful for me now, I couldn't lay my eyes on it. So I shut the house down and left it vacant.

I was driving by Doug's place with Hunter on the way back from hauling some stuff to the dump and decided to stop. I knew if I didn't make at least a few appearances, they'd never lay off me. I didn't tell him I was coming. Just sat on his porch until he saw my truck outside.

I heard the screen door slam, and a second later Doug was handing me a can of Coke.

"Thanks," I mumbled, taking it.

It was so humid you could've cut the air with a knife.

Doug sat down in the rocking chair next to me and opened his soda with a *pith*. "Don't like the looks of those clouds."

I didn't answer.

It had been pouring every day since Alexis left. It had been so miserable the town was almost empty of tourists. Couldn't use the bike trail or the river, couldn't walk around. All the weekenders had canceled. Even when it stopped, it didn't really stop. The sun never came out, nothing was ever dry. Then it would start again, like there was no limit to how much water could fall from the sky.

Hunter sat at my feet, his head on his paws. My dog had been good ever since Alexis had left. Like he knew I couldn't deal with his shit right now—or he was too sad to give me any. At home he kept staring at the driveway, waiting. Every time I tried to bring him in, he'd fight the leash. So I just left him out there.

"Did you eat today?" Doug asked.

I'd been losing weight. No appetite. He probably noticed it more than I did, not seeing me every day like he used to.

It was a moment before I gave him a slow head shake.

"You gotta eat, man. You get hungry, and you're gonna feel worse."

"Nothing can make me feel worse," I said, my voice rough. I was mortally wounded. A sandwich wasn't going to save me.

He didn't answer. He just procured a granola bar from somewhere and handed it to me. I took it slowly and just stared at it in my hand.

"This hurts so much," I said. "I can't breathe without her. I just want it to stop."

Doug peered out into the yard. "Maybe it's not meant to stop. Maybe this is supposed to make you strong."

"It's not making me strong. It's killing me."

He just looked out over the pastures. We went quiet for a few moments.

"I'm leaving," I said.

He turned to look at me. "What?"

"I've been thinking about it for a while. I can't be in this place without her. I can't breathe here."

Thunder rumbled overhead.

"But...you can't leave, man. What the hell are you gonna do somewhere else?"

I shrugged. The same thing I did here. I'd miss her. That's what

I'd do. But at least then I'd be missing her in a place that didn't remind me of her every second.

It was amazing that one season of someone could paint over a lifetime. This wasn't the place I grew up in anymore. It wasn't my home. It was just the last place I was with *her*. And why would I want to remember that?

A sharp gust cut through the property, and a bucket rolled across the yard. We watched it bounce like a white tumbleweed and then disappear behind the barn.

"I wasn't what she needed," I said so quietly I didn't think he heard me.

"Yeah, you were," Doug said. "She's just got other shit going on, shit that doesn't have anything to do with you."

I shook my head. "Yes, it does. She was embarrassed of me. I wasn't good enough. I wasn't worth the trade-off."

"You know what?" Doug said from next to me. "She loved you. I don't care what you think. I saw it. Everyone did."

I stayed quiet. She did love me. I knew that. I *believed* that. But what does love matter when it can't outweigh the rest of it?

The rain started to fall. It came down in heavy sheets so thick tiny creeks started to form in the grass. Dragonflies darted around in the downpour.

Doug squinted out at the yard. "What's up with this weather? I haven't seen it like this since the month your grandparents died. This shit's ridiculous."

I didn't answer. Because the answer didn't matter.

Nothing did.

"I'm going," I said, getting up. Hunter rose like his bones hurt and dragged after me.

"Well, when are you leaving?"

"I don't know. Tomorrow maybe. The day after. I need to pack up my tools."

"Don't go," Doug said. "Stay for dinner. Or let's go out, do something fun. We can go to Jane's."

It must speak to my mental state that Doug was the one worried about *me*.

I shook my head. "I'll call you when I land somewhere." I paused, looking at my friend. "Thank you. For everything."

He looked like he wanted to say something else, but he didn't. I turned and walked with Hunter through the rain to my truck. I got in, drenched.

I peered up at the clouds as I pulled off the property and started driving home along the river, my wet shirt clinging to me.

I didn't know where I would go when I left. South. That's all I had. South. I'd just drive until I ran out of gas or out-drove the rain. The thought of coming up with a plan felt so exhausting to me, I couldn't even consider it.

Maybe it would get better the farther away I got from here and her. Maybe it would lift like a fog, and I'd be able to breathe and think enough to function again.

When I got home, I peeled off my wet clothes and climbed into bed. It was only six o'clock and I was more weary than tired, but I didn't want to be awake anymore.

I fell into one of those sleeps of the brokenhearted. The kind that breathes in and out, between here and gone. You want to dream about them but then regret it when you do, because waking up hurts too much. So you hope for nothing but black. The temporary reprieve from existing without them.

It was dark outside when my phone rang. Rain was tapping on the roof.

I almost didn't answer the call. I was glad I did. Because it was *her*.

"Hello?" I said into the darkness.

There was a long pause before I got a quiet "Hi."

My heart didn't pound the way I would have thought at getting an unexpected phone call from her, a month since the last time I'd heard her voice. But it didn't feel like this was actually happening. It felt like a dream. Like I wasn't fully awake. And then when I started to realize that I *was* awake, my heart didn't pound because it was in pieces in my chest and it didn't work anymore.

We just sat there, quiet. Like just being on the phone not saying a word to each other was its own form of communication.

It was.

A thousand words passed through the silence.

She missed me.

She was thinking about me.

She loved me.

Not a single one of those things stopped being true when she ended us. And that was the most tragic thing of all.

"How have you been?" she asked into the silence.

"Fine," I lied.

A long pause.

"Did you save up enough for the house?"

I let out a breath. "Yeah. I did."

"You did?" She sounded genuinely happy for me. "That's amazing."

"Yeah, the Etsy store and Instagram page helped a lot. So thank you."

I could picture her nodding.

"You want to know how I did it?" I asked.

"Yes."

"I raised my prices. A lot. Like, twelve thousand dollars for that lightning strike table."

"You did?"

"Yeah. I realized when you hit zero fucks, that's when negotiations begin."

"What does *that* mean?" A small smile in her voice.

"It's just that I didn't care if they sold or not. When you don't care, everything's on your terms. They can take it or leave it. It doesn't matter to you, so ask for whatever the hell you want."

"Ahhh. Well, I always thought you were undercharging. I'd pay that for one of your tables."

"Yeah, well, you're a Kardashian, so..."

She gasped. "I am *not* a Kardashian."

I smiled a little. "Have you *seen* your house?"

She made a playful indignant noise.

"You even have a surgeon living in the basement."

She let out a laugh. The sound made me feel happier than I'd felt in weeks.

It amazed me how easily we just started again. But then it didn't. Because if I didn't see her for twenty years, it would still be like this. It was like this from the moment I'd met her, and it would always be like this between us. This was part of it. This is what made it easy.

This is what made it hard.

"Where are you?" I asked.

"In my room. In my bed."

The ache that I felt at this was almost more than I could stand.

I could picture that room now. Where she was lying, the blanket she was tucked under. I could be there. Or she could be *here*. Or we could be anywhere, as long as we were together, and everything would be okay again.

"Where are you?" she asked.

"In my bed."

Now she went quiet, and I wondered if she was thinking the same thing I had.

"Is your room dark?" she asked.

"Yeah. But I forgot to turn the light off in the bathroom, so there's a little light coming from under the door. Is yours dark?"

"Totally dark."

There was something intimate about calling someone in the pitch black of your bedroom in the middle of the night. It's like a whisper. It's private. It means something.

I wanted to ask her if the things I'd given her were still on the nightstand. If she was wearing one of my hoodies. But it would break my heart either way.

"So how is everyone?" she asked.

I rubbed my forehead. "They're good. Kevin Bacon has a hashtag on Instagram now. Doug just sort of gave up keeping him locked up, so Kevin hangs out by the fudge shop begging for handouts and taking selfies with tourists."

"So he's living his best life."

"Oh, yes."

"And Hunter?"

I paused, debating if I should tell her how he'd actually been. "He's good. He's here, with me."

He wasn't. He was sleeping on the porch of the house, waiting for her to come home.

"Liz left Jake," I said, changing the subject.

"She did?" Her voice brightened.

"Yeah. She showed up a few weeks ago with a black eye and Doreen. She took that stuff you were keeping for her. Brought it down to the police station in Rochester."

"She got a restraining order?"

"Yup." I scoffed. "But he violated it anyway. Came back looking for her. Pops pulled a gun on him."

"*What?*"

"Right in the middle of Main Street, in front of everyone. Told him he would shoot his balls off if he ever came back." I laughed a little. "Jake filed an assault charge, but nobody saw anything."

She snorted. "Of course they didn't."

"Anyway, Liz had him arrested for violating the restraining order. Then I guess she had a bunch of other dirt on him. He got fired. He'll be at least two years in jail. He won't be back."

"Good. What did Brian say?"

"He was happy. They went on a date last night, actually."

I felt her beaming through the phone.

"I have it on the highest authority that Liz's car was still parked outside of Brian's house this morning," I said.

"The highest authority?"

"Doug."

She laughed.

"So that's it then?" she said. "No more police presence in Wakan?"

"No, we have to have at least one. They sent us a new guy named Wade. He just parks the police cruiser by the walking path and plays on his phone. I think he's bored out of his mind."

"Well, maybe he'll be better than Jake at curbing the teenager crime wave," she said.

"Maybe."

We went quiet again.

"How's your new job?" I asked.

I pictured a shrug. "It's a lot. I work fourteen-hour days. My feet hurt all the time."

I didn't want to tell her that if I was there, I'd rub them every night. I'd have a bath ready for her when she got home, I'd have her scrubs for tomorrow washed and pressed and laid out, dinner ready. I'd take care of her.

I felt a lump form in my throat.

Nobody was taking care of her. That hurt almost as much as the thought of some other guy doing it.

Almost.

She got quiet on the other end. We were quiet for so long I'd have thought we'd lost the call if I didn't hear the occasional shift through the line. The rain outside my window filled the long silence, and I wished, so much, that she was with me. That she was lying next to me and I could smell her hair and wake up and make her breakfast. That all the things we talked about could be things we both already knew because we'd been together when they happened.

My chest felt tight, and I clutched a hand over my heart and squeezed.

I missed her so much it was physically painful. It was a form of grief. A withdrawal. Starvation.

It was unnatural. Because I wasn't supposed to be without her. My eyes started to tear up.

There's something more final than forever. It's never. Never is infinite.

I would never see her again. I would never touch her again. I would never make her lunch or listen to her breathing while she slept. We'd never get married or have children or die on the same day. And I wouldn't do those things with anyone because it would just be the poor man's version of what I'd had with her and I'd always know that.

"Daniel..."

I had to swallow hard to answer. "Yeah?"

I heard her sniff in the darkness.

"Will you still come for me?" she asked quietly.

"What?" I asked gently.

"If there's a zombie apocalypse. Will you come get me like you said?"

I had to move the phone away from my mouth. Tears squeezed from my eyes. "You mean if the world ends and none of this shit matters anymore?" I said, my voice thick.

"Yes," she whispered.

Hot tears slid down my cheeks.

"The world *is* ending, Alexis. That's what this feels like. So come with me now."

She started sobbing softly in the background, and I had to put my phone on mute so she wouldn't hear me cry.

The hole inside of me was so deep, it was all I was. I didn't know how I'd live the rest of my life without her. And then I knew unequivocally that leaving Wakan wouldn't change any of it. It wouldn't get better somewhere else. Because you carry love with you. And the realization that I couldn't escape this was so devastating, so overwhelming, I couldn't breathe.

"I have to go," she said.

Then she was gone.

I bawled into my pillow like a baby. And when I was done, I blocked her number so she could never do this to me again.

CHAPTER 36

ALEXIS

I'd cried all night.

Calling him made it a million times worse. I should have never done it. I'd just opened the wound, and now I was bleeding again. Hemorrhaging and I couldn't make it stop.

I dug in my closet with red, puffy eyes for what I planned on wearing for the gala tomorrow. It was a sleeveless, floor-length silver ball gown with a full, puffy tulle skirt. I'd bought it at Neiman Marcus last year on a girls' trip to New York with Jessica and Gabby. Just bought it, this four-thousand-dollar dress, for fun. No event planned, nowhere to go in it.

It occurred to me now how totally frivolous and ridiculous that was.

I was not the same woman I was back then.

I tossed it unceremoniously onto the bed and put the silver strappy heels I wanted next to it, picked out jewelry and set it in a little pile.

My makeup would be done and my hair would be swept into

a dramatic updo with a tiny diamond tiara that Mom insisted I wear. It was a family heirloom from my great-great-grandmother. She had worn it to the fifty-year Royaume Northwestern anniversary celebration, so my mother thought it was fitting.

I'd put all this on and go through the motions at this party. I'd smile and meet people. But I'd be empty inside the whole time, and nobody would be the wiser. Nobody would know that I'd lost an entire town, the man I loved, and most of myself.

Someone knocked on my bedroom door, and I dragged myself to open it. Neil was standing there.

"What," I said flatly.

"Briana's here," he said.

"Okay..."

"She's making you a drink in the kitchen. I was wondering if I could talk to you. Just for a minute."

I pressed my lips into a line and then pushed the door open, resigned. "Come in."

He stepped inside and closed the door behind him. He slipped his hands into his pockets. "Tomorrow your parents are seating me at the head table with them."

Which meant they were seating us together. Great.

I shook my head. "No. I'm not sitting with you like your date. I'll sit next to my mom, you sit next to my dad."

"Okay."

I eyed him. "Okay? You're not going to fight me? Force me?"

"Ali, I'm sorry."

I shook my head at him, annoyed. "What?"

"I'm sorry for everything I put you through."

I stared at him a moment before crossing my arms. "Which was what?"

This ought to be good.

He seemed to struggle with what he was going to say. "Ali, my life is not...happy. And I'm starting to realize that's my own fault. I've been really trying to understand why I do some of the things I do, and I think the therapy was the best thing you could have asked of me."

I scoffed, but his gaze was steady. "You know, I lost Rebecca too. This wasn't the only relationship I've struggled with."

Rebecca was his ex-wife. Cam's mom.

"Ali, you were—*are*—the most important person in my life. And I know that I didn't show you that very well, but I..." He paused. "When I was growing up, the relationship I saw with my parents was not healthy. My dad did some of the things to my mom that I did to you. And I think I did them because I was so afraid of losing you." He put a hand out. "I know that seems counterintuitive. But if I made you insecure, it meant you'd never leave. And I know that's not right. It's not an excuse. But it *is* the reason. I never did any of it because I didn't love you. I did it because I *did*. And I didn't know how to deal with that."

I shook my head at him. "You *cheated* on me."

His eyes were sad. "I know. I know that I royally, *royally* messed this up. I have issues, Ali. Abandonment issues, problems with confidence. I think I did what I did because I could see you getting ready to leave me, and if I sabotaged the relationship, I was still in control of how you left. It's the same thing I did to Rebecca. I just...I have problems. And I have a lot of work I still need to do about that. But if I don't, I'm never going to be happy and I'm never going to be able to make anyone else happy either." He paused. "I'm giving you the house."

My arms dropped.

"You can have it," he said. "You can have whatever you want."

I licked my lips. "You'll move out?"

He nodded. "If that's what you want, yes."

I narrowed my eyes. "And what do *you* want? Because I can't imagine this act of generosity comes without a price."

He looked at the floor. "All I want is for you to be open to not hating me." His eyes came back up to mine. "And maybe, in a few months, after I've figured out my life a little more, you might have room in your heart to come with me to a few couple's counseling sessions—not because I did my end of the bargain. Because you want to. Just to see. Because I know you loved me once, and I know I can be better. And I am so scared of losing you."

I realized then that I recognized the look on his face. I'd just never seen him wear it before. He was being genuine.

I let my hard expression soften a little. "I'll think about it."

He smiled gently. "Okay. Thank you."

I paused a moment. "Thank you for being nice to Daniel that day."

He looked away from me. "I knew you were seeing someone. I'm not an idiot." His eyes came back to mine. "But grace costs you nothing. Isn't that what you said? I figured that's what you'd want to see from me."

Something about it made my eyes tear up. It wasn't that Neil had transcended. It was that in a roundabout way, Daniel had caused it.

Daniel was a ripple on the water. He touched everyone. Even the people he'd never met.

Neil gave me one last lingering look. Then he let himself out. When he opened the door, Bri was standing there, her hand raised to knock. "Neil," she said, looking surprised. "You in the wrong room? There's some orphans downstairs. If you hurry you can catch them, tell them Santa isn't real."

He ignored the comment, and her dirty look, and left.

Bri came in with two salt-rimmed glasses and a pitcher of something that smelled like pure tequila.

"Margaritas!" she sang. "It's super strong. I measured the Patrón with my heart." She kicked the door closed behind her. "So what did Satan want?"

"He wanted to apologize."

She set the glasses on my nightstand. "Like, actually?"

"I think so." I sat on the bed. "He's giving me the house."

"Really?"

"That's what he said. Also, my dad put me next to him at dinner tomorrow," I added.

"Of course he did." She stuck a finger in her mouth like she was gagging.

She started pouring our drinks. "I wouldn't put too much stock in that apology. Just so you know, nine out of ten times, people like that don't actually change. They just learn to be better manipulators, so you *think* they did, and then they do allll the same shit."

I nodded. "I know. They don't always change." I paused. "But I *do* believe he wants to."

She thought about it for a moment and then bobbed her head. "Okay. I'll give him that much."

She handed me the pink concoction and plopped on the bed next to me with her own glass. "A toast," Bri said. "To my soon-to-be-ex-husband. May he get that antibiotic-resistant strain of chlamydia."

I laughed and we clinked our glasses. Then we took a sip and winced.

"Oh, my God." I coughed.

"Whooo!" She shook her head, choking. "Wow. My check-liver light just went on."

I laughed, making a face.

"I think we've already had enough." She took my glass from me and put it on the dresser next to hers before sitting back down.

I lay back on the bed on top of the skirt of my dress, and she lay with me. We both stared at the ceiling, in a cloud of tulle.

"I miss him..." I whispered.

She paused for a long beat. "I know."

We went quiet for a moment.

"I called him last night. I couldn't help it. It feels impossible, Bri. How am I going to get through this?"

She turned to look at me. "You know what's great about Derek and his wife? I've been thinking a lot about this."

"What."

"There's nothing in it for him except for *her*. Your parents hate her. His friends don't get it. He had to move to Cambodia to be with her. Nothing about their being together is simple. So you know he's with her because he really loves her. There's no other explanation." She looked back at my ceiling fan. "There's something so peaceful about that, to just hit zero fucks about everything else but the person you love." She paused. "I wish *I* had that."

"I love Daniel more than I've ever loved anyone, but it doesn't make the rest of it disappear."

"It's not supposed to make it disappear. It just prioritizes things."

I shook my head. "I should be happy right now," I whispered. "I got my house. I got the job I wanted. My parents are off my back. I'm fulfilling my obligation to Royaume. Neil is finally going to be out of my life. I'm going to be able to help thousands of people, save lives, make a difference. And I am absolutely, one hundred percent *miserable*. I am so unhappy, Bri, I can't even stand it. If all these things are so wonderful and so important and so meaningful, then why do I feel like this?"

"Because you can't breathe."

I lolled my head to look at her. "What?"

"You're dead inside. You've lost the thing that gives you life."

I watched her quietly. "Is that how you felt when Nick left?"

She scoffed. "Fuck no. You're way worse than I was."

I snorted.

"Seriously, I wouldn't give that jackass the satisfaction. But you? You're a mess."

I laughed a little.

She turned to look at me. "Can I ask you a question?"

"Yeah…"

"If you could wipe your whole life clean and rebuild it from scratch and nobody would question how you've done it, what order would you put it in? Royaume first? Then your parents? Then Daniel?"

I shook my head. "No…"

"Then what?"

I paused to think about it a moment. "Daniel. Then Wakan. Then Royaume and everything else."

She jabbed a finger at me. "*That's* why you feel like shit, Ali. You're all out of order."

I blinked at her. "What do you mean?"

She propped herself on her elbows. "What I mean is you have been conditioned your entire life to live for everyone else. To do what's expected of you, to blindly serve. You were promised to Royaume Northwestern before you were even *born*. And it's a super important thing and I'm not saying it isn't, but that doesn't mean you have to do it. You *can* decide to put yourself first— you do have a choice. It's not an easy choice. It's not without consequences. But you *do* have a choice.

"If your life is this bad without Daniel in it, then maybe you need to take another look at your priorities. Derek did. I mean, for him to do this Cambodia thing, he'd have to have felt like you feel right now, don't you think? I don't think he didn't care about Royaume or you or his parents. I just think at the end of the day he just didn't care more than he cared about *her*." She shrugged. "She was his nonnegotiable."

"His nonnegotiable..."

"Yeah. The one thing he couldn't live without. Everything else was just everything else."

I shook my head at her. "But...but I can't leave Royaume—"

"I mean, can't you? You're going to help people, no matter where you end up, Ali. Yeah, it's not gonna be on the scale that you can at Royaume. But you can still save lives. Derek is. He found a way. And personally, I think a hundred and twenty-five years is a nice round number to end it on, if you want my opinion."

I sat up and gawked at her.

"What? Seriously. If you left, would you feel worse than you do right now?" she asked. "If you just said 'Fuck it' and dipped, would you be as unhappy as you are today?"

I blinked at her. Because the answer was remarkably simple. "No."

"You don't have to feel like this. You literally don't. Quit. Leave. Pick him. Pick *yourself.*"

I stared at her a long moment. Then I started to breathe hard.

I wasn't allowed to think about leaving. *I* couldn't be the one to make this suggestion, because it was too selfish and too self-serving. It was a forbidden fantasy, too traitorous for me to even entertain. But the second Bri spoke it into the universe, my heart grabbed onto it and ran.

Because what if I did?

What if I quit?

What if just for once I did what *I* wanted? Instead of thinking about my parents or the legacy or the plethora of people I'd never met who would benefit one day from me staying where I was.

My mind immediately went there and played out quitting in my head, like a movie on fast forward.

I was mentally in my car, driving to Wakan, diving into Daniel's arms, sobbing into his neck, begging for his forgiveness.

The relief at just *thinking* this was palpable.

The thought that I could end my misery, stop my suffering, was such an enormous weight off my shoulders, I felt like I wanted to jump off the bed and bolt from the room. I could feel the idea getting so big and alive in just the few moments it was out, it no longer fit into the tiny box of impossible things that I had kept it in.

What if I *did*...

But I *couldn't*. Could I?

How could I live with the guilt? With the shame?

Without my parents...

Because for all their faults, they were still the only ones I'd ever have. And if I did this, they would never speak to me again. It would be worse than what Derek did. I'd be ending the legacy. It would never be forgiven. *Ever.* I would lose them forever.

But then how could I live with losing Daniel forever?

How could I wake up every day for the next fifty years and function like this, knowing that I didn't have to. That feeling this was a choice, a decision *I* made. That I'd picked this for me *and* him.

And that was the most crucial part of all.

How Daniel must feel, having this breakup thrust on him against his will. Having no say in any of it. Wasn't that worse than all the rest of it? Hurting someone I loved whose only crime had been unconditionally loving me back?

My parents had never loved me unconditionally. Never. So then why was *I* loving *them* that way? Why did they deserve that? Why did I think I had to sell my soul instead of them maybe learning to be open-minded or tolerant or just *quiet* about the choices their children were making?

But I knew why I thought I had to give them that...

I could hear my therapist in my head, breaking it down for me the way she probably would have been doing for weeks if I'd still been going to see her.

My dad was my abuser.

He was no different than Neil.

And my mom was his enabler.

I'd spent my whole life chasing my father's affection and approval, accepting his hurtful words, letting him get away with it. And I'd always thought Mom was a victim too, that we were in it together—and maybe in a way we were. But for the first time, maybe ever, I saw it differently.

Because she never protected us.

Mom had *normalized* this abuse. Indulged it. She'd made me a participant, reinforced this behavior by giving my father what he wanted when he acted this way. The most influential woman in my life had modeled this for me from the day I was born and told me to take it. She'd taught me this, primed me for my relationship with Neil. Made me believe that this was what love looked like.

Bri was right. I'd been taught to placate assholes.

I'd been taught by *Mom*.

My heart started to pound.

It was too much to unpack now, all the layers of dysfunction and the consequences of their existence. I couldn't think about who I'd be if I'd never been born to this family or if I'd been shown love without conditions or a mother with the strength to enforce the boundaries she never could. I couldn't go back. I didn't even want to.

I just wanted *out*.

I didn't want to coddle my toxic parents. I didn't want to die a martyr on the pyre of Royaume Northwestern, no matter how honorable that might be. I didn't want my eighty-hour-a-week job because even though it should be, it wasn't filling my well. I didn't want this house or this life.

All I wanted was Daniel.

Being without Daniel was worse than anything I'd ever experienced. And I couldn't have known this until I lived it. I couldn't in my wildest dreams have imagined how utterly unlivable this life would be without him in it, until it actually happened.

But Daniel could.

He knew, weeks ago, *months* ago, what this would feel like. It was why he'd been willing to leave Wakan for me. He'd known. And *I* hadn't.

I had to drown first.

And I was finally, *finally* ready to save myself.

Something flipped in my brain.

An enormous, stuck gear slowly turned inside of me, and an unmovable building block of my very makeup shifted. Daniel rose to the top, and everything else repositioned with a heavy metallic clank that echoed through my entire existence. For the first time in my life, my parents and Royaume Northwestern took second seat to something else, and the moment they did, a flood of new thinking poured out. Ideas I never would have considered began bubbling up, sloshing around, spilling into my mind. A mental clog disintegrated, and alternate pathways started to form.

And then I knew what to do. I knew it so clearly, I started to laugh.

I got up and darted across the room for my phone.

Bri twisted to watch me. "What are you doing?"

"I'm calling an emergency meeting of the hospital board," I said, pulling up my email.

She shook her head. "But—it's a *Friday*. They're not going to come talk to you tonight—"

"They will if they still want a Montgomery on staff this time tomorrow."

I hurriedly typed out the email and hit Send.

It was what Daniel had said last night. When you don't care, everything's on your terms. They can take it or leave it. It doesn't matter to you, so ask for whatever the hell you want.

It's not that I didn't care about Royaume. It's that I didn't care more about it than Daniel.

So let the negotiations begin…

CHAPTER 37

ALEXIS

I'd been calling Daniel since last night. His phone was going right to voicemail, and my texts were unread.

I was exhausted. I'd barely slept. My meeting with the hospital board went until almost midnight, and then I'd spent two hours on a satellite phone call with my brother and his wife. I had to rewrite my speech, get Daniel a ticket to the gala, and put a tux on hold for him at a shop in Minneapolis. Then I left him a message, begging him to come. When he didn't call me back or return my texts, I called the VFW looking for him. Hannah said he hadn't been there in weeks, so I called Doug.

Doug told me Daniel said he was moving out of Wakan. That he couldn't be there anymore. That he was probably already gone.

Because of *me*.

I'd broken his heart.

I'd thought letting him go was the most humane thing. The most humane thing would have been to let him stay.

Daniel had been ready to give up his whole world for me

once. He'd always known what came first. He was willing to trade Wakan, the Grant House, his legacy—all to join me in this shallow, hostile place, because being without me was unacceptable to him.

And I hadn't felt the same when it mattered.

I had allowed him to think I was embarrassed by him, that he wasn't worth any sacrifice, no matter how big. That he wasn't everything to me that I was to him. I'd had one foot out the door since the very beginning, I'd never given him everything, I'd denied him, hid him. And then I abandoned him.

I *betrayed* him.

So if he never wanted to speak to me again, could I even blame him?

I had to push it down. It wasn't going to help get me through what I had to do. And I was doing it whether he showed up or not.

It was six o'clock and I was at the quasquicentennial. I couldn't shake hands and hold a phone. My gown didn't have pockets, so my cell was back at the table in a clutch where I couldn't check it. I'd given Daniel's number to Bri and asked her to keep trying to get in touch with him. I didn't know how that was going, because she'd disappeared forty-five minutes ago, and I hadn't seen her since.

The event was well under way. More than five hundred were in attendance, a carefully cultivated invite-only list. A red carpet welcomed guests into a *Midsummer Night's Dream*–themed venue.

The ceiling had been transformed into a night sky complete with twinkling stars. Flowers dripped from the walls, and candles flickered on the linen-covered tables under towering floral centerpieces with bejeweled dragonflies in them. They'd even brought in trees. Servers in white gloves carried trays of appetizers and champagne around. Ice sculptures sat at every bar. There was a live band. Style magazines were here with other media. They were calling it the party of the century. I'd already posed for dozens of photos and done half a dozen interviews while Mom looked on, pleased.

My parents looked like the king and queen in a room full of their subjects. Everyone was shiny and glittery. Jessica and Gabby were standing in their gowns with their distinguished husbands over by the bar with Neil and Dad.

This was the first time in more than forty years that one of my parents wasn't the speaker for a big Royaume event. My doing it was a ceremonious passing of the torch, something Derek would have been doing without question if he hadn't left.

I could still picture how it would have gone if this gala had taken place a year ago. This alternate reality. My brother, handsome and charismatic, making everyone laugh during his speech that no doubt would have been equal parts charming and inspiring. I would have been here, but I would have been largely ignored. Insecure arm candy to Neil, who was a bigger deal than I was. Only halfheartedly introduced by my legendary father—and only when I was standing close enough that it was absolutely necessary.

So much had changed.

And it was going to change more still.

As people arrived, they had to make their way down an enormous marble staircase to the ballroom floor where the tables were. It made every entrance a grand one, and part of the fun was watching everyone. Mom and I stood at the base of the stairs, greeting people as they came in.

Mom knew everyone's name. She'd whisper it to me before they got to the bottom of the steps. Foreign princes and dignitaries, real estate moguls and politicians, actors. There was even a famous vlogger here, a big donor for the ALS clinical trials Royaume was doing.

There were billions of dollars in this room. Bottomless pockets. And for the first time, I knew *exactly* what I wanted to do with that money. I knew who I'd be to the Montgomery legacy, how Royaume would remember me, what the history books would write, and how I'd spend the rest of my life.

In the last twenty-four hours, I'd achieved a kind of clarity that I'd never thought possible.

My whole life I'd always felt a little fractured and scattered. Probably because it was always someone else trying to decide what I needed to be. I was a mosaic of someone else's design where none of the fragments were put in the right place. And now I had finally put myself together and I recognized myself for the very first time.

I'd made my arrangements with the board. I'd coordinated with my brother and his wife. Everything was in place. I just hoped Daniel showed up for it.

As the steady stream of arriving guests turned into a trickle, Mom leaned in. "I am so impressed, Alexis. I know this isn't usually what you're comfortable with, but you're doing so well."

I kept my eyes trained on the top of the steps, hoping that the next person to appear there would be Daniel.

"I think you'd be surprised at how motivated I am," I said.

Gabby and Jessica left their husbands at the bar with Neil and came over. Mom saw them coming and excused herself to chat with an old colleague and left me with them. This was the first time I'd spoken to either of them since the day Daniel came into the ER.

As soon as I was in earshot, Jessica sighed loudly. "How long are they going to make us wait for dinner? At five hundred dollars a seat you'd think they'd at least feed us at a reasonable hour."

Gabby stopped in front of me, poking at the ice in her mojito with a straw. "Your dress is pretty."

"Thanks," I mumbled, glancing at the top of the steps.

She put her straw to her mouth. "So Philip says Neil asked him to help him look for an apartment."

When I didn't answer she went on. "That's good, right?"

"It is," I said flatly.

"So, like, that's it then?" she asked, talking around her straw. "You guys are over?"

"We've *been* over," I reminded her.

"I know. It's just kind of romantic that he tried so hard to get you back. I was kind of rooting for him at the end."

I scoffed internally. Which part was romantic? Him holding me hostage in my own home? Or him finally getting the help he needed so he could be a halfway decent human being worth dating?

I didn't bother to reply.

She just wanted gossip. And she'd have plenty of it by the end of the night—but none of it would be about Neil.

Gabby shifted her feet like my silence was making her impatient. "So have you talked to that guy?" she asked.

I looked at her now and cocked my head. "You mean the squirrel guy?"

She blinked at me. "I—"

"You met him. You spent three days living in his home. You

know his name," I said. "Maybe you should check your one-star review for the Grant House and come back with it."

She gawked at me.

Even Jessica's jaw dropped.

A horn trumpeted. A cinematic touch to let everyone know it was time to head to the tables. Jessica cleared her throat. "Finally. Let's go." She turned to take her seat and Gabby scurried after her.

Dad made his way over in his tux, holding a whiskey, and Mom finished up her chat and joined us at the bottom of the steps. "Neil's getting you a glass of wine," Dad said, nodding at the line at the bar.

People were beginning to sit down, but Mom and Dad didn't move.

Mom probably wanted to be there to greet any stragglers, and Dad was either waiting on Neil or wanting to keep his imposing position over the room. Either way, it was a problem.

I wanted to get my purse and check my phone. But I was too afraid Daniel would show up and walk right into my parents without me there. So I stayed where I was too, chewing on my lip and nervously glancing at the top of the steps.

Every second that ticked by without Daniel arriving, I got more anxious. The gala started at five-thirty. He was over an hour late.

I began to get the sinking feeling that he wasn't coming.

I knew he missed me. I knew he still loved me. I could feel it when I was on the phone with him that night.

But that didn't mean he was going to forgive me.

A photo montage of the last hundred and twenty-five years of hospital history began to play as servers placed salads in front of guests. I would take the stage right after.

Dad took a swallow of his drink. "I trust your speech is ready," he said to me, his voice low. "This is a historic event. I hope you're adequately prepared."

I had to let a slow, calming breath out through my nose.

It was funny how these casual, careless jabs were so obvious to me now. I was so used to them growing up, I didn't even notice them. They were the building blocks of everything I'd accepted from Neil.

Instead of giving me words of encouragement before I stood in front of five hundred people, Dad chose to remind me just how little confidence he had in me. He wanted me to know that he assumed I didn't understand the significance of this gala and hadn't bothered to get ready for it. But mostly it annoyed me because it was a slight to Mom.

She'd been the one to coach and prepare me for this over the last few months, and he clearly didn't believe that Mom, who had been a professional public speaker for the last forty years, had done her due diligence before releasing me into the wild at arguably the most important Royaume event of her lifetime. It was insulting. And Mom ignored the implication, as usual, because she never chose to fight. For herself *or* me. But that was fine. Because for the first time in my life, I was ready to fight for myself.

I *was* prepared to give my speech. Though the one I was about to deliver wasn't the one we'd practiced. My parents had no idea what was about to happen. I'd asked the board to keep our discussion private, and they'd agreed.

Tonight would be full of surprises.

Black-and-white photos of the hospital's construction flickered across the jumbotrons. Then color photos. 1950s. 1960s. My family, featured in almost every single slide. We were at the mid

2000s in the montage when Neil started to make his way from the bar with my glass of wine. Dad leaned over. "Neil tells me you two had an encouraging discussion."

"It's good to hear the therapy's helping," I said dismissively, looking back to the top of the stairs.

"I'm glad you've come to your senses," he said, going on. "To think you could have been here with that boy." He chuckled into his glass.

I *snapped*.

My head whipped so fast I almost lost my tiara. "Don't you *ever* talk about Daniel like that in my presence ever again. Him *or* Nikki."

Mom's jaw dropped, and Dad lowered his glass and pinned me with a warning glare. "You be mindful of your tone, young lady," he said, his voice low.

I straightened my shoulders. *"No."*

Mom shifted uncomfortably. "Dear, I think they're about to call you up," she said quietly, putting a hand on my arm. "Maybe you should go stand by the stage. I'll make sure your drink makes it to the table—"

"I'm not sitting with you," I said sharply.

Mom blinked at me. "You're not sitting with us? Why not?"

"I bought new seats."

"You're not sitting with Neil?" Dad asked, looking confused.

"No, I am not. I've invited Daniel, and if I'm lucky he might actually show up, so I can *beg* him for forgiveness for the way I let you treat him."

The way *I* treated him.

The photo montage ended, and the CEO took the podium. I was on in two minutes.

I looked back and forth between my openmouthed parents, shaking my head. "Mom, I really hope you find your voice. I know it's in there. For your own sake, I hope to God you look for it."

I turned to my father.

"Dad, you are going to be a very lonely old man. Your world is about to be as small as your mind. You won't have your children. You won't get the privilege of knowing the people they love. You won't hold your grandchildren, you won't see them grow up." I shook my head. "But at least you'll have *Neil.*"

I turned and started for the stage. Then I stopped and looked back at them. "Also, you should know that effective tomorrow I've resigned from my position as chief."

Mom's face fell, and Dad went bright red.

"Do me a favor and let Neil know the house is his. I'll be moved out by the end of the week. I'll go ahead and disown myself to save you the trouble. Now excuse me. I have to go deliver a speech."

I picked up the skirt of my dress, made my way through the tables, and climbed the stage just as I was being introduced.

I took the podium to clapping, two large jumbotrons floating behind me. I thanked the CEO and adjusted my microphone as I looked out over the audience.

Even though my speech wasn't the one I'd practiced for months under Mom's tutelage, I didn't need a teleprompter or notes. I was ready. I felt completely and utterly calm. Like I was born to do this—and really, I *was.*

Dad never expected me to amount to much. And for a time, neither did I. My entire life, Dad made me feel like I was the weakest link, the most useless princess. A waste of my family's DNA.

But today I was a *Montgomery.*

It pulsed through my veins, poured out of me. It felt like I was the final form of everything my bloodline aspired to be. I was better at being a Montgomery than even Derek was—because I'd finally found the calling that anchored me to my birthright. It put fire in me. Gave me the tireless drive and razor-sharp focus of someone who believed in something.

And I couldn't wait to get started.

I scanned the crowd one more time for Bri and Daniel—and I saw that Bri had appeared at the back of the room. She waved and gave me a thumbs-up.

Was it a good-luck thumbs-up? Or a I-got-hold-of-Daniel thumbs-up? He wasn't with her...

I looked around the faces one more time, but I didn't see him. And I couldn't wait any longer to begin. So I did.

"Thank you for joining us on this historic milestone in Royaume Northwestern history." My voice was steady and confident. "On this day in 1897, the doors opened for the first time, and my great-great-great-grandfather Dr. Charles Edward Montgomery began his rounds. Today, a hundred and twenty-five years later, I am continuing a legacy that my family is unbelievably proud of, walking the halls of what's become one of the finest hospitals in the world.

"With your generous donations, we've pioneered medical breakthroughs, established ourselves as one of the leading research and training hospitals on the globe, and we've saved countless lives. Royaume is home to some of the best doctors ever to practice medicine. We are a destination for unparalleled talent, and we lead our industry in medical advancements. It is on the strength of this foundation that we are thrilled to announce to you tonight the new direction of the Montgomery Legacy and my family's relationship with Royaume Northwestern."

This was the moment my mother realized I was off script.

I watched her face register the last line, and she leaned over and said something hurried to my father.

"As you may know," I said, continuing, "I am the chief of emergency medicine here at Royaume. And if there's anything I've learned in my role, it's that in most cases, emergencies wouldn't be emergencies if patients had access to affordable routine medical care.

"Cost-prohibitive treatments cost lives.

"I have seen untreated cuts turn into sepsis. Sinus infections become pneumonia because a patient can't afford a simple doctor visit for antibiotics. I've had diabetic patients lose limbs because they're rationing insulin, stage-four terminal cancer that could have been detected earlier and treated with access to proper yearly screenings." I paused for effect and gave the audience an arched eyebrow. "I have seen patients stitch themselves up with gin and fishhooks because they can't afford a trip to the ER."

I gave the room a second to chuckle.

"There are only so many wings that we can add on to a building. So it's time for the healing power that is Royaume Northwestern to expand in a new way.

"Starting next week, we will be breaking ground on the first of Royaume's satellite clinic locations. These clinics will provide free medical care to underserved, low-income communities, beginning with a location in Grant County in the town of Wakan, and a second remote location in Cambodia, where my brother, Dr. Derek Montgomery, and his wife, Nikki, are already operating.

"I will be relocating to personally oversee the Wakan location.

"Over the next decade, it is our goal to expand this program to disadvantaged communities all over the world." I paused. "From this day forward, Royaume Northwestern will not just be here. It will be wherever we are needed most.

"It has been my absolute privilege to grow up a Montgomery in the Royaume Northwestern family. And I am excited and honored to continue our tradition of excellence by sharing the gift that is Royaume Northwestern beyond the walls that my forefathers built.

"Give generously today. Bid high. We are building a new beginning.

"Thank you."

Thunderous applause.

I could see Gabby and Jessica cheering and nodding. Neil was clapping. Bri was giving me a standing ovation, smiling so big, it looked like she was going to burst. And the funny thing was, my parents looked like that too. Mom was beaming, looking prouder than I'd ever seen her. Even Dad was grinning and clapping.

Ironically enough, this was probably the first time I'd actually impressed him. It was groundbreaking and innovative. Forward movement for the institution, something the hospital had never done before that brought Derek back into the fold and ensured the survival of the franchise for probably generations to come. And it hadn't even been hard to come up with it once I had my priorities straight, because it was in service to what I cared about most.

Daniel, Wakan, Royaume—and then everything else. In that order.

I went into that meeting ready to quit if they said no. But the board loved it. They got a big announcement for their anniversary gala, an exciting new initiative, and they got to keep two young and eager Montgomerys on staff—three. Because they were also getting Nikki.

Nikki would be adjacent to anything my brother did, and despite my father's shortsighted opinion about his daughter-in-law, Lola Simone was a powerful ally. Her fame gave her a global reach and hundreds of important connections— and she was very well respected for her humanitarian work. Nikki Montgomery would draw as many donors to Royaume Northwestern as my mother ever did. Her impact would be immeasurable and would ensure the success of this program. The board recognized this and had voted unanimously to support my proposal—and this was in part, because of *her*.

Maybe one day Dad would acknowledge that it was Nikki and Daniel that had led to all this. Maybe one day Dad would apologize and accept the lives Derek and I had chosen for ourselves and try to be a part of it. Learn some grace. I hoped he did. And I hoped that even if he didn't, Mom finally put her foot down and chose to do it anyway.

I knew from experience that sometimes when the wake-up call is big enough, you do, in fact, wake up.

Either way I was at peace with the choice I'd made. Derek and I both were.

But I still didn't see Daniel. He should have been here by now. If he was coming, he would have been.

My heart sank.

I didn't believe that he didn't know I was trying to reach him. Even if Bri and I couldn't get in touch with him and none of my texts or voicemails went through, Doug would have called him by now. He knew.

I had his answer. It was no.

I'd just hurt him too much, too many times. And I couldn't even blame him for being done.

But it didn't change anything. Because I would still move to Wakan.

I was a little more Grant than Montgomery, I realized. I wanted to change the world. But I wanted to start *there*. And I would.

Even if their mayor never spoke to me again.

I exited the podium to clapping. I was stopped by a few excited donors the second I got off the stage. Everyone wanted their name on a building, and we had two new clinics up for grabs. I was happy for the enthusiasm, but I just really wanted to go check my phone and talk to Bri. I was shaking hands and trying to break away when I saw a figure appear at the top of the marble staircase. I held my breath as he came into view.

Daniel...

My heart stopped at the sight of him.

He was in a black tux. One hand on the railing, and every woman in the room looking at him—but he was only looking at *me*. And I'd never seen him so handsome or so happy.

"Excuse me," I breathed.

I threaded through the crowd, picked up the skirt of my dress, and started to run. He grinned when he saw me coming and began jogging down the stairs.

I was so relieved to see him, I couldn't tell if I was laughing or crying or a little bit of both.

We collided in the middle of the dance floor. His world and mine, crashing together in front of everyone.

"You came," I said, my arms wrapped around him.

"Of course I came," he whispered.

"Daniel, I am so sorry," I gasped. "Please, *please* forgive me."

He pulled away and cupped my face in his hands.

I peered up at him with tears in my eyes. "I love you so much. I made the biggest mistake—"

"Shhhhhhh..."

"No. That day you came to my house, I should have packed a bag right there and then and left with you. I should have left months before that. I thought I'd ruined everything. I didn't think I was ever going to see you again."

"I'd like to tell you that I'm strong enough to stay mad at you," he said, his voice a little thick. "But I'm not. I came the second I got your message. Then my truck broke down outside of the tux shop and Bri had to come pick me up. I didn't know how to use Uber."

I laughed, tears pinching from my eyes.

"Did you hear my speech?" I asked, wiping my cheeks.

"I did. I watched from the top of the steps. I didn't want you to see me, didn't want to make you nervous."

"I was going to quit, Daniel. If they hadn't agreed to it, I was going to leave to be with you anyway. I was coming to Wakan with or without Royaume."

He smiled gently at me. "God, you look beautiful," he breathed.

I smiled at him through tears and we stood there, just being.

It was incredible how whole I felt. How he completed the final piece in my mosaic. I would have never been right without him. Even if I'd never met him or ever knew who he was.

The band started playing "True" by Spandau Ballet. Daniel raised an eyebrow. "I don't suppose you want to dance with me?"

I smiled. "Yes." I nodded. "Of course I want to dance with you."

I put an arm around his neck. He put a palm over the one

on his heart and started to turn me in this magical room full of flowers and twinkling stars.

It felt like a fairy tale. He looked like a prince in an enchanted forest.

But then he'd always been a prince. It was just the first time everyone else saw it too.

We were the only ones on the dance floor. The huge poof of my dress swept around as he spun me, and a spotlight clicked on and began to follow us.

The whole room was watching. I wanted them to.

I wanted everyone to see me with the man I loved. Because I was *proud* to love him in front of my world. I would have been proud if he'd come in his jeans and a T-shirt, mud on his boots, tattoos and all. He could have walked in with Kevin Bacon, and I would have smiled and dove into his arms.

"So what does this new job mean?" he asked, turning me. "Are you gonna have to travel to other clinics when they open? Are we nomads now?" he joked.

I laughed a little. "No. My job is just to make sure the clinics are funded. Basically, I have to go to a *lot* of parties. We should probably buy this tuxedo," I said, tugging on his lapel.

He pulled on the collar. "It's really uncomfortable. I've never worn one before."

"You should try Spanx."

He laughed.

"So, I guess I'll have to move you into the big house. You'll need the closet space for all the ball gowns."

I smiled. "Can we have the damask room?" I asked.

"Of course. But…" he said, giving me a stern look, "I can't live with you there unless we're married."

I gasped playfully. "What? Why not?"

"That's my grandparents' bedroom. Can't do the things I want to do with you in there unless you're my wife. Wouldn't feel right."

I pretended to think about it. "Hmmm. Plus, it's haunted. I'm not sure I should be in there alone. We should probably get married right away. I had to promise the hospital board not to drop my last name, but I think Dr. Alexis Montgomery Grant has a nice ring to it, don't you?"

He narrowed his eyes. "You wouldn't mind being married to a carpenter in a tiny town in the middle of nowhere?"

"I can't really think of a better way to spend the next fifty years. And anyway, we sort of have to. Doug bet me a hundred bucks that we wouldn't live happily ever after."

He laughed, and his whole face lit up.

Dr. Alexis Montgomery Grant.

It occurred to me that one day Daniel and I would be remembered with yellowing framed newspaper articles hung on the walls of the VFW like the Grants before us, and the idea made me feel so proud and complete, I couldn't even articulate it. It was better than stately paintings hung in hospital hallways or articles in *Forbes* or documentaries on the History Channel—though we'd probably have those too.

We would have the best of both worlds. I could dance the night away with him at an extravagant ball and then let him take me home to care for our town, our people—our *family.* Because sometimes family isn't what you're born into. Sometimes family is found.

And I'd found mine in Wakan.

I'd found mine in *him.*

I started to tear up again.

"Why are you crying?" he asked gently.

"Because I'm just so happy." I peered up at him through my wet lashes. "Let's never leave this place. Let's just stay here in this moment forever."

He peered around, bobbing his head. "Well, I'm not saying I'd like to build a summer home here. But the trees are actually quite lovely."

I laughed so hard, he pulled me closer to him by the waist to put his forehead to mine.

I beamed. "Kiss me, Daniel Grant."

He looked scandalized. "Right here? In front of everyone?"

"Right here. In front of *everyone*."

He stopped turning me, and we stood under the huge crystal chandelier in the middle of the room, the entire gala watching, all eyes on us. He hovered his lips an inch from mine.

"As. You. *Wish*."

EPILOGUE

DANIEL

Seven Months Later

Doug nodded at my wife across the VFW. "A hundred bucks if you can get her to give me Monday off."

I laughed, racking up the billiard balls. "That is between you and your boss."

"Come on, man. I've got a hot date."

I paused to look at him over my shoulder. "She's seen the pictures of you and she's still coming?"

Brian laughed.

Liz looked up from behind the bar and smiled at the sound, and Brian grinned back at her.

Doug worked part-time at the clinic. He got his EMT certificate and was the Royaume-Wakan clinic designated ambulance driver. It was an extremely part-time job that consisted mostly of making sure the rig was stocked with supplies and gas, and then driving someone to the hospital in Rochester, should the situation require it. They had inventory Monday.

Brian nodded at him. "Take her to work. Show her the ambulance. It'll make you look cool."

"Alexis won't let me. And this fucker won't get me the day off. Man, I wingmanned both of you idiots and this is the thanks I get?"

I looked at my watch. "If by wingmanning you mean you made us both look good in comparison, yes, you wingmanned us."

Brian snorted.

Doug took a swallow of his Fanta. "I don't even want to *think* about the shitty dick pics that'd be floating around if it wasn't for me. You owe your entire marriage to my expertise. You know what? Fuck you. And don't ask me to watch your dumb dog again. I'm not doing it."

I laughed.

Alexis finished up talking to Doreen over by the jukebox and started making her way across the bar to me. I smiled as I watched her coming.

We hadn't told anyone yet. She wanted to wait until she was twelve weeks along first. It was way too early to notice the bump, and she was wearing my camo hoodie so you wouldn't have seen it even if you could. But it made me grin ear to ear knowing what I knew, and that made *her* grin ear to ear too.

We'd already decided that our kids would be Montgomery Grants. That way they could pick whatever legacy they wanted.

It was almost a year from the day that I first laid eyes on my wife. A beautiful woman in a fancy car, nose first in a ditch, talking to me through a one-inch crack in the window.

My life was so different now. I couldn't have ever imagined how that chance encounter could lead to all this. How happy I'd be because of that damn raccoon.

We'd had the wedding three months after the gala. Alexis wanted to get married before the construction of the clinic was complete and she'd be too busy to leave for our honeymoon. The whole town shut down for it.

I'd made our wedding rings from the wood of the banister in the house. I etched them to match and waterproofed them. I thought maybe Alexis would want a diamond, and I could have sprung for one with how well my business was doing, but she loved the idea of me making the rings.

We got married at Doug's barn. Jane's catered, and Alexis ordered me a groom's cake from Nadia Cakes that looked like a raccoon to commemorate how we met.

Alexis's brother and his famous wife came, so we had to get three hundred and fifty NDAs signed.

I really liked Derek and Nikki. They flew in from Cambodia and stayed with us at the house for two weeks.

Alexis's dad didn't come to the wedding.

We knew he wouldn't. But her mom did, and we both appreciated that she had made the effort. We knew it wasn't easy for her to go against her husband. But she wasn't willing to lose her kids because of him. Alexis said her mom had been to therapy too, which my wife was really happy about.

Dr. Jennifer Montgomery was a nice woman. And I think she liked her daughter-in-law, Nikki, too. They had quite a bit in common, being the philanthropists that they are.

Alexis's mom stayed with us for a week. And when she left, she gifted us with a month-long honeymoon. It was a thoughtful present on many levels. But mostly because it was meant for *me*. Alexis told her mom I'd never been anywhere. So she sent us to Italy, Paris, Greece, London, and Ireland. It was all first-class and five-star hotels. A trip of a lifetime. We'd had a blast.

Alexis always gave me the window seat on the plane, since I'd never flown before. We ate at some of the best restaurants in the world. I'd learned which fork to use and I mastered Uber and those key card thingies that open hotel room doors. We saw ancient ruins and castles and spent days on white sand beaches. I came back even more in love with my wife than I was when we left, which was hard to imagine.

We were happy to be home though—and so was Doug, because he'd watched Hunter while we were away, and our stupid dog kept bringing live rodents into the house.

Alexis closed the distance between us, and I slipped a hand around her waist. "Ready to go?" I asked.

"Yeah. I'm feeling a little ick," she said quietly.

"Okay." I looked up at the guys. "Hey, we're heading out."

"See ya," Brian said, still smiling at his girlfriend.

Doug nodded at my wife. "So when's Briana coming down again? She still single?" He bounced his eyebrows.

Alexis laughed. "Doug, if she knew where you lived, she'd burn your house down."

"What?" He looked back and forth between us. "She was totally into me!"

Everyone started cracking up.

Doug had followed Briana around with his guitar at our wedding. She'd found a spray bottle full of water and used it for the rest of the night to squirt him when he got too close. At least Nikki showed him how to tune the guitar while she was here...

"I'll see you tomorrow," I said, still chuckling. I took my jacket off the back of the barstool and put it around my wife's shoulders and walked her out.

We pushed into the brisk April night air.

We'd walked here for the exercise, so we were walking home. I took her hand, and she hugged my arm and put her head on my shoulder.

"How you feeling?" I asked.

"I'm just tired."

"I think you should party less."

She laughed. "Ha. I had that vaccine clinic today. I must have done two hundred shots. And not the fun kind."

I kissed the top of her head. "I'll run you a bath when we get home."

Then I'd get the fireplace going in the bedroom while she soaked. When she got out, we'd curl up in bed with a book. In the morning I'd get up before she did and make her breakfast before she went into the clinic and I went to the garage to work on my latest commission.

At lunch I'd come meet her at Jane's or bring her something if she was too busy to take a break. Then for dinner we'd cook together, maybe watch a movie.

The house seemed so happy that we were in it. It sighed around us. And Wakan was happy too. And *healthy*. For the first time in the town's history, we had a real doctor. We didn't have to drive to Rochester. She did house calls for Pops. Alexis was able to monitor Doug's depression meds, so he got back on them and was doing better than ever. Lily had just come in for her one-year checkup. And the clinic helped with the tourists too. They didn't like having to drive forty-five minutes to get treatment either.

The clinic was so busy it was hard to imagine that we'd managed to not have one for the last hundred and twenty-five years. And all in exchange for us attending a few fund-raisers once in a while. A luncheon at a golf course, the gala that we'd do once a year, a private dinner now and then with big donors. I always went with her. They were fun. I got to meet Melinda Gates last month.

I always marveled at my wife. At the polished, sophisticated woman she was, explaining in articulate detail the statistics of underserved communities and the importance of their donations. And then she'd come home with me and put on her mud boots and go to Doug's farm and help him deliver a goat or something. I loved that she was so squarely a Montgomery *and* a Grant.

Kevin Bacon trotted across the street ahead of us wearing the reflective vest Doreen had made for him. "There he goes," Alexis said.

Kevin was our official town mascot now, allowed to wander Wakan with impunity. Tourists funded his escapades by sending Doug money via the Venmo on the side of Kevin's vest in exchange for taking pictures with our famous pig. It was Doug's most lucrative side hustle yet. He probably *could* give me the hundred bucks if I got him Monday off.

We crossed the bridge and started down the moonlit bike path under the apple trees.

"Huh," she said, hugging my arm.

"What?"

"I could swear those weren't blooming when we walked over."

I looked up. She was right. The trees were in full bloom. I couldn't remember either, though it seemed like something I would have noticed.

"Do you remember that night?" she asked. "When we were walking and the petals fell?"

I nodded. "Yup. The night with Liz and Jake. The night that you were going to tell me you couldn't see me anymore."

Even as far behind us as that was, it still made my chest get a little tight thinking about it.

"That was the night I think I realized I was in love with you," she said.

"Well. That explains why you tried to give me fifty thousand dollars. I'll take that now, by the way."

She laughed.

"It was the night you gave me the heart rock," she said, a little distantly. "The night of the spaghetti dinner, and I felt so loved and appreciated. I think I knew even then that I was supposed to be here."

A few petals began to drift down as we walked. Like a gentle snow made of springtime.

"I was one month in and I would have given you anything. Even then," I said, remembering how I felt. "And now I'll always have you and I can't even believe it's real."

She shook her head. "*I* can't believe the universe sent a raccoon and fog to put my car in a ditch so I'd end up there hitched to the mayor."

I gave her an amused glance. "Are you telling me that you, a woman of science, believes that God had nothing better to do than trap you in Wakan?"

She shrugged. "Maybe she didn't. And the town gets what it needs, doesn't it?"

"The town *does* get what it needs..."

She stopped walking and turned so she could wrap her arms around me. "I don't like that you think of me leaving you when you think of that night. That night was magic to me. Most of it."

I put her face into my hands. "We have a whole lifetime ahead of us full of magic nights. We don't need that one."

She smiled and I looked into her eyes and I saw everything. The rest of my life. I saw children and grandchildren and rocking chairs on the back porch of the house overlooking the river and two old people, dying on the same day because the world would never be cruel enough to make either one of us exist without the other.

The trees rustled in the wind, and petals floated down around us. They hovered in slow motion for a second time. The universe had dipped its snow globe again, just for us.

And we stood there in the magic, knowing full well what it was.

DON'T MISS BRI'S STORY,
COMING IN SPRING 2023!

ACKNOWLEDGMENTS

Thank you to beta readers Jeanette Theisen Jett, Kim Kao, Terri Puffer Burrell, Amy Edwards Norman, Dawn Cooper, Trish Grigorian, Lynn Fialkow, and sensitivity reader Leigh Kramer.

Thank you to George and Yasmin Eapen. Thank you to ER nurse Terri Saenz Martinez, ER doctor Brian Lovig, and his wife, Mackenzie, who relayed my weird ER questions to her husband. Thank you to firefighter paramedic Suzanna Hales Keeran, Dr. Pam Voelker, and Dr. Christine Muffoletto for answering questions about life on call and working in a hospital. Thank you to labor and delivery nurse Liesl Burnes and OB-GYN Susan Tran for helping me get the delivery scene right. Thank you to domestic violence advocates Ashlee Anderson and Virginia Gonzalez, a former board member for DVSAS, for helping me write about domestic violence with sensitivity and understanding. Thank you to Sue Lammert, a licensed clinical counselor specializing in trauma, for helping me to understand the psychological impact of the abuse cycle.

Please know that any errors in this book, should there be any, were fully my fault and not those of the professionals who loaned me their expertise.

A special thank-you to my best friend, Lindsay Van Horn, who has had many frank conversations with me about her harrowing experience with domestic violence. It was she who told me that nobody could save her until she was ready to save herself. She did, and she's happily remarried to a wonderful man.

Another thank-you to Ashley Spivey, who allowed me to use her words: I believe you, this is not your fault, and you don't deserve this. Ashley is a brave and vocal survivor of domestic violence. This was such a powerful statement that I asked if I could repeat it in this book. Thank you for letting me do so, so that this message can reach more of those who need to hear it.

The average abuse victim attempts to leave their abuser seven times before getting away for good. Many do not leave with their lives. If you or anyone you know is in need of help, please reach out to any of these organizations. There are resources available and there are people who understand.

National Domestic Violence Hotline
https://www.thehotline.org/
Tel: 1-800-799-7233
Text START to tel: 1-800-799-7233
National Resource Center on Domestic Violence
https://www.nrcdv.org/
The National Coalition Against Domestic Violence
https://ncadv.org/
Stronghearts Native Helpline
Tel: 1-844-7NATIVE (1-844-762-8483)
Love Is Respect
https://www.loveisrespect.org/
Tel: 1-866-331-9474
Text: LOVEIS 22522

YOUR BOOK CLUB RESOURCE

READING GROUP GUIDE

QUESTIONS FOR READERS

1. What are the pros and cons of Alexis's lifestyle versus Daniel's? Which would you choose? What is your definition of success?

2. Alexis is mistreated by Neil, and Liz by Jake. Compare and contrast those forms of abuse. What kind of impact does each have?

3. Alexis has a lot of expectations put on her by her family. Did you feel that was fair? Do you agree with how she handled the situation? How is that different from or similar to the pressures Daniel feels? Are there times in your own life when the pressure of expectation has conflicted with your own wants and needs?

4. In some ways Wakan feels like a place out of time, its own separate world. Do you think that's part of its protection? Do you believe that a place can have a spirit, the way Pops explained?

5. What are some of the fairy-tale similarities you could find in the story?

6. Gabby's behavior during the girls' weekend is the first time Alexis has thought about the power of her privilege. Do you think Gabby was right to leave a poor rating for their stay at Grant House? What would you have done in the same situation? Or at a restaurant? Or for an Etsy shop?

7. Alexis refers to herself as Dr. Alexis through most of the book...until she decides to marry Daniel. Then she becomes Dr. Alexis Montgomery Grant. How do you think that reflects the way she felt about her identity and family legacy?

8. Who would be on your zombie apocalypse team?

Q & A WITH ABBY

What made you want to tell this story?

My best friend was in an incredibly abusive marriage before we met. She barely escaped with her life. She has since gone on to be an advocate for survivors of domestic violence and she speaks openly about what she lived through.

I didn't understand the cycle of abuse before I met Lindsay. I couldn't wrap my brain around why a woman wouldn't just leave. Many people are unaware of the power dynamic that takes place in an abusive relationship and how to help someone enduring it. It wasn't until Lindsay began to talk to me about it that I could grasp how complicated the situation was and how hard it is to get out. Here was this intelligent, capable, strong woman who ended up in this awful marriage that she felt powerless to escape. It shattered all the preconceived notions I had about who this happens to and why. It was very eye-opening.

I can't think of a better way to educate than to put a reader right into the brain of someone living it. I did a lot of due diligence in writing this to make sure the advice Alexis gives Liz is accurate. My hope is that it can act as a road map out to those witnessing it or surviving it.

In what ways do you relate to Alexis? To Daniel?

I can relate to both of them. I grew up without money. I never went to college. I had to start working at sixteen, which planted me in the service industry where I could get a job without any advanced education. I have cried in many a walk-in freezer—LOL. Alexis is closer to my age, and now that I'm more financially secure, I can afford some nicer things. So I really was able to live in both of their heads pretty easily. But if I had to pick one, I'd say I related most to Daniel.

Daniel is just so salt of the earth. And I loved seeing Alexis's house through Daniel's eyes. Alexis was completely oblivious to her own lifestyle. We never understand when we're in her POV just how opulent and extravagant her life is—because she doesn't realize it herself. She's so used to it, none of it even warrants a mental mention. And then Daniel shows up there and he's floored by the way she's living. I feel like no matter how many luxuries I'm able to one day afford, I'll never not appreciate it. And I don't think Daniel ever will either. He'll always appreciate the privileges in his life, because he comes from such a humble upbringing. And I can very much relate to that.

How did you decide on the name Wakan for Daniel's town?

For the name of Daniel's town I wanted it to be a word local Indigenous people would use, since so many places in Minnesota are still called by their original names. For this I contacted Native Languages of the Americas and made a donation to their Naming Fundraiser to have the town named. This fund-raiser benefits the preservation of native languages, which I loved. I wanted the name of the town to be something that indicated its magical properties. The area south of Minneapolis is traditional Dakota Sioux land. The best-known Dakota word for "magic" is "Wakan" (pronounced wah-kahn). This word means not only magic, but spiritual, sacred, or wondrous.

I also wanted Alexis's world to have a hidden meaning. Royaume means "kingdom" or "realm" in French.

Things in Wakan aren't always what they seem—the dragon-flies, the changing stained-glass window at Grant House, the freak storms. What was your purpose in these details, and how does the town become a character in its own right?

Pops said it best: Things happen in Wakan that can't be explained.

I wanted the town to have a touch of "maybe" magic. I loved the idea that Alexis and Daniel meeting was more than luck or fate—it was divine intervention. The spirit of the town sensing her presence, knowing she belonged there, and finding a way to stop her from driving on. And whatever omnipresent entity is guarding the town, it has a deep interest in Daniel.

Daniel has so much to do with the well-being of Wakan. He's the groundskeeper in a long line of groundskeepers. And I think the magic would have a vested interest in his happiness and would do whatever needed to be done to help him. It's protective over him and very much tied to Daniel's emotions—and isn't above playing wingman when needed.

There were a lot of little nuanced things I put in the book that you had to really be paying attention to notice. The stained glass on the landing is one of them. It's never described the same way twice, because it's changing, and nobody remembers what it used to be except for the reader who isn't under the spell. It also has the ability to make you forget what you've seen, and it doesn't allow itself to be photographed.

The dragonflies mean change is coming. We see the first dragonfly in the very first chapter when Daniel is towing Alexis out of the ditch. Once these two meet, wheels are already turning. We continue to see dragonflies throughout the book. They disappear in the tubing scene when Jake shows up because there's no change in Liz's situation, as she doesn't feel able to leave him—but afterward one lands on her knee, giving us hope that maybe the idea is planted and there might be hope for change after all.

There's a strong royalty component and a touch of Disney in this book. Tell us about that.

Daniel and Alexis are both royalty. He's the last in his line, an impoverished prince on the cusp of losing his castle. She's a wealthy, albeit reluctant, princess with an enormous and powerful kingdom, the heir to a prestigious throne. I *loved* drawing that dynamic throughout the book. Derek's exit is very similar to Edward VIII's abdication of the British throne to marry American divorcee Wallis Simpson. This was a huge scandal at the time, covered ruthlessly in the tabloids. Wallis was considered socially and morally unsuitable for the king, like Lola was for Derek, and Edward's exodus left his younger brother George VI to take the throne, much to his dismay.

And I had a blast incorporating all the Disney elements into it as well. We have Alexis losing a shoe right out of the gate. She's a redheaded, fish-out-of-water princess with a controlling father—

The Little Mermaid, anyone? There's some serious *Aladdin* vibes. The street that Alexis lives on, Chateau de Chambord, is named after the castle that inspired both the 1991 cartoon and the 2017 live-action film of *Beauty and the Beast*. I did this because Alexis is a beautiful, intelligent woman trapped in a castle with a monster. And of course we have *The Princess Bride* nods. I just had so much fun writing this book.

Is Hunter based on one of your own dogs, the way Stuntman Mike was in *The Friend Zone*?

Hunter is loosely based on my husband's hunting dog, Tess—who has brought me several mostly dead animals, including one that made it into the living room. She always looks totally perplexed when I'm screaming.

Which three of your characters would you choose for your zombie apocalypse team?

If I'm dipping into my other books, I'd have to say Jason. He hunts. Then Alexis, of course, because we need a doctor, and Daniel because he knows how to can food, garden, and build a deer stand. And I'm assuming by picking these characters their spouses are automatically on the team because no way am I separating them!

DANIEL'S CREPE RECIPE

- ¾ cup milk
- 1 teaspoon vanilla extract
- ½ teaspoon almond extract (optional)
- ¾ cup water
- ½ cup granulated sugar
- 4 tablespoons butter, melted
- ½ teaspoon salt
- 3 eggs
- 1½ cups all-purpose flour

Toppings:

- Jam or berries of your choice
- ¼ cup powdered sugar
- Whipped cream
- Chocolate, caramel sauce, or other sauce as desired (optional)

Step 1

In a large mixing bowl, whisk together the milk, extracts, water, granulated sugar, butter, salt, and the eggs. Gradually add in the flour, stirring to combine. Mix until smooth.

Step 2

Heat a lightly oiled griddle or frying pan over medium-high heat. Using a ¼-cup measuring cup for each crepe, ladle batter into the pan. Tilt the pan with a circular motion so that the batter coats the surface evenly.

Step 3

Cook the crepe for 1–2 minutes, until the bottom is light brown. Loosen with a spatula, turn, and cook the other side.

Step 4

Fill the crepes with a smear of your favorite jam or fresh berries. Fold in the bottom, then the sides, then tuck in the top, like you're folding a burrito. Sprinkle with powdered sugar and top with a dollop of whipped cream with the option to add more berries or a drizzle of chocolate, caramel, or some other kind of sauce.

ABOUT THE AUTHOR

Abby Jimenez is a Food Network champion and *New York Times* bestselling contemporary romance novelist living in Minnesota. Abby founded Nadia Cakes out of her home kitchen in 2007. The bakery has since expanded to multiple locations in two states, won numerous Food Network competitions, and amassed an international cult following. She loves a good book, coffee, doglets, and not leaving the house.

You can learn more at:
AuthorAbbyJimenez.com
Twitter @AuthorAbbyJim
Facebook.com/AuthorAbbyJimenez
Instagram @AuthorAbbyJimenez
Tik Tok @AuthorAbbyJimenez